THE

CENTENARY EDITION

OF THE WORKS OF

NATHANIEL HAWTHORNE

Volume XI

THE SNOW-IMAGE

EDITORS

General Editors

WILLIAM CHARVAT, 1905–1966
ROY HARVEY PEARCE
CLAUDE M. SIMPSON

FREDSON BOWERS, *Textual Editor*

L. NEAL SMITH, *Associate Textual Editor*

JOHN MANNING, *Assistant Textual Editor*

J. DONALD CROWLEY, *Editor for the Tales*

A PUBLICATION OF
THE OHIO STATE UNIVERSITY CENTER
FOR TEXTUAL STUDIES

NATHANIEL HAWTHORNE

THE SNOW-IMAGE
And Uncollected Tales

Ohio State University Press

CENTER FOR EDITIONS OF
AMERICAN AUTHORS

AN APPROVED TEXT

MODERN LANGUAGE
ASSOCIATION OF AMERICA

*Editorial expenses for this volume have been supported by
grants from the National Endowment for the Humanities
administered through the
Center for Editions of American Authors of the
Modern Language Association*

*International Standard Book Number 0-8142-0204-7
Library of Congress Catalogue Card Number 73-5365
Copyright© 1974 by the Ohio State University Press
All Rights Reserved
Printed in the United States of America*

ACKNOWLEDGEMENTS

THE EDITORS express their gratitude for the generous assistance of scholars, librarians, and bibliophiles. Particular thanks are offered to Nelson F. Adkins, New York University, and to Norman Holmes Pearson, Yale University. Permission to edit manuscript material was graciously given by the Henry E. Huntington Library; the Berg Collection, New York Public Library, Astor, Lenox, and Tilden Foundations; the University of Virginia Library; and the Pierpont Morgan Library. In the preparation of *The Snow-Image, and Uncollected Tales,* the work of Marianne Bailey, Frances Lappe, Nancy Long, and Don Nigro is appreciated, and the special contributions of Ann Jackowski and Nolan Smith.

We are grateful for support from the National Endowment for the Humanities of the National Foundation on the Arts and Humanities, the University of Missouri Research Council, and the following divisions of the Ohio State University: the Department of English, the Graduate School, the University Libraries, and the Research Foundation.

THE EDITORS

CONTENTS

The Snow-Image

Uncollected Tales

CONTENTS

THE SNOW-IMAGE

PREFACE

TO HORATIO BRIDGE, ESQ., U. S. N.

M Y DEAR BRIDGE:

Some of the more crabbed of my critics, I understand, have pronounced your friend egotistical, indiscreet, and even impertinent, on account of the Prefaces and Introductions with which, on several occasions, he has seen fit to pave the reader's way into the interior edifice of a book. In the justice of this censure I do not exactly concur, for the reasons, on the one hand, that the public generally has negatived the idea of undue freedom on the author's part, by evincing, it seems to me, rather more interest in these aforesaid Introductions than in the stories which followed,—and that, on the other hand, with whatever appearance of confidential intimacy, I have been especially careful to make no disclosures respecting myself which the most indifferent observer might not have been acquainted with, and which I was not perfectly willing that my worst enemy should know. I might further justify myself, on the plea that, ever since my youth, I have been addressing a very limited circle of friendly readers, without much danger of being overheard by the public at large; and that the habits thus acquired might pardonably continue, although strangers may have begun to mingle with my audience.

But the charge, I am bold to say, is not a reasonable one, in any view which we can fairly take of it. There is no harm, but, on the contrary, good, in arraying some of the ordinary facts of life in a slightly idealized and artistic guise. I have taken facts which relate to myself, because they chance to be nearest at hand, and likewise are my own property. And, as for egotism, a person, who has been burrowing, to his utmost ability, into the depths of our common nature, for the purposes of psychological romance,—and who pursues his researches in that dusky region, as he needs must, as well by the tact of sympathy as by the light of observation,—will smile at incurring such an imputation in virtue of a little preliminary talk about his external habits, his abode, his casual associates, and other matters entirely upon the surface. These things hide the man, instead of displaying him. You must make quite another kind of inquest, and look through the whole range of his fictitious characters, good and evil, in order to detect any of his essential traits.

Be all this as it may, there can be no question as to the propriety of my inscribing this volume of earlier and later sketches to you, and pausing here, a few moments, to speak of them, as friend speaks to friend; still being cautious, however, that the public and the critics shall overhear nothing which we care about concealing. On you, if on no other person, I am entitled to rely, to sustain the position of my Dedicatee. If anybody is responsible for my being at this day an author, it is yourself. I know not whence your faith came; but, while we were lads together at a country college,— gathering blue-berries, in study-hours, under those tall academic pines; or watching the great logs, as they tumbled along the current of the Androscoggin; or shooting pigeons and gray squirrels in the woods; or bat-fowling in the summer twilight; or catching trouts in that shadowy little stream which, I suppose, is still wandering riverward through the forest,—though you and I will never cast a line in it again,—

two idle lads, in short (as we need not fear to acknowledge now), doing a hundred things that the Faculty never heard of, or else it had been the worse for us,—still it was your prognostic of your friend's destiny, that he was to be a writer of fiction.

And a fiction-monger, in due season, he became. But, was there ever such a weary delay in obtaining the slightest recognition from the public, as in my case? I sat down by the wayside of life, like a man under enchantment, and a shrubbery sprung up around me, and the bushes grew to be saplings, and the saplings became trees, until no exit appeared possible, through the entangling depths of my obscurity. And there, perhaps, I should be sitting at this moment, with the moss on the imprisoning tree-trunks, and the yellow leaves of more than a score of autumns piled above me, if it had not been for you. For it was through your interposition,— and that, moreover, unknown to himself,—that your early friend was brought before the public, somewhat more prominently than theretofore, in the first volume of Twice-told Tales. Not a publisher in America, I presume, would have thought well enough of my forgotten or never noticed stories, to risk the expense of print and paper; nor do I say this with any purpose of casting odium on the respectable fraternity of book-sellers, for their blindness to my wonderful merit. To confess the truth, I doubted of the public recognition quite as much as they could do. So much the more generous was your confidence; and knowing, as I do, that it was founded on old friendship rather than cold criticism, I value it only the more for that.

So, now, when I turn back upon my path, lighted by a transitory gleam of public favor, to pick up a few articles which were left out of my former collections, I take pleasure in making them the memorial of our very long and unbroken connection. Some of these sketches were among the earliest that I wrote, and, after lying for years in manuscript, they at last skulked into the Annuals or Magazines, and have hidden themselves there ever since. Others were the productions of a later period; others, again, were written recently. The comparison of these various trifles—the indices of intellectual condition at far separated epochs—affects me with a singular complexity of regrets. I am disposed to quarrel with the earlier sketches, both because a mature judgment discerns so many faults, and still more because they come so nearly up to the standard of the best that I can achieve now. The ripened autumnal fruit tastes but little better than the early windfalls. It would, indeed, be mortifying to believe that the summertime of life has passed away, without any greater progress and improvement than is indicated here. But,—at least, so I would fain hope,—these things are scarcely to be depended upon, as measures of the intellectual and moral man. In youth, men are apt to write more wisely than they really know or feel; and the remainder of life may be not idly spent in realizing and convincing themselves of the wisdom which they uttered long ago. The truth that was only in the fancy then may have since become a substance in the mind and heart.

I have nothing further, I think, to say; unless it be that the public need not dread my again trespassing on its kindness, with any more of these musty and mouse-nibbled leaves of old periodicals, transformed, by the magic arts of my friendly publishers, into a new book. These are the last. Or, if a few still remain, they are either such as no paternal partiality could induce the author to think worth preserving, or else they have got into some very dark and dusty hiding-place, quite out of my own remembrance and whence no researches can avail to unearth them. So there let them rest.

Very sincerely yours,

N. H.

Lenox, November 1st, 1851.

THE SNOW-IMAGE

A CHILDISH MIRACLE

ONE AFTERNOON of a cold winter's day, when the sun shone forth with chilly brightness, after a long storm, two children asked leave of their mother to run out and play in the new-fallen snow. The elder child was a little girl, whom, because she was of a tender and modest disposition, and was thought to be very beautiful, her parents, and other people that were familiar with her, used to call Violet. But her brother was known by the style and title of Peony, on account of the ruddiness of his broad and round little phiz, which made everybody think of sunshine and great scarlet flowers. The father of these two children, a certain Mr. Lindsey, it is important to say, was an excellent, but exceedingly matter-of-fact sort of man, a dealer in hardware, and was sturdily accustomed to take what is called the common-sense view of all matters that came under his consideration. With a heart about as tender as other people's, he had a head as hard and impenetrable, and therefore perhaps as empty, as one of the iron-pots which it was a part of his business to sell. The mother's character, on the other hand, had a strain of poetry in it, a trait of unworldly beauty, a delicate and dewy flower, as it were, that had survived out of her imaginative youth, and still kept itself alive amid the dusty realities of matrimony and motherhood.

So, Violet and Peony, as I began with saying, besought their mother to let them run out and play in the new snow; for, though it had looked so dreary and dismal, drifting downward out of the grey sky, it had a very cheerful aspect, now that the sun was shining on it. The children dwelt in a city, and had no wider play-place than a little garden before the house, divided by a white fence from the street, and with a pear-tree and two or three plum-trees overshadowing it, and some rose-bushes just in front of the parlor-windows. The trees and shrubs, however, were now leafless, and their twigs were enveloped in the light snow, which thus made a kind of wintry foliage, with here-and-there a pendant icicle for the fruit.

"Yes, Violet—yes, my little Peony," said their kind mother, "you may go out and play in the new snow."

Accordingly, the good lady bundled up her darlings in woollen jackets and wadded sacks, and put comforters round their necks, and a pair of striped gaiters on each little pair of legs, and worsted mittens on their hands, and gave them a kiss apiece, by way of a spell to keep away Jack Frost. Forth sallied the two children with a hop-skip-and-jump, that carried them at once into the very heart of a huge snow-drift, whence Violet emerged like a snow-bunting, while little Peony floundered out with his round face in full bloom. Then what a merry time had they! To look at them, frolicking in the wintry garden, you would have thought that the dark and pitiless storm had been sent for no other purpose but to provide a new plaything for Violet and Peony; and that they themselves had been created, as the snow-birds were, to take delight only in the tempest, and in the white mantle which it spread over the earth.

At last, when they had frosted one another all over with handfulls of snow, Violet, after laughing heartily at little Peony's figure, was struck with a new thought.

"You look exactly like a snow-image, Peony," said she, "if your cheeks were not so red. And that puts me in mind! Let us make an image out of snow—an image of a little girl—and it shall be our sister, and shall run about and play with us, all winter long. Won't it be nice?"

"Oh, yes!" cried Peony, as plainly as he could speak, for he was but a little boy. "That will be nice! And mamma shall see it!"

"Yes," answered Violet, "mamma shall see the new little girl. But she must not make her come into the warm parlor; for, you know, our little snow-sister will not love the warmth."

And, forthwith, the children began this great business of making a snow-image that should run about; while their mother, who was sitting at the window and overheard some of their talk, could not help smiling at the gravity with which they set about it. They really seemed to imagine that there would be no difficulty whatever in creating a live little girl out of the snow. And, to say the truth, if miracles are ever to be wrought, it will be by putting our hands to the work, in precisely such a simple and undoubting frame of mind as that in which Violet and Peony now undertook to perform one, without so much as knowing that it was a miracle. So thought the mother, and thought, likewise, that the new snow, just fallen from heaven, would be excellent material to make new beings of, if it were not so very cold. She gazed at the children, a moment longer, delighting to watch their little figures—the girl, tall for her age, graceful and agile, and so delicately colored that she looked like a cheerful Thought, more than a physical reality—while Peony expanded in breadth rather than height, and rolled along on his short and sturdy legs, as substantial as an elephant, though not quite so big. Then the mother resumed her work; what it was I forget; but she was either trimming a silken bonnet for Violet, or darning a pair of stockings for little Peony's short legs. Again, however, and again, and yet other agains, she could not help turning her head to the window, to see how the children got on with their snow-image.

Indeed, it was an exceedingly pleasant sight, those bright little souls at their tasks! Moreover, it was really wonderful to observe how knowingly and skilfully they managed the matter. Violet assumed the chief direction, and told Peony what to do, while, with her own delicate fingers, she shaped out all the nicer parts of the snow-figure. It seemed, in fact, not so much to be made by the children, as to grow up under their hands, while they were playing and prattling about it. Their mother was quite surprised at this; and the longer she looked, the more and more surprised she grew.

"What remarkable children mine are!" thought she, smiling with a mother's pride, and smiling at herself, too, for being so proud of them. What other children could have made anything so like a little girl's figure out of snow, at the first trial? Well;—but now I must finish Peony's new frock; for his grandfather is coming tomorrow, and I want the little fellow to look as handsome as possible."

So she took up the frock, and was soon as busily at work again with her needle, as the two children with their snow-image. But still, as the needle travelled hither and thither through the seams of the dress, the mother made her toil light and happy by listening to the airy voices of Violet and Peony. They kept talking to one another all the time, their tongues being quite as active as their feet and hands. Except at intervals, she could not distinctly hear what was said, but had merely a sweet impression that they were in a most loving mood, and were enjoying themselves highly, and that the business of making the snow-image went prosperously on. Now and then, however, when Violet and Peony happened to raise their voices, the words were as audible as if they had been spoken in the very parlor, where the mother sat.

Oh, how delightfully those words echoed in her heart, even though they meant nothing so very wise or wonderful, after all!

But, you must know, a mother listens with her heart, much more than with her ears; and thus she is often delighted with the trills of celestial music, when other people can hear nothing of the kind.

"Peony, Peony!" cried Violet to her brother, who had gone to another part of the garden. "Bring me some of that fresh snow, Peony, from the very furthest corner, where we have not been trampling. I want it to shape our little snow-sister's bosom with. You know that part must be quite pure, just as it came out of the sky!"

"Here it is, Violet!" answered Peony, in his bluff tone—but a very sweet tone too—as he came floundering through the half-trodden drifts. "Here is the snow for her 'ittle bosom. Oh, Violet, how beau-ti-ful she begins to look!"

"Yes," said Violet, thoughtfully and quietly, "our snow-sister does look very lovely. I did not quite know, Peony, that we could make such a sweet little girl as this."

The mother, as she listened, thought how fit and delightful an incident it would be, if fairies, or, still better, if angel-children were to come from Paradise, and play invisibly with her own darlings, and help them to make their snow-image, giving it the features of celestial babyhood! Violet and Peony would not be aware of their immortal playmates; only they would see that the image grew very beautiful, while they worked at it, and would think that they themselves had done it all.

"My little girl and boy deserve such playmates, if mortal children ever did!" said the mother to herself; and then she smiled again at her own motherly pride.

Nevertheless, the idea seized upon her imagination; and, ever and anon, she took a glimpse out of the window, half-dreaming that she might see the golden-haired children of Paradise, sporting with her own golden-haired Violet and bright-cheeked Peony.

Now, for a few moments, there was a busy and earnest, but indistinct hum of the two children's voices, as Violet and Peony wrought together with one happy consent. Violet still seemed to be the guiding spirit; while Peony acted rather as a laborer, and brought her the snow from far and near. And yet the little urchin evidently had a proper understanding of the matter, too!

"Peony, Peony!" cried Violet; for her brother was again at the other side of the garden. "Bring me those light wreaths of snow that have rested on the lower branches of the pear-tree. You can clamber on the snow-drift, Peony, and reach them easily. I must have them to make some ringlets for our snow-sister's head!"

"Here they are, Violet!" answered the little boy. "Take care you do not break them. Well done! Well done! How pretty!"

"Does she not look sweetly?" said Violet, with a very satisfied tone. "And now we must have some little shining bits of ice, to make the brightness of her eyes. She is not finished yet. Mamma will see how very beautiful she is; but papa will say, 'Tush!—nonsense!—come in out of the cold!'"

"Let us call mamma to look out," said Peony; and then he shouted lustily, "Mamma! Mamma!! Mamma!!! Look out, and see what a nice 'ittle girl we are making!"

The mother put down her work, for an instant, and looked out of the window. But it so happened that the sun—for this was one of the shortest days of the whole year—had sunken so nearly to the edge of the world, that his setting shine came obliquely into the lady's eyes. So she was dazzled, you must understand, and could not very distinctly observe what was in the garden. Still, however, through all that bright, blinding dazzle of the sun and the new snow, she beheld a small white figure in the garden, that seemed to have a wonderful deal of human likeness about it. And she saw Violet and Peony—indeed, she looked more at them than at the image—she saw the two children still at work; Peony bringing fresh snow, and Violet applying it to the figure, as scientifically as a sculptor adds clay to his model. Indistinctly as she discerned the snow-child, the mother thought to herself, that never before was there a snow-figure so cunningly made, nor ever such a dear little girl and boy to make it.

"They do everything better than other children," said she, very complacently. "Then no wonder they make better snow-images!"

She sate down again to her work, and made as much haste with it as possible; because twilight would soon come, and Peony's frock was not yet finished, and grandfather was expected, by railroad, pretty early in the morning. Faster and faster, therefore, went her flying fingers. The children, like-wise, kept busily at work in the garden, and still the mother listened, whenever she could catch a word. She was amused to observe how their little imaginations had got mixed up with what they were doing, and were carried away by it.—They seemed positively to think that the snow-child would run about and play with them.

"What a nice playmate she will be for us, all winter long!" said Violet. "I hope papa will not be afraid of her giving us a cold! Shan't you love her dearly, Peony?"

"Oh, yes!" cried Peony. "And I will hug her, and she shall sit down close by me, and drink some of my warm milk!"

"Oh, no, Peony!" answered Violet, with grave wisdom. "That will not do at all. Warm milk will not be wholesome for our little snow-sister. Little snow-people, like her, eat nothing but icicles. No, no, Peony;—we must not give her anything warm to drink!"

There was a minute or two of silence; for Peony, whose short legs were never weary, had gone on pilgrimage again to the other side of the garden. All of a sudden, Violet cried out, loudly and joyfully:—

"Look here, Peony! Come quickly! A light has been shining on her cheek out of that rose-colored cloud!—and the color does not go away! Is not that beautiful?"

"Yes; it is beau-ti-ful," answered Peony, pronouncing the three syllables with deliberate accuracy. "Oh, Violet, only look at her hair! It is all like gold!"

"Oh, certainly," said Violet, with tranquillity, as if it were very much a matter of course. "That color, you know, comes from the golden clouds, that we see up there in the sky. She is almost finished now. But her lips must be made very red—redder than her cheeks. Perhaps, Peony, it will make them red, if we both kiss them!"

Accordingly, the mother heard two smart little smacks, as if both her children were kissing the snow-image on its frozen mouth. But, as this did not seem to make the lips quite red enough, Violet next proposed that the snow-child should be invited to kiss Peony's scarlet cheek.

"Come, 'ittle snow-sister, kiss me!" cried Peony.

"There! She has kissed you," added Violet, "and now her lips are very red. And she blushed a little, too!"

"Oh, what a cold kiss!" cried Peony.

Just then, there came a breeze of the pure west-wind, sweeping through the garden and rattling the parlor-windows. It sounded so wintry cold, that the mother was about to tap on the window-pane with her thimbled finger, to summon the two children in; when they both cried out to her with one voice. The tone was not a tone of surprise, although they were evidently a good deal excited; it appeared rather as if they were very much rejoiced at some event that had now happened, but which they had been looking for, and had reckoned upon all along.

"Mamma! Mamma! We have finished our little snow-sister, and she is running about the garden with us!"

"What imaginative little beings my children are!" thought the mother, putting the last few stitches into Peony's frock. "And it is strange, too, that they make me almost as much a child as they themselves are! I can hardly help believing, now, that the snow-image has really come to life!"

"Dear mamma," cried Violet, "pray look out, and see what a sweet playmate we have!"

The mother, being thus entreated, could no longer delay to look forth from the window. The sun was now gone out of the sky, leaving, however, a rich inheritance of his brightness among those purple and golden clouds which make the sunsets of winter so magnificent. But there was not the slightest gleam or dazzle, either on the window or on the snow; so that the good lady could look all over the garden, and see everything and everybody in it. And what do you think she saw there? Violet and Peony, of course, her own two darling children. Ah, but whom or what did she see besides? Why, if you will believe me, there was a small figure of a girl, dressed all in white, with rose-tinged cheeks and ringlets of golden hair, playing about the garden with the two children. A stranger though she was, the child seemed to be on as familiar terms with Violet and Peony, and they with her, as if all the three had been playmates during the whole of their little lives. The mother thought to herself, that it must certainly be the daughter of one of the neighbors, and that, seeing Violet and Peony in the garden, the child had run across the street to play with them. So this kind lady went to the door, intending to invite the little runaway into her comfortable parlor; for, now that the sunshine was withdrawn, the atmosphere, out of doors, was already growing very cold.

But, after opening the house-door, she stood an instant on the threshold, hesitating whether she ought to ask the child to come in, or whether she should even speak to her. Indeed, she almost doubted whether it were a real child, after all, or only a light wreath of the new-fallen snow, blown hither and thither about the garden by the intensely cold west-wind. There was certainly something very singular in the aspect of the little stranger. Among all the children of the neighborhood, the lady could remember no such face, with its pure white, and delicate rose-color, and the golden ringlets tossing about the forehead and cheeks. And as for her dress, which was entirely of white, and fluttering in the breeze, it was such as no reasonable woman would put upon a little girl, when sending her out to play, in the depth of winter. It made this kind and careful mother shiver only to look at those small feet, with nothing in the world on them, except a very thin pair of white slippers. Nevertheless, airily as she was clad, the child seemed to feel not the slightest inconvenience from the cold, but danced so lightly over the snow that the tips of her toes left hardly a print in its surface; while Violet could but just keep pace with her, and Peony's short legs compelled him to lag behind.

Once, in the course of their play, the strange child placed herself between Violet and Peony, and taking a hand of each, skipt merrily forward, and they along with her. Almost immediately, however, Peony pulled away his little fist, and began to rub it as if the fingers were tingling with cold; while Violet also released herself, though with less abruptness, gravely remarking that it was better not to take hold of hands. The white-robed damsel said not a word, but danced about, just as merrily as before. If Violet and Peony did not choose

to play with her, she could make just as good a playmate
of the brisk and cold west-wind, which kept blowing her all
about the garden, and took such liberties with her that they
seemed to have been friends for a long time. All this while,
the mother stood on the threshold, wondering how a little
girl could look so much like a flying snow-drift, or how a
snow-drift could look so very like a little girl.

She called Violet, and whispered to her.

"Violet, my darling, what is this child's name?" asked she.
"Does she live near us?"

"Why, dearest mamma," answered Violet, laughing to
think that her mother did not comprehend so very plain an
affair, "this is our little snow-sister, whom we have just
been making!"

"Yes, dear mamma," cried Peony, running to his mother
and looking up simply into her face. "This is our snow-image!
Is it not a nice 'ittle child?"

At this instant, a flock of snow-birds came flitting through
the air. As was very natural, they avoided Violet and Peony.
But—and this looked strange—they flew at once to the
white-robed child, fluttered eagerly about her head, alighted
on her shoulders, and seemed to claim her as an old acquaintance. She, on her part, was evidently as glad to see these
little birds, old Winter's grandchildren, as they were to see
her, and welcomed them by holding out both her hands.
Hereupon, they each and all tried to alight on her two palms
and ten small fingers and thumbs, crowding one another off,
with an immense fluttering of their tiny wings. One dear
little bird nestled tenderly in her bosom; another put its bill
to her lips. They were as joyous, all the while, and seemed
as much in their element, as you may have seen them when
sporting with a snow-storm.

Violet and Peony stood laughing at this pretty sight; for
they enjoyed the merry time which their new playmate was

having with these small winged visitants, almost as much as if they themselves took part in it.

"Violet," said her mother, greatly perplexed, "tell me the truth, without any jest. Who is this little girl?"

"My darling mamma," answered Violet, looking seriously into her mother's face, and apparently surprised that she should need any further explanation, "I have told you truly who she is. It is our little snow-image, which Peony and I have been making. Peony will tell you so, as well as I."

"Yes, mamma!" asseverated Peony, with much gravity in his crimson little phiz. "This is 'ittle snow-child. Is not she a nice one. But, mamma, her hand is, oh, so very cold!"

While mamma still hesitated what to think and what to do, the street-gate was thrown open, and the father of Violet and Peony appeared, wrapt in a pilot-cloth sack, with a fur-cap drawn down over his ears, and the thickest of gloves upon his hands. Mr. Lindsey was a middle-aged man, with a weary, and yet a happy look in his wind-flushed and frost-pinched face, as if he had been busy all day long, and was glad to get back to his quiet home. His eyes brightened at sight of his wife and children, although he could not help uttering a word or two of surprise, at finding the whole family in the open air, on so bleak a day, and after sunset too. He soon perceived the little white stranger, sporting to-and-fro in the garden, like a dancing snow-wreath, and the flock of snow-birds fluttering about her head.

"Pray what little girl may that be?" inquired this very sensible man. "Surely her mother must be crazy, to let her go out in such bitter weather as it has been to-day, with only that flimsy white gown, and those thin slippers!"

"My dear husband," said his wife, "I know no more about the little thing than you do. Some neighbor's child, I suppose. Our Violet and Peony," she added, laughing at herself for repeating so absurd a story, "insist that she is nothing but a snow-image, which they have been busy about in the garden, almost all the afternoon."

As she said this, the mother glanced her eyes towards the spot where the children's snow-image had been made. What was her surprise, on perceiving that there was not the slightest trace of so much labor!—no image at all!—no piled-up heap of snow!—nothing whatever, save the prints of little footsteps around a vacant space.

"This is very strange!" said she.

"What is strange, dear mother?" asked Violet. "Dear father, do not you see how it is? This is our snow-image, which Peony and I have made, because we wanted another play-mate. Did not we, Peony?"

"Yes, papa," said crimson Peony. "This be our 'ittle snow-sister. Is not she beau-ti-ful? But she gave me such a cold kiss!"

"Poh, nonsense, children!" cried their good, honest father, who, as we have already intimated, had an exceedingly common-sensible way of looking at matters. "Do not tell me of making live figures out of snow! Come, wife; this little stranger must not stay out in the bleak air a moment longer. We will bring her into the parlor; and you shall give her a supper of warm bread and milk, and make her as comfortable as you can. Meanwhile, I will inquire among the neighbors; or, if necessary, send the city-crier about the streets, to give notice of a lost child."

So saying, this honest and very kind-hearted man was going towards the little white damsel, with the best intentions in the world. But Violet and Peony, each seizing their father by a hand, earnestly besought him not to make her come in.

"Dear father," cried Violet, putting herself before him, "it is true, what I have been telling you! This is our little snow-girl, and she cannot live any longer than while she breathes the cold west-wind. Do not make her come into the hot room!"

"Yes, father!" shouted Peony, stamping his little foot, so mightily was he in earnest.—"This be nothing but our 'ittle snow-child! She will not love the hot fire!"

"Nonsense, children, nonsense, nonsense!" cried the father, half-vexed, half-laughing at what he considered their foolish obstinacy. "Run into the house, this moment! It is too late to play any longer, now. I must take care of this little girl immediately, or she will catch her death-a-cold!"

"Husband!—dear husband!" said his wife, in a low voice; for she had been looking narrowly at the snow-child, and was more perplexed than ever.—"There is something very singular in all this. You will think me foolish—but—but— may it not be that some invisible angel has been attracted by the simplicity and good faith with which our children set about their undertaking? May he not have spent an hour of his immortality in playing with those dear little souls?—and so the result is what we call a miracle. No, no! Do not laugh at me. I see what a foolish thought it is!"

"My dear wife," replied the husband, laughing heartily, "you are as much a child as Violet and Peony."

And, in one sense, so she was; for, all through life, she had kept her heart full of childlike simplicity, and faith, which was as pure and clear as crystal; and, looking at all matters through this transparent medium, she sometimes saw truths so profound, that other people laughed at them as nonsense and absurdity.

But, now, kind Mr. Lindsey had entered the garden, breaking away from his two children, who still sent their shrill voices after him, beseeching him to let the snow-child stay and enjoy herself in the cold west-wind. As he approached, the snow-birds took to flight. The little white damsel, also, fled backward, shaking her head as if to say—'Pray do not touch me!'—and roguishly, as it appeared, leading him through the deepest of the snow. Once, the good man stumbled, and floundered down upon his face; so that, gathering himself up again, with the snow sticking to his rough pilot-cloth sack, he looked as white and wintry as a snow-image of the largest size. Some of the neighbors, meanwhile, seeing him from their windows, wondered what could possess poor Mr. Lindsey to be running about his garden in pursuit of a snow-drift, which the west-wind was driving hither and thither! At length, after a vast deal of trouble, he chased the little stranger into a corner, where she could not possibly escape him. His wife had been looking on, and, it being now nearly twilight, was wonder-struck to observe how the snow-child gleamed and sparkled, and how she seemed to shed a glow all roundabout her, and how, when driven into the corner, she positively glistened like a star! It was a frosty kind of brightness, too, like that of an icicle in the moonlight. The wife thought it strange, that good Mr. Lindsey should see nothing remarkable in the snow-child's appearance.

"Come, you odd little thing!" cried the honest man, seizing her by the hand. "I have caught you at last, and will make you comfortable in spite of yourself. We will put a nice warm pair of worsted stockings on your frozen little feet; and you shall have a good thick shawl to wrap yourself in. Your poor, white nose, I am afraid, is actually frost-bitten. But we will make it all right. Come along in!"

And so, with a most benevolent smile on his sagacious visage, all purple as it was with the cold, this very well-meaning gentleman took the snow-child by the hand and led her towards the house. She followed him, droopingly and reluctant; for all the glow and sparkle was gone out of her figure; and, whereas, just before, she had resembled a bright, frosty, star-gemmed evening, with a crimson gleam on the cold horizon, she now looked as dull and languid as a thaw. As kind Mr. Lindsey led her up the steps of the door, Violet and Peony looked into his face—their eyes full of tears, which froze before they could run down their cheeks—and again entreated him not to bring their snow-image into the house.

"Not bring her in!" exclaimed the kind-hearted man. "Why, you are crazy, my little Violet!—quite crazy, my small Peony! She is so cold, already, that her hand has almost frozen mine, in spite of my thick gloves. Would you have her freeze to death?"

His wife, as he came up the steps, had been taking another long, earnest, almost awe-stricken gaze at the little white stranger. She hardly knew whether it were a dream or no; but she could not help fancying that she saw the delicate print of Violet's fingers on the child's neck. It looked just as if, while Violet was shaping out the image, she had given it a gentle pat with her hand, and had neglected to smooth the impression quite away.

"After all, husband," said the mother, recurring to her idea, that the angels would be as much delighted to play with Violet and Peony, as she herself was, "after all, she does look strangely like a snow-image! I do believe she is made of snow!"

A puff of the west-wind blew against the snow-child; and again she sparkled like a star.

"Snow!" repeated good Mr. Lindsey, drawing the reluctant guest over his hospitable threshold. "No wonder she looks like snow. She is half-frozen, poor little thing! But a good fire will put everything to rights."

Without further talk, and always with the very best intentions, this highly benevolent and common-sensible individual led the little white damsel—drooping, drooping, drooping, more and more—out of the frosty air, and into his comfortable parlor. A Heidenberg stove, filled to the brim with intensely burning anthracite, was sending a bright gleam through the isinglass of its iron-door, and causing the vase of water on its top to fume and bubble with excitement. A warm, sultry smell was diffused throughout the room. A thermometer, on the wall farthest from the stove, stood at eighty degrees. The parlor was hung with red curtains, and covered with a red carpet, and looked just as warm as it felt. The difference betwixt the atmosphere here, and the cold, wintry twilight, out of doors, was like stepping at once from Nova Zembla to the hottest part of India, or from the North-pole into an oven. Oh, this was a fine place for the little white stranger!

The common-sensible man placed the snow-child on the hearth-rug, right in front of the hissing and fuming stove.

"Now she will be comfortable!" cried kind Mr. Lindsey, rubbing his hands and looking about him, with the pleasantest smile you ever saw. "Make yourself at home, my child!"

Sad, sad, and drooping, looked the little white maiden, as she stood on the hearth-rug, with the hot blast of the stove striking through her like a pestilence. Once, she threw a glance wistfully towards the window, and caught a glimpse, through its red curtains, of the snow-covered roofs, and the stars glimmering frostily, and all the delicious intensity of the cold night. The bleak wind rattled the window-panes, as if it were summoning her to come forth. But there stood the snow-child, drooping, before the hot stove!

But the common-sensible man saw nothing amiss.

"Come, wife," said he, "let her have a pair of thick stockings and a woollen shawl or blanket directly; and tell Dora to give her some warm supper as soon as the milk boils. You, Violet and Peony, amuse your little friend. She is out of spirits, you see, at finding herself in a strange place. For my part, I will go round among the neighbors, and find out where she belongs."

The mother, meanwhile, had gone in search of the shawl and stockings; for her own view of the matter, however subtle and delicate, had given way, as it always did, to the stubborn materialism of her husband. Without heeding the remonstrances of his two children, who still kept murmuring that their little snow-sister did not love the warmth, good Mr. Lindsey took his departure, shutting the parlor-door carefully behind him. Turning up the collar of his sack over his ears, he emerged from the house, and had barely reached the street-gate, when he was recalled by the screams of Violet and Peony, and the rapping of a thimbled finger against the parlor-window.

"Husband! Husband!" cried his wife, showing her horror-stricken face through the window-panes. "There is no need of going for the child's parents!"

"We told you so, father!" screamed Violet and Peony, as he re-entered the parlor. "You would bring her in; and now our poor—dear—beau-ti-ful little snow-sister is thawed!"

And their own sweet little faces were already dissolved in tears; so that their father, seeing what strange things occasionally happen in this every-day world, felt not a little anxious lest his children might be going to thaw too! In the utmost perplexity, he demanded an explanation of his wife. She could only reply, that, being summoned to the parlor by the cries of Violet and Peony, she found no trace of the little white maiden, unless it were the remains of a heap of snow, which, while she was gazing at it, melted quite away upon the hearth-rug.

"And there you see all that is left of it!" added she, pointing to a pool of water, in front of the stove.

"Yes, father," said Violet, looking reproachfully at him, through her tears, "there is all that is left of our dear little snow-sister!"

"Naughty father!" cried Peony, stamping his foot, and—I shudder to say—shaking his little fist at the common-sensible man. "We told you how it would be! What for did you bring her in?"

And the Heidenberg stove, through the isinglass of its door, seemed to glare at good Mr. Lindsey, like a red-eyed demon, triumphing in the mischief which it had done!

This, you will observe, was one of those rare cases, which yet will occasionally happen, where common-sense finds itself at fault. The remarkable story of the snow-image, though, to that sagacious class of people to whom good Mr. Lindsey belongs, it may seem but a childish affair, is nevertheless capable of being moralized in various methods, greatly for their edification. One of its lessons, for instance, might be, that it behoves men, and especially men of benevolence, to consider well what they are about, and, before acting on their philanthropic purposes, to be quite sure that they comprehend the nature and all the relations of the business in hand. What has been established as an element of good to one being, may prove absolute mischief to another; even as the warmth of the parlor was proper enough for children of flesh and blood, like Violet and Peony—though by no means very wholesome, even for them—but involved nothing short of annihilation to the unfortunate snow-image.

But, after all, there is no teaching anything to wise men of good Mr. Lindsey's stamp. They know everything—Oh, to be sure!—everything that has been, and everything that is, and everything that, by any future possibility, can be. And, should some phenomenon of Nature or Providence transcend their system, they will not recognize it, even if it come to pass under their very noses.

"Wife," said Mr. Lindsey, after a fit of silence, "see what a quantity of snow the children have brought in on their feet! It has made quite a puddle here before the stove. Pray tell Dora to bring some towels and sop it up!"

THE GREAT STONE FACE

ONE AFTERNOON, when the sun was going down, a mother and her little boy sat at the door of their cottage, talking about the Great Stone Face. They had but to lift their eyes, and there it was plainly to be seen, though miles away, with the sunshine brightening all its features.

And what was the Great Stone Face?

Embosomed amongst a family of lofty mountains, there was a valley so spacious that it contained many thousand inhabitants. Some of these good people dwelt in log huts, with the black forest all around them, on the steep and difficult hill-sides. Others had their homes in comfortable farm-houses, and cultivated the rich soil on the gentle slopes or level surfaces of the valley. Others, again, were congregated into populous villages, where some wild, highland rivulet, tumbling down from its birth-place in the upper mountain region, had been caught and tamed by human cunning, and compelled to turn the machinery of cotton factories. The inhabitants of this valley, in short, were numerous, and of many modes of life. But all of them, grown people and children, had a kind of familiarity with the Great Stone Face, although some possessed the gift of distinguishing this grand natural phenomenon more perfectly than many of their neighbors.

The Great Stone Face, then, was a work of Nature in her mood of majestic playfulness, formed on the perpendicular side of a mountain by some immense rocks, which had been thrown together in such a position, as, when viewed at a proper distance, precisely to resemble the features of the human countenance. It seemed as if an enormous giant, or a Titan, had sculptured his own likeness on the precipice. There was the broad arch of the forehead, a hundred feet in height, the nose, with its long bridge, and the vast lips, which, if they could have spoken, would have rolled their thunder accents from one end of the valley to the other. True it is, that if the spectator approached too near, he lost the outline of the gigantic visage, and could discern only a heap of ponderous and gigantic rocks, piled in chaotic ruin one upon another. Retracing his steps, however, the wondrous features would again be seen, and the farther he withdrew from them, the more like a human face, with all its original divinity intact, did they appear; until, as it grew dim in the distance, with the clouds and glorified vapor of the mountains clustering about it, the Great Stone Face seemed positively to be alive.

It was a happy lot for children to grow up to manhood or womanhood, with the Great Stone Face before their eyes, for all the features were noble, and the expression was at once grand and sweet, as if it were the glow of a vast, warm heart, that embraced all mankind in its affections, and had room for more. It was an education only to look at it. According to the belief of many people, the valley owed much of its fertility to this benign aspect that was continually beaming over it, illuminating the clouds, and infusing its tenderness into the sunshine.

As we began with saying, a mother and her little boy sat at their cottage door, gazing at the Great Stone Face, and talking about it. The child's name was Ernest.

"Mother," said he, while the Titanic visage smiled on him, "I wish that it could speak, for it looks so very kindly that its voice must needs be pleasant. If I were to see a man with such a face, I should love him dearly."

"If an old prophecy should come to pass," answered his mother, "we may see a man, some time or other, with exactly such a face as that."

"What prophecy do you mean, dear mother?" eagerly inquired Ernest. "Pray tell me all about it!"

So his mother told him a story that her own mother had told to her, when she herself was younger than little Ernest; a story, not of things that were past, but of what was yet to come; a story, nevertheless, so very old, that even the Indians, who formerly inhabited this valley, had heard it from their forefathers, to whom, as they affirmed, it had been murmured by the mountain streams, and whispered by the wind among the tree-tops. The purport was, that, at some future day, a child should be born hereabouts, who was destined to become the greatest and noblest personage of his time, and whose countenance, in manhood, should bear an exact resemblance to the Great Stone Face. Not a few old-fashioned people, and young ones likewise, in the ardor of their hopes, still cherished an enduring faith in this old prophecy. But others—who had seen more of the world, had watched and waited till they were weary, and had beheld no man with such a face, nor any man that proved to be much greater or nobler than his neighbors—concluded it to be nothing but an idle tale. At all events, the great man of the prophecy had not yet appeared.

"Oh, mother, dear mother," cried Ernest, clapping his hands above his head, "I do hope that I shall live to see him!"

His mother was an affectionate and thoughtful woman, and felt that it was wisest not to discourage the generous hopes of her little boy. So she only said to him—"Perhaps you may!"

And Ernest never forgot the story that his mother told him. It was always in his mind whenever he looked upon the Great Stone Face. He spent his childhood in the log-cottage where he was born, and was dutiful to his mother, and helpful to her in many things, assisting her much with his little hands, and more with his loving heart. In this manner, from a happy yet often pensive child, he grew up to be a mild, quiet, unobtrusive boy, and sun-browned with labor in the fields, but with more intelligence brightening his aspect than is seen in many lads who have been taught at famous schools. Yet Ernest had had no teacher, save only that the Great Stone Face became one to him. When the toil of the day was over, he would gaze at it for hours, until he began to imagine that those vast features recognized him, and gave him a smile of kindness and encouragement, responsive to his own look of veneration. We must not take upon us to affirm that this was a mistake, although the Face may have looked no more kindly at Ernest than at all the world besides. But the secret was, that the boy's tender and confiding simplicity discerned what other people could not see; and thus the love, which was meant for all, became his peculiar portion.

About this time, there went a rumor throughout the valley, that the great man, foretold from ages long ago, who was to bear a resemblance to the Great Stone Face, had appeared at last. It seems that, many years before, a young man had migrated from the valley and settled at a distant seaport, where, after getting together a little money, he had set up as a shopkeeper. His name—but I could never learn whether it was his real one, or a nickname that had grown out of his habits and success in life—was Gathergold. Being shrewd and active, and endowed by Providence with that inscrutable faculty which developes itself in what the world calls luck, he became an exceedingly rich merchant, and owner of a whole fleet of bulky-bottomed ships. All the countries of the globe appeared to join hands for the mere purpose of adding heap after heap to the mountainous accumulation of this one man's wealth. The cold regions of the north, almost within the gloom and shadow of the Arctic Circle, sent him their tribute in the shape of furs; hot Africa sifted for him the golden sands of her rivers, and gathered up the ivory tusks of her great elephants out of the forests; the East came bringing him the rich shawls, and spices, and teas, and the effulgence of diamonds, and the gleaming purity of large pearls. The ocean, not to be behindhand with the earth, yielded up her mighty whales, that Mr. Gathergold might sell their oil, and make a profit on it. Be the original commodity what it might, it was gold within his grasp. It might be said of him, as of Midas in the fable, that whatever he touched with his finger immediately glistened, and grew yellow, and was changed at once into sterling metal, or, which suited him still better, into piles of coin. And, when Mr. Gathergold had become so very rich that it would have taken him a hundred years only to count his wealth, he bethought himself of his native valley, and resolved to go back thither, and end his days where he was born. With this purpose in view, he sent a skilful architect to build him such a palace as should be fit for a man of his vast wealth to live in.

As I have said above, it had already been rumored in the valley that Mr. Gathergold had turned out to be the prophetic personage, so long and vainly looked for, and that his visage was the perfect and undeniable similitude of the Great Stone Face. People were the more ready to believe that this must needs be the fact, when they beheld the splendid edifice that rose, as if by enchantment, on the site of his father's old weather-beaten farm-house. The exterior was of marble, so dazzlingly white that it seemed as though the whole structure might melt away in the sunshine, like those humbler ones which Mr. Gathergold, in his young play-days, before his fingers were gifted with the touch of transmutation, had been accustomed to build of snow. It had a richly ornamented portico, supported by tall pillars, beneath which was a lofty door, studded with silver knobs, and made of a kind of variegated wood that had been brought from beyond the sea. The windows, from the floor to the ceiling of each stately apartment, were composed, respectively, of but one enormous pane of glass, so transparently pure that it was said to be a finer medium than even the vacant atmosphere. Hardly anybody had been permitted to see the interior of this palace; but it was reported, and with good semblance of truth, to be far more gorgeous than the outside, insomuch that, whatever was iron or brass in other houses, was silver or gold in this; and Mr. Gathergold's bed-chamber, especially, made such a glittering appearance that no ordinary man would have been able to close his eyes there. But, on the other hand, Mr. Gathergold was now so inured to wealth, that perhaps he could not have closed his eyes, unless where the gleam of it was certain to find its way beneath his eyelids.

In due time, the mansion was finished; next came the upholsterers, with magnificent furniture; then, a whole troop of black and white servants, the harbingers of Mr. Gathergold, who, in his own majestic person, was expected to arrive at sunset. Our friend Ernest, meanwhile, had been deeply stirred by the idea that the great man, the noble man, the Man of Prophecy, after so many ages of delay, was at length to be made manifest to his native valley. He knew, boy as he was, that there were a thousand ways in which Mr. Gathergold, with his vast wealth, might transform himself into an angel of beneficence, and assume a control over human affairs as wide and benignant as the smile of the Great Stone Face. Full of faith and hope, Ernest doubted not that what the people said was true, and that now he was to behold the living likeness of those wondrous features on the mountain-side. While the boy was still gazing up the valley, and fancying, as he always did, that the Great Stone Face returned his gaze and looked kindly at him, the rumbling of wheels was heard, approaching swiftly along the winding road.

"Here he comes!" cried a group of people who were assembled to witness the arrival—"Here comes the great Mr. Gathergold!"

A carriage, drawn by four horses, dashed round the turn of the road. Within it, thrust partly out of the window, appeared the physiognomy of a little old man, with a skin as yellow as if his own Midas-hand had transmuted it. He had a low forehead, small, sharp eyes, puckered about with innumerable wrinkles, and very thin lips, which he made still thinner by pressing them forcibly together.

"The very image of the Great Stone Face!" shouted the people. "Sure enough, the old prophecy is true; and here we have the great man, come at last!"

And, what greatly perplexed Ernest, they seemed actually to believe that here was the likeness which they spoke of. By the road-side there chanced to be an old beggar-woman and two little beggar-children, stragglers from some far-off region, who, as the carriage rolled onward, held out their hands and lifted up their doleful voices, most piteously beseeching charity. A yellow claw—the very same that had clawed together so much wealth—poked itself out of the coach-window, and dropt some copper coins upon the ground; so that, though the great man's name seems to have been Gathergold, he might just as suitably have been nicknamed Scattercopper! Still, nevertheless, with an earnest shout, and evidently with as much good faith as ever, the people bellowed—

"He is the very image of the Great Stone Face!"

But Ernest turned sadly from the wrinkled shrewdness of that sordid visage, and gazed up the valley, where, amid a gathering mist, gilded by the last sunbeams, he could still distinguish those glorious features which had impressed themselves into his soul. Their aspect cheered him. What did the benign lips seem to say?

"He will come! Fear not, Ernest—the man will come!"

The years went on, and Ernest ceased to be a boy. He had grown to be a young man now. He attracted little notice from the other inhabitants of the valley; for they saw nothing remarkable in his way of life, save that when the labor of the day was over, he still loved to go apart and gaze and meditate upon the Great Stone Face. According to their idea of the matter, it was a folly, indeed, but pardonable, inasmuch as Ernest was industrious, kind, and neighborly, and neglected no duty for the sake of indulging this idle habit. They knew not that the Great Stone Face had become a teacher to him, and that the sentiment, which was expressed in it, would enlarge the young man's heart, and fill it with wider and deeper sympathies than other hearts. They knew not that thence would come a better wisdom than could be learned from books, and a better life than could be moulded on the defaced example of other human lives. Neither did Ernest know that the thoughts and affections which came to him so naturally, in the fields and at the fireside, and wherever he communed with himself, were of a higher tone than those which all men shared with him. A simple soul— simple as when his mother first taught him the old prophecy —he beheld the marvellous features beaming adown the valley, and still wondered that their human counterpart was so long in making his appearance.

By this time poor Mr. Gathergold was dead and buried; and the oddest part of the matter was, that his wealth, which was the body and spirit of his existence, had disappeared before his death, leaving nothing of him but a living skeleton, covered over with a wrinkled yellow skin. Since the melting away of his gold, it had been very generally conceded that there was no such striking resemblance, after all, betwixt the ignoble features of the ruined merchant and that majestic face upon the mountain-side. So the people ceased to honor him during his lifetime, and quietly consigned him to forgetfulness after his decease. Once in a while, it is true, his memory was brought up in connection with the magnificent palace which he had built, and which had long ago been turned into a hotel for the accommodation of strangers, multitudes of whom came, every summer, to visit that famous natural curiosity—the Great Stone Face. Thus, Mr. Gathergold being discredited and thrown into the shade, the Man of Prophecy was yet to come.

It so happened that a native-born son of the valley, many years before, had enlisted as a soldier, and, after a great deal of hard fighting, had now become an illustrious commander. Whatever he may be called in history, he was known in camps and on the battle-field, under the nickname of Old Blood-and-Thunder. This war-worn veteran, being now infirm with age and wounds, and weary of the turmoil of a military life, and of the roll of the drum and the clangor of the trumpet, that had so long been ringing in his ears, had lately signified a purpose of returning to his native valley, hoping to find repose where he remembered to have left it. The inhabitants, his old neighbors and their grown-up children, were resolved to welcome the renowned warrior with a salute of cannon and a public dinner; and all the more enthusiastically, it being affirmed that now, at last, the likeness of the Great Stone Face had actually appeared. An aid-de-camp of old Blood-and-Thunder, travelling through the valley, was said to have been struck with the resemblance. Moreover, the schoolmates and early acquaintances of the General were ready to testify on oath that, to the best of their recollection, the aforesaid General had been exceedingly like the majestic image, even when a boy, only that the idea had never occurred to them at that period. Great, therefore, was the excitement throughout the valley; and many people, who had never once thought of glancing at the Great Stone Face for years before, now spent their time in gazing at it, for the sake of knowing exactly how General Blood-and-Thunder looked.

On the day of the grand festival, Ernest, with all the other people of the valley, left their work, and proceeded to the spot where the sylvan banquet was prepared. As he approached, the loud voice of the Reverend Doctor Battle-blast was heard, beseeching a blessing on the good things set before them, and on the distinguished Friend of Peace, in whose honor they were assembled. The tables were arranged in a cleared space of the woods, shut in by the surrounding trees, except where a vista opened eastward, and afforded a distant view of the Great Stone Face. Over the General's chair, which was a relic from the home of Washington, there was an arch of verdant boughs, with the laurel profusely intermixed, and surmounted by his country's banner, beneath which he had won his victories. Our friend Ernest raised himself on his tip-toes, in hopes to get a glimpse of the cele-brated guest; but there was a mighty crowd about the tables, anxious to hear the toasts and speeches, and to catch any word that might fall from the General in reply; and a volun-teer company, doing duty as a guard, pricked ruthlessly with their bayonets at any particularly quiet person among the throng. So Ernest, being of an unobtrusive character, was thrust quite into the background, where he could see no more of Old Blood-and-Thunder's physiognomy than if it had been still blazing on the battle-field. To console himself, he turned towards the Great Stone Face, which, like a faithful and long-remembered friend, looked back and smiled upon him through the vista of the forest. Meantime, however, he could overhear the remarks of various individuals, who were comparing the features of the hero with the face on the distant mountain-side.

" 'Tis the same face, to a hair!" cried one man, cutting a caper for joy.

"Wonderfully like, that's a fact!" responded another.

"Like!—why, I call it Old Blood-and-Thunder himself, in a monstrous looking-glass!" cried a third. "And why not? He's the greatest man of this or any other age, beyond a doubt."

And then, all three of the speakers gave a great shout, which communicated electricity to the crowd, and called forth a roar from a thousand voices, that went reverberating for miles among the mountains, until you might have supposed that the Great Stone Face had poured its thunder-breath into the cry. All these comments, and this vast enthusiasm, served the more to interest our friend; nor did he think of questioning that now, at length, the mountain-visage had found its human counterpart. It is true, Ernest had imagined that this long-looked-for personage would appear in the character of a Man of Peace, uttering wisdom, and doing good, and making people happy. But, taking a habitual breadth of view, with all his simplicity, he contended that Providence should choose its own method of blessing mankind, and could conceive that this great end might be effected even by a warrior and a bloody sword, should Inscrutable Wisdom see fit to order matters so.

"The General! the General!" was now the cry. "Hush! silence! Old Blood-and-Thunder's going to make a speech."

Even so; for, the cloth being removed, the General's health had been drunk amid shouts of applause, and he now stood upon his feet to thank the company. Ernest saw him! There he was, over the shoulders of the crowd, from the two glittering epaulets and embroidered collar upward, beneath the arch of green boughs with intertwined laurel, and the banner drooping as if to shade his brow! And there, too, visible in the same glance, through the vista of the forest, appeared the Great Stone Face! And was there, indeed, such a resemblance as the crowd had testified? Alas, Ernest could not recognize it! He beheld a war-worn and weather-beaten countenance, full of energy, and expressive of an iron will; but the gentle wisdom, the deep, broad, tender sympathies, were altogether wanting in Old Blood-and-Thunder's visage; and even if the Great Stone Face had assumed his look of stern command, the milder traits would still have tempered it.

"This is not the Man of Prophecy," sighed Ernest to himself, as he made his way out of the throng. "And must the world wait longer yet?"

The mists had congregated about the distant mountain-side, and there were seen the grand and awful features of the Great Stone Face, awful but benignant, as if a mighty angel were sitting among the hills, and enrobing himself in a cloud-vesture of gold and purple. As he looked, Ernest could hardly believe but that a smile beamed over the whole visage, with a radiance still brightening, although without motion of the lips. It was probably the effect of the western sunshine, melting through the thinly diffused vapors that had swept between him and the object that he gazed at. But—as it always did—the aspect of his marvellous friend made Ernest as hopeful as if he had never hoped in vain.

"Fear not, Ernest," said his heart, even as if the Great Face were whispering him, "fear not, Ernest, he will come."

More years sped swiftly and tranquilly away. Ernest still dwelt in his native valley, and was now a man of middle age. By imperceptible degrees, he had become known among the people. Now, as heretofore, he labored for his bread, and was the same simple-hearted man that he had always been. But he had thought and felt so much—he had given so many of the best hours of his life to unworldly hopes for some great good to mankind, that it seemed as though he had been talking with the angels, and had imbibed a portion of their wisdom unawares. It was visible in the calm and well-considered beneficence of his daily life, the quiet stream of which had made a wide green margin all along its course. Not a day passed by, that the world was not the better because this man, humble as he was, had lived. He never stepped aside from his own path, yet would always reach a blessing to his neighbor. Almost involuntarily, too, he had become a preacher. The pure and high simplicity of his thought, which, as one of its manifestations, took shape in the good deeds that dropped silently from his hand, flowed also forth in speech. He uttered truths that wrought upon and moulded the lives of those who heard him. His auditors, it may be, never suspected that Ernest, their own neighbor and familiar friend, was more than an ordinary man; least of all, did Ernest himself suspect it; but, inevitably as the murmur of a rivulet, came thoughts out of his mouth that no other human lips had spoken.

When the people's minds had had a little time to cool, they were ready enough to acknowledge their mistake in imagining a similarity between General Blood-and-Thunder's truculent physiognomy and the benign visage on the mountain-side. But now, again, there were reports and many paragraphs in the newspapers, affirming that the likeness of the Great Stone Face had appeared upon the broad shoulders of a certain eminent statesman. He, like Mr. Gathergold and Old Blood-and-Thunder, was a native of the valley, but had left it in his early days, and taken up the trades of law and politics. Instead of the rich man's wealth and the warrior's sword, he had but a tongue, and it was mightier than both together. So wonderfully eloquent was he, that whatever he might choose to say, his auditors had no choice but to believe him; wrong looked like right, and right like wrong; for when it pleased him, he could make a kind of illuminated fog with his mere breath, and obscure the natural daylight with it.

His tongue, indeed, was a magic instrument; sometimes it rumbled like the thunder; sometimes it warbled like the sweetest music. It was the blast of war—the song of peace; and it seemed to have a heart in it, when there was no such matter. In good truth, he was a wondrous man; and when his tongue had acquired him all other imaginable success— when it had been heard in halls of state, and in the courts of princes and potentates—after it had made him known all over the world, even as a voice crying from shore to shore— it finally persuaded his countrymen to select him as a candidate for the Presidency. Before this time—indeed, as soon as he began to grow celebrated—his admirers had found out the resemblance between him and the Great Stone Face; and so much were they struck by it, that throughout the country this distinguished gentleman was known by the name of Old Stony Phiz. The phrase was considered as giving a highly favorable aspect to his political prospects; for as is likewise the case with the Popedom, nobody ever becomes President without taking a name other than his own.

While his friends were doing their best to make him President, Old Stony Phiz, as he was called, set out on a visit to the valley where he was born. Of course, he had no other object than to shake hands with his fellow-citizens, and neither thought nor cared about any effect which his progress through the country might have upon the election. Magnificent preparations were made to receive the illustrious statesman; a cavalcade of horsemen set forth to meet him at the boundary line of the State; and all the people left their business and gathered along the wayside to see him pass. Among these was Ernest. Though more than once disappointed, as we have seen, he had such a hopeful and confiding nature, that he was always ready to believe in whatever seemed beautiful and good. He kept his heart continually open, and thus was sure to catch the blessing from on high, when it should come. So now again, as buoyantly as ever, he went forth to behold the likeness of the Great Stone Face.

The cavalcade came prancing along the road, with a great clattering of hoofs and a mighty cloud of dust, which rose up so dense and high that the visage of the mountain-side was completely hidden from Ernest's eyes. All the great men of the neighborhood were there on horseback; militia officers, in uniform; the member of Congress; the sheriff of the county; the editors of newspapers; and many a farmer, too, had mounted his patient steed, with his Sunday coat upon his back. It really was a very brilliant spectacle, especially as there were numerous banners flaunting over the cavalcade, on some of which were gorgeous portraits of the illustrious statesman and the Great Stone Face, smiling familiarly at one another, like two brothers. If the pictures were to be trusted, the mutual resemblance, it must be confessed, was marvellous. We must not forget to mention, that there was a band of music, which made the echoes of the mountains ring and reverberate with the loud triumph of its strains; so that airy and soul-thrilling melodies broke out among all the heights and hollows, as if every nook of his native valley had found a voice, to welcome the distinguished guest. But the grandest effect was when the far-off mountain precipice flung back the music; for then the Great Stone Face itself seemed to be swelling the triumphant chorus, in acknowledgment that, at length, the Man of Prophecy was come.

All this while the people were throwing up their hats and shouting, with enthusiasm so contagious that the heart of Ernest kindled up, and he likewise threw up his hat, and shouted, as loudly as the loudest—"Huzza for the great man! Huzza for Old Stony Phiz!" But as yet he had not seen him.

"Here he is now!" cried those who stood near Ernest. "There! There! Look at Old Stony Phiz and then at the Old Man of the Mountain, and see if they are not as like as two twin-brothers!"

In the midst of all this gallant array, came an open barouche, drawn by four white horses; and in the barouche, with his massive head uncovered, sat the illustrious statesman, Old Stony Phiz himself.

"Confess it," said one of Ernest's neighbors to him, "the Great Stone Face has met its match at last!"

Now, it must be owned that, at his first glimpse of the countenance which was bowing and smiling from the barouche, Ernest did fancy that there was a resemblance between it and the old familiar face upon the mountain-side. The brow, with its massive depth and loftiness, and all the other features, indeed, were boldly and strongly hewn, as if in emulation of a more than heroic, of a Titanic model. But the sublimity and stateliness, the grand expression of a divine sympathy, that illuminated the mountain visage, and ethere- alized its ponderous granite substance into spirit, might here be sought in vain. Something had been originally left out, or had departed. And therefore the marvellously gifted states- man had always a weary gloom in the deep caverns of his eyes, as of a child that has outgrown its playthings, or a man of mighty faculties and little aims, whose life, with all its high performances, was vague and empty, because no high purpose had endowed it with reality.

Still, Ernest's neighbor was thrusting his elbow into his side, and pressing him for an answer—

"Confess! Confess! Is not he the very picture of your Old Man of the Mountain?"

"No!" said Ernest, bluntly, "I see little or no likeness."

"Then so much the worse for the Great Stone Face!" answered his neighbor; and again he set up a shout for Old Stony Phiz.

But Ernest turned away, melancholy, and almost despon- dent; for this was the saddest of his disappointments, to behold a man who might have fulfilled the prophecy, and had not willed to do so. Meantime, the cavalcade, the banners, the music, and the barouches swept past him, with the vociferous crowd in the rear, leaving the dust to settle down, and the Great Stone Face to be revealed again, with the grandeur that it had worn for untold centuries.

"Lo, here I am, Ernest!" the benign lips seemed to say. "I have waited longer than thou, and am not yet weary. Fear not; the man will come."

The years hurried onward, treading in their haste on one another's heels. And now they began to bring white hairs, and scatter them over the head of Ernest; they made reverend wrinkles across his forehead, and furrows in his cheeks. He was an aged man. But not in vain had he grown old; more than the white hairs on his head were the sage thoughts in his mind; his wrinkles and furrows were inscriptions that Time had graved, and in which he had written legends of wisdom that had been tested by the tenor of a life. And Ernest had ceased to be obscure. Unsought for, undesired, had come the fame which so many seek, and made him known in the great world, beyond the limits of the valley in which he had dwelt so quietly. College professors, and even the active men of cities, came from far to see and converse with Ernest; for the report had gone abroad that this simple husbandman had ideas unlike those of other men, not gained from books, but of a higher tone—a tranquil and familiar majesty, as if he had been talking with the angels as his daily friends. Whether it were sage, statesman, or philanthropist, Ernest received these visiters with the gentle sincerity that had characterized him from boyhood, and spoke freely with them of whatever came uppermost, or lay deepest in his heart or their own. While they talked together, his face would kindle, unawares, and shine upon them, as with a mild evening light. Pensive with the fulness of such discourse, his guests took leave and went their way; and, passing up the valley, paused to look at the Great Stone Face, imagining that they had seen its likeness in a human countenance, but could not remember where.

While Ernest had been growing up and growing old, a bountiful Providence had granted a new poet to this earth. He, likewise, was a native of the valley, but had spent the greater part of his life at a distance from that romantic region, pouring out his sweet music amid the bustle and din of cities. Often, however, did the mountains which had been familiar to him in his childhood, lift their snowy peaks into the clear atmosphere of his poetry. Neither was the Great Stone Face forgotten, for the poet had celebrated it in an ode, which was grand enough to have been uttered by its own majestic lips. This man of genius, we may say, had come down from heaven with wonderful endowments. If he sang of a mountain, the eyes of all mankind beheld a mightier grandeur reposing on its breast or soaring to its summit, than had before been seen there. If his theme were a lovely lake, a celestial smile had now been thrown over it, to gleam forever on its surface. If it were the vast, old sea, even the deep immensity of its dread bosom seemed to swell the higher, as if moved by the emotions of the song. Thus the world assumed another and a better aspect from the hour that the poet blessed it with his happy eyes. The Creator had bestowed him, as the last, best touch to his own handiwork. Creation was not finished till the poet came to interpret, and so complete it.

The effect was no less high and beautiful, when his human brethren were the subject of his verse. The man or woman, sordid with the common dust of life, who crossed his daily path, and the little child who played in it, were glorified if he beheld them in his mood of poetic faith. He showed the golden links of the great chain that intertwined them with an angelic kindred; he brought out the hidden traits of a celestial birth that made them worthy of such kin. Some, indeed, there were, who thought to show the soundness of their judgment by affirming that all the beauty and dignity of the natural world existed only in the poet's fancy. Let such men speak for themselves, who undoubtedly appear to have been spawned forth by Nature with a contemptuous bitterness; she having plastered them up out of her refuse stuff, after all the swine were made. As respects all things else, the poet's ideal was the truest truth.

The songs of this poet found their way to Ernest. He read them, after his customary toil, seated on the bench before his cottage door, where, for such a length of time, he had filled his repose with thought, by gazing at the Great Stone Face. And now, as he read stanzas that caused the soul to thrill within him, he lifted his eyes to the vast countenance beaming on him so benignantly.

"Oh, majestic friend," he murmured, addressing the Great Stone Face, "is not this man worthy to resemble thee?"

The Face seemed to smile, but answered not a word.

Now it happened that the poet, though he dwelt so far away, had not only heard of Ernest, but had meditated much upon his character, until he deemed nothing so desirable as to meet this man, whose untaught wisdom walked hand in hand with the noble simplicity of his life. One summer morning, therefore, he took passage by the railroad, and, in the decline of the afternoon, alighted from the cars at no great distance from Ernest's cottage. The great hotel, which had formerly been the palace of Mr. Gathergold, was close at hand, but the poet, with his carpet-bag on his arm, inquired at once where Ernest dwelt, and was resolved to be accepted as his guest.

Approaching the door, he there found the good old man, holding a volume in his hand, which alternately he read, and then, with a finger between the leaves, looked lovingly at the Great Stone Face.

"Good evening," said the poet. "Can you give a traveller a night's lodging?"

"Willingly," answered Ernest; and then he added, smiling, "methinks I never saw the Great Stone Face look so hospitably at a stranger."

The poet sat down on the bench beside him, and he and Ernest talked together. Often had the poet held intercourse with the wittiest and the wisest, but never before with a man like Ernest, whose thoughts and feelings gushed up with such a natural freedom, and who made great truths so familiar by his simple utterance of them. Angels, as had been so often said, seemed to have wrought with him at his labor in the fields; angels seemed to have sat with him by the fireside; and, dwelling with angels as friend with friends, he had imbibed the sublimity of their ideas, and imbued it with the sweet and lowly charm of household words. So thought the poet. And Ernest, on the other hand, was moved and agitated by the living images which the poet flung out of his mind, and which peopled all the air about the cottage door with shapes of beauty, both gay and pensive. The sympathies of these two men instructed them with a profounder sense than either could have attained alone. Their minds accorded into one strain, and made delightful music which neither of them could have claimed as all his own, nor distinguished his own share from the other's. They led one another, as it were, into a high pavilion of their thoughts, so remote, and hitherto so dim that they had never entered it before, and so beautiful, that they desired to be there always.

As Ernest listened to the poet, he imagined that the Great Stone Face was bending forward to listen too. He gazed earnestly into the poet's glowing eyes.

"Who are you, my strangely gifted guest?" he said.

The poet laid his finger on the volume that Ernest had been reading.

"You have read these poems," said he. "You know me, then—for I wrote them!"

Again, and still more earnestly than before, Ernest examined the poet's features; then turned towards the Great Stone Face; then back, with an uncertain aspect, to his guest. But his countenance fell; he shook his head, and sighed.

"Wherefore are you sad?" inquired the poet.

"Because," replied Ernest, "all through life, I have awaited the fulfilment of a prophecy; and, when I read these poems, I hoped that it might be fulfilled in you."

"You hoped," answered the poet, faintly smiling, "to find in me the likeness of the Great Stone Face! And you are disappointed, as formerly with Mr. Gathergold, and Old Blood-and-Thunder, and Old Stony Phiz! Yes, Ernest, it is my doom. You must add my name to those of the illustrious Three, and record another failure of your hopes. For—in shame and sadness do I speak it, Ernest—I am not worthy to be typified by yonder benign and majestic image!"

"And why?" asked Ernest; he pointed to the volume. "Are not those thoughts divine?"

"They have a strain of the Divinity," replied the poet. "You can hear in them the far-off echo of a heavenly song. But my life, dear Ernest, has not corresponded with my thought. I have had grand dreams, but they have been only dreams, because I have lived—and that, too, by my own choice—among poor and mean realities. Sometimes even—shall I dare to say it?—I lack faith in the grandeur, the beauty, and the goodness, which my own works are said to have made more evident in nature and in human life. Why, then, pure Seeker of the Good and True, should'st thou hope to find me, in yonder image of the Divine!"

The poet spoke sadly, and his eyes were dim with tears. So, likewise, were those of Ernest.

At the hour of sunset, as had long been his frequent custom, Ernest was to discourse to an assemblage of the neighboring inhabitants, in the open air. He and the poet, arm in arm, still talking together as they went along, proceeded to the spot. It was a small nook among the hills, with a gray precipice behind, the stern front of which was relieved by the pleasant foliage of many creeping plants, that made a tapestry for the naked rock, by hanging their festoons from all its rugged angles. At a small elevation above the ground, set in a rich frame-work of verdure, there appeared a niche, spacious enough to admit a human figure, with freedom for such gestures as spontaneously accompany earnest thought and genuine emotion. Into this natural pulpit Ernest ascended, and threw a look of familiar kindness around upon his audience. They stood, or sat, or reclined upon the grass, as seemed good to each, with the departing sunshine falling obliquely over them, and mingling its subdued cheerfulness with the solemnity of a grove of ancient trees, beneath and amid the boughs of which the golden rays were constrained to pass. In another direction was seen the Great Stone Face, with the same cheer, combined with the same solemnity, in its benignant aspect.

Ernest began to speak, giving to the people of what was in his heart and mind. His words had power, because they accorded with his thoughts, and his thoughts had reality and depth, because they harmonized with the life which he had always lived. It was not mere breath that this preacher uttered; they were the words of life, because a life of good deeds and holy love was melted into them. Pearls, pure and rich, had been dissolved into this precious draught. The poet, as he listened, felt that the being and character of Ernest were a nobler strain of poetry than he had ever written. His eyes glistening with tears, he gazed reverentially at the venerable man, and said within himself, that never was there an aspect so worthy of a prophet and a sage as that mild, sweet, thoughtful countenance, with the glory of white hair diffused about it. At a distance, but distinctly to be seen, high up in the golden light of the setting sun, appeared the Great Stone Face, with hoary mists around it, like the white hairs around the brow of Ernest. Its look of grand beneficence seemed to embrace the world.

At that moment, in sympathy with a thought which he was about to utter, the face of Ernest assumed a grandeur of expression, so imbued with benevolence, that the poet, by an irresistible impulse, threw his arms aloft, and shouted—

"Behold! Behold! Ernest is himself the likeness of the Great Stone Face!"

Then all the people looked, and saw that what the deep-sighted poet said was true. The prophecy was fulfilled. But Ernest, having finished what he had to say, took the poet's arm, and walked slowly homeward, still hoping that some wiser and better man than himself would by-and-by appear, bearing a resemblance to the GREAT STONE FACE.

MAIN-STREET

A RESPECTABLE-LOOKING individual makes his bow, and addresses the public. In my daily walks along the principal street of my native town, it has often occurred to me, that, if its growth from infancy upward, and the vicissitude of characteristic scenes that have passed along this thoroughfare, during the more than two centuries of its existence, could be presented to the eye in a shifting panorama, it would be an exceedingly effective method of illustrating the march of time. Acting on this idea, I have contrived a certain pictorial exhibition, somewhat in the nature of a puppet-show, by means of which I propose to call up the multiform and many-colored Past before the spectator, and show him the ghosts of his forefathers, amid a succession of historic incidents, with no greater trouble than the turning of a crank. Be pleased, therefore, my indulgent patrons, to walk into the show-room, and take your seats before yonder mysterious curtain. The little wheels and springs of my machinery have been well oiled; a multitude of puppets are dressed in character, representing all varieties of fashion, from the Puritan cloak and jerkin to the latest Oak Hall coat; the lamps are trimmed, and shall brighten into noontide sunshine, or fade away in moonlight, or muffle their brilliancy in a November cloud, as the nature of the scene may require; and, in short, the exhibition is just ready to commence. Unless something should go wrong,—as, for instance, the misplacing of a picture, whereby the people and events of one century might be thrust into the middle of another; or the breaking of a wire, which would bring the course of time to a sudden period,—barring, I say, the casualties to which such a complicated piece of mechanism is liable, I flatter myself, ladies and gentlemen, that the performance will elicit your generous approbation.

Ting-a-ting-ting! goes the bell; the curtain rises; and we behold—not, indeed, the Main-street—but the tract of leaf-strewn forest-land, over which its dusty pavement is hereafter to extend.

You perceive, at a glance, that this is the ancient and primitive wood,—the ever-youthful and venerably old,—verdant with new twigs, yet hoary, as it were, with the snowfall of innumerable years, that have accumulated upon its intermingled branches. The white man's axe has never smitten a single tree; his footstep has never crumpled a single one of the withered leaves, which all the autumns since the flood have been harvesting beneath. Yet, see! along through the vista of impending boughs, there is already a faintly-traced path, running nearly east and west, as if a prophecy or foreboding of the future street had stolen into the heart of the solemn old wood. Onward goes this hardly perceptible track, now ascending over a natural swell of land, now subsiding gently into a hollow; traversed here by a little streamlet, which glitters like a snake through the gleam of sunshine, and quickly hides itself among the underbrush, in its quest for the neighboring cove; and impeded there by the massy corpse of a giant of the forest, which had lived out its incalculable term of life, and been overthrown by mere old age, and lies buried in the new vegetation that is born of its decay. What footsteps can have worn this half-seen path? Hark! Do we not hear them now rustling softly over the leaves? We discern an Indian woman—a majestic and queenly woman, or else her spectral image does not represent her truly—for this is the great Squaw Sachem, whose rule, with that of her sons, extends from Mystic to Agawam. That red chief, who stalks by her side, is Wappacowet, her second husband, the priest and magician, whose incantations shall hereafter affright the pale-faced settlers with grisly phantoms, dancing and shrieking in the woods, at midnight. But greater would be the affright of the Indian necromancer, if, mirrored in the pool of water at his feet, he could catch a prophetic glimpse of the noon-day marvels which the white man is destined to achieve; if he could see, as in a dream, the stone-front of the stately hall, which will cast its shadow over this very spot; if he could be aware that the future edifice will contain a noble Museum, where, among countless curiosities of earth and sea, a few Indian arrow-heads shall be treasured up as memorials of a vanished race!

No such forebodings disturb the Squaw Sachem and Wappacowet. They pass on, beneath the tangled shade, holding high talk on matters of state and religion, and imagine, doubtless, that their own system of affairs will endure for ever. Meanwhile, how full of its own proper life is the scene that lies around them! The gray squirrel runs up the trees, and rustles among the upper branches. Was not that the leap of a deer? And there is the whirr of a partridge! Methinks, too, I catch the cruel and stealthy eye of a wolf, as he draws back into yonder impervious density of underbrush. So, there, amid the murmur of boughs, go the Indian queen and the Indian priest; while the gloom of the broad wilderness impends over them, and its sombre mystery invests them as with something preternatural; and only momentary streaks of quivering sunlight, once in a great while, find their way down, and glimmer among the feathers in their dusky hair. Can it be that the thronged street of a city will ever pass into this twilight solitude,—over those soft heaps of the decaying tree-trunks,—and through the swampy places, green with water-moss,—and penetrate that hopeless entanglement of great trees, which have been uprooted and tossed together by a whirlwind! It has been a wilderness from the creation. Must it not be a wilderness for ever?

Here an acidulous-looking gentleman in blue glasses, with bows of Berlin steel, who has taken a seat at the extremity of the front row, begins, at this early stage of the exhibition, to criticise.

"The whole affair is a manifest catch-penny," observes he, scarcely under his breath. "The trees look more like weeds in a garden, than a primitive forest; the Squaw Sachem and Wappacowet are stiff in their pasteboard joints; and the squirrels, the deer, and the wolf, move with all the grace of a child's wooden monkey, sliding up and down a stick."

"I am obliged to you, sir, for the candor of your remarks," replies the showman, with a bow. "Perhaps they are just. Human art has its limits, and we must now and then ask a little aid from the spectator's imagination."

"You will get no such aid from mine," responds the critic. "I make it a point to see things precisely as they are. But come! go ahead!—the stage is waiting!"

The showman proceeds.

Casting our eyes again over the scene, we perceive that strangers have found their way into the solitary place. In more than one spot, among the trees, an upheaved axe is glittering in the sunshine. Roger Conant, the first settler in Naumkeag, has built his dwelling, months ago, on the border of the forest-path; and at this moment he comes eastward through the vista of woods, with his gun over his shoulder, bringing home the choice portions of a deer. His stalwart figure, clad in a leathern jerkin and breeches of the same, strides sturdily onward, with such an air of physical force and energy, that we might almost expect the very trees to stand aside, and give him room to pass. And so, indeed, they must; for, humble as is his name in history, Roger Conant still is of that class of men who do not merely find, but make, their place in the system of human affairs: a man of thoughtful strength, he has planted the germ of a city. There stands his habitation, showing in its rough architecture some features of the Indian wigwam, and some of the log-cabin, and somewhat, too, of the straw-thatched cottage in Old England, where this good yeoman had his birth and breeding. The dwelling is surrounded by a cleared space of a few acres, where Indian corn grows thrivingly among the stumps of the trees; while the dark forest hems it in, and seems to gaze silently and solemnly, as if wondering at the breadth of sunshine which the white man spreads around him. An Indian, half hidden in the dusky shade, is gazing and wondering too.

Within the door of the cottage, you discern the wife, with her ruddy English cheek. She is singing, doubtless, a psalm-tune, at her household work; or perhaps she sighs at the remembrance of the cheerful gossip, and all the merry social life, of her native village beyond the vast and melancholy sea. Yet the next moment she laughs, with sympathetic glee, at the sports of her little tribe of children, and soon turns round, with the home-look in her face, as her husband's foot is heard approaching the rough-hewn threshold. How sweet must it be for those who have an Eden in their hearts, like Roger Conant and his wife, to find a new world to project it into, as they have; instead of dwelling among old haunts of men, where so many household fires have been kindled and burnt out, that the very glow of happiness has something dreary in it! Not that this pair are alone in their wild Eden; for here comes Goodwife Massey, the young spouse of Jeffrey Massey, from her home hard by, with an infant at her breast.

Dame Conant has another of like age; and it shall hereafter be one of the disputed points of history, which of these two babies was the first town-born child.

But see! Roger Conant has other neighbors within view. Peter Palfrey likewise has built himself a house, and so has Balch and Norman and Woodbury. Their dwellings, indeed, —such is the ingenious contrivance of this piece of pictorial mechanism,—seem to have arisen, at various points of the scene, even while we have been looking at it. The forest-track, trodden more and more by the hob-nailed shoes of these sturdy and ponderous Englishmen, has now a distinct-ness which it never could have acquired from the light tread of a hundred times as many Indian moccasins. It will be a street, anon. As we observe it now, it goes onward from one clearing to another, here plunging into a shadowy strip of woods, there open to the sunshine, but everywhere showing a decided line, along which human interests have begun to hold their career. Over yonder swampy spot, two trees have been felled, and laid side by side, to make a causeway. In another place, the axe has cleared away a confused intricacy of fallen trees and clustered boughs, which had been tossed together by a hurricane. So, now, the little children, just beginning to run alone, may trip along the path, and not often stumble over an impediment, unless they stray from it to gather wood-berries beneath the trees. And, besides the feet of grown people and children, there are the cloven hoofs of a small herd of cows, who seek their subsistence from the native grasses, and help to deepen the track of the future thoroughfare. Goats also browse along it, and nibble at the twigs that thrust themselves across the way. Not seldom, in its more secluded portions, where the black shadow of the forest strives to hide the trace of human footsteps, stalks a gaunt wolf, on the watch for a kid or a young calf; or fixes his hungry gaze on the group of children gathering berries, and can hardly forbear to rush upon them. And the Indians, coming from their distant wigwams to view the white man's settlement, marvel at the deep track which he makes, and perhaps are saddened by a flitting presentiment, that this heavy tread will find its way over all the land; and that the wild woods, the wild wolf, and the wild Indian, will alike be trampled beneath it. Even so shall it be. The pavements of the Main-street must be laid over the red man's grave.

Behold! here is a spectacle which should be ushered in by the peal of trumpets, if Naumkeag had ever yet heard that cheery music, and by the roar of cannon, echoing among the woods. A procession—for, by its dignity, as marking an epoch in the history of the street, it deserves that name— a procession advances along the pathway. The good ship Abigail has arrived from England, bringing wares and merchandise, for the comfort of the inhabitants, and traffic with the Indians; bringing passengers too, and, more important than all, a Governor for the new settlement. Roger Conant and Peter Palfrey, with their companions, have been to the shore to welcome him; and now, with such honor and triumph as their rude way of life permits, are escorting the sea-flushed voyagers to their habitations. At the point where Endicott enters upon the scene, two venerable trees unite their branches high above his head; thus forming a triumphal arch of living verdure, beneath which he pauses, with his wife leaning on his arm, to catch the first impression of their new-found home. The old settlers gaze not less earnestly at him, than he at the hoary woods and the rough surface of the clearings. They like his bearded face, under the shadow of the broad-brimmed and steeple-crowned Puritan hat;—a visage, resolute, grave, and thoughtful, yet apt to kindle with that glow of a cheerful spirit, by which men of strong character are enabled to go joyfully on their proper tasks. His form, too, as you see it, in a doublet and hose of sad-colored cloth, is of a manly make, fit for toil and hardship, and fit to wield the heavy sword that hangs from his leathern belt. His aspect is a better warrant for the ruler's office, than the parchment commission which he bears, however fortified it may be with the broad seal of the London council. Peter Palfrey nods to Roger Conant. "The worshipful Court of Assistants have done wisely," say they between themselves. "They have chosen for our governor a man out of a thousand." Then they toss up their hats,—they, and all the uncouth figures of their company, most of whom are clad in skins, inasmuch as their old kersey and linsey-woolsey garments have been torn and tattered by many a long month's wear,—they all toss up their hats, and salute their new governor and captain with a hearty English shout of welcome. We seem to hear it with our own ears; so perfectly is the action represented in this life-like, this almost magic picture!

But have you observed the lady who leans upon the arm of Endicott?—a rose of beauty from an English garden, now to be transplanted to a fresher soil. It may be, that, long years—centuries, indeed—after this fair flower shall have decayed, other flowers of the same race will appear in the same soil, and gladden other generations with hereditary beauty. Does not the vision haunt us yet? Has not Nature kept the mould unbroken, deeming it a pity that the idea should vanish from mortal sight for ever, after only once assuming earthly substance? Do we not recognize, in that fair woman's face, the model of features which still beam, at happy moments, on what was then the woodland pathway, but has long since grown into a busy street?

"This is too ridiculous!—positively insufferable!" mutters the same critic who had before expressed his disapprobation. "Here is a pasteboard figure, such as a child would cut out of a card, with a pair of very dull scissors; and the fellow modestly requests us to see in it the prototype of hereditary beauty!"

"But, sir, you have not the proper point of view," remarks the showman. "You sit altogether too near to get the best effect of my pictorial exhibition. Pray, oblige me by removing to this other bench; and, I venture to assure you, the proper light and shadow will transform the spectacle into quite another thing."

"Pshaw!" replies the critic: "I want no other light and shade. I have already told you, that it is my business to see things just as they are."

"I would suggest to the author of this ingenious exhibition," observes a gentlemanly person, who has shown signs of being much interested,—"I would suggest, that Anna Gower, the first wife of Governor Endicott, and who came with him from England, left no posterity; and that, consequently, we cannot be indebted to that honorable lady for any specimens of feminine loveliness, now extant among us."

Having nothing to allege against this genealogical objection, the showman points again to the scene.

During this little interruption, you perceive that the Anglo-Saxon energy—as the phrase now goes—has been at work in the spectacle before us. So many chimneys now send up their smoke, that it begins to have the aspect of a village street; although every thing is so inartificial and inceptive, that it seems as if one returning wave of the wild nature might overwhelm it all. But the one edifice, which gives the pledge of permanence to this bold enterprise, is seen at the central point of the picture. There stands the meeting-house, a small structure, low-roofed, without a spire, and built of rough timber, newly hewn, with the sap still in the logs, and here and there a strip of bark adhering to them. A meaner temple was never consecrated to the worship of the Deity. With the alternative of kneeling beneath the awful vault of the firmament, it is strange that men should creep into this pent-up nook, and expect God's presence there. Such, at least, one would imagine, might be the feeling of these forest-settlers, accustomed, as they had been, to stand under the dim arches of vast cathedrals, and to offer up their hereditary worship in the old, ivy-covered churches of rural England, around which lay the bones of many generations of their forefathers. How could they dispense with the carved altar-work?—how, with the pictured windows, where the light of common day was hallowed by being transmitted through the glorified figures of saints?—how, with the lofty roof, imbued, as it must have been, with the prayers that had gone upward for centuries?—how, with the rich peal of the solemn organ, rolling along the aisles, pervading the whole church, and sweeping the soul away on a flood of audible religion? They needed nothing of all this. Their house of worship, like their ceremonial, was naked, simple, and severe. But the zeal of a recovered faith burned like a lamp within their hearts, enriching every thing around them with its radiance; making of these new walls, and this narrow compass, its own cathedral; and being, in itself, that spiritual mystery and experience, of which sacred architecture, pictured windows, and the organ's grand solemnity, are remote and imperfect symbols. All was well, so long as their lamps were freshly kindled at the heavenly flame. After a while, however, whether in their time or their children's, these lamps began to burn more dimly, or with a less genuine lustre; and then it might be seen, how hard, cold, and confined, was their system,—how like an iron cage was that which they called Liberty!

Too much of this. Look again at the picture, and observe how the aforesaid Anglo-Saxon energy is now trampling along the street, and raising a positive cloud of dust beneath its sturdy footsteps. For there the carpenters are building a new house, the frame of which was hewn and fitted in England, of English oak, and sent hither on shipboard; and here a blacksmith makes huge clang and clatter on his anvil, shaping out tools and weapons; and yonder a wheelwright, who boasts himself a London workman, regularly bred to his handicraft, is fashioning a set of wagon-wheels, the track of which shall soon be visible. The wild forest is shrinking back; the street has lost the aromatic odor of the pine-trees, and of the sweet fern that grew beneath them. The tender and modest wild-flowers, those gentle children of savage nature that grew pale beneath the ever-brooding shade, have shrunk away and disappeared, like stars that vanish in the breadth of light. Gardens are fenced in, and display pumpkin-beds and rows of cabbages and beans; and, though the governor and the minister both view them with a disapproving eye, plants of broad-leaved tobacco, which the cultivators are enjoined to use privily, or not at all. No wolf, for a year past, has been heard to bark, or known to range among the dwellings, except that single one whose grisly head, with a plash of blood beneath it, is now affixed to the portal of the meeting-house. The partridge has ceased to run across the too-frequented path. Of all the wild life that used to throng here, only the Indians still come into the settlement, bringing the skins of beaver and otter, bear and elk, which they sell to Endicott for the wares of England. And there is little John Massey, the son of Jeffrey Massey and first-born of Naumkeag, playing beside his father's threshold, a child of six or seven years old. Which is the better-grown infant,—the town or the boy?

The red men have become aware, that the street is no longer free to them, save by the sufferance and permission of the settlers. Often, to impress them with an awe of English power, there is a muster and training of the town-forces, and a stately march of the mail-clad band, like this which we now see advancing up the street. There they come, fifty of them, or more; all with their iron breastplates and steel-caps well burnished, and glimmering bravely against the sun; their ponderous muskets on their shoulders, their bandaliers about their waists, their lighted matches in their hands, and the drum and fife playing cheerily before them. See! do they not step like martial men? Do they not manœuvre like soldiers who have seen stricken fields? And well they may; for this band is composed of precisely such materials as those with which Cromwell is preparing to beat down the strength of a kingdom; and his famous regiment of Ironsides might be recruited from just such men. In every thing, at this period, New England was the essential spirit and flower of that which was about to become uppermost in the mother-country. Many a bold and wise man lost the fame which would have accrued to him in English history, by crossing the Atlantic with our forefathers. Many a valiant captain, who might have been foremost at Marston Moor or Naseby, exhausted his martial ardor in the command of a log-built fortress, like that which you observe on the gently rising ground at the right of the pathway,—its banner fluttering in the breeze, and the culverins and sakers showing their deadly muzzles over the rampart.

A multitude of people were now thronging to New England; some, because the ancient and ponderous framework of Church and State threatened to crumble down upon their heads; others, because they despaired of such a downfall. Among those who came to Naumkeag were men of history and legend, whose feet leave a track of brightness along any pathway which they have trodden. You shall behold their life-like images,—their spectres, if you choose so to call them,—passing, encountering with a familiar nod, stopping to converse together, praying, bearing weapons, laboring or resting from their labors, in the Main-street. Here, now, comes Hugh Peters, an earnest, restless man, walking swiftly, as being impelled by that fiery activity of nature which shall hereafter thrust him into the conflict of dangerous affairs, make him the chaplain and counsellor of Cromwell, and finally bring him to a bloody end. He pauses, by the meeting-house, to exchange a greeting with Roger Williams, whose face indicates, methinks, a gentler spirit, kinder and more expansive, than that of Peters; yet not less active for what he discerns to be the will of God, or the welfare of mankind. And look! here is a guest for Endicott, coming forth out of the forest, through which he has been journeying from Boston, and which, with its rude branches, has caught hold of his attire, and has wet his feet with its swamps and streams. Still there is something in his mild and venerable, though not aged presence,—a propriety, an equilibrium in Governor Winthrop's nature,—that causes the disarray of his costume to be unnoticed, and gives us the same impression as if he were clad in such grave and rich attire as we may suppose him to have worn in the Council Chamber of the colony. Is not this characteristic wonderfully perceptible in our spectral representative of his person? But what dignitary is this crossing from the other side to greet the governor? A stately personage, in a dark velvet cloak, with a hoary beard, and a gold chain across his breast; he has the authoritative port of one who has filled the highest civic station in the first of cities. Of all men in the world, we should least expect to meet the Lord Mayor of London—as Sir Richard Saltonstall has been, once and again—in a forest-bordered settlement of the western wilderness.

Farther down the street, we see Emanuel Downing, a grave and worthy citizen, with his son George, a stripling who has a career before him; his shrewd and quick capacity and pliant conscience shall not only exalt him high, but secure him from a downfall. Here is another figure, on whose characteristic make and expressive action I will stake the credit of my pictorial puppet-show. Have you not already detected a quaint, sly humor in that face,—an eccentricity in the manner,—a certain indescribable waywardness,—all the marks, in short, of an original man, unmistakeably impressed, yet kept down by a sense of clerical restraint? That is Nathaniel Ward, the minister of Ipswich, but better remembered as the simple cobbler of Agawam. He hammered his sole so faithfully, and stitched his upper-leather so well, that the shoe is hardly yet worn out, though thrown aside for some two centuries past. And next, among these Puritans and Roundheads, we observe the very model of a Cavalier, with the curling lovelock, the fantastically trimmed beard, the embroidery, the ornamented rapier, the gilded dagger, and all other foppishnesses that distinguished the wild gallants who rode headlong to their overthrow in the cause of King Charles. This is Morton of Merry Mount, who has come hither to hold a council with Endicott, but will shortly be his prisoner. Yonder pale, decaying figure of a white-robed woman who glides slowly along the street, is the Lady Arabella, looking for her own grave in the virgin soil. That other female form, who seems to be talking—we might almost say preaching or expounding—in the centre of a group of profoundly attentive auditors, is Ann Hutchinson. And here comes Vane.——

"But, my dear sir," interrupts the same gentleman who before questioned the showman's genealogical accuracy, "allow me to observe, that these historical personages could not possibly have met together in the Main-street. They might, and probably did, all visit our old town, at one time or another, but not simultaneously; and you have fallen into anachronisms that I positively shudder to think of!"

"The fellow," adds the scarcely civil critic, "has learned a bead-roll of historic names, whom he lugs into his pictorial puppet-show, as he calls it, helter-skelter, without caring whether they were contemporaries or not,—and sets them all by the ears together. But was there ever such a fund of impudence! To hear his running commentary, you would suppose that these miserable slips of painted pasteboard, with hardly the remotest outlines of the human figure, had all the character and expression of Michael Angelo's pictures. Well!—go on, sir!"

"Sir, you break the illusion of the scene," mildly remonstrates the showman.

"Illusion! What illusion?" rejoins the critic, with a contemptuous snort. "On the word of a gentleman, I see nothing illusive in the wretchedly bedaubed sheet of canvass that forms your back-ground, or in these pasteboard slips that hitch and jerk along the front. The only illusion, permit me to say, is in the puppet-showman's tongue,—and that but a wretched one, into the bargain!"

"We public men," replies the showman, meekly, "must lay our account, sometimes, to meet an uncandid severity of criticism. But—merely for your own pleasure, sir—let me entreat you to take another point of view. Sit further back, by that young lady, in whose face I have watched the reflection of every changing scene; only oblige me by sitting there; and, take my word for it, the slips of pasteboard shall assume spiritual life, and the bedaubed canvass become an airy and changeable reflex of what it purports to represent."

"I know better," retorts the critic, settling himself in his seat, with sullen, but self-complacent immovableness. "And, as for my own pleasure, I shall best consult it by remaining precisely where I am."

The showman bows, and waves his hand; and, at the signal, as if time and vicissitude had been awaiting his permission to move onward, the mimic street becomes alive again.

Years have rolled over our scene, and converted the forest-track into a dusty thoroughfare, which, being intersected with lanes and cross-paths, may fairly be designated as the Main-street. On the ground-sites of many of the log-built sheds, into which the first settlers crept for shelter, houses of quaint architecture have now risen. These later edifices are built, as you see, in one generally accordant style, though with such subordinate variety as keeps the beholder's curiosity excited, and causes each structure, like its owner's character, to produce its own peculiar impression. Most of them have one huge chimney in the centre, with flues so vast that it must have been easy for the witches to fly out of them, as they were wont to do, when bound on an aerial visit to the Black Man in the forest. Around this great chimney the wooden house clusters itself, in a whole community of gable-ends, each ascending into its own separate peak; the second story, with its lattice-windows, projecting over the first; and the door, which is perhaps arched, provided on the outside with an iron hammer, wherewith the visitor's hand may give a thundering rat-a-tat. The timber frame-work of these houses, as compared with those of recent date, is like the skeleton of an old giant, beside the frail bones of a modern man of fashion. Many of them, by the vast strength and soundness of their oaken substance, have been preserved through a length of time which would have tried the stability of brick and stone; so that, in all the progressive decay and continual reconstruction of the street, down to our own days, we shall still behold these old edifices occupying their long-accustomed sites. For instance, on the upper corner of that green lane which shall hereafter be North-street, we see the Curwen House, newly built, with the carpenters still at work on the roof, nailing down the last sheaf of shingles. On the lower corner stands another dwelling,—destined, at some period of its existence, to be the abode of an unsuccessful alchymist,— which shall likewise survive to our own generation, and perhaps long outlive it. Thus, through the medium of these patriarchal edifices, we have now established a sort of kindred and hereditary acquaintance with the Main-street.

Great as is the transformation produced by a short term of years, each single day creeps through the Puritan settlement sluggishly enough. It shall pass before your eyes, condensed into the space of a few moments. The gray light of early morning is slowly diffusing itself over the scene; and the bellman, whose office it is to cry the hour at the street-corners, rings the last peal upon his hand-bell, and goes wearily homewards, with the owls, the bats, and other creatures of the night. Lattices are thrust back on their hinges, as if the town were opening its eyes, in the summer morning. Forth stumbles the still drowsy cow-herd, with his horn; putting which to his lips, it emits a bellowing bray, impossible to be represented in the picture, but which reaches the pricked-up ears of every cow in the settlement, and tells her that the dewy pasture-hour is come. House after house awakes, and sends the smoke up curling from its chimney, like frosty breath from living nostrils; and as those white wreaths of smoke, though impregnated with earthy admixtures, climb skyward, so, from each dwelling, does the morning worship— its spiritual essence bearing up its human imperfection—find its way to the heavenly Father's throne.

The breakfast-hour being past, the inhabitants do not, as usual, go to their fields or workshops, but remain within doors; or perhaps walk the street, with a grave sobriety, yet a disengaged and unburthened aspect, that belongs neither to a holiday nor a Sabbath. And, indeed, this passing day is neither, nor is it a common week-day, although partaking of all the three. It is the Thursday Lecture; an institution which New England has long ago relinquished, and almost forgotten, yet which it would have been better to retain, as bearing relations to both the spiritual and ordinary life, and bringing each acquainted with the other. The tokens of its observance, however, which here meet our eyes, are of rather a questionable cast. It is, in one sense, a day of public shame; the day on which transgressors, who have made themselves liable to the minor severities of the Puritan law, receive their reward of ignominy. At this very moment, the constable has bound an idle fellow to the whipping-post, and is giving him his deserts with a cat-o'-nine-tails. Ever since sunrise, Daniel Fairfield has been standing on the steps of the meeting-house, with a halter about his neck, which he is condemned to wear visibly throughout his lifetime; Dorothy Talby is chained to a post at the corner of Prison Lane, with the hot sun blazing on her matronly face, and all for no other offence than lifting her hand against her husband; while, through the bars of that great wooden cage, in the centre of the scene, we discern either a human being or a wild beast, or both in one, whom this public infamy causes to roar, and gnash his teeth, and shake the strong oaken bars, as if he would break forth, and tear in pieces the little children who have been peeping at him. Such are the profitable sights that serve the good people to while away the earlier part of lecture-day. Betimes in the forenoon, a traveller—the first traveller that has come hither-ward this morning—rides slowly into the street, on his patient steed. He seems a clergyman; and, as he draws near, we recognize the minister of Lynn, who was pre-engaged to lecture here, and has been revolving his discourse, as he rode through the hoary wilderness. Behold, now, the whole town thronging into the meeting-house, mostly with such sombre visages, that the sunshine becomes little better than a shadow, when it falls upon them. There go the Thirteen Men, grim rulers of a grim community! There goes John Massey, the first town-born child, now a youth of twenty, whose eye wanders with peculiar interest towards that buxom damsel who comes up the steps at the same instant. There hobbles

Goody Foster, a sour and bitter old beldam, looking as if she went to curse, and not to pray, and whom many of her neighbors suspect of taking an occasional airing on a broom-stick. There, too, slinking shamefacedly in, you observe that same poor do-nothing and good-for-nothing, whom we saw castigated just now at the whipping-post. Last of all, there goes the tithing-man, lugging in a couple of small boys, whom he has caught at play beneath God's blessed sunshine, in a back lane. What native of Naumkeag, whose recollections go back more than thirty years, does not still shudder at that dark ogre of his infancy, who perhaps had long ceased to have an actual existence, but still lived in his childish belief, in a horrible idea, and in the nurse's threat, as the Tidy Man!

It will be hardly worth our while to wait two, or it may be three, turnings of the hour-glass, for the conclusion of the lecture. Therefore, by my control over light and darkness, I cause the dusk, and then the starless night, to brood over the street; and summon forth again the bellman, with his lantern casting a gleam about his footsteps, to pace wearily from corner to corner, and shout drowsily the hour to drowsy or dreaming ears. Happy are we, if for nothing else, yet because we did not live in those days. In truth, when the first novelty and stir of spirit had subsided,—when the new settlement, between the forest-border and the sea, had become actually a little town,—its daily life must have trudged onward with hardly any thing to diversify and enliven it, while also its rigidity could not fail to cause miserable distortions of the moral nature. Such a life was sinister to the intellect, and sinister to the heart; especially when one generation had bequeathed its religious gloom, and the counterfeit of its religious ardor, to the next; for these characteristics, as was inevitable, assumed the form both of hypocrisy and exaggeration, by being inherited from the example and precept of other human beings, and not from an original and spiritual source. The sons and grandchildren of the first settlers were a race of lower and narrower souls than their progenitors had been. The latter were stern, severe, intolerant, but not superstitious, not even fanatical; and endowed, if any men of that age were, with a far-seeing worldly sagacity. But it was impossible for the succeeding race to grow up, in Heaven's freedom, beneath the discipline which their gloomy energy of character had established; nor, it may be, have we even yet thrown off all the unfavorable influences which, among many good ones, were bequeathed to us by our Puritan forefathers. Let us thank God for having given us such ancestors; and let each successive generation thank him, not less fervently, for being one step further from them in the march of ages.

"What is all this?" cries the critic. "A sermon? If so, it is not in the bill."

"Very true," replies the showman; "and I ask pardon of the audience."

Look now at the street, and observe a strange people entering it. Their garments are torn and disordered, their faces haggard, their figures emaciated; for they have made their way hither through pathless deserts, suffering hunger and hardship, with no other shelter than a hollow tree, the lair of a wild beast, or an Indian wigwam. Nor, in the most inhospitable and dangerous of such lodging-places, was there half the peril that awaits them in this thoroughfare of Christian men, with those secure dwellings and warm hearths on either side of it, and yonder meeting-house as the central object of the scene. These wanderers have received from Heaven a gift that, in all epochs of the world, has brought with it the penalties of mortal suffering and persecution, scorn, enmity, and death itself;—a gift that, thus terrible to its possessors, has ever been most hateful to all other men, since its very existence seems to threaten the overthrow of whatever

else the toilsome ages have built up;—the gift of a new idea.
You can discern it in them, illuminating their faces—their
whole persons, indeed, however earthly and cloddish—with
a light that inevitably shines through, and makes the startled
community aware that these men are not as they themselves
are; not brethren nor neighbors of their thought. Forthwith,
it is as if an earthquake rumbled through the town, making
its vibrations felt at every hearthstone, and especially causing the spire of the meeting-house to totter. The Quakers
have come! We are in peril! See! they trample upon our wise
and well-established laws in the person of our chief magistrate;
for Governor Endicott is passing, now an aged man, and
dignified with long habits of authority,—and not one of the
irreverent vagabonds has moved his hat! Did you note the
ominous frown of the white-bearded Puritan governor, as he
turned himself about, and, in his anger, half uplifted the staff
that has become a needful support to his old age? Here
comes old Mr. Norris, our venerable minister. Will they doff
their hats, and pay reverence to him? No: their hats stick fast
to their ungracious heads, as if they grew there; and—impious
varlets that they are, and worse than the heathen Indians!—
they eye our reverend pastor with a peculiar scorn, distrust,
unbelief, and utter denial of his sanctified pretensions, of
which he himself immediately becomes conscious; the more
bitterly conscious, as he never knew nor dreamed of the
like before.

But look yonder! Can we believe our eyes? A Quaker
woman, clad in sackcloth, and with ashes on her head, has
mounted the steps of the meeting-house. She addresses the
people in a wild, shrill voice,—wild and shrill it must be, to
suit such a figure,—which makes them tremble and turn
pale, although they crowd open-mouthed to hear her. She is
bold against established authority; she denounces the priest
and his steeple-house. Many of her hearers are appalled; some

weep; and others listen with a rapt attention, as if a living truth had now, for the first time, forced its way through the crust of habit, reached their hearts, and awakened them to life. This matter must be looked to; else we have brought our faith across the seas with us in vain; and it had been better that the old forest were still standing here, waving its tangled boughs, and murmuring to the sky out of its desolate recesses, instead of this goodly street, if such blasphemies be spoken in it.

So thought the old Puritans. What was their mode of action may be partly judged from the spectacles which now pass before your eyes. Joshua Buffum is standing in the pillory. Cassandra Southwick is led to prison. And there a woman,—it is Ann Coleman,—naked from the waist upward, and bound to the tail of a cart, is dragged through the Main-street at the pace of a brisk walk, while the constable follows with a whip of knotted cords. A strong-armed fellow is that constable; and each time that he flourishes his lash in the air, you see a frown wrinkling and twisting his brow, and, at the same instant, a smile upon his lips. He loves his business, faithful officer that he is, and puts his soul into every stroke, zealous to fulfil the injunction of Major Hawthorne's warrant, in the spirit and to the letter. There came down a stroke that has drawn blood! Ten such stripes are to be given in Salem, ten in Boston, and ten in Dedham; and, with those thirty stripes of blood upon her, she is to be driven into the forest. The crimson trail goes wavering along the Main-street; but Heaven grant, that, as the rain of so many years has wept upon it, time after time, and washed it all away, so there may have been a dew of mercy, to cleanse this cruel blood-stain out of the record of the persecutor's life!

Pass on, thou spectral constable, and betake thee to thine own place of torment! Meanwhile, by the silent operation of the mechanism behind the scenes, a considerable space of time would seem to have lapsed over the street. The older dwellings now begin to look weather-beaten, through the effect of the many eastern storms that have moistened their unpainted shingles and clapboards, for not less than forty years. Such is the age we would assign to the town, judging by the aspect of John Massey, the first town-born child, whom his neighbors now call Goodman Massey, and whom we see yonder, a grave, almost autumnal-looking man, with children of his own about him. To the patriarchs of the settlement, no doubt, the Main-street is still but an affair of yesterday, hardly more antique, even if destined to be more permanent, than a path shovelled through the snow. But to the middle-aged and elderly men who came hither in childhood or early youth, it presents the aspect of a long and well-established work, on which they have expended the strength and ardor of their life. And the younger people, native to the street, whose earliest recollections are of creeping over the paternal threshold, and rolling on the grassy margin of the track, look at it as one of the perdurable things of our mortal state,—as old as the hills of the great pasture, or the headland at the harbor's mouth. Their fathers and grandsires tell them, how, within a few years past, the forest stood here with but a lonely track beneath its tangled shade. Vain legend! They cannot make it true and real to their conceptions. With them, moreover, the Main-street is a street indeed, worthy to hold its way with the thronged and stately avenues of cities beyond the sea. The old Puritans tell them of the crowds that hurry along Cheapside and Fleet-street and the Strand, and of the rush of tumultuous life at Temple Bar. They describe London Bridge, itself a street, with a row of houses on each side. They speak of the vast structure of the Tower, and the solemn grandeur of Westminster Abbey. The children listen, and still inquire if the streets of London are longer and broader than the one before their father's door; if the Tower is bigger than the jail in Prison Lane; if the old Abbey will hold a larger congregation than our meeting-house. Nothing impresses them, except their own experience.

It seems all a fable, too, that wolves have ever prowled here; and not less so, that the Squaw Sachem, and the Sagamore her son, once ruled over this region, and treated as sovereign potentates with the English settlers, then so few and storm-beaten, now so powerful. There stand some school-boys, you observe, in a little group around a drunken Indian, himself a prince of the Squaw Sachem's lineage. He brought hither some beaver-skins for sale, and has already swallowed the larger portion of their price, in deadly draughts of fire-water. Is there not a touch of pathos in that picture? and does it not go far towards telling the whole story of the vast growth and prosperity of one race, and the fated decay of another?—the children of the stranger making game of the great Squaw Sachem's grandson!

But the whole race of red men have not vanished with that wild princess and her posterity. This march of soldiers along the street betokens the breaking out of King Philip's war; and these young men, the flower of Essex, are on their way to defend the villages on the Connecticut; where, at Bloody Brook, a terrible blow shall be smitten, and hardly one of that gallant band be left alive. And there, at that stately mansion, with its three peaks in front, and its two little peaked towers, one on either side of the door, we see brave Captain Gardner issuing forth, clad in his embroidered buff-coat, and his plumed cap upon his head. His trusty sword, in its steel scabbard, strikes clanking on the door-step. See how the people throng to their doors and windows, as the cavalier rides past, reining his mettled steed so gallantly, and looking so like the very soul and emblem of martial achievement,—destined, too, to meet a warrior's fate, at the desperate assault on the fortress of the Narragansetts!

"The mettled steed looks like a pig," interrupts the critic, "and Captain Gardner himself like the devil, though a very tame one, and on a most diminutive scale."

"Sir, sir!" cries the persecuted showman, losing all patience, —for, indeed, he had particularly prided himself on these figures of Captain Gardner and his horse,—"I see that there is no hope of pleasing you. Pray, sir, do me the favor to take back your money, and withdraw!"

"Not I!" answers the unconscionable critic. "I am just beginning to get interested in the matter. Come! turn your crank, and grind out a few more of these fooleries!"

The showman rubs his brow impulsively, whisks the little rod with which he points out the notabilities of the scene,— but, finally, with the inevitable acquiescence of all public servants, resumes his composure, and goes on.

Pass onward, onward, Time! Build up new houses here, and tear down thy works of yesterday, that have already the rusty moss upon them! Summon forth the minister to the abode of the young maiden, and bid him unite her to the joyful bridegroom! Let the youthful parents carry their first-born to the meeting-house, to receive the baptismal rite! Knock at the door, whence the sable line of the funeral is next to issue! Provide other successive generations of men, to trade, talk, quarrel, or walk in friendly intercourse along the street, as their fathers did before them! Do all thy daily and accustomed business, Father Time, in this thoroughfare, which thy footsteps, for so many years, have now made dusty! But here, at last, thou leadest along a procession which, once witnessed, shall appear no more, and be remembered only as a hideous dream of thine, or a frenzy of thy old brain.

"Turn your crank, I say," bellows the remorseless critic, "and grind it out, whatever it be, without further preface!"

The showman deems it best to comply.

Then, here comes the worshipful Captain Curwen, Sheriff

of Essex, on horseback, at the head of an armed guard, escorting a company of condemned prisoners from the jail to their
place of execution on Gallows Hill. The witches! There is no
mistaking them! The witches! As they approach up Prison
Lane, and turn into the Main-street, let us watch their faces,
as if we made a part of the pale crowd that presses so eagerly
about them, yet shrinks back with such shuddering dread,
leaving an open passage betwixt a dense throng on either
side. Listen to what the people say.

There is old George Jacobs, known hereabouts, these sixty
years, as a man whom we thought upright in all his way of
life, quiet, blameless, a good husband before his pious wife
was summoned from the evil to come, and a good father to
the children whom she left him. Ah! but when that blessed
woman went to heaven, George Jacobs' heart was empty, his
hearth lonely, his life broken up; his children were married,
and betook themselves to habitations of their own; and Satan,
in his wanderings up and down, beheld this forlorn old man,
to whom life was a sameness and a weariness, and found the
way to tempt him. So the miserable sinner was prevailed with
to mount into the air, and career among the clouds; and he is
proved to have been present at a witch-meeting as far off as
Falmouth, on the very same night that his next neighbors
saw him, with his rheumatic stoop, going in at his own door.
There is John Willard too; an honest man we thought him,
and so shrewd and active in his business, so practical, so intent
on every-day affairs, so constant at his little place of trade,
where he bartered English goods for Indian corn and all kinds
of country produce! How could such a man find time, or what
could put it into his mind, to leave his proper calling, and
become a wizard? It is a mystery, unless the Black Man
tempted him with great heaps of gold. See that aged couple,
—a sad sight truly,—John Proctor, and his wife Elizabeth. If

there were two old people in all the County of Essex who seemed to have led a true Christian life, and to be treading hopefully the little remnant of their earthly path, it was this very pair. Yet have we heard it sworn, to the satisfaction of the worshipful Chief Justice Sewall, and all the Court and Jury, that Proctor and his wife have shown their withered faces at children's bedsides, mocking, making mouths, and affrighting the poor little innocents in the night-time. They, or their spectral appearances, have stuck pins into the Afflicted Ones, and thrown them into deadly fainting-fits with a touch, or but a look. And, while we supposed the old man to be reading the Bible to his old wife,—she meanwhile knitting in the chimney-corner,—the pair of hoary reprobates have whisked up the chimney, both on one broomstick, and flown away to a witch-communion, far into the depths of the chill, dark forest. How foolish! Were it only for fear of rheumatic pains in their old bones, they had better have stayed at home. But away they went; and the laughter of their decayed, cackling voices has been heard at midnight, aloft in the air. Now, in the sunny noontide, as they go tottering to the gallows, it is the devil's turn to laugh.

Behind these two,—who help one another along, and seem to be comforting and encouraging each other, in a manner truly pitiful, if it were not a sin to pity the old witch and wizard,—behind them comes a woman, with a dark, proud face that has been beautiful, and a figure that is still majestic. Do you know her? It is Martha Carrier, whom the devil found in a humble cottage, and looked into her discontented heart, and saw pride there, and tempted her with his promise that she should be Queen of Hell. And now, with that lofty demeanor, she is passing to her kingdom, and, by her unquenchable pride, transforms this escort of shame into a triumphal procession, that shall attend her to the gates of her

infernal palace, and seat her upon the fiery throne. Within
this hour, she shall assume her royal dignity.

Last of the miserable train comes a man clad in black,
of small stature and a dark complexion, with a clerical band
about his neck. Many a time, in the years gone by, that face
has been uplifted heavenward from the pulpit of the East
Meeting-house, when the Reverend Mr. Burroughs seemed to
worship God. What!—he? The holy man!—the learned!—
the wise! How has the devil tempted him? His fellow-crim-
inals, for the most part, are obtuse, uncultivated creatures,
some of them scarcely half-witted by nature, and others
greatly decayed in their intellects through age. They were an
easy prey for the destroyer. Not so with this George Burroughs, as we judge by the inward light which glows through
his dark countenance, and, we might almost say, glorifies
his figure, in spite of the soil and haggardness of long im-
prisonment,—in spite of the heavy shadow that must fall on
him, while Death is walking by his side. What bribe could
Satan offer, rich enough to tempt and overcome this man?
Alas! it may have been in the very strength of his high and
searching intellect, that the Tempter found the weakness
which betrayed him. He yearned for knowledge; he went
groping onward into a world of mystery; at first, as the witnesses have sworn, he summoned up the ghosts of his two
dead wives, and talked with them of matters beyond the
grave; and, when their responses failed to satisfy the intense
and sinful craving of his spirit, he called on Satan, and was
heard. Yet—to look at him—who, that had not known the
proof, could believe him guilty? Who would not say, while
we see him offering comfort to the weak and aged partners
of his horrible crime,—while we hear his ejaculations of
prayer, that seem to bubble up out of the depths of his
heart, and fly heavenward, unawares,—while we behold a
radiance brightening on his features as from the other world,

which is but a few steps off,—who would not say, that, over
the dusty track of the Main-street, a Christian saint is now
going to a martyr's death? May not the Arch Fiend have
been too subtle for the court and jury, and betrayed them—
laughing in his sleeve the while—into the awful error of
pouring out sanctified blood as an acceptable sacrifice upon
God's altar? Ah! no; for listen to wise Cotton Mather, who,
as he sits there on his horse, speaks comfortably to the perplexed multitude, and tells them that all has been religiously
and justly done, and that Satan's power shall this day receive
its death-blow in New England.

Heaven grant it be so!—the great scholar must be right!
so, lead the poor creatures to their death! Do you see that
group of children and half-grown girls, and, among them, an
old, hag-like Indian woman, Tituba by name? Those are the
Afflicted Ones. Behold, at this very instant, a proof of Satan's
power and malice! Mercy Parris, the minister's daughter, has
been smitten by a flash of Martha Carrier's eye, and falls
down in the street, writhing with horrible spasms and foam-
ing at the mouth, like the possessed ones spoken of in Scripture. Hurry on the accursed witches to the gallows, ere they
do more mischief!—ere they fling out their withered arms,
and scatter pestilence by handfuls among the crowd!—ere, as
their parting legacy, they cast a blight over the land, so that
henceforth it may bear no fruit nor blade of grass, and be fit
for nothing but a sepulchre for their unhallowed carcasses!
So, on they go; and old George Jacobs has stumbled by
reason of his infirmity; but Goodman Proctor and his wife
lean on one another, and walk at a reasonably steady pace,
considering their age. Mr. Burroughs seems to administer
counsel to Martha Carrier, whose face and mien, methinks,
are milder and humbler than they were. Among the multitude, meanwhile, there is horror, fear, and distrust; and
friend looks askance at friend, and the husband at his wife,

and the wife at him, and even the mother at her little child; as if, in every creature that God has made, they suspected a witch, or dreaded an accuser. Never, never again, whether in this or any other shape, may Universal Madness riot in the Main-street!

I perceive in your eyes, my indulgent spectators, the criticism which you are too kind to utter. These scenes, you think, are all too sombre. So, indeed, they are; but the blame must rest on the sombre spirit of our forefathers, who wove their web of life with hardly a single thread of rose-color or gold, and not on me, who have a tropic love of sunshine, and would gladly gild all the world with it, if I knew where to find so much. That you may believe me, I will exhibit one of the only class of scenes, so far as my investigation has taught me, in which our ancestors were wont to steep their tough old hearts in wine and strong drink, and indulge an outbreak of grisly jollity.

Here it comes, out of the same house whence we saw brave Captain Gardner go forth to the wars. What! A coffin, borne on men's shoulders, and six aged gentlemen as pall-bearers, and a long train of mourners, with black gloves and black hat-bands, and every thing black, save a white handkerchief in each mourner's hand, to wipe away his tears withal. Now, my kind patrons, you are angry with me. You were bidden to a bridal-dance, and find yourselves walking in a funeral procession. Even so; but look back through all the social customs of New England, in the first century of her existence, and read all her traits of character; and if you find one occasion, other than a funeral-feast, where jollity was sanctioned by universal practice, I will set fire to my puppet-show without another word. These are the obsequies of old Governor Bradstreet, the patriarch and survivor of the first settlers, who, having intermarried with the Widow Gardner, is now resting from his labors, at the great age of ninety-four. The white-bearded corpse, which was his spirit's earthly garniture, now lies beneath yonder coffin-lid. Many a cask of ale and cider is on tap, and many a draught of spiced wine and aquavitæ has been quaffed. Else why should the bearers stagger, as they tremulously uphold the coffin?—and the aged pall-bearers, too, as they strive to walk solemnly beside it?—and wherefore do the mourners tread on one another's heels?—and why, if we may ask without offence, should the nose of the Reverend Mr. Noyes, through which he has just been delivering the funeral discourse, glow like a ruddy coal of fire? Well, well, old friends! Pass on, with your burthen of mortality, and lay it in the tomb with jolly hearts. People should be permitted to enjoy themselves in their own fashion; every man to his taste; but New England must have been a dismal abode for the man of pleasure, when the only boon-companion was Death!

Under cover of a mist that has settled over the scene, a few years flit by, and escape our notice. As the atmosphere becomes transparent, we perceive a decrepit grandsire, hobbling along the street. Do you recognize him? We saw him, first as the baby in Goodwife Massey's arms, when the primeval trees were flinging their shadow over Roger Conant's cabin; we have seen him, as the boy, the youth, the man, bearing his humble part in all the successive scenes, and forming the index-figure whereby to note the age of his coeval town. And here he is, old Goodman Massey, taking his last walk,—often pausing,—often leaning over his staff,—and calling to mind whose dwelling stood at such and such a spot, and whose field or garden occupied the site of those more recent houses. He can render a reason for all the bends and deviations of the thoroughfare, which, in its flexible and plastic infancy, was made to swerve aside from a straight line, in order to visit every settler's door. The Main-street is still youthful; the coeval Man is in his latest age. Soon he will be gone, a patriarch of fourscore, yet shall retain a sort of infantine life in our local history, as the first town-born child.

Behold here a change, wrought in the twinkling of an eye, like an incident in a tale of magic, even while your observation has been fixed upon the scene. The Main-street has vanished out of sight. In its stead appears a wintry waste of snow, with the sun just peeping over it, cold and bright, and tinging the white expanse with the faintest and most ethereal rose-color. This is the Great Snow of 1717, famous for the mountain-drifts in which it buried the whole country. It would seem as if the street, the growth of which we have noted so attentively,—following it from its first phase, as an Indian track, until it reached the dignity of side-walks,— were all at once obliterated, and resolved into a drearier pathlessness than when the forest covered it. The gigantic swells and billows of the snow have swept over each man's metes and bounds, and annihilated all the visible distinctions of human property. So that now, the traces of former times and hitherto accomplished deeds being done away, mankind should be at liberty to enter on new paths, and guide themselves by other laws than heretofore; if, indeed, the race be not extinct, and it be worth our while to go on with the march of life, over the cold and desolate expanse that lies before us. It may be, however, that matters are not so desperate as they appear. That vast icicle, glittering so cheerlessly in the sunshine, must be the spire of the meeting-house, incrusted with frozen sleet. Those great heaps, too, which we mistook for drifts, are houses, buried up to their eaves, and with their peaked roofs rounded by the depth of snow upon them. There, now, comes a gush of smoke from what I judge to be the chimney of the Ship Tavern—and another— another—and another—from the chimneys of other dwellings, where fireside comfort, domestic peace, the sports of children, and the quietude of age, are living yet, in spite of the frozen crust above them.

But it is time to change the scene. Its dreary monotony shall not test your fortitude like one of our actual New England winters, which leave so large a blank—so melancholy a death-spot—in lives so brief that they ought to be all summer-time. Here, at least, I may claim to be ruler of the seasons. One turn of the crank shall melt away the snow from the Main-street, and show the trees in their full foliage, the rose-bushes in bloom, and a border of green grass along the side-walk. There! But what! How! The scene will not move. A wire is broken. The street continues buried beneath the snow, and the fate of Herculaneum and Pompeii has its parallel in this catastrophe.

Alas! my kind and gentle audience, you know not the extent of your misfortune. The scenes to come were far better than the past. The street itself would have been more worthy of pictorial exhibition; the deeds of its inhabitants, not less so. And how would your interest have deepened, as, passing out of the cold shadow of antiquity, in my long and weary course, I should arrive within the limits of man's memory, and, leading you at last into the sunshine of the present, should give a reflex of the very life that is flitting past us! Your own beauty, my fair townswomen, would have beamed upon you, out of my scene. Not a gentleman that walks the street but should have beheld his own face and figure, his gait, the peculiar swing of his arm, and the coat that he put on yesterday. Then, too,—and it is what I chiefly regret,—I had expended a vast deal of light and brilliancy on a representation of the street in its whole length, from Buffum's Corner downward, on the night of the grand illumination for General Taylor's triumph. Lastly, I should have given the crank one other turn, and have brought out the future, showing you who shall walk the Main-street tomorrow, and, perchance, whose funeral shall pass through it!

But these, like most other human purposes, lie unaccomplished; and I have only further to say, that any lady or gentleman, who may feel dissatisfied with the evening's entertainment, shall receive back the admission fee at the door.

"Then give me mine," cries the critic, stretching out his palm. "I said that your exhibition would prove a humbug, and so it has turned out. So hand over my quarter!"

ETHAN BRAND

A CHAPTER FROM AN ABORTIVE ROMANCE

BARTRAM, the lime-burner, a rough, heavy-looking man, begrimed with charcoal, sat watching his kiln, at nightfall, while his little son played at building houses with the scattered fragments of marble; when, on the hill-side below them, they heard a roar of laughter, not mirthful, but slow, and even solemn, like a wind shaking the boughs of the forest.

"Father, what is that?" asked the little boy, leaving his play, and pressing betwixt his father's knees.

"Oh, some drunken man, I suppose," answered the lime-burner;—"some merry fellow from the bar-room in the village, who dared not laugh loud enough within doors, lest he should blow the roof of the house off. So here he is, shaking his jolly sides, at the foot of Graylock."

"But, father," said the child, more sensitive than the obtuse, middle-aged clown, "he does not laugh like a man that is glad. So the noise frightens me!"

"Don't be a fool, child!" cried his father, gruffly. "You will never make a man, I do believe; there is too much of your mother in you. I have known the rustling of a leaf startle you. Hark! Here comes the merry fellow now. You shall see that there is no harm in him."

Bartram and his little son, while they were talking thus, sat watching the same lime-kiln that had been the scene of Ethan Brand's solitary and meditative life, before he began his search for the Unpardonable Sin. Many years, as we have seen, had now elapsed, since that portentous night when the IDEA was first developed. The kiln, however, on the mountain-side, stood unimpaired, and was in nothing changed, since he had thrown his dark thoughts into the intense glow of its furnace, and melted them, as it were, into the one thought that took possession of his life. It was a rude, round, tower-like structure, about twenty feet high, heavily built of rough stones, and with a hillock of earth heaped about the larger part of its circumference; so that blocks and fragments of marble might be drawn by cart-loads, and thrown in at the top. There was an opening at the bottom of the tower, like an oven-mouth, but large enough to admit a man in a stooping posture, and provided with a massive iron door. With the smoke and jets of flame issuing from the chinks and crevices of this door, which seemed to give admittance into the hill-side, it resembled nothing so much as the private entrance to the infernal regions, which the shepherds of the Delectable Mountains were accustomed to show to pilgrims.

There are many such lime-kilns in that tract of country, for the purpose of burning the white marble which composes a large part of the substance of the hills. Some of them, built years ago, and long deserted, with weeds growing in the vacant round of the interior, which is open to the sky, and grass and wild flowers rooting themselves into the chinks of the stones, look already like relics of antiquity, and may yet be overspread with the lichens of centuries to come. Others, where the lime-burner still feeds his daily and night-long fire, afford points of interest to the wanderer among the hills, who seats himself on a log of wood or a fragment of marble, to hold chat with the solitary man. It is a lonesome, and, when the character is inclined to thought, may be an intensely thoughtful occupation; as it proved in the case of Ethan Brand, who had mused to such strange purpose, in days gone by, while the fire in this very kiln was burning.

The man, who now watched the fire, was of a different order, and troubled himself with no thoughts save the very few that were requisite to his business. At frequent intervals he flung back the clashing weight of the iron door, and, turning his face from the insufferable glare, thrust in huge logs of oak, or stirred the immense brands with a long pole. Within the furnace, was seen the curling and riotous flames, and the burning marble, almost molten with the intensity of heat; while, without, the reflection of the fire quivered on the dark intricacy of the surrounding forest, and showed, in the foreground, a bright and ruddy little picture of the hut, the spring beside its door, the athletic and coal-begrimed figure of the lime-burner, and the half-frightened child, shrinking into the protection of his father's shadow. And when, again, the iron door was closed, then re-appeared the tender light of the half-full moon, which vainly strove to trace out the indistinct shapes of the neighboring mountains; and, in the upper sky, there was a flitting congregation of clouds, still faintly tinged with the rosy sunset, though, thus far down into the valley, the sunshine had vanished long and long ago.

The little boy now crept still closer to his father, as footsteps were heard ascending the hill-side, and a human form thrust aside the bushes that clustered beneath the trees.

"Halloo! who is it?" cried the lime-burner, vexed at his son's timidity, yet half-infected by it. "Come forward, and show yourself, like a man; or I'll fling this chunk of marble at your head!"

"You offer me a rough welcome," said a gloomy voice, as the unknown man drew nigh. "Yet I neither claim nor desire a kinder one, even at my own fireside."

To obtain a distincter view, Bartram threw open the iron door of the kiln, whence immediately issued a gush of fierce light, that smote full upon the stranger's face and figure. To a careless eye, there appeared nothing very remarkable in his aspect, which was that of a man in a coarse, brown, country-made suit of clothes, tall and thin, with the staff and heavy shoes of a wayfarer. As he advanced, he fixed his eyes, which were very bright, intently upon the brightness of the furnace, as if he beheld, or expected to behold, some object worthy of note within it.

"Good evening, stranger," said the lime-burner, "whence come you, so late in the day?"

"I come from my search," answered the wayfarer; "for, at last, it is finished."

"Drunk, or crazy!" muttered Bartram to himself. "I shall have trouble with the fellow. The sooner I drive him away, the better."

The little boy, all in a tremble, whispered to his father, and begged him to shut the door of the kiln, so that there might not be so much light; for that there was something in the man's face which he was afraid to look at, yet could not look away from. And, indeed, even the lime-burner's dull and torpid sense began to be impressed by an indescribable something in that thin, rugged, thoughtful visage, with the grizzled hair hanging wildly about it, and those deeply sunken eyes, which gleamed like fires within the entrance of a mysterious cavern. But, as he closed the door, the stranger turned towards him, and spoke in a quiet, familiar way, that made Bartram feel as if he were a sane and sensible man, after all.

"Your task draws to an end, I see," said he. "This marble has already been burning three days. A few hours more will convert the stone to lime."

"Why, who are you?" exclaimed the lime-burner. "You seem as well acquainted with my business as I myself."

"And well I may be," said the stranger, "for I followed the same craft, many a long year; and here, too, on this very spot. But you are a new comer in these parts. Did you never hear of Ethan Brand?"

"The man that went in search of the Unpardonable Sin?" asked Bartram, with a laugh.

"The same," answered the stranger. "He has found what he sought, and therefore he comes back again."

"What! then you are Ethan Brand, himself?" cried the lime-burner in amazement. "I am a new comer here, as you say; and they call it eighteen years since you left the foot of Graylock. But, I can tell you, the good folks still talk about Ethan Brand, in the village yonder, and what a strange errand took him away from his lime-kiln. Well, and so you have found the Unpardonable Sin?"

"Even so!" said the stranger, calmly.

"If the question is a fair one," proceeded Bartram, "where might it be?"

Ethan Brand laid his finger on his own heart. "Here!" replied he.

And then, without mirth in his countenance, but as if moved by an involuntary recognition of the infinite absurdity of seeking throughout the world for what was the closest of all things to himself, and looking into every heart, save his own, for what was hidden in no other breast, he broke into a laugh of scorn. It was the same slow, heavy laugh, that had almost appalled the lime-burner, when it heralded the way-farer's approach.

The solitary mountain-side was made dismal by it. Laughter, when out of place, mistimed, or bursting forth from a disordered state of feeling, may be the most terrible modulation of the human voice. The laughter of one asleep, even if it be a little child—the madman's laugh—the wild, screaming laugh of a born idiot, are sounds that we sometimes tremble to hear, and would always willingly forget. Poets have imagined no utterance of fiends or hobgoblins so fearfully appropriate as a laugh. And even the obtuse lime-burner felt his nerves shaken, as this strange man looked inward at his own heart, and burst into laughter that rolled away into the night, and was indistinctly reverberated among the hills.

"Joe," said he to his little son, "scamper down to the tavern in the village, and tell the jolly fellows there that Ethan Brand has come back, and that he has found the Unpardonable Sin!"

The boy darted away on his errand, to which Ethan Brand made no objection, nor seemed hardly to notice it. He sat on a log of wood, looking steadfastly at the iron door of the kiln. When the child was out of sight, and his swift and light footsteps ceased to be heard, treading first on the fallen leaves, and then on the rocky mountain-path, the lime-burner began to regret his departure. He felt that the little fellow's presence had been a barrier between his guest and himself, and that he must now deal, heart to heart, with a man who, on his own confession, had committed the only crime for which Heaven could afford no mercy. That crime, in its indistinct blackness, seemed to overshadow him. The lime-burner's own sins rose up within him, and made his memory riotous with a throng of evil shapes that asserted their kindred with the Master Sin, whatever it might be, which it was within the scope of man's corrupted nature to conceive and cherish. They were all of one family; they went to and fro between his breast and Ethan Brand's, and carried dark greetings from one to the other.

Then Bartram remembered the stories which had grown traditionary in reference to this strange man, who had come upon him like a shadow of the night, and was making himself at home in his old place, after so long absence that the dead people, dead and buried for years, would have had more right to be at home, in any familiar spot, than he. Ethan Brand, it was said, had conversed with Satan himself, in the lurid blaze of this very kiln. The legend had been matter of mirth heretofore, but looked grisly now. According to this tale, before Ethan Brand departed on his search, he had been accustomed to evoke a fiend from the hot furnace of the lime-kiln, night after night, in order to confer with him about the Unpardonable Sin; the Man and the Fiend each laboring to frame the image of some mode of guilt, which could neither be atoned for, nor forgiven. And, with the first gleam of light upon the mountain-top, the fiend crept in at the iron door, there to abide in the intensest element of fire, until again summoned forth to share in the dreadful task of extending man's possible guilt beyond the scope of Heaven's else infinite mercy.

While the lime-burner was struggling with the horror of these thoughts, Ethan Brand rose from the log and flung open the door of the kiln. The action was in such accordance with the idea in Bartram's mind, that he almost expected to see the Evil One issue forth, red-hot from the raging furnace.

"Hold, hold!" cried he, with a tremulous attempt to laugh; for he was ashamed of his fears, although they overmastered him. "Don't, for mercy's sake, bring out your devil now!"

"Man!" sternly replied Ethan Brand, "what need have I of the devil? I have left him behind me on my track. It is with such half-way sinners as you that he busies himself. Fear not, because I open the door. I do but act by old custom, and am going to trim your fire, like a lime-burner, as I was once."

He stirred the vast coals, thrust in more wood, and bent forward to gaze into the hollow prison-house of the fire, regardless of the fierce glow that reddened upon his face. The lime-burner sat watching him, and half suspected his strange guest of a purpose, if not to evoke a fiend, at least to plunge bodily into the flames, and thus vanish from the sight of man. Ethan Brand, however, drew quietly back, and closed the door of the kiln.

"I have looked," said he, "into many a human heart that was seven times hotter with sinful passions than yonder furnace is with fire. But I found not there what I sought. No; not the Unpardonable Sin!"

"What is the Unpardonable Sin?" asked the lime-burner; and then he shrank farther from his companion, trembling lest his question should be answered.

"It is a sin that grew within my own breast," replied Ethan Brand, standing erect, with the pride that distinguishes all enthusiasts of his stamp. "A sin that grew nowhere else! The sin of an intellect that triumphed over the sense of brotherhood with man, and reverence for God, and sacrificed everything to its own mighty claims! The only sin that deserves a recompense of immortal agony! Freely, were it to do again, would I incur the guilt. Unshrinkingly, I accept the retribution!"

"The man's head is turned," muttered the lime-burner to himself. "He may be a sinner, like the rest of us—nothing more likely—but I'll be sworn, he is a madman, too."

Nevertheless, he felt uncomfortable at his situation, alone with Ethan Brand on the wild mountain-side, and was right glad to hear the rough murmur of tongues, and the footsteps of what seemed a pretty numerous party, stumbling over the stones, and rustling through the underbrush. Soon appeared the whole lazy regiment that was wont to infest the village tavern, comprehending three or four individuals who had drunk flip beside the bar-room fire, through all the winters, and smoked their pipes beneath the stoop, through all the summers since Ethan Brand's departure. Laughing boisterously, and mingling all their voices together in unceremonious talk, they now burst into the moonshine and narrow streaks of fire-light that illuminated the open space before the lime-kiln. Bartram set the door ajar again, flooding the spot with light, that the whole company might get a fair view of Ethan Brand, and he of them.

There, among other old acquaintances, was a once ubiquitous man, now almost extinct, but whom we were formerly sure to encounter at the hotel of every thriving village throughout the country. It was the stage-agent. The present specimen of the genus was a wilted and smoke-dried man, wrinkled and red-nosed, in a smartly cut, brown, bob-tailed coat, with brass buttons, who, for a length of time unknown, had kept his desk and corner in the bar-room, and was still puffing what seemed to be the same cigar that he had lighted twenty years before. He had great fame as a dry joker, though, perhaps, less on account of any intrinsic humor, than from a certain flavor of brandy-toddy and tobacco-smoke, which impregnated all his ideas and expressions, as well as his person. Another well-remembered, though strangely-altered face was that of Lawyer Giles, as people still called him in courtesy; an elderly ragamuffin, in his soiled shirt-sleeves and tow-cloth trowsers. This poor fellow had been an attorney, in what he called his better days, a sharp practitioner, and in great vogue among the village litigants; but flip, and sling, and toddy, and cocktails, imbibed at all hours, morning, noon, and night, had caused him to slide from intellectual, to various kinds and degrees of bodily labor, till, at last, to adopt his own phrase, he slid into a soap-vat. In other words, Giles was now a soap-boiler, in a small way. He had come to be but the fragment of a human being, a part of one foot having been chopped off by an axe, and an entire hand torn away by the devilish gripe of a steam-engine. Yet, though the corporeal hand was gone, a spiritual member remained; for, stretching forth the stump, Giles steadfastly averred, that he felt an invisible thumb and fingers, with as vivid a sensation as before the real ones were amputated. A maimed and miserable wretch he was; but one, nevertheless, whom the world could not trample on, and had no right to scorn, either in this or any previous stage of his misfortunes, since he had still kept up the courage and spirit of a man, asked nothing in charity, and, with his one hand—and that the left one—fought a stern battle against want and hostile circumstances.

Among the throng, too, came another personage, who, with certain points of similarity to Lawyer Giles, had more of difference. It was the village Doctor, a man of some fifty years, whom, at an earlier period of his life, we should have introduced as paying a professional visit to Ethan Brand, during the latter's supposed insanity. He was now a purple-visaged, rude, and brutal, yet half-gentlemanly figure, with something wild, ruined, and desperate in his talk, and in all the details of his gesture and manners. Brandy possessed this man like an evil spirit, and made him as surly and savage as a wild beast, and as miserable as a lost soul; but there was supposed to be in him such wonderful skill, such native gifts of healing, beyond any which medical science could impart, that society caught hold of him, and would not let him sink out of its reach. So, swaying to and fro upon his horse, and grumbling thick accents at the bedside, he visited all the sick chambers for miles about among the mountain towns; and sometimes raised a dying man, as it were, by miracle, or, quite as often, no doubt, sent his patient to a grave that was dug many a year too soon. The Doctor had an everlasting pipe in his mouth, and, as somebody said, in allusion to his habit of swearing, it was always alight with hell-fire.

These three worthies pressed forward, and greeted Ethan Brand, each after his own fashion, earnestly inviting him to partake of the contents of a certain black bottle; in which, as they averred, he would find something far better worth seeking for, than the Unpardonable Sin. No mind, which has wrought itself, by intense and solitary meditation, into a high state of enthusiasm, can endure the kind of contact with low and vulgar modes of thought and feeling, to which Ethan Brand was now subjected. It made him doubt—and, strange to say, it was a painful doubt—whether he had indeed found the Unpardonable Sin, and found it within himself. The whole question on which he had exhausted life, and more than life, looked like a delusion.

"Leave me," he said bitterly, "ye brute beasts, that have made yourselves so, shrivelling up your souls with fiery liquors! I have done with you. Years and years ago, I groped into your hearts and found nothing there for my purpose. Get ye gone!"

"Why, you uncivil scoundrel," cried the fierce Doctor, "is that the way you respond to the kindness of your best friends? Then let me tell you the truth. You have no more found the Unpardonable Sin than yonder boy Joe has. You are but a crazy fellow—I told you so, twenty years ago—neither better nor worse than a crazy fellow, and the fit companion of old Humphrey, here!"

He pointed to an old man, shabbily dressed, with long white hair, thin visage, and unsteady eyes. For some years past, this aged person had been wandering about among the hills, inquiring of all travellers whom he met, for his daughter. The girl, it seemed, had gone off with a company of circus-performers; and, occasionally, tidings of her came to the village, and fine stories were told of her glittering appearance, as she rode on horseback in the ring, or performed marvellous feats on the tight-rope.

The white-haired father now approached Ethan Brand, and gazed unsteadily into his face.

"They tell me you have been all over the earth," said he, wringing his hands with earnestness. "You must have seen my daughter; for she makes a grand figure in the world, and everybody goes to see her. Did she send any word to her old father, or say when she is coming back?"

Ethan Brand's eye quailed beneath the old man's. That daughter, from whom he so earnestly desired a word of greeting, was the Esther of our tale; the very girl whom, with such cold and remorseless purpose, Ethan Brand had made the subject of a psychological experiment, and wasted, absorbed, and perhaps annihilated her soul, in the process.

"Yes," murmured he, turning away from the hoary wanderer; "it is no delusion. There is an Unpardonable Sin!"

While these things were passing, a merry scene was going forward in the area of cheerful light, besides the spring and before the door of the hut. A number of the youth of the village, young men and girls, had hurried up the hill-side, impelled by curiosity to see Ethan Brand, the hero of so many a legend familiar to their childhood. Finding nothing, however, very remarkable in his aspect—nothing but a sun-burnt wayfarer, in plain garb and dusty shoes, who sat looking into the fire, as if he fancied pictures among the coals—these young people speedily grew tired of observing him. As it happened, there was other amusement at hand. An old German Jew, travelling with a diorama on his back, was passing down the mountain-road towards the village, just as the party turned aside from it; and, in hopes of eking out the profits of the day, the showman had kept them company to the lime-kiln.

"Come, old Dutchman," cried one of the young men, "let us see your pictures, if you can swear they are worth looking at!"

"Oh, yes, Captain," answered the Jew—whether as a matter of courtesy or craft, he styled everybody Captain—"I shall show you, indeed, some very superb pictures!"

So, placing his box in a proper position, he invited the young men and girls to look through the glass orifices of the machine, and proceeded to exhibit a series of the most outrageous scratchings and daubings, as specimens of the fine arts, that ever an itinerant showman had the face to impose upon his circle of spectators. The pictures were worn out, moreover, tattered, full of cracks and wrinkles, dingy with tobacco-smoke, and otherwise in a most pitiable condition. Some purported to be cities, public edifices, and ruined castles, in Europe; others represented Napoleon's battles, and Nelson's sea-fights; and in the midst of these would be seen a gigantic, brown, hairy hand—which might have been mistaken for the Hand of Destiny, though, in truth, it was only the showman's—pointing its forefinger to various scenes of the conflict, while its owner gave historical illustrations. When, with much merriment at its abominable deficiency of merit, the exhibition was concluded, the German bade little Joe put his head into the box. Viewed through the magnifying glasses, the boy's round, rosy visage assumed the strangest imaginable aspect of an immense, Titanic child, the mouth grinning broadly, and the eyes, and every other feature, overflowing with fun at the joke. Suddenly, however, that merry face turned pale, and its expression changed to horror; for this easily impressed and excitable child had become sensible that the eye of Ethan Brand was fixed upon him through the glass.

"You make the little man to be afraid, Captain," said the German Jew, turning up the dark and strong outline of his visage, from his stooping posture. "But, look again; and, by chance, I shall cause you to see somewhat that is very fine, upon my word!"

Ethan Brand gazed into the box for an instant, and then starting back, looked fixedly at the German. What had he seen? Nothing, apparently; for a curious youth, who had peeped in, almost at the same moment, beheld only a vacant space of canvass.

"I remember you now," muttered Ethan Brand to the showman.

"Ah, Captain," whispered the Jew of Nuremberg, with a dark smile, "I find it to be a heavy matter in my show-box— this Unpardonable Sin! By my faith, Captain, it has wearied my shoulders, this long day, to carry it over the mountain."

"Peace!" answered Ethan Brand, sternly, "or get thee into the furnace yonder!"

The Jew's exhibition had scarcely concluded, when a great, elderly dog—who seemed to be his own master, as no person in the company laid claim to him—saw fit to render himself the object of public notice. Hitherto, he had shown himself a very quiet, well-disposed old dog, going round from one to another, and, by way of being sociable, offering his rough head to be patted by any kindly hand that would take so much trouble. But, now, all of a sudden, this grave and venerable quadruped, of his own mere notion, and without the slightest suggestion from anybody else, began to run round after his tail, which, to heighten the absurdity of the proceeding, was a great deal shorter than it should have been. Never was seen such headlong eagerness in pursuit of an object that could not possibly be attained; never was heard such a tremendous outbreak of growling, snarling, barking, and snapping—as if one end of the ridiculous brute's body were at deadly and most unforgivable enmity with the other. Faster and faster, roundabout went the cur; and faster and still faster fled the unapproachable brevity of his tail; and louder and fiercer grew his yells of rage and animosity; until, utterly exhausted, and as far from the goal as ever, the foolish old dog ceased his performance as suddenly as he had begun it. The next moment, he was as mild, quiet, sensible, and respectable in his deportment, as when he first scraped acquaintance with the company.

As may be supposed, the exhibition was greeted with universal laughter, clapping of hands, and shouts of encore; to which the canine performer responded by wagging all that there was to wag of his tail, but appeared totally unable to repeat his very successful effort to amuse the spectators.

Meanwhile, Ethan Brand had resumed his seat upon the log; and, moved, it might be, by a perception of some remote analogy between his own case and that of this self-pursuing cur, he broke into the awful laugh, which, more than any other token, expressed the condition of his inward being. From that moment, the merriment of the party was at an end; they stood aghast, dreading lest the inauspicious sound should be reverberated around the horizon, and that mountain would thunder it to mountain, and so the horror be prolonged upon their ears. Then, whispering one to another, that it was late—that the moon was almost down—that the August night was growing chill—they hurried homeward, leaving the lime-burner and little Joe to deal as they might with their unwelcome guest. Save for these three human beings, the open space on the hill-side was a solitude, set in a vast gloom of forest. Beyond that darksome verge, the fire-light glimmered on the stately trunks and almost black foliage of pines, intermixed with the lighter verdure of sapling oaks, maples, and poplars, while, here and there, lay the gigantic corpses of dead trees, decaying on the leaf-strewn soil. And it seemed to little Joe—a timorous and imaginative child—that the silent forest was holding its breath, until some fearful thing should happen.

Ethan Brand thrust more wood into the fire, and closed the door of the kiln; then looking over his shoulder at the lime-burner and his son, he bade, rather than advised, them to retire to rest.

"For myself I cannot sleep," said he. "I have matters that it concerns me to meditate upon. I will watch the fire, as I used to do in the old time."

"And call the devil out of the furnace to keep you company, I suppose," muttered Bartram, who had been making intimate acquaintance with the black bottle above-mentioned. "But watch, if you like, and call as many devils as you like! For my part, I shall be all the better for a snooze. Come, Joe!"

As the boy followed his father into the hut, he looked back to the wayfarer, and the tears came into his eyes; for his tender spirit had an intuition of the bleak and terrible loneliness in which this man had enveloped himself.

When they had gone, Ethan Brand sat listening to the crackling of the kindled wood, and looking at the little spirts of fire that issued through the chinks of the door. These trifles, however, once so familiar, had but the slightest hold of his attention; while deep within his mind, he was reviewing the gradual, but marvellous change, that had been wrought upon him by the search to which he had devoted himself. He remembered how the night-dew had fallen upon him—how the dark forest had whispered to him—how the stars had gleamed upon him—a simple and loving man, watching his fire in the years gone by, and ever musing as it burned. He remembered with what tenderness, with what love and sympathy for mankind, and what pity for human guilt and wo, he had first begun to contemplate those ideas which afterwards became the inspiration of his life; with what reverence he had then looked into the heart of man, viewing it as a temple originally divine, and however desecrated, still to be held sacred by a brother; with what awful fear he had deprecated the success of his pursuit, and prayed that the Unpardonable Sin might never be revealed to him. Then ensued that vast intellectual development, which, in its progress, disturbed the counterpoise between his mind and heart. The Idea that possessed his life had operated as a means of education; it had gone on cultivating his powers to the highest point of which they were susceptible; it had raised him from the level of an unlettered laborer, to stand on a star-light eminence, whither the philosophers of the earth, laden with the lore of universities, might vainly strive to clamber after him. So much for the intellect! But where was the heart? That, indeed, had withered—had contracted—had hardened—had perished! It had ceased to partake of the universal throb. He had lost his hold of the magnetic chain of humanity. He was no longer a brother-man, opening the chambers or the dungeons of our common nature by the key of holy sympathy, which gave him a right to share in all its secrets; he was now a cold observer, looking on mankind as the subject of his experiment, and, at length, converting man and woman to be his puppets, and pulling the wires that moved them to such degrees of crime as were demanded for his study.

Thus Ethan Brand became a fiend. He began to be so from the moment that his moral nature had ceased to keep the pace of improvement with his intellect. And now, as his highest effort and inevitable development—as the bright and gorgeous flower, and rich, delicious fruit of his life's labor— he had produced the Unpardonable Sin!

"What more have I to seek? What more to achieve?" said Ethan Brand to himself. "My task is done, and well done!"

Starting from the log with a certain alacrity in his gait, and ascending the hillock of earth that was raised against the stone circumference of the lime-kiln, he thus reached the top of the structure. It was a space of perhaps ten feet across, from edge to edge, presenting a view of the upper surface of the immense mass of broken marble with which the kiln was heaped. All these innumerable blocks and fragments of marble were red-hot, and vividly on fire, sending up great spouts of blue flame, which quivered aloft and danced madly, as within a magic circle, and sank and rose again, with continual and multitudinous activity. As the lonely man bent forward over this terrible body of fire, the blasting heat smote up against his person with a breath that, it might be supposed, would have scorched and shrivelled him up in a moment.

Ethan Brand stood erect and raised his arms on high. The blue flames played upon his face, and imparted the wild and ghastly light which alone could have suited its expression; it was that of a fiend on the verge of plunging into his gulf of intensest torment.

"Oh, Mother Earth," cried he, "who art no more my Mother, and into whose bosom this frame shall never be resolved! Oh, mankind, whose brotherhood I have cast off, and trampled thy great heart beneath my feet! Oh, stars of Heaven, that shone on me of old, as if to light me onward and upward!—farewell all, and forever! Come, deadly element of Fire—henceforth my familiar friend! Embrace me as I do thee!"

That night the sound of a fearful peal of laughter rolled heavily through the sleep of the lime-burner and his little son; dim shapes of horror and anguish haunted their dreams, and seemed still present in the rude hovel when they opened their eyes to the daylight.

"Up, boy, up!" cried the lime-burner, staring about him. "Thank Heaven, the night is gone at last; and rather than pass such another, I would watch my lime-kiln, wide awake, for a twelvemonth. This Ethan Brand, with his humbug of an Unpardonable Sin, has done me no such mighty favor in taking my place!"

He issued from the hut, followed by little Joe, who kept fast hold of his father's hand. The early sunshine was already pouring its gold upon the mountain-tops, and though the valleys were still in shadow, they smiled cheerfully in the promise of the bright day that was hastening onward. The village, completely shut in by hills, which swelled away gently about it, looked as if it had rested peacefully in the hollow of the great hand of Providence. Every dwelling was distinctly visible; the little spires of the two churches pointed upward, and caught a fore-glimmering of brightness from the sun-gilt skies upon their gilded weathercocks. The tavern was astir, and the figure of the old, smoke-dried stage-agent, cigar in mouth, was seen beneath the stoop. Old Graylock was glorified with a golden cloud upon his head. Scattered, likewise, over the breasts of the surrounding mountains, there were heaps of hoary mist, in fantastic shapes, some of them far down into the valley, others high up towards the summits, and still others, of the same family of mist or cloud, hovering in the gold radiance of the upper atmosphere. Stepping from one to another of the clouds that rested on the hills, and thence to the loftier brotherhood that sailed in air, it seemed almost as if a mortal man might thus ascend into the heavenly regions. Earth was so mingled with sky that it was a day-dream to look at it.

To supply that charm of the familiar and homely, which Nature so readily adopts into a scene like this, the stage-coach was rattling down the mountain-road, and the driver sounded his horn; while echo caught up the notes and inter-twined them into a rich, and varied, and elaborate harmony, of which the original performer could lay claim to little share. The great hills played a concert among themselves, each contributing a strain of airy sweetness.

Little Joe's face brightened at once.

"Dear father," cried he, skipping cheerily to and fro, "that strange man is gone, and the sky and the mountains all seem glad of it!"

"Yes," growled the lime-burner with an oath, "but he has let the fire go down, and no thanks to him, if five hundred bushels of lime are not spoilt. If I catch the fellow here-abouts again I shall feel like tossing him into the furnace!"

With his long pole in his hand he ascended to the top of the kiln. After a moment's pause he called to his son.

"Come up here, Joe!" said he.

So little Joe ran up the hillock and stood by his father's side. The marble was all burnt into perfect, snow-white lime. But on its surface, in the midst of the circle—snow-white too, and thoroughly converted into lime—lay a human skeleton, in the attitude of a person who, after long toil, lies down to long repose. Within the ribs—strange to say—was the shape of a human heart.

"Was the fellow's heart made of marble?" cried Bartram, in some perplexity at this phenomenon. "At any rate, it is burnt into what looks like special good lime; and, taking all the bones together, my kiln is half a bushel the richer for him."

So saying, the rude lime-burner lifted his pole, and letting it fall upon the skeleton, the relics of Ethan Brand were crumbled into fragments.

A BELL'S BIOGRAPHY

HEARKEN to our neighbor with the iron tongue! While I sit musing over my sheet of foolscap, he emphatically tells the hour, in tones loud enough for all the town to hear, though doubtless intended only as a gentle hint to myself, that I may begin his biography before the evening shall be farther wasted. Unquestionably, a personage in such an elevated position, and making so great a noise in the world, has a fair claim to the services of a biographer. He is the representative and most illustrious member of that innumerable class, whose characteristic feature is the tongue, and whose sole business, to clamor for the public good. If any of his noisy brethren, in our tongue-governed democracy, be envious of the superiority which I have assigned him, they have my free consent to hang themselves as high as he. And for his history, let not the reader apprehend an empty repetition of ding-dong-bell. He has been the passive hero of wonderful vicissitudes, with which I have chanced to become acquainted, possibly from his own mouth; while the careless multitude supposed him to be talking merely of the time of day, or calling them to dinner or to church, or bidding drowsy people go bedward, or the dead to their graves. Many a revolution has it been his fate to go through, and invariably with a prodigious uproar. And whether or no he have told me his reminiscences, this at least is true, that the more I study his deep-toned language, the more sense, and sentiment, and soul, do I discover in it.

This bell—for we may as well drop our quaint personification—is of antique French manufacture, and the symbol of the cross betokens that it was meant to be suspended in the belfry of a Romish place of worship. The old people hereabout have a tradition, that a considerable part of the metal was supplied by a brass cannon, captured in one of the victories of Louis the Fourteenth over the Spaniards, and that a Bourbon princess threw her golden crucifix into the molten mass. It is said, likewise, that a bishop baptized and blessed the bell, and prayed that a heavenly influence might mingle with its tones. When all due ceremonies had been performed, the Grand Monarque bestowed the gift—than which none could resound his beneficence more loudly—on the Jesuits, who were then converting the American Indians to the spiritual dominion of the Pope. So the bell—our self-same bell, whose familiar voice we may hear at all hours, in the streets—this very bell sent forth its first-born accents from the tower of a log-built chapel, westward of Lake Champlain, and near the mighty stream of the Saint Lawrence. It was called Our Lady's Chapel of the Forest. The peal went forth as if to redeem and consecrate the heathen wilderness. The wolf growled at the sound, as he prowled stealthily through the underbrush—the grim bear turned his back, and stalked sullenly away—the startled doe leaped up, and led her fawn into a deeper solitude. The red men wondered what awful voice was speaking amid the wind that roared through the tree-tops; and following reverentially its summons, the dark-robed fathers blessed them, as they drew near the cross-crowned chapel. In a little time, there was a crucifix on every dusky bosom. The Indians knelt beneath the lowly roof, worshipping in the same forms that were observed under the vast dome of Saint Peter's, when the Pope performed high mass in the presence of kneeling princes. All the religious festivals, that awoke the chiming bells of lofty cathedrals, called forth a peal from Our Lady's Chapel of the Forest. Loudly rang the bell of the wilderness, while the streets of Paris echoed with rejoicings for the birthday of the Bourbon, or whenever France had triumphed on some European battle-field. And the solemn woods were saddened with a melancholy knell, as often as the thick-strewn leaves were swept away from the virgin soil, for the burial of an Indian chief.

Meantime, the bells of a hostile people and a hostile faith were ringing on Sabbaths and lecture-days, at Boston and other Puritan towns. Their echoes died away hundreds of miles south-eastward of Our Lady's Chapel. But scouts had threaded the pathless desert that lay between, and, from behind the huge tree-trunks, perceived the Indians assembling at the summons of the bell. Some bore flaxen-haired scalps at their girdles, as if to lay those bloody trophies on Our Lady's altar. It was reported, and believed, all through New-England, that the Pope of Rome, and the King of France, had established this little chapel in the forest, for the purpose of stirring up the red men to a crusade against the English settlers. The latter took energetic measures to secure their religion and their lives. On the eve of an especial fast of the Romish church, while the bell tolled dismally, and the priests were chanting a doleful stave, a band of New-England rangers rushed from the surrounding woods. Fierce shouts, and the report of musketry, pealed suddenly within the chapel. The ministering priests threw themselves before the altar, and were slain even on its steps. If, as antique traditions tell us, no grass will grow where the blood of martyrs has been shed, there should be a barren spot, to this very day, on the site of that desecrated altar.

While the blood was still plashing from step to step, the leader of the rangers seized a torch, and applied it to the drapery of the shrine. The flame and smoke arose, as from a burnt-sacrifice, at once illuminating and obscuring the whole interior of the chapel, now hiding the dead priests in a sable shroud, now revealing them and their slayers in one terrific glare. Some already wished that the altar-smoke could cover the deed from the sight of Heaven. But one of the rangers—a man of sanctified aspect, though his hands were bloody—approached the captain.

'Sir,' said he, 'our village meeting-house lacks a bell, and hitherto we have been fain to summon the good people to worship, by beat of drum. Give me, I pray you, the bell of this popish chapel, for the sake of the godly Mr. Rogers, who doubtless hath remembered us in the prayers of the congregation, ever since we began our march. Who can tell what share of this night's good success we owe to that holy man's wrestling with the Lord?'

'Nay, then,' answered the captain, 'if good Mr. Rogers hath holpen our enterprise, it is right that he should share the spoil. Take the bell and welcome, Deacon Lawson, if you will be at the trouble of carrying it home. Hitherto it hath spoken nothing but papistry, and that too in the French or Indian gibberish; but I warrant me, if Mr. Rogers consecrate it anew, it will talk like a good English and Protestant bell.'

So Deacon Lawson and half a score of his townsmen took down the bell, suspended it on a pole, and bore it away on their sturdy shoulders, meaning to carry it to the shore of Lake Champlain, and thence homeward by water. Far through the woods gleamed the flames of Our Lady's Chapel, flinging fantastic shadows from the clustered foliage, and glancing on brooks that had never caught the sunlight. As the rangers traversed the midnight forest, staggering under their heavy burden, the tongue of the bell gave many a tremendous stroke—clang, clang, clang!—a most doleful sound, as if it were tolling for the slaughter of the priests and the ruin of the chapel. Little dreamed Deacon Lawson and his townsmen that it was their own funeral knell. A war-party of Indians had heard the report of musketry, and seen the blaze of the chapel, and now were on the track of the rangers, summoned to vengeance by the bell's dismal murmurs. In the midst of a deep swamp, they made a sudden onset on the retreating foe. Good Deacon Lawson battled stoutly, but had his skull cloven by a tomahawk, and sank into the depths of the morass, with the ponderous bell above him. And, for many a year thereafter, our hero's voice was heard no more on earth, neither at the hour of worship, nor at festivals nor funerals.

And is he still buried in that unknown grave? Scarcely so, dear reader. Hark! How plainly we hear him at this moment, the spokesman of Time, proclaiming that it is nine o'clock at night! We may therefore safely conclude, that some happy chance has restored him to upper air.

But there lay the bell, for many silent years; and the wonder is, that he did not lie silent there a century, or perhaps a dozen centuries, till the world should have forgotten not only his voice, but the voices of the whole brotherhood of bells. How would the first accent of his iron tongue have startled his resurrectionists! But he was not fated to be a subject of discussion among the antiquaries of far posterity. Near the close of the Old French War, a party of New-England axe-men, who preceded the march of Colonel Bradstreet towards Lake Ontario, were building a bridge of logs through a swamp. Plunging down a stake, one of these pioneers felt it graze against some hard, smooth substance. He called his comrades, and by their united efforts, the top of the bell was raised to the surface, a rope made fast to it, and thence passed over the horizontal limb of a tree. Heave-oh! up they hoisted their prize, dripping with moisture, and festooned with verdant water-moss. As the base of the bell emerged from the swamp, the pioneers perceived that a skeleton was clinging with its bony fingers to the clapper, but immediately relaxing its nerveless grasp, sank back into the stagnant water. The bell then gave forth a sullen clang. No wonder that he was in haste to speak, after holding his tongue for such a length of time! The pioneers shoved the bell to-and-fro, thus ringing a loud and heavy peal, which echoed widely through the forest, and reached the ears of Colonel Bradstreet, and his three thousand men. The soldiers paused on their march; a feeling of religion, mingled with home-tenderness, overpowered their rude hearts; each seemed to hear the clangor of the old church-bell, which had been familiar to him from infancy, and had tolled at the funerals of all his forefathers. By what magic had that holy sound strayed over the wide-murmuring ocean, and become audible amid the clash of arms, the loud crashing of the artillery over the rough wilderness-path, and the melancholy roar of the wind among the boughs!

The New-Englanders hid their prize in a shadowy nook, betwixt a large gray stone and the earthy roots of an overthrown tree; and when the campaign was ended, they conveyed our friend to Boston, and put him up at auction on the side-walk of King-street. He was suspended, for the nonce, by a block and tackle, and being swung backward and forward, gave such loud and clear testimony to his own merits, that the auctioneer had no need to say a word. The highest bidder was a rich old representative from our town, who piously bestowed the bell on the meeting-house where he had been a worshipper for half a century. The good man had his reward. By a strange coincidence, the very first duty of the sexton, after the bell had been hoisted into the belfry, was to toll the funeral knell of the donor. Soon, however, those doleful echoes were drowned by a triumphant peal for the surrender of Quebec.

Ever since that period, our hero has occupied the same elevated station, and has put in his word on all matters of public importance, civil, military, or religious. On the day when Independence was first proclaimed in the street beneath, he uttered a peal which many deemed ominous and fearful, rather than triumphant. But he has told the same story these sixty years, and none mistake his meaning now. When Washington, in the fullness of his glory, rode through our flower-strewn streets, this was the tongue that bade the Father of his Country welcome! Again the same voice was heard when La Fayette came to gather in his half-century's harvest of gratitude. Meantime, vast changes have been going on below. His voice, which once floated over a little provincial sea-port, is now reverberated between brick edifices, and strikes the ear amid the buzz and tumult of a city. On the Sabbaths of olden time, the summons of the bell was obeyed by a picturesque and varied throng; stately gentlemen in purple velvet coats, embroidered waistcoats, white wigs, and gold-laced hats, stepping with grave courtesy beside ladies in flowered satin gowns, and hoop-petticoats of majestic circumference; while behind followed a liveried slave or bondsman, bearing the psalm-book and a stove for his mistress's feet. The commonalty, clad in homely garb, gave precedence to their betters at the door of the meeting-house, as if admitting that there were distinctions between them, even in the sight of God. Yet, as their coffins were borne one after another through the street, the bell has tolled a requiem for all alike. What mattered it, whether or no there were a silver scutcheon on the coffin-lid? 'Open thy bosom, Mother Earth!' Thus spake the bell. 'Another of thy children is coming to his long rest. Take him to thy bosom, and let him slumber in peace.' Thus spake the bell, and Mother Earth received her child. With the self-same tones will the present generation be ushered to the embraces of their mother; and Mother Earth will still receive her children. Is not thy tongue a-weary, mournful talker of two centuries? Oh, funeral bell! wilt thou never be shattered with thine own melancholy strokes? Yea; and a trumpet-call shall arouse the sleepers, whom thy heavy clang could awake no more!

Again—again, thy voice, reminding me that I am wasting the 'midnight oil.' In my lonely fantasy, I can scarce believe that other mortals have caught the sound, or that it vibrates elsewhere than in my secret soul. But to many hast thou spoken. Anxious men have heard thee on their sleepless pillows, and bethought themselves anew of to-morrow's care. In a brief interval of wakefulness, the sons of toil have heard thee, and say, 'Is so much of our quiet slumber spent?—is the morning so near at hand?' Crime has heard thee, and mutters, 'Now is the very hour!' Despair answers thee, 'Thus much of this weary life is gone!' The young mother, on her bed of pain and ecstasy, has counted thy echoing strokes, and dates from them her first-born's share of life and immortality. The bride-groom and the bride have listened, and feel that their night of rapture flits like a dream away. Thine accents have fallen faintly on the ear of the dying man, and warned him that, ere thou speakest again, his spirit shall have passed whither no voice of time can ever reach. Alas for the departing traveller, if thy voice—the voice of fleeting time—have taught him no lessons for Eternity!

SYLPH ETHEREGE

ON A BRIGHT summer evening, two persons stood among the shrubbery of a garden, stealthily watching a young girl, who sat in the window-seat of a neighbouring mansion. One of these unseen observers, a gentleman, was youthful, and had an air of high breeding and refinement, and a face marked with intellect, though otherwise of unprepossessing aspect. His features wore even an ominous, though somewhat mirthful expression, while he pointed his long forefinger at the girl, and seemed to regard her as a creature completely within the scope of his influence.

"The charm works!" said he, in a low, but emphatic whisper.

"Do you know, Edward Hamilton,—since so you choose to be named,—do you know," said the lady beside him, "that I have almost a mind to break the spell at once? What if the lesson should prove too severe! True; if my ward could be thus laughed out of her fantastic nonsense, she might be the better for it through life. But then she is such a delicate creature! And besides, are you not ruining your own chance, by putting forward this shadow of a rival?"

"But will he not vanish into thin air, at my bidding?" rejoined Edward Hamilton. "Let the charm work!"

The girl's slender and sylph-like figure, tinged with radiance from the sunset clouds, and overhung with the rich drapery of the silken curtains, and set within the deep frame of the window, was a perfect picture; or rather, it was like the original loveliness in a painter's fancy, from which the most finished picture is but an imperfect copy. Though her occupation excited so much interest in the two spectators, she was merely gazing at a miniature which she held in her hand, encased in white satin and red morocco; nor did there appear to be any other cause for the smile of mockery and malice with which Hamilton regarded her.

"The charm works!" muttered he, again. "Our pretty Sylvia's scorn will have a dear retribution!"

At this moment the girl raised her eyes, and, instead of a lifelike semblance of the miniature, beheld the ill-omened shape of Edward Hamilton, who now stepped forth from his concealment in the shrubbery.

Sylvia Etherege was an orphan girl, who had spent her life, till within a few months past, under the guardianship, and in the secluded dwelling, of an old bachelor uncle. While yet in her cradle, she had been the destined bride of a cousin, who was no less passive in the betrothal than herself. Their future union had been projected, as the means of uniting two rich estates, and was rendered highly expedient, if not indispensable, by the testamentary dispositions of the parents on both sides. Edgar Vaughan, the promised bridegroom, had been bred from infancy in Europe, and had never seen the beautiful girl, whose heart he was to claim as his inheritance. But already, for several years, a correspondence had been kept up between the cousins, and had produced an intellectual intimacy, though it could but imperfectly acquaint them with each other's character.

Sylvia was shy, sensitive, and fanciful; and her guardian's secluded habits had shut her out from even so much of the world as is generally open to maidens of her age. She had been left to seek associates and friends for herself, in the haunts of imagination, and to converse with them, sometimes in the language of dead poets, oftener in the poetry of her own mind. The companion whom she chiefly summoned up, was the cousin, with whose idea her earliest thoughts had been connected. She made a vision of Edgar Vaughan, and tinted it with stronger hues than a mere fancy-picture, yet graced it with so many bright and delicate perfections, that her cousin could nowhere have encountered so dangerous a rival. To this shadow she cherished a romantic fidelity. With its airy presence sitting by her side, or gliding along her favorite paths, the loneliness of her young life was blissful; her heart was satisfied with love, while yet its virgin purity was untainted by the earthliness that the touch of a real lover would have left there. Edgar Vaughan seemed to be conscious of her character; for, in his letters, he gave her a name that was happily appropriate to the sensitiveness of her disposition, the delicate peculiarity of her manners, and the ethereal beauty both of her mind and person. Instead of Sylvia, he called her Sylph,—with the prerogative of a cousin and a lover,—his dear Sylph Etherege.

When Sylvia was seventeen her guardian died, and she passed under the care of Mrs. Grosvenor, a lady of wealth and fashion, and Sylvia's nearest relative, though a distant one. While an inmate of Mrs. Grosvenor's family, she still pre-served somewhat of her life-long habits of seclusion, and shrank from a too familiar intercourse with those around her. Still, too, she was faithful to her cousin, or to the shadow which bore his name.

The time now drew near, when Edgar Vaughan, whose education had been completed by an extensive range of travel, was to revisit the soil of his nativity. Edward Hamilton, a young gentleman, who had been Vaughan's companion, both in his studies and rambles, had already recrossed the Atlantic, bringing letters to Mrs. Grosvenor and Sylvia Etherege. These credentials insured him an earnest welcome, which, however, on Sylvia's part, was not followed by personal partiality, or even the regard that seemed due to her cousin's most intimate friend. As she herself could have assigned no cause for her repugnance, it might be termed instinctive. Hamilton's person, it is true, was the reverse of attractive, especially when beheld for the first time. Yet, in the eyes of the most fastidious judges, the defect of natural grace was compensated by the polish of his manners, and by the intellect which so often gleamed through his dark features. Mrs. Grosvenor, with whom he immediately became a prodigious favorite, exerted herself to overcome Sylvia's dislike. But, in this matter, her ward could neither be reasoned with, nor persuaded. The presence of Edward Hamilton was sure to render her cold, shy, and distant, abstracting all the vivacity from her deportment, as if a cloud had come betwixt her and the sunshine.

The simplicity of Sylvia's demeanor rendered it easy for so keen an observer as Hamilton to detect her feelings. Whenever any slight circumstance made him sensible of them, a smile might be seen to flit over the young man's sallow visage. None, that had once beheld this smile, were in any danger of forgetting it; whenever they recalled to memory the features of Edward Hamilton, they were always duskily illuminated by this expression of mockery and malice.

In a few weeks after Hamilton's arrival, he presented to Sylvia Etherege a miniature of her cousin, which, as he informed her, would have been delivered sooner, but was detained with a portion of his baggage. This was the miniature, in the contemplation of which we beheld Sylvia so absorbed, at the commencement of our story. Such, in truth, was too often the habit of the shy and musing girl. The beauty of the pictured countenance was almost too perfect to represent a human creature, that had been born of a fallen and world-worn race, and had lived to manhood amid ordinary troubles and enjoyments, and must become wrinkled with age and care. It seemed too bright for a thing formed of dust, and doomed to crumble into dust again. Sylvia feared that such a being would be too refined and delicate to love a simple girl like her. Yet, even while her spirit drooped with that apprehension, the picture was but the masculine counterpart of Sylph Etherege's sylph-like beauty. There was that resemblance between her own face and the miniature, which is said often to exist between lovers whom Heaven has destined for each other, and which, in this instance, might be owing to the kindred blood of the two parties. Sylvia felt, indeed, that there was something familiar in the countenance, so like a friend did the eyes smile upon her, and seem to imply a knowledge of her thoughts. She could account for this impression only by supposing, that, in some of her day-dreams, imagination had conjured up the true similitude of her distant and unseen lover.

But now could Sylvia give a brighter semblance of reality to those day-dreams. Clasping the miniature to her heart, she could summon forth, from that haunted cell of pure and blissful fantasies, the life-like shadow, to roam with her in the moonlight garden. Even at noontide it sat with her in the arbour, when the sunshine threw its broken flakes of gold into the clustering shade. The effect upon her mind was hardly less powerful, than if she had actually listened to, and reciprocated, the vows of Edgar Vaughan; for, though the illusion never quite deceived her, yet the remembrance was as distinct as of a remembered interview. Those heavenly eyes gazed for ever into her soul, which drank at them as at a fountain, and was disquieted if reality threw a momentary cloud between. She heard the melody of a voice breathing sentiments with which her own chimed in like music. Oh, happy, yet hapless girl! Thus to create the being whom she loves, to endow him with all the attributes that were most fascinating to her heart, and then to flit with the airy creature into the realm of fantasy and moonlight, where dwelt his dreamy kindred! For her lover wiled Sylvia away from earth, which seemed strange, and dull, and darksome, and lured her to a country where her spirit roamed in peaceful rapture, deeming that it had found its home. Many, in their youth, have visited that land of dreams, and wandered so long in its enchanted groves, that, when banished thence, they feel like exiles everywhere.

The dark-browed Edward Hamilton, like the villain of a tale, would often glide through the romance wherein poor Sylvia walked. Sometimes, at the most blissful moment of her ecstasy, when the features of the miniature were pictured brightest in the air, they would suddenly change, and darken, and be transformed into his visage. And always, when such change occurred, the intrusive visage wore that peculiar smile, with which Hamilton had glanced at Sylvia.

Before the close of summer, it was told Sylvia Etherege, that Vaughan had arrived from France, and that she would meet him,—would meet, for the first time, the loved of years,—that very evening. We will not tell how often and how earnestly she gazed upon the miniature, thus endeavouring to prepare herself for the approaching interview, lest the throbbing of her timorous heart should stifle the words of welcome. While the twilight grew deeper and duskier, she sat with Mrs. Grosvenor in an inner apartment, lighted only by the softened gleam from an alabaster lamp, which was burning at a distance, on the centre-table of the drawing-room. Never before had Sylph Etherege looked so sylph-like. She had communed with a creature of imagination, till her own loveliness seemed but the creation of a delicate and dreamy fancy. Every vibration of her spirit was visible in her frame, as she listened to the rattling of wheels and the tramp upon the pavement, and deemed that even the breeze bore the sound of her lover's footsteps, as if he trode upon the viewless air. Mrs. Grosvenor, too, while she watched the tremulous flow of Sylvia's feelings, was deeply moved; she looked uneasily at the agitated girl, and was about to speak, when the opening of the street door arrested the words upon her lips.

Footsteps ascended the staircase, with a confident and familiar tread, and some one entered the drawing-room. From the sofa where they sat, in the inner apartment, Mrs. Grosvenor and Sylvia could not discern the visiter.

"Sylph!" cried a voice. "Dearest Sylph! Where are you, sweet Sylph Etherege? Here is your Edgar Vaughan!"

But instead of answering, or rising to meet her lover,—who had greeted her by the sweet and fanciful name, which, appropriate as it was to her character, was known only to him,—Sylvia grasped Mrs. Grosvenor's arm, while her whole frame shook with the throbbing of her heart.

"Who is it?" gasped she. "Who calls me Sylph?"

Before Mrs. Grosvenor could reply, the stranger entered the room, bearing the lamp in his hand. Approaching the sofa, he displayed to Sylvia the features of Edward Hamilton, illuminated by that evil smile, from which his face derived so marked an individuality.

"Is not the miniature an admirable likeness?" inquired he.

Sylvia shuddered, but had not power to turn away her white face from his gaze. The miniature, which she had been holding in her hand, fell down upon the floor, where Hamilton, or Vaughan, set his foot upon it, and crushed the ivory counterfeit to fragments.

"There, my sweet Sylph!" he exclaimed. "It was I that created your phantom-lover, and now I annihilate him! Your dream is rudely broken. Awake, Sylph Etherege, awake to truth! I am the only Edgar Vaughan."

"We have gone too far, Edgar Vaughan," said Mrs. Grosvenor, catching Sylvia in her arms. The revengeful freak, which Vaughan's wounded vanity had suggested, had been countenanced by this lady, in the hope of curing Sylvia of her romantic notions, and reconciling her to the truths and realities of life. "Look at the poor child!" she continued. "I protest I tremble for the consequences!"

"Indeed, Madam!" replied Vaughan, sneeringly, as he threw the light of the lamp on Sylvia's closed eyes and marble features. "Well, my conscience is clear. I did but look into this delicate creature's heart; and with the pure fantasies that I found there, I made what seemed a man,— and the delusive shadow has wiled her away to Shadow-land, and vanished there! It is no new tale. Many a sweet maid has shared the lot of poor Sylph Etherege!"

"And now, Edgar Vaughan," said Mrs. Grosvenor, as Sylvia's heart began faintly to throb again, "now try, in good earnest, to win back her love from the phantom which you conjured up. If you succeed, she will be the better her whole life long, for the lesson we have given her."

Whether the result of the lesson corresponded with Mrs. Grosvenor's hopes, may be gathered from the closing scene of our story. It had been made known to the fashionable world, that Edgar Vaughan had returned from France, and, under the assumed name of Edward Hamilton, had won the affections of the lovely girl, to whom he had been affianced in his boyhood. The nuptials were to take place at an early date. One evening, before the day of anticipated bliss arrived, Edgar Vaughan entered Mrs. Grosvenor's drawing-room, where he found that lady and Sylph Etherege.

"Only that Sylvia makes no complaint," remarked Mrs. Grosvenor, "I should apprehend that the town air is ill suited to her constitution. She was always, indeed, a delicate creature; but now she is a mere gossamer. Do but look at her! Did you ever imagine any thing so fragile?"

Vaughan was already attentively observing his mistress, who sat in a shadowy and moonlighted recess of the room, with her dreamy eyes fixed steadfastly upon his own. The bough of a tree was waving before the window, and sometimes enveloped her in the gloom of its shadow, into which she seemed to vanish.

"Yes," he said, to Mrs. Grosvenor. "I can scarcely deem her 'of the earth, earthy.' No wonder that I call her Sylph! Methinks she will fade into the moonlight, which falls upon her through the window. Or, in the open air, she might flit away upon the breeze, like a wreath of mist!"

Sylvia's eyes grew yet brighter. She waved her hand to Edgar Vaughan, with a gesture of ethereal triumph.

"Farewell!" she said. "I will neither fade into the moonlight, nor flit away upon the breeze. Yet you cannot keep me here!"

There was something in Sylvia's look and tones, that startled Mrs. Grosvenor with a terrible apprehension. But, as she was rushing towards the girl, Vaughan held her back.

"Stay!" cried he, with a strange smile of mockery and anguish. "Can our sweet Sylph be going to Heaven, to seek the original of the miniature?"

THE CANTERBURY PILGRIMS

THE SUMMER moon, which shines in so many a tale, was beaming over a broad extent of uneven country. Some of its brightest rays were flung into a spring of water, where no traveller, toiling up the hilly road beside which it gushes, ever failed to quench his thirst. The work of neat hands and considerate art, was visible about this blessed fountain. An open cistern, hewn and hollowed out of solid stone, was placed above the waters, which filled it to the brim, but, by some invisible outlet, were conveyed away without dripping down its sides. Though the basin had not room for another drop, and the continual gush of water made a tremor on the surface, there was a secret charm that forbade it to overflow. I remember, that when I had slaked my summer thirst, and sat panting by the cistern, it was my fanciful theory, that Nature could not afford to lavish so pure a liquid, as she does the waters of all meaner fountains.

While the moon was hanging almost perpendicularly over this spot, two figures appeared on the summit of the hill, and came with noiseless footsteps down towards the spring. They were then in the first freshness of youth; nor is there a wrinkle now on either of their brows, and yet they wore a strange old fashioned garb. One, a young man with ruddy cheeks, walked beneath the canopy of a broad brimmed gray hat; he seemed to have inherited his great-grand-sire's square skirted coat, and a waistcoat that extended its immense flaps to his knees; his brown locks, also, hung down behind, in a mode unknown to our times. By his side was a sweet young damsel, her fair features sheltered by a prim little bonnet, within which appeared the vestal muslin of a cap; her close, long waisted gown, and indeed her whole attire, might have been worn by some rustic beauty who had faded half a century before. But that there was something too warm and life-like in them, I would here have compared this couple to the ghosts of two young lovers, who had died long since in the glow of passion, and now were straying out of their graves, to renew the old vows, and shadow forth the unforgotten kiss of their earthly lips, beside the moonlit spring.

'Thee and I will rest here a moment, Miriam,' said the young man, as they drew near the stone cistern, 'for there is no fear that the elders know what we have done; and this may be the last time we shall ever taste this water.'

Thus speaking, with a little sadness in his face, which was also visible in that of his companion, he made her sit down on a stone, and was about to place himself very close to her side; she, however, repelled him, though not unkindly.

'Nay, Josiah,' said she, giving him a timid push with her maiden hand, 'thee must sit farther off, on that other stone, with the spring between us. What would the sisters say, if thee were to sit so close to me?'

'But we are of the world's people now, Miriam,' answered Josiah.

The girl persisted in her prudery, nor did the youth, in fact, seem altogether free from a similar sort of shyness; so they sat apart from each other, gazing up the hill, where the moonlight discovered the tops of a group of buildings. While their attention was thus occupied, a party of travellers, who had come wearily up the long ascent, made a halt to refresh themselves at the spring. There were three men, a woman, and a little girl and boy. Their attire was mean, covered with the dust of the summer's day, and damp with the night dew; they all looked woe begone, as if the cares and sorrows of the world had made their steps heavier as they climbed the hill; even the two little children appeared older in evil days, than the young man and maiden who had first approached the spring.

'Good evening to you, young folks,' was the salutation of the travellers; and 'Good evening, friends,' replied the youth and damsel.

'Is that white building the Shaker meeting house?' asked one of the strangers. 'And are those the red roofs of the Shaker village?'

'Friend, it is the Shaker village,' answered Josiah, after some hesitation.

The travellers, who, from the first had looked suspiciously at the garb of these young people, now taxed them with an intention, which all the circumstances, indeed, rendered too obvious to be mistaken.

'It is true, friends,' replied the young man, summoning up his courage. 'Miriam and I have a gift to love each other, and we are going among the world's people, to live after their fashion. And ye know that we do not transgress the law of the land; and neither ye, nor the elders themselves, have a right to hinder us.'

'Yet you think it expedient to depart without leave taking,' remarked one of the travellers.

'Yea, ye–a,' said Josiah, reluctantly, 'because father Job is a very awful man to speak with, and being aged himself, he has but little charity for what he calls the iniquities of the flesh.'

'Well,' said the stranger, 'we will neither use force to bring you back to the village, nor will we betray you to the elders. But sit you here awhile, and when you have heard what we shall tell you of the world which we have left, and into which you are going, perhaps you will turn back with us of your own accord. What say you?' added he, turning to his companions. 'We have travelled thus far without becoming known to each other. Shall we tell our stories, here by this pleasant spring, for our own pastime, and the benefit of these misguided young lovers?'

In accordance with this proposal, the whole party stationed themselves round the stone cistern; the two children, being very weary, fell asleep upon the damp earth, and the pretty Shaker girl, whose feelings were those of a nun or a Turkish lady, crept as close as possible to the female traveller, and as far as she well could from the unknown men. The same person who had hitherto been the chief spokesman, now stood up, waving his hat in his hand, and suffered the moonlight to fall full upon his front.

'In me,' said he, with a certain majesty of utterance, 'in me, you behold a poet.'

Though a lithographic print of this gentleman is extant, it may be well to notice that he was now nearly forty, a thin and stooping figure, in a black coat, out at elbows; notwithstanding the ill condition of his attire, there were about him several tokens of a peculiar sort of foppery, unworthy of a mature man, particularly in the arrangement of his hair, which was so disposed as to give all possible loftiness and breadth to his forehead. However, he had an intelligent eye, and on the whole a marked countenance.

'A poet!' repeated the young Shaker, a little puzzled how to understand such a designation, seldom heard in the utilitarian community where he had spent his life. 'Oh, ay, Miriam, he means a varse maker, thee must know.'

This remark jarred upon the susceptible nerves of the poet; nor could he help wondering what strange fatality had put into this young man's mouth an epithet, which ill natured people had affirmed to be more proper to his merit than the one assumed by himself.

'True, I am a verse maker,' he resumed, 'but my verse is no more than the material body into which I breathe the celestial soul of thought. Alas! how many a pang has it cost me, this same insensibility to the ethereal essence of poetry, with which you have here tortured me again, at the moment when I am to relinquish my profession forever! Oh, Fate! why hast thou warred with Nature, turning all her higher and more perfect gifts to the ruin of me, their possessor? What is the voice of song, when the world lacks the ear of taste? How can I rejoice in my strength and delicacy of feeling, when they have but made great sorrows out of little ones? Have I dreaded scorn like death, and yearned for fame as others pant for vital air, only to find myself in a middle state between obscurity and infamy? But I have my revenge! I could have given existence to a thousand bright creations. I crush them into my heart, and there let them putrify! I shake off the dust of my feet against my countrymen! But posterity, tracing my footsteps up this weary hill, will cry shame upon the unworthy age that drove one of the fathers of American song to end his days in a Shaker village!'

During this harangue, the speaker gesticulated with great energy, and, as poetry is the natural language of passion, there appeared reason to apprehend his final explosion into an ode extempore. The reader must understand, that for all these bitter words, he was a kind, gentle, harmless, poor fellow enough, whom Nature, tossing her ingredients together without looking at her recipe, had sent into the world with too much of one sort of brain and hardly any of another.

'Friend,' said the young Shaker, in some perplexity, 'thee seemest to have met with great troubles, and, doubtless, I should pity them, if—if I could but understand what they were.'

'Happy in your ignorance!' replied the poet, with an air of sublime superiority. 'To your coarser mind, perhaps, I may seem to speak of more important griefs, when I add, what I had well nigh forgotten, that I am out at elbows, and almost starved to death. At any rate, you have the advice and example of one individual to warn you back; for I am come hither, a disappointed man, flinging aside the fragments of my hopes, and seeking shelter in the calm retreat which you are so anxious to leave.'

'I thank thee, friend,' rejoined the youth, 'but I do not mean to be a poet, nor, Heaven be praised! do I think Miriam ever made a varse in her life. So we need not fear thy disappointments. But, Miriam,' he added, with real concern, 'thee knowest that the elders admit nobody that has not a gift to be useful. Now, what under the sun can they do with this poor varse maker?'

'Nay, Josiah, do not thee discourage the poor man,' said the girl, in all simplicity and kindness. 'Our hymns are very rough, and perhaps they may trust him to smooth them.'

Without noticing this hint of professional employment, the poet turned away, and gave himself up to a sort of vague reverie, which he called thought. Sometimes he watched the moon, pouring a silvery liquid on the clouds, through which it slowly melted till they became all bright; then he saw the same sweet radiance dancing on the leafy trees which rustled as if to shake it off, or sleeping on the high tops of hills, or hovering down in distant vallies, like the material of unshaped dreams; lastly, he looked into the spring, and there the light was mingling with the water. In its crystal bosom, too, beholding all heaven reflected there, he found an emblem of a pure and tranquil breast. He listened to that most ethereal of all sounds, the song of crickets, coming in full choir upon the wind, and fancied, that, if moonlight could be heard, it would sound just like that. Finally he took a draught at the Shaker spring, and, as if it were the true Castalia, was forthwith moved to compose a lyric, a Farewell to his Harp, which he swore should be its closing strain, the last verse that an ungrateful world should have from him. This effusion, with two or three other little pieces, subsequently written, he took the first opportunity to send by one of the Shaker brethren to Concord, where they were published in the New Hampshire Patriot.

Meantime, another of the Canterbury Pilgrims, one so different from the poet, that the delicate fancy of the latter could hardly have conceived of him, began to relate his sad experience. He was a small man, of quick and unquiet gestures, about fifty years old, with a narrow forehead, all wrinkled and drawn together. He held in his hand a pencil, and a card of some commission merchant in foreign parts, on the back of which, for there was light enough to read or write by, he seemed ready to figure out a calculation.

'Young man,' said he abruptly, 'what quantity of land do the Shakers own here, in Canterbury?'

'That is more than I can tell thee, friend,' answered Josiah, 'but it is a very rich establishment, and for a long way by the road-side, thee may guess the land to be ours, by the neatness of the fences.'

'And what may be the value of the whole,' continued the stranger, 'with all the buildings and improvements, pretty nearly, in round numbers?'

'Oh, a monstrous sum, more than I can reckon,' replied the young Shaker.

'Well, sir,' said the pilgrim, 'there was a day, and not very long ago, neither, when I stood at my counting room window, and watched the signal flags of three of my own ships entering the harbour, from the East Indies, from Liverpool, and from up the Straits; and I would not have given the invoice of the least of them for the title deeds of this whole Shaker settlement. You stare. Perhaps, now, you won't

believe that I could have put more value on a little piece of
paper, no bigger than the palm of your hand, than all these
solid acres of grain, grass and pasture land, would sell for?'

'I won't dispute it, friend,' answered Josiah, 'but I know
I had rather have fifty acres of this good land, than a whole
sheet of thy paper.'

'You may say so now,' said the ruined merchant, bitterly,
'for my name would not be worth the paper I should write
it on. Of course, you must have heard of my failure?'

And the stranger mentioned his name, which, however
mighty it might have been in the commercial world, the
young Shaker had never heard of among the Canterbury hills.

'Not heard of my failure!' exclaimed the merchant, considerably piqued. 'Why, it was spoken of on 'Change in London,
and from Boston to New Orleans, men trembled in their
shoes. At all events I did fail, and you see me here on my
road to the Shaker village, where, doubtless, (for the Shakers
are a shrewd sect,) they will have a due respect for my
experience, and give me the management of the trading part
of the concern, in which case, I think I can pledge myself
to double their capital in four or five years. Turn back with
me, young man, for though you will never meet with my
good luck, you can hardly escape my bad.'

'I will not turn back for this,' replied Josiah, calmly, 'any
more than for the advice of the varse maker, between whom
and thee, friend, I see a sort of likeness, though I can't justly
say where it lies. But Miriam and I can earn our daily bread
among the world's people, as well as in the Shaker village.
And do we want any thing more, Miriam?'

'Nothing more, Josiah,' said the girl quietly.

'Yea, Miriam, and daily bread for some other little mouths,
if God send them,' observed the simple Shaker lad.

Miriam did not reply, but looked down into the spring,
where she encountered the image of her own pretty face,

blushing within the prim little bonnet. The third pilgrim now took up the conversation. He was a sunburnt country-man, of tall frame and bony strength, on whose rude and manly face there appeared a darker, more sullen and obsti-nate despondency, than on those of either the poet or the merchant.

'Well now, youngster,' he began, 'these folks have had their say, so I'll take my turn. My story will cut but a poor figure by the side of theirs; for I never supposed that I could have a right to meat and drink, and great praise besides, only for tagging rhymes together, as it seems this man does; nor ever tried to get the substance of hundreds into my own hands, like the trader there. When I was about of your years, I married me a wife, just such a neat and pretty young woman as Miriam, if that's her name, and all I asked of Providence was an ordinary blessing on the sweat of my brow, so that we might be decent and comfortable, and have daily bread for ourselves, and for some other little mouths that we soon had to feed. We had no very great prospects before us; but I never wanted to be idle, and I thought it a matter of course that the Lord would help me, because I was willing to help myself.'

'And didn't He help thee, friend?' demanded Josiah, with some eagerness.

'No,' said the yeoman, sullenly; 'for then you would not have seen me here. I have labored hard for years; and my means have been growing narrower, and my living poorer, and my heart colder and heavier, all the time; till at last I could bear it no longer. I set myself down to calculate whether I had best go on the Oregon expedition, or come here to the Shaker village; but I had not hope enough left in me to begin the world over again; and, to make my story short, here I am. And now, youngster, take my advice, and turn back; or else, some few years hence, you'll have to climb this hill, with as heavy a heart as mine.'

This simple story had a strong effect on the young fugitives. The misfortunes of the poet and merchant had won little sympathy from their plain good sense and unworldly feelings, qualities which made them such unprejudiced and inflexible judges, that few men would have chosen to take the opinion of this youth and maiden, as to the wisdom or folly of their pursuits. But here was one whose simple wishes had resembled their own, and who, after efforts which almost gave him a right to claim success from fate, had failed in accomplishing them.

'But thy wife, friend?' exclaimed the young man, 'What became of the pretty girl, like Miriam? Oh, I am afraid she is dead!'

'Yea, poor man, she must be dead, she and the children too,' sobbed Miriam.

The female pilgrim had been leaning over the spring, wherein latterly a tear or two might have been seen to fall, and form its little circle on the surface of the water. She now looked up, disclosing features still comely, but which had acquired an expression of fretfulness, in the same long course of evil fortune that had thrown a sullen gloom over the temper of the unprosperous yeoman.

'I am his wife,' said she, a shade of irritability just perceptible in the sadness of her tone. 'These poor little things, asleep on the ground, are two of our children. We had two more, but God has provided better for them than we could, by taking them to himself.'

'And what would thee advise Josiah and me to do?' asked Miriam, this being the first question which she had put to either of the strangers.

' 'Tis a thing almost against nature, for a woman to try to part true lovers,' answered the yeoman's wife, after a pause; 'but I'll speak as truly to you as if these were my dying words. Though my husband told you some of our troubles, he didn't mention the greatest, and that which makes all the rest so hard to bear. If you and your sweet-heart marry, you'll be kind and pleasant to each other for a year or two, and while that's the case, you never will repent; but by-and-by, he'll grow gloomy, rough, and hard to please, and you'll be peevish, and full of little angry fits, and apt to be complaining by the fireside, when he comes to rest himself from his troubles out of doors; so your love will wear away by little and little, and leave you miserable at last. It has been so with us; and yet my husband and I were true lovers once, if ever two young folks were.'

As she ceased, the yeoman and his wife exchanged a glance, in which there was more and warmer affection than they had supposed to have escaped the frost of a wintry fate, in either of their breasts. At that moment, when they stood on the utmost verge of married life, one word fitly spoken, or perhaps one peculiar look, had they had mutual confidence enough to reciprocate it, might have renewed all their old feelings, and sent them back, resolved to sustain each other amid the struggles of the world. But the crisis past, and never came again. Just then, also, the children, roused by their mother's voice, looked up, and added their wailing accents to the testimony borne by all the Canterbury Pilgrims against the world from which they fled.

'We are tired and hungry!' cried they. 'Is it far to the Shaker village?'

The Shaker youth and maiden looked mournfully into each other's eyes. They had but stepped across the threshold of their homes, when lo! the dark array of cares and sorrows that rose up to warn them back. The varied narratives of the strangers had arranged themselves into a parable; they seemed not merely instances of woeful fate that had befallen others, but shadowy omens of disappointed hope, and unavailing toil, domestic grief, and estranged affection, that would cloud the onward path of these poor fugitives. But after one instant's hesitation, they opened their arms, and sealed their resolve with as pure and fond an embrace as ever youthful love had hallowed.

'We will not go back,' said they. 'The world never can be dark to us, for we will always love one another.'

Then the Canterbury Pilgrims went up the hill, while the poet chanted a drear and desperate stanza of the Farewell to his Harp, fitting music for that melancholy band. They sought a home where all former ties of nature or society would be sundered, and all old distinctions levelled, and a cold and passionless security be substituted for human hope and fear, as in that other refuge of the world's weary outcasts, the grave. The lovers drank at the Shaker spring, and then, with chastened hopes, but more confiding affections, went on to mingle in an untried life.

OLD NEWS

I

H ERE IS a volume of what were once newspapers
—each on a small half-sheet, yellow and time-
stained, of a coarse fabric, and imprinted with a
rude old type. Their aspect conveys a singular impression of
antiquity, in a species of literature which we are accustomed
to consider as connected only with the present moment.
Ephemeral as they were intended and supposed to be, they
have long outlived the printer and his whole subscription
list, and have proved more durable, as to their physical existence, than most of the timber, bricks, and stone, of the town
where they were issued. These are but the least of their
triumphs. The government, the interests, the opinions—in
short, all the moral circumstances that were contemporary
with their publication, have passed away, and left no better
record of what they were, than may be found in these frail
leaves. Happy are the editors of newspapers! Their productions excel all others in immediate popularity, and are certain
to acquire another sort of value with the lapse of time. They
scatter their leaves to the wind, as the sybil did, and posterity
collects them, to be treasured up among the best materials of
its wisdom. With hasty pens, they write for immortality.

It is pleasant to take one of these little dingy half-sheets
between the thumb and finger, and picture forth the per-

sonage, who, above ninety years ago, held it, wet from the press, and steaming, before the fire. Many of the numbers bear the name of an old colonial dignitary. There he sits, a major, a member of the council, and a weighty merchant, in his high-backed arm-chair, wearing a solemn wig and grave attire, such as befits his imposing gravity of mien, and displaying but little finery, except a huge pair of silver shoe-buckles, curiously carved. Observe the awful reverence of his visage, as he reads His Majesty's most gracious speech, and the deliberate wisdom with which he ponders over some paragraph of provincial politics, and the keener intelligence with which he glances at the ship-news and commercial advertisements. Observe, and smile! He may have been a wise man in his day; but, to us, the wisdom of the politician appears like folly, because we can compare its prognostics with actual results; and the old merchant seems to have busied himself about vanities, because we know that the expected ships have been lost at sea, or mouldered at the wharves; that his imported broadcloths were long ago worn to tatters, and his cargoes of wine quaffed to the lees; and that the most precious leaves of his leger have become waste-paper. Yet, his avocations were not so vain as our philosophic moralizing. In this world, we are the things of a moment, and are made to pursue momentary things, with here and there a thought that stretches mistily towards eternity, and perhaps may endure as long. All philosophy, that would abstract mankind from the present, is no more than words.

The first pages, of most of these old papers, are as soporific as a bed of poppies. Here we have an erudite clergyman, or perhaps a Cambridge professor, occupying several successive weeks with a criticism on Tate and Brady, as compared with the New-England version of the Psalms. Of course, the preference is given to the native article. Here are doctors disagreeing about the treatment of a putrid fever, then prevalent, and blackguarding each other with a characteristic virulence, that renders the controversy not altogether unreadable. Here are President Wigglesworth and the Rev. Dr. Colman, endeavoring to raise a fund for the support of missionaries among the Indians of Massachusetts Bay. Easy would be the duties of such a mission, now! Here—for there is nothing new under the sun—are frequent complaints of the disordered state of the currency, and the project of a bank with a capital of five hundred thousand pounds, secured on lands. Here are literary essays, from the Gentleman's Magazine; and squibs against the Pretender, from the London newspapers. And here, occasionally, are specimens of New-England humor —laboriously light and lamentably mirthful; as if some very sober person, in his zeal to be merry, were dancing a jig to the tune of a funeral-psalm. All this is wearisome, and we must turn the leaf.

There is a good deal of amusement, and some profit, in the perusal of those little items, which characterize the manners and circumstances of the country. New-England was then in a state incomparably more picturesque than at present, or than it has been within the memory of man; there being, as yet, only a narrow strip of civilization along the edge of a vast forest, peopled with enough of its original race to contrast the savage life with the old customs of another world. The white population, also, was diversified by the influx of all sorts of expatriated vagabonds, and by the continual importation of bond-servants from Ireland and elsewhere; so that there was a wild and unsettled multitude, forming a strong minority to the sober descendants of the Puritans. Then, there were the slaves, contributing their dark shade to the picture of society. The consequence of all this was, a great variety and singularity of action and incident—many instances of which, might be selected from these columns, where they are told with a simplicity and quaintness of style, that bring the striking points into very strong relief.

It is natural to suppose, too, that these circumstances affected the body of the people, and made their course of life generally less regular than that of their descendants. There is no evidence that the moral standard was higher then than now; or, indeed, that morality was so well defined as it has since become. There seem to have been quite as many frauds and robberies, in proportion to the number of honest deeds; there were murders, in hot blood and in malice; and bloody quarrels, over liquor. Some of our fathers, also, appear to have been yoked to unfaithful wives—if we may trust the frequent notices of elopements from bed and board. The pillory, the whipping-post, the prison, and the gallows, each, had their use in those old times; and, in short, as often as our imagination lives in the past, we find it a ruder and rougher age than our own, with hardly any perceptible advantages, and much that gave life a gloomier tinge.

In vain, we endeavor to throw a sunny and joyous air over our picture of this period; nothing passes before our fancy but a crowd of sad-visaged people, moving duskily through a dull gray atmosphere. It is certain, that winter rushed upon them with fiercer storms than now—blocking up the narrow forest-paths, and overwhelming the roads, along the sea-coast, with mountain snow-drifts; so that weeks elapsed before the newspaper could announce how many travellers had perished, or what wrecks had strewn the shore. The cold was more piercing then, and lingered farther into the spring—making the chimney-corner a comfortable seat till long past May-day. By the number of such accidents on record, we might suppose that the thunder-stone, as they termed it, fell oftener and deadlier, on steeples, dwellings, and unsheltered wretches. In fine, our fathers bore the brunt of more raging and pitiless elements than we. There were forebodings, also, of a more fearful tempest than those of the elements. At two or three dates, we have stories of drums, trumpets, and all sorts of martial music, passing athwart the midnight sky, accompanied with the roar of cannon and rattle of musketry, prophetic echoes of the sounds that were soon to shake the land. Besides these airy prognostics, there were rumors of French fleets on the coast, and of the march of French and Indians through the wilderness, along the borders of the settlements. The country was saddened, moreover, with grievous sickness. The small-pox raged in many of the towns, and seems, though so familiar a scourge, to have been regarded with as much affright as that which drove the throng from Wall-street and Broadway, at the approach of a new pestilence. There were autumnal fevers, too; and a contagious and destructive throat-distemper—diseases unwritten in medical books. The dark superstition of former days had not yet been so far dispelled, as not to heighten the gloom of the present times. There is an advertisement, indeed, by a committee of the Legislature, calling for information as to the circumstances of sufferers in the 'late calamity of 1692,' with a view to reparation for their losses and misfortunes. But the tenderness, with which, after above forty years, it was thought expedient to allude to the witchcraft delusion, indicates a good deal of lingering error, as well as the advance of more enlightened opinions. The rigid hand of Puritanism might yet be felt upon the reins of government, while some of the ordinances intimate a disorderly spirit on the part of the people. The Suffolk justices, after a preamble that great disturbances have been committed by persons entering town and leaving it in coaches, chaises, calashes, and other wheel-carriages, on the evening before the Sabbath, give notice that a watch will hereafter be set at the 'fortification-gate,' to prevent these outrages. It is amusing to see Boston assuming the aspect of a walled city— guarded, probably, by a detachment of church-members, with a deacon at their head. Governor Belcher makes proclamation

against certain 'loose and dissolute people,' who have been
wont to stop passengers in the streets, on the Fifth of November, 'otherwise called Pope's Day,' and levy contributions for
the building of bonfires. In this instance, the populace are
more puritanic than the magistrate.

The elaborate solemnities of funerals were in accordance
with the sombre character of the times. In cases of ordinary
death, the printer seldom fails to notice that the corpse was
'very decently interred.' But when some mightier mortal has
yielded to his fate, the decease of the 'worshipful' such-a-one
is announced, with all his titles of deacon, justice, councillor,
and colonel; then follows an heraldic sketch of his honorable
ancestors, and lastly an account of the black pomp of his
funeral, and the liberal expenditure of scarfs, gloves, and
mourning-rings. The burial train glides slowly before us, as
we have seen it represented in the wood-cuts of that day,
the coffin, and the bearers, and the lamentable friends, trail-
ing their long black garments, while grim Death, a most
mis-shapen skeleton, with all kinds of doleful emblems, stalks
hideously in front. There was a coachmaker at this period,
one John Lucas, who seems to have gained the chief of his
living by letting out a sable coach to funerals.

It would not be fair, however, to leave quite so dismal an
impression on the reader's mind; nor should it be forgotten
that happiness may walk soberly in dark attire as well as
dance lightsomely in a gala-dress. And this reminds us that
there is an incidental notice of the 'dancing-school near the
Orange-Tree,' whence we may infer, that the saltatory art
was occasionally practised, though perhaps chastened into a
characteristic gravity of movement. This pastime was probably confined to the aristocratic circle, of which the royal
Governor was the centre. But we are scandalized, at the
attempt of Jonathan Furness to introduce a more reprehen-
sible amusement: he challenges the whole country to match

his black gelding in a race for a hundred pounds, to be decided on Metonomy Common or Chelsea Beach. Nothing, as to the manners of the times, can be inferred from this freak of an individual. There were no daily and continual opportunities of being merry; but sometimes the people rejoiced, in their own peculiar fashion, oftener with a calm religious smile, than with a broad laugh; as when they feasted, like one great family, at Thanksgiving time; or indulged a livelier mirth throughout the pleasant days of Election-week. This latter, was the true holyday-season of New-England. Military musters were too seriously important, in that warlike time, to be classed among amusements; but they stirred up and enlivened the public mind, and were occasions of solemn festival to the Governor and great men of the Province, at the expense of the field-officers. The Revolution blotted a feast-day out of our calendar; for the anniversary of the King's birth appears to have been celebrated with most imposing pomp, by salutes from Castle William, a military parade, a grand dinner at the town-house, and a brilliant illumination in the evening. There was nothing forced nor feigned in these testimonials of loyalty to George the Second. So long as they dreaded the re-establishment of a popish dynasty, the people were fervent for the house of Hanover; and, besides, the immediate magistracy of the country was a barrier between the monarch and the occasional discontents of the colonies; the waves of faction sometimes reached the governor's chair, but never swelled against the throne. Thus, until oppression was felt to proceed from the King's own hand, New-England rejoiced with her whole heart on His Majesty's birth-day.

But the slaves, we suspect, were the merriest part of the population—since it was their gift to be merry in the worst of circumstances; and they endured, comparatively, few hardships, under the domestic sway of our fathers. There seems to have been a great trade in these human commodities. No advertisements are more frequent than those of 'a negro fellow, fit for almost any household work;' 'a negro woman, honest, healthy, and capable;' 'a young negro wench, of many desirable qualities;' 'a negro man, very fit for a taylor.' We know not in what this natural fitness for a taylor consisted, unless it were some peculiarity of conformation that enabled him to sit cross-legged. When the slaves of a family were inconveniently prolific, it being not quite orthodox to drown the superfluous offspring, like a litter of kittens, notice was promulgated of 'a negro child to be given away.' Sometimes the slaves assumed the property of their own persons, and made their escape: among many such instances, the Governor raises a hue-and-cry after his negro Juba. But, without venturing a word in extenuation of the general system, we confess our opinion, that Cæsar, Pompey, Scipio, and all such great Roman namesakes, would have been better advised had they staid at home, foddering the cattle, cleaning dishes—in fine, performing their moderate share of the labors of life without being harassed by its cares. The sable inmates of the mansion were not excluded from the domestic affections: in families of middling rank, they had their places at the board; and when the circle closed round the evening hearth, its blaze glowed on their dark shining faces, intermixed familiarly with their master's children. It must have contributed to reconcile them to their lot, that they saw white men and women imported from Europe, as they had been from Africa, and sold, though only for a term of years, yet as actual slaves to the highest bidder. Slave labor being but a small part of the industry of the country, it did not change the character of the people; the latter, on the contrary, modified and softened the institution, making it a patriarchal, and almost a beautiful, peculiarity of the times.

Ah! We had forgotten the good old merchant, over whose shoulder we were peeping, while he read the newspaper. Let us now suppose him putting on his three-cornered, gold-laced hat, grasping his cane, with a head inlaid of ebony and mother-of-pearl, and setting forth, through the crooked streets of Boston, on various errands, suggested by the advertisements of the day. Thus he communes with himself: I must be mindful, says he, to call at Captain Scut's, in Creek-lane, and examine his rich velvet, whether it be fit for my apparel on Election-day—that I may wear a stately aspect in presence of the Governor and my brethren of the council. I will look in, also, at the shop of Michael Cario, the jeweller; he has silver buckles of a new fashion; and mine have lasted me some half score years. My fair daughter, Miriam, shall have an apron of gold brocade, and a velvet mask—though it would be a pity the wench should hide her comely visage; and also a French cap, from Robert Jenkins's, on the north side of the town-house. He hath beads, too, and ear-rings, and necklaces, of all sorts; these are but vanities—nevertheless, they would please the silly maiden well. My dame desireth another female in the kitchen; wherefore, I must inspect the lot of Irish lasses, for sale by Samuel Waldo, aboard the schooner Endeavor; as also the likely negro wench, at Captain Bulfinch's. It were not amiss, that I took my daughter, Miriam, to see the royal wax-work, near the town-dock, that she may learn to honour our most gracious King and Queen, and their royal progeny, even in their waxen images; not that I would approve of image-worship. The camel, too, that strange beast from Africa, with two great humps, to be seen near the common; methinks I would fain go thither, and see how the old patriarchs were wont to ride. I will tarry awhile in Queen-street, at the book-store of my good friends, Kneeland & Green, and purchase Doctor Colman's new sermon, and the volume of discourses, by Mr. Henry Flynt; and look over the controversy on baptism, between the Reverend Peter Clarke and an unknown adversary; and see whether this George Whitefield be as great in print as he is famed to be in the pulpit. By that time, the auction will have commenced at the Royal Exchange, in King-street. Moreover, I must look to the disposal of my last cargo of West-India rum and muscovado sugar; and also the lot of choice Cheshire cheese, lest it grow mouldy. It were well that I ordered a cask of good English beer, at the lower end of Milk-street. Then am I to speak with certain dealers about the lot of stout old Vidonia, rich Canary, and Oporto wines, which I have now lying in the cellar of the Old South meeting-house. But, a pipe or two of the rich Canary shall be reserved, that it may grow mellow in mine own wine-cellar, and gladden my heart when it begins to droop with old-age.

Provident old gentleman! But, was he mindful of his sepulchre? Did he bethink him to call at the workshop of Timothy Sheaffe, in Cold-lane, and select such a grave-stone as would best please him? There wrought the man, whose handiwork, or that of his fellow-craftsmen, was ultimately in demand by all the busy multitude, who have left a record of their earthly toil in these old time-stained papers. And now, as we turn over the volume, we seem to be wandering among the mossy stones of a burial-ground.

II The Old French War

At a period about twenty years subsequent to that of our former sketch, we again attempt a delineation of some of the characteristics of life and manners in New-England. Our text-book, as before, is a file of antique newspapers. The volume, which serves us for a writing-desk, is a folio of larger dimensions than the one before described; and the papers are generally printed on a whole sheet, sometimes with a supplemental leaf of news and advertisements. They have a venerable appearance, being overspread with the duskiness of more than seventy years; and discolored, here and there, with the deeper stains of some liquid, as if the contents of a wine-glass had long since been splashed upon the page. Still, the old book conveys an impression, that, when the separate numbers were flying about town, in the first day or two of their respective existences, they might have been fit reading for very stylish people. Such newspapers could have been issued nowhere but in a metropolis, the centre, not only of public and private affairs, but of fashion and gaiety. Without any discredit to the colonial press, these might have been, and probably were, spread out on the tables of the British coffee-house, in King-street, for the perusal of the throng of officers who then drank their wine at that celebrated establishment. To interest these military gentlemen, there were bulletins of the war between Prussia and Austria; between England and France, on the old battle-plains of Flanders; and between the same antagonists, in the newer fields of the East-Indies—and in our own trackless woods, where white men never trod until they came to fight there. Or, the travelled American, the petit-maitre of the colonies—the ape of London foppery, as the newspaper was the semblance of the London journals—he, with his gray-powdered periwig, his embroidered coat, lace ruffles, and glossy silk stockings, golden-clocked—his buckles, of glittering paste, at knee-band and shoe-strap—his scented handkerchief, and chapeau beneath his arm—even such a dainty figure need not have disdained to glance at these old yellow pages, while they were the mirror of passing times. For his amusement, there were essays of wit and humor, the light literature of the day, which, for breadth and license, might have proceeded from the pen of Fielding or Smollett; while, in other columns, he would delight his imagination

with the enumerated items of all sorts of finery, and with the
rival advertisements of half a dozen peruke-makers. In short,
newer manners and customs had almost entirely superseded
those of the Puritans, even in their own city of refuge.

It was natural that, with the lapse of time and increase
of wealth and population, the peculiarities of the early settlers
should have waxed fainter and fainter through the generations of their descendants, who also had been alloyed by a
continual accession of emigrants from many countries and of
all characters. It tended to assimilate the colonial manners to
those of the mother-country, that the commercial intercourse
was great, and that the merchants often went thither in their
own ships. Indeed, almost every man of adequate fortune felt
a yearning desire, and even judged it a filial duty, at least
once in his life, to visit the home of his ancestors. They still
called it their own home, as if New-England were to them,
what many of the old Puritans had considered it, not a
permanent abiding-place, but merely a lodge in the wilderness, until the trouble of the times should be passed. The
example of the royal governors must have had much influence
on the manners of the colonists; for these rulers assumed a
degree of state and splendor, which had never been practised
by their predecessors, who differed in nothing from republican chief-magistrates, under the old charter. The officers of
the crown, the public characters in the interest of the administration, and the gentlemen of wealth and good descent,
generally noted for their loyalty, would constitute a dignified
circle, with the governor in the centre, bearing a very passable
resemblance to a court. Their ideas, their habits, their code
of courtesy, and their dress, would have all the fresh glitter
of fashions immediately derived from the fountain-head, in
England. To prevent their modes of life from becoming the
standard, with all who had the ability to imitate them, there
was no longer an undue severity of religion, nor as yet any

disaffection to British supremacy, nor democratic prejudices against pomp. Thus, while the colonies were attaining that strength which was soon to render them an independent republic, it might have been supposed that the wealthier classes were growing into an aristocracy, and ripening for hereditary rank, while the poor were to be stationary in their abasement, and the country, perhaps, to be a sister-monarchy with England. Such, doubtless, were the plausible conjectures, deduced from the superficial phenomena of our connexion with a monarchical government, until the prospective nobility were leveled with the mob, by the mere gathering of winds that preceded the storm of the Revolution. The portents of that storm were not yet visible in the air. A true picture of society, therefore, would have the rich effect, produced by distinctions of rank that seemed permanent, and by appropriate habits of splendor on the part of the gentry.

The people at large had been somewhat changed in character, since the period of our last sketch, by their great exploit, the conquest of Louisburg. After that event, the New-Englanders never settled into precisely the same quiet race, which all the world had imagined them to be. They had done a deed of history, and were anxious to add new ones to the record. They had proved themselves powerful enough to influence the result of a war, and were thenceforth called upon, and willingly consented, to join their strength against the enemies of England; on those fields, at least, where victory would redound to their peculiar advantage. And now, in the heat of the Old French War, they might well be termed a martial people. Every man was a soldier, or the father or brother of a soldier; and the whole land literally echoed with the roll of the drum, either beating up for recruits among the towns and villages, or striking the march towards the frontiers. Besides the provincial troops, there were twenty-three British regiments in the northern colonies. The country has never known a period of such excitement and warlike life, except during the Revolution—perhaps scarcely then; for that was a lingering war, and this a stirring and eventful one.

One would think, that no very wonderful talent was requisite for an historical novel, when the rough and hurried paragraphs of these newspapers can recall the past so magically. We seem to be waiting in the street for the arrival of the post-rider—who is seldom more than twelve hours beyond his time—with letters, by way of Albany, from the various departments of the army. Or, we may fancy ourselves in the circle of listeners, all with necks stretched out towards an old gentleman in the centre, who deliberately puts on his spectacles, unfolds the wet newspaper, and gives us the details of the broken and contradictory reports, which have been flying from mouth to mouth, ever since the courier alighted at Secretary Oliver's office. Sometimes we have an account of the Indian skirmishes near Lake George, and how a ranging party of provincials were so closely pursued, that they threw away their arms, and eke their shoes, stockings, and breeches, barely reaching the camp in their shirts, which also were terribly tattered by the bushes. Then, there is a journal of the siege of Fort Niagara, so minute, that it almost numbers the cannon-shot and bombs, and describes the effect of the latter missiles on the French commandant's stone-mansion, within the fortress. In the letters of the provincial officers, it is amusing to observe how some of them endeavor to catch the careless and jovial turn of old campaigners. One gentleman tells us, that he holds a brimming glass in his hand, intending to drink the health of his correspondent, unless a cannon ball should dash the liquor from his lips; in the midst of his letter, he hears the bells of the French churches ringing, in Quebec, and recollects that it is Sunday; whereupon, like a good Protestant, he resolves to disturb the

Catholic worship by a few thirty-two pound shot. While this wicked man of war was thus making a jest of religion, his pious mother had probably put up a note, that very Sabbath-day, desiring the 'prayers of the congregation for a son gone a soldiering.' We trust, however, that there were some stout old worthies, who were not ashamed to do as their fathers did, but went to prayer, with their soldiers, before leading them to battle; and doubtless fought none the worse for that. If we had enlisted in the Old French War, it should have been under such a captain; for we love to see a man keep the characteristics of his country.*

These letters, and other intelligence from the army, are pleasant and lively reading, and stir up the mind like the music of a drum and fife. It is less agreeable, to meet with accounts of women slain and scalped, and infants dashed against trees, by the Indians on the frontiers. It is a striking circumstance, that innumerable bears, driven from the woods, by the uproar of contending armies in their accustomed haunts, broke into the settlements and committed great ravages, among children as well as sheep and swine. Some of them prowled where bears had never been for a century— penetrating within a mile or two of Boston; a fact, that gives a strong and gloomy impression of something very terrific going on in the forest, since these savage beasts fled town-ward to avoid it. But it is impossible to moralize about such trifles, when every newspaper contains tales of military enterprize, and often a huzza for victory; as, for instance, the taking of Ticonderoga, long a place of awe to the provincials, and one of the bloodiest spots in the present war. Nor is it

* The contemptuous jealousy of the British army, from the general downwards, was very galling to the provincial troops. In one of the news-papers, there is an admirable letter of a New-Englandman, copied from the London Chronicle, defending the provincials with an ability worthy of Franklin, and somewhat in his style. The letter is remarkable, also, because it takes up the cause of the whole range of colonies, as if the writer looked upon them all as constituting one country, and that his own. Colonial patriotism had not hitherto been so broad a sentiment.

unpleasant, among whole pages of exultation, to find a note of sorrow for the fall of some brave officer; it comes wailing in, like a funeral strain amidst a peal of triumph, itself triumphant too. Such was the lamentation over Wolfe. Somewhere, in this volume of newspapers, though we cannot now lay our finger upon the passage, we recollect a report, that General Wolfe was slain, not by the enemy, but by a shot from his own soldiers.

In the advertising columns, also, we are continually reminded that the country was in a state of war. Governor Pownall makes proclamation for the enlisting of soldiers, and directs the militia colonels to attend to the discipline of their regiments, and the selectmen of every town to replenish their stocks of ammunition. The magazine, by the way, was generally kept in the upper loft of the village meeting-house. The provincial captains are drumming up for soldiers, in every newspaper. Sir Jeffrey Amherst advertises for batteaux-men, to be employed on the lakes; and gives notice to the officers of seven British regiments, dispersed on the recruiting service, to rendezvous in Boston. Captain Hallowell, of the province ship-of-war King George, invites able-bodied seamen to serve his Majesty, for fifteen pounds, old tenor, per month. By the rewards offered, there would appear to have been frequent desertions from the New-England forces; we applaud their wisdom, if not their valor or integrity. Cannon, of all calibres, gunpowder and balls, firelocks, pistols, swords, and hangers, were common articles of merchandise. Daniel Jones, at the sign of the hat and helmet, offers to supply officers with scarlet broadcloth, gold-lace for hats and waist-coats, cockades, and other military foppery, allowing credit until the pay-rolls shall be made up. This advertisement gives us quite a gorgeous idea of a provincial captain in full dress.

At the commencement of the campaign of 1759, the British general informs the farmers of New-England that a regular market will be established at Lake George, whither they are

invited to bring provisions and refreshments of all sorts, for
the use of the army. Hence, we may form a singular picture
of petty traffic, far away from any permanent settlements,
among the hills which border that romantic lake, with the
solemn woods overshadowing the scene. Carcasses of bullocks
and fat porkers are placed upright against the huge trunks of
the trees; fowls hang from the lower branches, bobbing
against the heads of those beneath; butter-firkins, great
cheeses, and brown loaves of household bread, baked in
distant ovens, are collected under temporary shelters of pine-
boughs, with gingerbread, and pumpkin-pies, perhaps, and
other toothsome dainties. Barrels of cider and spruce-beer
are running freely into the wooden canteens of the soldiers.
Imagine such a scene, beneath the dark forest canopy, with
here and there a few struggling sunbeams, to dissipate the
gloom. See the shrewd yeomen, haggling with their scarlet-
coated customers, abating somewhat in their prices, but still
dealing at monstrous profit; and then complete the picture
with circumstances that bespeak war and danger. A cannon
shall be seen to belch its smoke from among the trees, against
some distant canoes on the lake; the traffickers shall pause,
and seem to hearken, at intervals, as if they heard the rattle
of musketry or the shout of Indians; a scouting-party shall be
driven in, with two or three faint and bloody men among
them. And, in spite of these disturbances, business goes on
briskly in the market of the wilderness.

It must not be supposed, that the martial character of the
times interrupted all pursuits except those connected with
war. On the contrary, there appears to have been a general
vigor and vivacity diffused into the whole round of colonial
life. During the winter of 1759, it was computed that about
a thousand sled-loads of country produce were daily brought
into Boston market. It was a symptom of an irregular and
unquiet course of affairs, that innumerable lotteries were

projected, ostensibly for the purpose of public improvements, such as roads and bridges. Many females seized the opportunity to engage in business; as, among others, Alice Quick, who dealt in crockery and hosiery, next door to Deacon Beautineau's; Mary Jackson, who sold butter, at the Brazen-Head, in Cornhill; Abigail Hiller, who taught ornamental-work, near the Orange-Tree, where also were to be seen the King and Queen, in wax-work; Sarah Morehead, an instructer in glass-painting, drawing, and japanning; Mary Salmon, who shod horses, at the south-end; Harriet Pain, at the Buck and Glove, and Mrs. Henrietta Maria Caine, at the Golden Fan, both fashionable milliners; Anna Adams, who advertises Quebec and Garrick bonnets, Prussian cloaks, and scarlet cardinals, opposite the old brick meeting-house; besides a lady at the head of a wine and spirit establishment. Little did these good dames expect to re-appear before the public, so long after they had made their last courtesies behind the counter. Our great-grandmothers were a stirring sisterhood, and seem not to have been utterly despised by the gentlemen at the British coffee-house; at least, some gracious bachelor, there resident, gives public notice of his willingness to take a wife, provided she be not above twenty-three, and possess brown hair, regular features, a brisk eye, and a fortune. Now, this was great condescension towards the ladies of Massachusetts-Bay, in a threadbare lieutenant of foot.

Polite literature was beginning to make its appearance. Few native works were advertised, it is true, except sermons and treatises of controversial divinity; nor were the English authors of the day much known, on this side of the Atlantic. But, catalogues were frequently offered at auction or private sale, comprising the standard English books, history, essays, and poetry, of Queen Anne's age, and the preceding century. We see nothing in the nature of a novel, unless it be 'The

Two Mothers, price four coppers.' There was an American poet, however, of whom Mr. Kettell has preseved no specimen—the author of 'War, an Heroic Poem;' he publishes by subscription, and threatens to prosecute his patrons for not taking their books. We have discovered a periodical, also, and one that has a peculiar claim to be recorded here, since it bore the title of 'THE NEW-ENGLAND MAGAZINE,' a forgotten predecessor, for which we should have a filial respect, and take its excellence on trust. The fine arts, too, were budding into existence. At the 'old glass and picture shop,' in Cornhill, various maps, plates, and views, are advertised, and among them a 'Prospect of Boston,' a copper-plate engraving of Quebec, and the effigies of all the New-England ministers ever done in mezzotinto. All these must have been very saleable articles. Other ornamental wares were to be found at the same shop; such as violins, flutes, hautboys, musical books, English and Dutch toys, and London babies. About this period, Mr. Dipper gives notice of a concert of vocal and instrumental music. There had already been an attempt at theatrical exhibitions.

There are tokens, in every newspaper, of a style of luxury and magnificence, which we do not usually associate with our ideas of the times. When the property of a deceased person was to be sold, we find, among the household furniture, silk beds and hangings, damask table-cloths, Turkey carpets, pictures, pier-glasses, massive plate, and all things proper for a noble mansion. Wine was more generally drunk than now, though by no means to the neglect of ardent spirits. For the apparel of both sexes, the mercers and milliners imported good store of fine broadcloths—especially scarlet, crimson, and sky-blue, silks, satins, lawns, and velvets, gold brocade, and gold and silver lace, and silver tassels, and silver spangles, until Cornhill shone and sparkled with their merchandise. The gaudiest dress, permissible by modern taste, fades into a Quaker-like sobriety, compared with the deep, rich, glowing splendor of our ancestors. Such figures were almost too fine to go about town on foot; accordingly, carriages were so numerous as to require a tax; and it is recorded that, when Governor Bernard came to the province, he was met, between Dedham and Boston, by a multitude of gentlemen in their coaches and chariots.

Take my arm, gentle reader, and come with me into some street, perhaps trodden by your daily footsteps, but which now has such an aspect of half-familiar strangeness, that you suspect yourself to be walking abroad in a dream. True; there are some brick edifices which you remember from childhood, and which your father and grandfather remembered as well; but you are perplexed by the absence of many that were here, only an hour or two since; and still more amazing is the presence of whole rows of wooden and plastered houses, projecting over the sidewalks, and bearing iron figures on their fronts, which prove them to have stood on the same sites above a century. Where have your eyes been, that you never saw them before? Along the ghostly street—for at length, you conclude that all is unsubstantial, though it be so good a mockery of an antique town—along the ghostly street, there are ghostly people too. Every gentleman has his three-cornered hat, either on his head or under his arm, and all wear wigs, in infinite variety,—the Tie, the Brigadier, the Spencer, the Albemarle, the Major, the Ramillies, the grave Full-bottom, or the giddy Feather-top. Look at the elaborate lace-ruffles, and the square-skirted coats of gorgeous hues, bedizzened with silver and gold! Make way for the phantom-ladies, whose hoops require such breadth of passage, as they pace majestically along, in silken gowns, blue, green, or yellow, brilliantly embroidered, and with small satin hats surmounting their powdered hair. Make way; for the whole spectral show will vanish, if your earthly garments brush against their robes. Now that the scene is brightest, and the whole street glitters with imaginary sunshine—now hark to the bells of the Old South and the Old North, ringing out with a sudden and merry peal, while the cannon of Castle William thunder below the town, and those of the Diana frigate repeat the sound, and the Charlestown batteries reply with a nearer roar! You see the crowd toss up their hats, in visionary joy. You hear of illuminations and fire-works, and of bonfires, built on scaffolds, raised several stories above the ground, that are to blaze all night, in King-street, and on Beacon-hill. And here come the trumpets and kettle-drums, and the tramping hoofs of the Boston troop of horse-guards, escorting the governor to King's Chapel, where he is to return solemn thanks for the surrender of Quebec. March on, thou shadowy troop! and vanish, ghostly crowd! and change again, old street! for those stirring times are gone.

Opportunely for the conclusion of our sketch, a fire broke out, on the twentieth of March, 1760, at the Brazen-Head in Cornhill, and consumed nearly four hundred buildings. Similar disasters have always been epochs in the chronology of Boston. That of 1711, had hitherto been termed the Great Fire, but now resigned its baleful dignity to one which has ever since retained it. Did we desire to move the reader's sympathies, on this subject, we would not be grandiloquent about the sea of billowy flame, the glowing and crumbling streets, the broad, black firmament of smoke, and the blast of wind, that sprang up with the conflagration and roared behind it. It would be more effective, to mark out a single family, at the moment when the flames caught upon an angle of their dwelling; then would ensue the removal of the bed-ridden grandmother, the cradle with the sleeping infant, and, most dismal of all, the dying man, just at the extremity of a lingering disease. Do but imagine the confused agony of one thus awfully disturbed in his last hour; his fearful glance behind at the consuming fire, raging after him, from house to house, as its devoted victim; and finally, the almost eagerness with which he would seize some calmer interval to die! The Great Fire must have realized many such a scene.

Doubtless, posterity has acquired a better city by the calamity of that generation. None will be inclined to lament it, at this late day, except the lover of antiquity, who would have been glad to walk among those streets of venerable houses, fancying the old inhabitants still there, that he might commune with their shadows, and paint a more vivid picture of their times.

III THE OLD TORY

Again we take a leap, of about twenty years, and alight in the midst of the Revolution. Indeed, having just closed a volume of colonial newspapers, which represented the period when monarchical and aristocratic sentiments were at the highest; and now opening another volume, printed in the same metropolis, after such sentiments had long been deemed a sin and shame, we feel as if the leap were more than figurative. Our late course of reading has tinctured us, for the moment, with antique prejudices, and we shrink from the strangely-contrasted times, into which we emerge, like one of those immutable old Tories, who acknowledge no oppression in the Stamp-act. It may be the most effective method of going through the present file of papers, to follow out this idea, and transform ourself, perchance, from a modern Tory into such a sturdy King-man, as once wore that pliable nickname.

Well then, here we sit, an old, gray, withered, sour-visaged, threadbare sort of gentleman, erect enough, here in our solitude, but marked out by a depressed and distrustful mien abroad—as one conscious of a stigma upon his forehead, though for no crime. We were already in the decline of life, when the first tremors of the earthquake, that has convulsed the continent, were felt. Our mind had grown too rigid to change any of its opinions, when the voice of the people demanded, that all should be changed. We are an Episcopalian, and sat under the high-church doctrines of Doctor Caner; we have been a captain of the provincial forces, and love our King the better, for the blood that we shed in his cause, on the Plains of Abraham. Among all the refugees, there is not one more loyal, to the back-bone, than we. Still we lingered behind, when the British army evacuated Boston, sweeping in its train most of those with whom we held communion—the old, loyal gentlemen, the aristocracy of the colonies, the hereditary Englishman, imbued with more than native zeal and admiration for the glorious island and its monarch, because the far intervening ocean threw a dim reverence around them. When our brethren departed, we could not tear our aged roots out of the soil. We have remained, therefore, enduring to be outwardly a freeman, but idolizing King George, in secresy and silence—one true old heart, amongst a host of enemies. We watch, with a weary hope, for the moment when all this turmoil shall subside, and the impious novelty, that has distracted our latter years, like a wild dream, give place to the blessed quietude of royal sway, with the King's name in every ordinance, his prayer in the church, his health at the board, and his love in the people's heart. Meantime, our old age finds little honor. Hustled have we been, till driven from town-meetings; dirty water has been cast upon our ruffles, by a Whig chambermaid; John Hancock's coachman seizes every opportunity to be-spatter us with mud; daily are we hooted by the unbreeched rebel brats; and narrowly, once, did our gray hairs escape the ignominy of tar and feathers. Alas! only that we cannot bear to die till the next royal Governor comes over, we would fain be in our quiet grave.

Such an old man among new things are we, who now hold, at arm's length, the rebel newspaper of the day. The very figure-head, for the thousandth time, elicits a groan of spiteful lamentation. Where are the united heart and crown, the loyal emblem, that used to hallow the sheet, on which it was impressed, in our younger days? In its stead, we find a continental officer, with the Declaration of Independence in one hand, a drawn sword in the other, and, above his head, a scroll, bearing the motto 'WE APPEAL TO HEAVEN.' Then say we, with a prospective triumph, let Heaven judge, in its own good time! The material of the sheet attracts our scorn. It is a fair specimen of rebel manufacture, thick and coarse, like wrapping-paper, all overspread with little knobs, and of such a deep, dingy blue color, that we wipe our spectacles thrice before we can distinguish a letter of the wretched print. Thus, in all points, the newspaper is a type of the times, far more fit for the rough hands of a democratic mob, than for our own delicate, though bony fingers. Nay; we will not handle it without our gloves!

Glancing down the page, our eyes are greeted everywhere by the offer of lands at auction, for sale or to be leased— not by the rightful owners, but a rebel committee; notices of the town constable, that he is authorized to receive the taxes on such an estate, in default of which, that also is to be knocked down to the highest bidder; and notifications of complaints, filed by the Attorney-general, against certain traitorous absentees, and of confiscations that are to ensue. And who are these traitors? Our own best friends—names as old, once as honored, as any in the land, where they are no longer to have a patrimony, nor to be remembered as good men, who have passed away. We are ashamed of not relinquishing our little property, too; but comfort ourselves, because we still keep our principles, without gratifying the rebels with our plunder. Plunder, indeed, they are seizing, everywhere, by the strong hand at sea, as well as by legal forms on shore. Here are prize-vessels for sale—no French nor Spanish merchantmen, whose wealth is the birthright of British subjects, but hulls of British oak, from Liverpool, Bristol, and the Thames, laden with the King's own stores, for his army in New-York. And what a fleet of privateers—pirates, say we—are fitting out for new ravages, with rebellion in their very names! The Free Yankee, the General Green, the Saratoga, the Lafayette, and the Grand Monarch! Yes, the Grand Monarch; so is a French King styled, by the sons of Englishmen. And here we have an ordinance, from the Court of Versailles, with the Bourbon's own signature affixed, as if New-England were already a French province. Everything is French. French soldiers, French sailors, French surgeons—and French diseases, too, I trow—besides, French dancing-masters and French milliners, to debauch our daughters with French fashions! Everything in America is French, except the Canadas—the loyal Canadas—which we helped to wrest from France. And to that old French province, the Englishman of the colonies must go to find his country!

Oh, the misery of seeing the whole system of things changed in my old days, when I would be loth to change even a pair of buckles! The British coffee-house—where oft we sat, brimfull of wine and loyalty, with the gallant gentlemen of Amherst's army, when we wore a red-coat, too—the British coffee-house, forsooth, must now be styled the American, with a golden eagle, instead of the royal arms, above the door. Even the street it stands in, is no longer King-street! Nothing is the King's, except this heavy heart, in my old bosom. Wherever I glance my eyes, they meet something that pricks them like a needle. This soapmaker, for instance, this Robert Hewes, has conspired against my peace, by notifying that his shop is situated near Liberty Stump. But when will their mis-named liberty have its true emblem in that Stump, hewn down by British steel!

Where shall we buy our next year's Almanac? Not this of Weatherwise's, certainly; for it contains a likeness of George Washington, the upright rebel, whom we most hate, though reverentially, as a fallen angel, with his heavenly brightness undiminished, evincing pure fame in an unhallowed cause. And here is a new book, for my evening's recreation—a History of the War till the close of the year 1779, with the heads of thirteen distinguished officers engraved on copper-plate. A plague upon their heads! We desire not to see them, till they grin at us from the balcony before the townhouse, fixed on spikes, as the heads of traitors. How bloody-minded the villains make a peaceable old man! What next? An Oration, on the Horrid Massacre of 1770. When that blood was shed—the first that the British soldier ever drew from the bosoms of our countrymen—we turned sick at heart, and do so still, as often as they make it reek anew from among the stones in King-street. The pool, that we saw that night, has swelled into a lake—English blood and American—no!—all British, all blood of my brethren. And here come down tears. Shame on me, since half of them are shed for rebels! Who are not rebels now? Even the women are thrusting their white hands into the war, and come out in this very paper with proposals to form a society—the lady of George Washington at their head—for clothing the continental troops. They will strip off their stiff petticoats to cover the ragged rascals, and then enlist in the ranks themselves.

What have we here? Burgoyne's proclamation turned into Hudibrastic rhyme! And here, some verses against the King, in which the scribbler leaves a blank for the name of George, as if his doggerel might yet exalt him to the pillory. Such, after years of rebellion, is the heart's unconquerable reverence for the Lord's anointed! In the next column, we have Scripture parodied in a squib against his sacred Majesty. What would our Puritan great-grand-sires have said to that? They never laughed at God's word, though they cut off a King's head.

Yes; it was for us to prove how disloyalty goes hand in hand with irreligion, and all other vices come trooping in the train. Now-a-days, men commit robbery and sacrilege, for the mere luxury of wickedness, as this advertisement testifies. Three hundred pounds reward, for the detection of the villains who stole and destroyed the cushions and pulpit drapery of the Brattle-street and Old South churches. Was it a crime? I can scarcely think our temples hallowed, since the King ceased to be prayed for. But it is not temples only, that they rob. Here a man offers a thousand dollars—a thousand dollars, in Continental rags!—for the recovery of his stolen cloak, and other articles of clothing. Horse thieves are innumerable. Now is the day, when every beggar gets on horse-back. And is not the whole land like a beggar on horse-back, riding post to the devil? Ha! Here is a murder, too. A woman slain at midnight, by an unknown ruffian, and found cold, stiff, and bloody, in her violated bed! Let the hue-and-cry follow hard after the man in the uniform of blue and buff, who last went by that way. My life on it, he is the blood-stained ravisher! These deserters, whom we see proclaimed in every column— proof, that the banditti are as false to their stars and stripes, as to the Holy Red-Cross—they bring the crimes of a rebel camp into a soil well suited to them; the bosom of a people, without the heart that kept them virtuous—their King!

Here, flaunting down a whole column, with official seal and signature, here comes a proclamation. By whose authority? Ah! the United States—those thirteen little anarchies, assembled in that one grand anarchy, their Congress. And

what the import? A general Fast. By Heaven! for once, the
traitorous blockheads have legislated wisely! Yea; let a misguided people kneel down in sackcloth and ashes, from end
to end, from border to border, of their wasted country. Well
may they fast, where there is no food—and cry aloud, for
whatever remnant of God's mercy their sins may not have
exhausted. We, too, will fast, even at a rebel summons. Pray
others as they will, there shall be, at least, an old man
kneeling for the righteous cause. Lord, put down the rebels!
God save the King!

Peace to the good old Tory! One of our objects has been
to exemplify, without softening a single prejudice proper to
the character which we assumed, that the Americans, who
clung to the losing side, in the Revolution, were men greatly
to be pitied, and often worthy of our sympathy. It would be
difficult to say whose lot was most lamentable—that of the
active Tories, who gave up their patrimonies, for a pittance
from the British pension-roll and their native land, for a cold
reception in their mis-called home; or the passive ones, who
remained behind to endure the coldness of former friends,
and the public opprobrium, as despised citizens, under a government which they abhorred. In justice to the old gentleman, who has favored us with his discontented musings, we
must remark, that the state of the country, so far as can be
gathered from these papers, was of dismal augury, for the
tendencies of democratic rule. It was pardonable, in the con-
servative of that day, to mistake the temporary evils of a
change, for permanent diseases of the system which that
change was to establish. A revolution, or anything, that interrupts social order, may afford opportunities for the individual display of eminent virtue; but, its effects are pernicious
to general morality. Most people are so constituted, that they
can be virtuous only in a certain routine; and an irregular
course of public affairs demoralizes them. One great source

of disorder, was the multitude of disbanded troops, who were continually returning home, after terms of service just long enough to give them a distaste to peaceable occupations; neither citizens nor soldiers, they were very liable to become ruffians. Almost all our impressions, in regard to this period are unpleasant, whether referring to the state of civil society, or to the character of the contest, which, especially where native Americans were opposed to each other, was waged with the deadly hatred of fraternal enemies. It is the beauty of war, for men to commit mutual havoc with undisturbed good humor.

The present volume of newspapers contains fewer characteristic traits than any which we have looked over. Except for the peculiarities attendant on the passing struggle, manners seem to have taken a modern cast. Whatever antique fashions lingered into the war of the Revolution, or beyond it, they were not so strongly marked as to leave their traces in the public journals. Moreover, the old newspapers had an indescribable picturesqueness, not to be found in the later ones. Whether it be something in the literary execution, or the ancient print and paper, and the idea, that those same musty pages have been handled by people—once alive and bustling amid the scenes there recorded, yet now in their graves beyond the memory of man—so it is, that in those elder volumes, we seem to find the life of a past age preserved between the leaves, like a dry specimen of foliage. It is so difficult to discover what touches are really picturesque, that we doubt whether our attempts have produced any similar effect.

THE MAN OF ADAMANT

AN APOLOGUE

I N THE OLD TIMES of religious gloom and intoler-
ance, lived Richard Digby, the gloomiest and most intolerant of a stern brotherhood. His plan of salvation
was so narrow, that, like a plank in a tempestuous sea, it
could avail no sinner but himself, who bestrode it triumphantly, and hurled anathemas against the wretches whom he
saw struggling with the billows of eternal death. In his view
of the matter, it was a most abominable crime—as, indeed,
it is a great folly—for men to trust to their own strength, or
even to grapple to any other fragment of the wreck, save
this narrow plank, which, moreover, he took special care to
keep out of their reach. In other words, as his creed was like
no man's else, and being well pleased that Providence had
entrusted him, alone of mortals, with the treasure of a true
faith, Richard Digby determined to seclude himself to the
sole and constant enjoyment of his happy fortune.

'And verily,' thought he, 'I deem it a chief condition of
Heaven's mercy to myself, that I hold no communion with
those abominable myriads which it hath cast off to perish.
Peradventure, were I to tarry longer in the tents of Kedar,
the gracious boon would be revoked, and I also be swallowed
up in the deluge of wrath, or consumed in the storm of fire

and brimstone, or involved in whatever new kind of ruin is ordained for the horrible perversity of this generation.'

So Richard Digby took an axe, to hew space enough for a tabernacle in the wilderness, and some few other necessaries, especially a sword and gun, to smite and slay any intruder upon his hallowed seclusion; and plunged into the dreariest depths of the forest. On its verge, however, he paused a moment, to shake off the dust of his feet against the village where he had dwelt, and to invoke a curse on the meeting-house, which he regarded as a temple of heathen idolatry. He felt a curiosity, also, to see whether the fire and brimstone would not rush down from Heaven at once, now that the one righteous man had provided for his own safety. But, as the sunshine continued to fall peacefully on the cottages and fields, and the husbandmen labored and children played, and as there were many tokens of present happiness, and nothing ominous of a speedy judgment, he turned away, somewhat disappointed. The further he went, however, and the lonelier he felt himself, and the thicker the trees stood along his path, and the darker the shadow overhead, so much the more did Richard Digby exult. He talked to himself, as he strode onward; he read his Bible to himself, as he sat beneath the trees; and, as the gloom of the forest hid the blessed sky, I had almost added, that, at morning, noon, and eventide, he prayed to himself. So congenial was this mode of life to his disposition, that he often laughed to himself, but was displeased when an echo tossed him back the long, loud roar.

In this manner, he journeyed onward three days and two nights, and came, on the third evening, to the mouth of a cave, which, at first sight, reminded him of Elijah's cave at Horeb, though perhaps it more resembled Abraham's sepulchral cave, at Machpelah. It entered into the heart of a rocky hill. There was so dense a veil of tangled foliage about it, that none but a sworn lover of gloomy recesses would have

discovered the low arch of its entrance, or have dared to step
within its vaulted chamber, where the burning eyes of a
panther might encounter him. If Nature meant this remote
and dismal cavern for the use of man, it could only be, to
bury in its gloom the victims of a pestilence, and then to
block up its mouth with stones, and avoid the spot forever
after. There was nothing bright nor cheerful near it, except
a bubbling fountain, some twenty paces off, at which Richard
Digby hardly threw away a glance. But he thrust his head
into the cave, shivered, and congratulated himself.

'The finger of Providence hath pointed my way!' cried
he, aloud, while the tomb-like den returned a strange echo, as
if some one within were mocking him. 'Here my soul will
be at peace; for the wicked will not find me. Here I can
read the Scriptures, and be no more provoked with lying in-
terpretations. Here I can offer up acceptable prayers, because
my voice will not be mingled with the sinful supplications of
the multitude. Of a truth, the only way to Heaven leadeth
through the narrow entrance of this cave—and I alone have
found it!'

In regard to this cave, it was observable that the roof, so
far as the imperfect light permitted it to be seen, was hung
with substances resembling opaque icicles; for the damps of
unknown centuries, dripping down continually, had become
as hard as adamant; and wherever that moisture fell, it
seemed to possess the power of converting what it bathed to
stone. The fallen leaves and sprigs of foliage, which the wind
had swept into the cave, and the little feathery shrubs, rooted
near the threshold, were not wet with a natural dew, but had
been embalmed by this wondrous process. And here I am put
in mind, that Richard Digby, before he withdrew himself
from the world, was supposed by skilful physicians to have
contracted a disease, for which no remedy was written in their
medical books. It was a deposition of calculous particles within

his heart, caused by an obstructed circulation of the blood, and unless a miracle should be wrought for him, there was danger that the malady might act on the entire substance of the organ, and change his fleshly heart to stone. Many, indeed, affirmed that the process was already near its consummation. Richard Digby, however, could never be convinced that any such direful work was going on within him; nor when he saw the sprigs of marble foliage, did his heart even throb the quicker, at the similitude suggested by these once tender herbs. It may be, that this same insensibility was a symptom of the disease.

Be that as it might, Richard Digby was well contented with his sepulchral cave. So dearly did he love this congenial spot, that, instead of going a few paces to the bubbling spring for water, he allayed his thirst with now and then a drop of moisture from the roof, which, had it fallen any where but on his tongue, would have been congealed into a pebble. For a man predisposed to stoniness of the heart, this surely was unwholesome liquor. But there he dwelt, for three days more, eating herbs and roots, drinking his own destruction, sleeping, as it were, in a tomb, and awaking to the solitude of death, yet esteeming this horrible mode of life as hardly inferior to celestial bliss. Perhaps superior; for, above the sky, there would be angels to disturb him. At the close of the third day, he sat in the portal of his mansion, reading the Bible aloud, because no other ear could profit by it, and reading it amiss, because the rays of the setting sun did not penetrate the dismal depth of shadow roundabout him, nor fall upon the sacred page. Suddenly, however, a faint gleam of light was thrown over the volume, and raising his eyes, Richard Digby saw that a young woman stood before the mouth of the cave, and that the sunbeams bathed her white garment, which thus seemed to possess a radiance of its own.

'Good evening, Richard,' said the girl, 'I have come from afar to find thee.'

The slender grace and gentle loveliness of this young woman were at once recognized by Richard Digby. Her name was Mary Goffe. She had been a convert to his preaching of the word in England, before he yielded himself to that exclusive bigotry, which now enfolded him with such an iron grasp, that no other sentiment could reach his bosom. When he came a pilgrim to America, she had remained in her father's hall, but now, as it appeared, had crossed the ocean after him, impelled by the same faith that led other exiles hither, and perhaps by love almost as holy. What else but faith and love united could have sustained so delicate a creature, wandering thus far into the forest, with her golden hair dishevelled by the boughs, and her feet wounded by the thorns! Yet, weary and faint though she must have been, and affrighted at the dreariness of the cave, she looked on the lonely man with a mild and pitying expression, such as might beam from an angel's eyes, towards an afflicted mortal. But the recluse, frowning sternly upon her, and keeping his finger between the leaves of his half closed Bible, motioned her away with his hand.

'Off!' cried he. 'I am sanctified, and thou art sinful. Away!'

'Oh, Richard,' said she, earnestly, 'I have come this weary way, because I heard that a grievous distemper had seized upon thy heart; and a great Physician hath given me the skill to cure it. There is no other remedy than this which I have brought thee. Turn me not away, therefore, nor refuse my medicine; for then must this dismal cave be thy sepulchre.'

'Away!' replied Richard Digby, still with a dark frown. 'My heart is in better condition than thine own. Leave me, earthly one; for the sun is almost set; and when no light reaches the door of the cave, then is my prayer time!'

Now, great as was her need, Mary Goffe did not plead with this stony hearted man for shelter and protection, nor ask any thing whatever for her own sake. All her zeal was for his welfare.

'Come back with me!' she exclaimed, clasping her hands—'Come back to thy fellow men; for they need thee, Richard; and thou hast tenfold need of them. Stay not in this evil den; for the air is chill, and the damps are fatal; nor will any, that perish within it, ever find the path to Heaven. Hasten hence, I entreat thee, for thine own soul's sake; for either the roof will fall upon thy head, or some other speedy destruction is at hand.'

'Perverse woman!' answered Richard Digby, laughing aloud; for he was moved to bitter mirth by her foolish vehemence. 'I tell thee that the path to Heaven leadeth straight through this narrow portal, where I sit. And, moreover, the destruction thou speakest of, is ordained, not for this blessed cave, but for all other habitations of mankind, throughout the earth. Get thee hence speedily, that thou may'st have thy share!'

So saying, he opened his Bible again, and fixed his eyes intently on the page, being resolved to withdraw his thoughts from this child of sin and wrath, and to waste no more of his holy breath upon her. The shadow had now grown so deep, where he was sitting, that he made continual mistakes in what he read, converting all that was gracious and merciful, to denunciations of vengeance and unutterable woe, on every created being but himself. Mary Goffe, meanwhile, was leaning against a tree, beside the sepulchral cave, very sad, yet with something heavenly and ethereal in her unselfish sorrow. The light from the setting sun still glorified her form, and was reflected a little way within the darksome den, discovering so terrible a gloom, that the maiden shuddered for its self-doomed inhabitant. Espying the bright fountain near at hand, she hastened thither, and scooped up a portion of its water, in a cup of birchen bark. A few tears mingled with the draught, and perhaps gave it all its efficacy. She then returned to the mouth of the cave, and knelt down at Richard Digby's feet.

'Richard,' she said, with passionate fervor, yet a gentleness in all her passion, 'I pray thee, by thy hope of Heaven, and as thou wouldst not dwell in this tomb forever, drink of this hallowed water, be it but a single drop! Then, make room for me by thy side, and let us read together one page of that blessed volume—and, lastly, kneel down with me and pray! Do this; and thy stony heart shall become softer than a babe's, and all be well.'

But Richard Digby, in utter abhorrence of the proposal, cast the Bible at his feet, and eyed her with such a fixed and evil frown, that he looked less like a living man than a marble statue, wrought by some dark imagined sculptor to express the most repulsive mood that human features could assume. And, as his look grew even devilish, so, with an equal change, did Mary Goffe become more sad, more mild, more pitiful, more like a sorrowing angel. But, the more heavenly she was, the more hateful did she seem to Richard Digby, who at length raised his hand, and smote down the cup of hallowed water upon the threshold of the cave, thus rejecting the only medicine that could have cured his stony heart. A sweet perfume lingered in the air for a moment, and then was gone.

'Tempt me no more, accursed woman,' exclaimed he, still with his marble frown, 'lest I smite thee down also! What hast thou to do with my Bible?—what with my prayers?—what with my Heaven?'

No sooner had he spoken these dreadful words, than Richard's Digby's heart ceased to beat; while—so the legend says—the form of Mary Goffe melted into the last sunbeams, and returned from the sepulchral cave to Heaven. For Mary Goffe had been buried in an English churchyard, months before; and either it was her ghost that haunted the wild forest, or else a dreamlike spirit, typifying pure Religion.

Above a century afterwards, when the trackless forest of Richard Digby's day had long been interspersed with settlements, the children of a neighbouring farmer were playing at the foot of a hill. The trees, on account of the rude and broken surface of this acclivity, had never been felled, and were crowded so densely together, as to hide all but a few rocky prominences, wherever their roots could grapple with the soil. A little boy and girl, to conceal themselves from their playmates, had crept into the deepest shade, where not only the darksome pines, but a thick veil of creeping plants suspended from an overhanging rock, combined to make a twilight at noonday, and almost a midnight at all other seasons. There the children hid themselves, and shouted, repeating the cry at intervals, till the whole party of pursuers were drawn thither, and pulling aside the matted foliage, let in a doubtful glimpse of daylight. But scarcely was this accomplished, when the little group uttered a simultaneous shriek and tumbled headlong down the hill, making the best of their way homeward, without a second glance into the gloomy recess. Their father, unable to comprehend what had so startled them, took his axe, and by felling one or two trees, and tearing away the creeping plants, laid the mystery open to the day. He had discovered the entrance of a cave, closely resembling the mouth of a sepulchre, within which sat the figure of a man, whose gesture and attitude warned the father and children to stand back, while his visage wore a most forbidding frown. This repulsive personage seemed to have been carved in the same gray stone that formed the walls and portal of the cave. On minuter inspection, indeed, such blemishes were observed, as made it doubtful whether the figure were really a statue, chiselled by human art, and somewhat worn and defaced by the lapse of ages, or a freak of Nature, who might have chosen to imitate, in stone, her usual handiwork of flesh. Perhaps it was the least unreasonable idea, suggested by this strange spectacle, that the moisture of the cave possessed a petrifying quality, which had thus awfully embalmed a human corpse.

There was something so frightful in the aspect of this Man of Adamant, that the farmer, the moment that he recovered from the fascination of his first gaze, began to heap stones into the mouth of the cavern. His wife, who had followed him to the hill, assisted her husband's efforts. The children, also, approached as near as they durst, with their little hands full of pebbles, and cast them on the pile. Earth was then thrown into the crevices, and the whole fabric overlaid with sods. Thus all traces of the discovery were obliterated, leaving only a marvellous legend, which grew wilder from one generation to another, as the children told it to their grandchildren, and they to their posterity, till few believed that there had ever been a cavern or a statue, where now they saw but a grassy patch on the shadowy hill-side. Yet, grown people avoid the spot, nor do children play there. Friendship, and Love, and Piety, all human and celestial sympathies, should keep aloof from that hidden cave; for there still sits, and, unless an earthquake crumble down the roof upon his head, shall sit forever, the shape of Richard Digby, in the attitude of repelling the whole race of mortals —not from Heaven—but from the horrible loneliness of his dark, cold sepulchre.

THE DEVIL IN MANUSCRIPT

ON A BITTER evening of December, I arrived by mail in a large town, which was then the residence of an intimate friend, one of those gifted youths who cultivate poetry and the belles lettres, and call themselves students at law. My first business, after supper, was to visit him at the office of his distinguished instructer. As I have said, it was a bitter night, clear starlight, but cold as Nova Zembla—the shop-windows along the street being frosted, so as almost to hide the lights, while the wheels of coaches thundered equally loud over frozen earth and pavements of stone. There was no snow, either on the ground or the roofs of the houses. The wind blew so violently, that I had but to spread my cloak like a mainsail, and scud along the street at the rate of ten knots, greatly envied by other navigators who were beating slowly up, with the gale right in their teeth. One of these I capsized, but was gone on the wings of the wind before he could even vociferate an oath.

After this picture of an inclement night, behold us seated by a great blazing fire, which looked so comfortable and delicious that I felt inclined to lie down and roll among the hot coals. The usual furniture of a lawyer's office was around us—rows of volumes in sheepskin, and a multitude of writs, summonses, and other legal papers, scattered over the desks and tables. But there were certain objects which seemed to intimate that we had little dread of the intrusion of clients, or of the learned counsellor himself, who, indeed, was attending court in a distant town. A tall, decanter-shaped bottle stood on the table, between two tumblers, and beside a pile of blotted manuscripts, altogether dissimilar to any law documents recognized in our courts. My friend, whom I shall call Oberon—it was a name of fancy and friendship between him and me—my friend Oberon looked at these papers with a peculiar expression of disquietude.

'I do believe,' said he, soberly, 'or, at least, I would believe, if I chose, that there is a devil in this pile of blotted papers. You have read them, and know what I mean—that conception, in which I endeavored to embody the character of a fiend, as represented in our traditions and the written records of witchcraft. Oh! I have a horror of what was created in my own brain, and shudder at the manuscripts in which I gave that dark idea a sort of material existence. Would they were out of my sight!'

'And of mine too,' thought I.

'You remember,' continued Oberon, 'how the hellish thing used to suck away the happiness of those who, by a simple concession that seemed almost innocent, subjected themselves to his power. Just so my peace is gone, and all by these accursed manuscripts. Have you felt nothing of the same influence?'

'Nothing,' replied I, 'unless the spell be hid in a desire to turn novelist, after reading your delightful tales.'

'Novelist!' exclaimed Oberon, half seriously. 'Then, indeed, my devil has his claw on you! You are gone! You cannot even pray for deliverance! But we will be the last and only victims; for this night I mean to burn the manuscripts, and commit the fiend to his retribution in the flames.'

'Burn your tales!' repeated I, startled at the desperation of the idea.

'Even so,' said the author, despondingly. 'You cannot conceive what an effect the composition of these tales has had on me. I have become ambitious of a bubble, and careless of solid reputation. I am surrounding myself with shadows, which bewilder me, by aping the realities of life. They have drawn me aside from the beaten path of the world, and led me into a strange sort of solitude—a solitude in the midst of men—where nobody wishes for what I do, nor thinks nor feels as I do. The tales have done all this. When they are ashes, perhaps I shall be as I was before they had existence. Moreover, the sacrifice is less than you may suppose; since nobody will publish them.'

'That does make a difference, indeed,' said I.

'They have been offered, by letter,' continued Oberon, reddening with vexation, 'to some seventeen booksellers. It would make you stare to read their answers; and read them you should, only that I burnt them as fast as they arrived. One man publishes nothing but school-books; another has five novels already under examination—'

'What a voluminous mass the unpublished literature of America must be!' cried I.

'Oh! the Alexandrian manuscripts were nothing to it,' said my friend. 'Well; another gentleman is just giving up business, on purpose, I verily believe, to escape publishing my book. Several, however, would not absolutely decline the agency, on my advancing half the cost of an edition, and giving bonds for the remainder, besides a high percentage to themselves, whether the book sells or not. Another advises a subscription.'

'The villain!' exclaimed I.

'A fact!' said Oberon. 'In short, of all the seventeen booksellers, only one has vouchsafed even to read my tales; and he—a literary dabbler himself, I should judge—has the impertinence to criticize them, proposing what he calls vast improvements, and concluding, after a general sentence of condemnation, with the definitive assurance that he will not be concerned on any terms.'

'It might not be amiss to pull that fellow's nose,' remarked I.

'If the whole "trade" had one common nose, there would be some satisfaction in pulling it,' answered the author. 'But, there does seem to be one honest man among these seventeen unrighteous ones, and he tells me fairly, that no American publisher will meddle with an American work, seldom if by a known writer, and never if by a new one, unless at the writer's risk.'

'The paltry rogues!' cried I. 'Will they live by literature, and yet risk nothing for its sake? But, after all, you might publish on your own account.'

'And so I might,' replied Oberon. 'But the devil of the business is this. These people have put me so out of conceit with the tales, that I loathe the very thought of them, and actually experience a physical sickness of the stomach, whenever I glance at them on the table. I tell you there is a demon in them! I anticipate a wild enjoyment in seeing them in the blaze; such as I should feel in taking vengeance on an enemy, or destroying something noxious.'

I did not very strenuously oppose this determination, being privately of opinion, in spite of my partiality for the author, that his tales would make a more brilliant appearance in the fire than anywhere else. Before proceeding to execution, we broached the bottle of champagne, which Oberon had provided for keeping up his spirits in this doleful business. We swallowed each a tumblerfull, in sparkling commotion; it went bubbling down our throats, and brightened my eyes at once, but left my friend sad and heavy as before. He drew the tales towards him, with a mixture of natural affection and natural disgust, like a father taking a deformed infant into his arms.

'Pooh! Pish! Pshaw!' exclaimed he, holding them at arm's length. 'It was Gray's idea of Heaven, to lounge on a sofa and read new novels. Now, what more appropriate torture would Dante himself have contrived, for the sinner who perpetrates a bad book, than to be continually turning over the manuscript?'

'It would fail of effect,' said I, 'because a bad author is always his own great admirer.'

'I lack that one characteristic of my tribe, the only desirable one,' observed Oberon. 'But how many recollections throng upon me, as I turn over these leaves! This scene came into my fancy as I walked along a hilly road, on a starlight October evening; in the pure and bracing air, I became all soul, and felt as if I could climb the sky and run a race along the Milky Way. Here is another tale, in which I wrapt myself during a dark and dreary night-ride in the month of March, till the rattling of the wheels and the voices of my companions seemed like faint sounds of a dream, and my visions a bright reality. That scribbled page describes shadows which I summoned to my bedside at midnight; they would not depart when I bade them; the gray dawn came, and found me wide awake and feverish, the victim of my own enchantments!'

'There must have been a sort of happiness in all this,' said I, smitten with a strange longing to make proof of it.

'There may be happiness in a fever fit,' replied the author. 'And then the various moods in which I wrote! Sometimes my ideas were like precious stones under the earth, requiring toil to dig them up, and care to polish and brighten them; but often, a delicious stream of thought would gush out upon the page at once, like water sparkling up suddenly in the desert; and when it had passed, I gnawed my pen hopelessly, or blundered on with cold and miserable toil, as if there were a wall of ice between me and my subject.'

'Do you now perceive a corresponding difference,' inquired I, 'between the passages which you wrote so coldly, and those fervid flashes of the mind?'

'No,' said Oberon, tossing the manuscripts on the table. 'I find no traces of the golden pen, with which I wrote in characters of fire. My treasure of fairy coin is changed to worthless dross. My picture, painted in what seemed the loveliest hues, presents nothing but a faded and indistinguishable surface. I have been eloquent and poetical and humorous in a dream—and behold! it is all nonsense, now that I am awake.'

My friend now threw sticks of wood and dry chips upon the fire, and seeing it blaze like Nebuchadnezzar's furnace, seized the champagne bottle, and drank two or three brimming bumpers, successively. The heady liquor combined with his agitation to throw him into a species of rage. He laid violent hands on the tales. In one instant more, their faults and beauties would alike have vanished in a glowing purgatory. But, all at once, I remembered passages of high imagination, deep pathos, original thoughts, and points of such varied excellence, that the vastness of the sacrifice struck me most forcibly. I caught his arm.

'Surely, you do not mean to burn them!' I exclaimed.

'Let me alone!' cried Oberon, his eyes flashing fire. 'I will burn them! Not a scorched syllable shall escape! Would you have me a damned author?—To undergo sneers, taunts, abuse, and cold neglect, and faint praise, bestowed, for pity's sake, against the giver's conscience! A hissing and a laughing-stock to my own traitorous thoughts! An outlaw from the protection of the grave—one whose ashes every careless foot might spurn, unhonored in life, and remembered scornfully in death! Am I to bear all this, when yonder fire will ensure me from the whole? No! There go the tales! May my hand wither when it would write another!'

The deed was done. He had thrown the manuscripts into the hottest of the fire, which at first seemed to shrink away, but soon curled around them, and made them a part of its own fervent brightness. Oberon stood gazing at the conflagration, and shortly began to soliloquize, in the wildest strain, as if Fancy resisted and became riotous, at the moment when he would have compelled her to ascend that funeral pile. His words described objects which he appeared to discern in the fire, fed by his own precious thoughts; perhaps the thousand visions, which the writer's magic had incorporated with those pages, became visible to him in the dissolving heat, brightening forth ere they vanished forever; while the smoke, the vivid sheets of flame, the ruddy and whitening coals, caught the aspect of a varied scenery.

'They blaze,' said he, 'as if I had steeped them in the intensest spirit of genius. There I see my lovers clasped in in each other's arms. How pure the flame that bursts from their glowing hearts! And yonder the features of a villain, writhing in the fire that shall torment him to eternity. My holy men, my pious and angelic women, stand like martyrs amid the flames, their mild eyes lifted heavenward. Ring out the bells! A city is on fire. See!—destruction roars through my dark forests, while the lakes boil up in steaming billows, and the mountains are volcanoes, and the sky kindles with a lurid brightness! All elements are but one pervading flame! Ha! The fiend!'

I was somewhat startled by this latter exclamation. The tales were almost consumed, but just then threw forth a broad sheet of fire, which flickered as with laughter, making the whole room dance in its brightness, and then roared portentously up the chimney.

'You saw him? You must have seen him!' cried Oberon. 'How he glared at me and laughed, in that last sheet of flame, with just the features that I imagined for him! Well! The tales are gone.'

The papers were indeed reduced to a heap of black cinders, with a multitude of sparks hurrying confusedly among them, the traces of the pen being now represented by white lines, and the whole mass fluttering to and fro, in the draughts of air. The destroyer knelt down to look at them.

'What is more potent than fire!' said he, in his gloomiest tone. 'Even thought, invisible and incorporeal as it is, cannot escape it. In this little time, it has annihilated the creations of long nights and days, which I could no more reproduce, in their first glow and freshness, than cause ashes and whitened bones to rise up and live. There, too, I sacrificed the unborn children of my mind. All that I had accomplished —all that I planned for future years—has perished by one common ruin, and left only this heap of embers. The deed has been my fate. And what remains? A weary and aimless life—a long repentance of this hour—and at last an obscure grave, where they will bury and forget me.'

As the author concluded his dolorous moan, the extinguished embers arose and settled down and arose again, and finally flew up the chimney, like a demon with sable wings. Just as they disappeared, there was a loud and solitary cry in the street below us. 'Fire! Fire!' Other voices caught up that terrible word, and it speedily became the shout of a multitude. Oberon started to his feet, in fresh excitement.

'A fire on such a night!' cried he. 'The wind blows a gale, and wherever it whirls the flames, the roofs will flash up like gunpowder. Every pump is frozen up, and boiling water would turn to ice the moment it was flung from the engine. In an hour, this wooden town will be one great bonfire! What a glorious scene for my next——Pshaw!'

The street was now all alive with footsteps, and the air full of voices. We heard one engine thundering round a corner, and another rattling from a distance over the pavements. The bells of three steeples clanged out at once, spreading the alarm to many a neighboring town, and expressing hurry, confusion and terror, so inimitably that I could almost distinguish in their peal the burthen of the universal cry—'Fire! Fire! Fire!'

'What is so eloquent as their iron tongues!' exclaimed Oberon. 'My heart leaps and trembles, but not with fear. And that other sound, too—deep and awful as a mighty organ— the roar and thunder of the multiude on the pavement below! Come! We are losing time. I will cry out in the loudest of the uproar, and mingle my spirit with the wildest of the confusion, and be a bubble on the top of the ferment!'

From the first outcry, my forebodings had warned me of the true object and centre of alarm. There was nothing now but uproar—above, beneath, and around us; footsteps stumbling pell-mell up the public stair-case, eager shouts and heavy thumps at the door, the whiz and dash of water from the engines, and the crash of furniture thrown upon the pavement. At once, the truth flashed upon my friend. His frenzy took the hue of joy, and, with a wild gesture of exultation, he leaped almost to the ceiling of the chamber.

'My tales!' cried Oberon. 'The chimney! The roof! The Fiend has gone forth by night, and startled thousands in fear and wonder from their beds! Here I stand—a triumphant author! Huzza! Huzza! My brain has set the town on fire! Huzza!'

JOHN INGLEFIELD'S THANKSGIVING

O N THE EVENING of Thanksgiving day, John Inglefield, the blacksmith, sat in his elbow-chair, among those who had been keeping festival at his board. Being the central figure of the domestic circle, the fire threw its strongest light on his massive and sturdy frame, reddening his rough visage, so that it looked like the head of an iron statue, all a-glow from his own forge, and with its features rudely fashioned on his own anvil. At John Inglefield's right hand was an empty chair. The other places round the hearth were filled by the members of the family, who all sat quietly, while, with a semblance of fantastic merriment, their shadows danced on the wall behind them. One of the group was John Inglefield's son, who had been bred at college, and was now a student of theology at Andover. There was also a daughter of sixteen, whom nobody could look at without thinking of a rose-bud almost blossomed. The only other person at the fireside was Robert Moore, formerly an apprentice of the blacksmith, but now his journeyman, and who seemed more like an own son of John Inglefield than did the pale and slender student.

Only these four had kept New England's festival beneath that roof. The vacant chair at John Inglefield's right hand, was in memory of his wife, whom death had snatched

from him since the previous Thanksgiving. With a feeling
that few would have looked for in his rough nature, the bereaved husband had himself set the chair in its place next
his own; and often did his eye glance thitherward, as if he
deemed it possible that the cold grave might send back its
tenant to the cheerful fireside, at least for that one evening.
Thus did he cherish the grief that was dear to him. But
there was another grief which he would fain have torn from
his heart; or, since that could never be, have buried it too
deep for others to behold, or for his own remembrance.
Within the past year another member of his household had
gone from him—but not to the grave. Yet they kept no
vacant chair for her.

While John Inglefield and his family were sitting round
the hearth, with the shadows dancing behind them on the
wall, the outer door was opened, and a light footstep came
along the passage. The latch of the inner door was lifted by
some familiar hand, and a young girl came in, wearing a
cloak and hood, which she took off, and laid on the table
beneath the looking-glass. Then, after gazing a moment at
the fireside circle, she approached, and took the seat at John
Inglefield's right hand, as if it had been reserved on purpose
for her.

"Here I am at last, father," said she. "You ate your
Thanksgiving dinner without me; but I have come back
to spend the evening with you."

Yes—it was Prudence Inglefield. She wore the same neat
and maidenly attire, which she had been accustomed to put
on when the household work was over for the day, and her
hair was parted from her brow, in the simple and modest
fashion that became her best of all. If her cheek might
otherwise have been pale, yet the glow of the fire suffused it
with a healthful bloom. If she had spent the many months
of her absence in guilt and infamy, yet they seemed to have

left no traces on her gentle aspect. She could not have looked
less altered, had she merely stept away from her father's
fireside for half an hour, and returned while the blaze was
quivering upwards from the same brands that were burning
at her departure. And to John Inglefield she was the very
image of his buried wife, such as he remembered her on the
first Thanksgiving which they had passed under their own
roof. Therefore, though naturally a stern and rugged man, he
could not speak unkindly to his sinful child, nor yet could
he take her to his bosom.

"You are welcome home, Prudence," said he, glancing
sideways at her, and his voice faltered. "Your mother would
have rejoiced to see you, but she has been gone from us
these four months."

"I know it, father, I know it," replied Prudence quickly.
"And yet when I first came in, my eyes were so dazzled by
the fire-light, that she seemed to be sitting in this very chair!"

By this time the other members of the family had begun
to recover from their surprise, and became sensible that it
was no ghost from the grave, nor vision of their vivid recollections, but Prudence her own self. Her brother was the
next that greeted her. He advanced and held out his hand
affectionately, as a brother should; yet not entirely like a
brother, for, with all his kindness, he was still a clergyman,
and speaking to a child of sin.

"Sister Prudence," said he earnestly, "I rejoice that a
merciful Providence has turned your steps homeward, in
time for me to bid you a last farewell. In a few weeks, sister,
I am to sail as a missionary to the far islands of the Pacific.
There is not one of these beloved faces, that I shall ever hope
to behold again on this earth. Oh, may I see all of them—
yours and all—beyond the grave!"

A shadow flitted across the girl's countenance.

"The grave is very dark, brother," answered she, withdrawing her hand somewhat hastily from his grasp. "You must look your last at me by the light of this fire."

While this was passing, the twin-girl—the rose-bud that had grown on the same stem with the cast-away—stood gazing at her sister, longing to fling herself upon her bosom, so that the tendrils of their hearts might intertwine again. At first she was restrained by mingled grief and shame, and by a dread that Prudence was too much changed to respond to her affection, or that her own purity would be felt as a reproach by the lost one. But as she listened to the familiar voice, while the face grew more and more familiar, she forgot everything, save that Prudence had come back. Springing forward, she would have clasped her in a close embrace. At that very instant, however, Prudence started from her chair, and held out both her hands, with a warning gesture.

"No, Mary—no, my sister," cried she, "do not you touch me. Your bosom must not be pressed to mine!"

Mary shuddered, and stood still, for she felt that something darker than the grave was between Prudence and herself, though they seemed so near each other in the light of their father's hearth, where they had grown up together. Meanwhile Prudence threw her eyes around the room, in search of one who had not yet bidden her welcome. He had withdrawn from his seat by the fireside, and was standing near the door, with his face averted, so that his features could be discerned only by the flickering shadow of the profile upon the wall. But Prudence called to him, in a cheerful and kindly tone:

"Come, Robert," said she, "won't you shake hands with your old friend?"

Robert Moore held back for a moment; but affection struggled powerfully, and overcame his pride and resentment; he rushed towards Prudence, seized her hand, and pressed it to his bosom.

"There, there, Robert!" said she, smiling sadly as she withdrew her hand, "you must not give me too warm a welcome."

And now, having exchanged greetings with each member of the family, Prudence again seated herself in the chair at John Inglefield's right hand. She was naturally a girl of quick and tender sensibilities, gladsome in her general mood, but with a bewitching pathos interfused among her merriest words and deeds. It was remarked of her, too, that she had a faculty, even from childhood, of throwing her own feelings like a spell over her companions. Such as she had been in her days of innocence, so did she appear this evening. Her friends, in the surprise and bewilderment of her return, almost forgot that she had ever left them, or that she had forfeited any of her claims to their affection. In the morning, perhaps, they might have looked at her with altered eyes, but by the Thanksgiving fireside they felt only that their own Prudence had come back to them, and were thankful. John Inglefield's rough visage brightened with the glow of his heart, as it grew warm and merry within him; once or twice, even, he laughed till the room rang again, yet seemed startled by the echo of his own mirth. The grave young minister became as frolicsome as a school-boy. Mary, too, the rose-bud, forgot that her twin blossom had ever been torn from the stem, and trampled in the dust. And as for Robert Moore, he gazed at Prudence with the bashful earnestness of love new-born, while she, with sweet maiden coquetry, half smiled upon, and half discouraged him.

In short, it was one of those intervals when sorrow vanishes in its own depth of shadow, and joy starts forth in transitory brightness. When the clock struck eight, Prudence poured out her father's customary draught of herb tea, which had been steeping by the fireside ever since twilight.

"God bless you, child," said John Inglefield, as he took the cup from her hand; "you have made your old father happy again. But we miss your mother sadly, Prudence—sadly. It seems as if she ought to be here now."

"Now, father, or never," replied Prudence.

It was now the hour for domestic worship. But while the family were making preparations for this duty, they suddenly perceived that Prudence had put on her cloak and hood, and was lifting the latch of the door.

"Prudence, Prudence! where are you going?" cried they all with one voice.

As Prudence passed out of the door, she turned towards them, and flung back her hand with a gesture of farewell. But her face was so changed that they hardly recognized it. Sin and evil passions glowed through its comeliness, and wrought a horrible deformity; a smile gleamed in her eyes, as of triumphant mockery at their surprise and grief.

"Daughter," cried John Inglefield, between wrath and sorrow, "stay and be your father's blessing—or take his curse with you!"

For an instant Prudence lingered and looked back into the fire-lighted room, while her countenance wore almost the expression as if she were struggling with a fiend, who had power to seize his victim even within the hallowed precincts of her father's hearth. The fiend prevailed; and Prudence vanished into the outer darkness. When the family rushed to the door, they could see nothing, but heard the sound of wheels rattling over the frozen ground.

That same night, among the painted beauties at the theatre of a neighboring city, there was one whose dissolute mirth seemed inconsistent with any sympathy for pure affections, and for the joys and griefs which are hallowed by them. Yet this was Prudence Inglefield. Her visit to the Thanksgiving fireside was the realization of one of those waking dreams in which the guilty soul will sometimes stray back to its innocence. But Sin, alas! is careful of her bond-slaves; they hear her voice, perhaps at the holiest moment, and are constrained to go whither she summons them. The same dark power that drew Prudence Inglefield from her father's hearth —the same in its nature, though heightened then to a dread necessity—would snatch a guilty soul from the gate of Heaven, and make its sin and its punishment alike eternal.

OLD TICONDEROGA

A PICTURE OF THE PAST

THE GREATEST ATTRACTION, in this vicinity, is the famous old fortress of Ticonderoga; the remains of which are visible from the piazza of the tavern, on a swell of land that shuts in the prospect of the lake. Those celebrated heights, Mount Defiance and Mount Independence, familiar to all Americans in history, stand too prominent not to be recognized, though neither of them precisely correspond to the images excited by their names. In truth, the whole scene, except the interior of the fortress, disappointed me. Mount Defiance, which one pictures as a steep, lofty, and rugged hill, of most formidable aspect, frowning down with the grim visage of a precipice on old Ticonderoga, is merely a long and wooded ridge; and bore, at some former period, the gentle name of Sugar Hill. The brow is certainly difficult to climb, and high enough to look into every corner of the fortress. St. Clair's most probable reason, however, for neglecting to occupy it, was the deficiency of troops to man the works already constructed, rather than the supposed inaccessibility of Mount Defiance. It is singular that the French never fortified this height, standing, as it does, in the quarter whence they must have looked for the advance of a British army.

In my first view of the ruins I was favored with the scientific guidance of a young lieutenant of engineers, recently from West Point, where he had gained credit for great military genius. I saw nothing but confusion in what chiefly interested him; straight lines and zigzags, defence within defence, wall opposed to wall, and ditch intersecting ditch; oblong squares of masonry below the surface of the earth, and huge mounds, or turf-covered hills of stone, above it. On one of these artificial hillocks, a pine-tree has rooted itself, and grown tall and strong, since the banner-staff was levelled. But where my unmilitary glance could trace no regularity, the young lieutenant was perfectly at home. He fathomed the meaning of every ditch, and formed an entire plan of the fortress from its half-obliterated lines. His description of Ticonderoga would be as accurate as a geometrical theorem, and as barren of the poetry that has clustered round its decay. I viewed Ticonderoga as a place of ancient strength, in ruins for half a century; where the flags of three nations had successively waved, and none waved now; where armies had struggled, so long ago that the bones of the slain were mouldered; where Peace had found a heritage in the forsaken haunts of War. Now the young West Pointer, with his lectures on ravelins, counterscarps, angles, and covered ways, made it an affair of brick and mortar and hewn stone, arranged on certain regular principles, having a good deal to do with mathematics but nothing at all with poetry.

I should have been glad of a hoary veteran to totter by my side, and tell me, perhaps, of the French garrisons and their Indian allies—of Abercrombie, Lord Howe, and Amherst— of Ethan Allen's triumph and St. Clair's surrender. The old soldier and the old fortress would be emblems of each other. His reminiscences, though vivid as the image of Ticonderoga in the lake, would harmonize with the gray influence of the scene. A survivor of the long-disbanded garrisons, though but a private soldier, might have mustered his dead chiefs and comrades—some from Westminster Abbey, and English church-yards, and battle-fields in Europe—others from their graves here in America—others, not a few, who lie sleeping round the fortress; he might have mustered them all, and bid them march through the ruined gateway, turning their old historic faces on me as they passed. Next to such a companion, the best is one's own fancy.

At another visit I was alone, and, after rambling all over the ramparts, sat down to rest myself in one of the roofless barracks. These are old French structures, and appear to have occupied three sides of a large area, now overgrown with grass, nettles, and thistles. The one, in which I sat, was long and narrow, as all the rest had been, with peaked gables. The exterior walls were nearly entire, constructed of gray, flat, unpicked stones, the aged strength of which promised long to resist the elements, if no other violence should precipitate their fall. The roof, floors, partitions, and the rest of the wood-work, had probably been burnt, except some bars of stanch old oak, which were blackened with fire but still remained embedded into the window-sills and over the doors. There were a few particles of plastering near the chimney, scratched with rude figures, perhaps by a soldier's hand. A most luxuriant crop of weeds had sprung up within the edifice and hid the scattered fragments of the wall. Grass and weeds grew in the windows, and in all the crevices of the stone, climbing, step by step, till a tuft of yellow flowers was waving on the highest peak of the gable. Some spicy herb diffused a pleasant odor through the ruin. A verdant heap of vegetation had covered the hearth of the second floor, clustering on the very spot where the huge logs had mouldered to glowing coals, and flourished beneath the broad flue, which had so often puffed the smoke over a circle of French or English soldiers. I felt that there was no other token of decay so impressive as that bed of weeds in the place of the back-log.

Here I sat, with those roofless walls about me, the clear sky over my head, and the afternoon sunshine falling gently bright through the window-frames and doorway. I heard the tinkling of a cow-bell, the twittering of birds, and the pleasant hum of insects. Once a gay butterfly, with four gold-speckled wings, came and fluttered about my head, then flew up and lighted on the highest tuft of yellow flowers, and at last took wing across the lake. Next a bee buzzed through the sunshine, and found much sweetness among the weeds. After watching him till he went off to his distant hive, I closed my eyes on Ticonderoga in ruins, and cast a dream-like glance over pictures of the past, and scenes of which this spot had been the theatre.

At first, my fancy saw only the stern hills, lonely lakes, and venerable woods. Not a tree, since their seeds were first scattered over the infant soil, had felt the axe, but had grown up and flourished through its long generation, had fallen beneath the weight of years, been buried in green moss, and nourished the roots of others as gigantic. Hark! A light paddle dips into the lake, a birch canoe glides round the point, and an Indian chief has passed, painted and feather-crested, armed with a bow of hickory, a stone tomahawk, and flint-headed arrows. But the ripple had hardly vanished from the water, when a white flag caught the breeze, over a castle in the wilderness with frowning ramparts and a hundred cannon. There stood a French chevalier, commandant of the fortress, paying court to a copper-colored lady, the princess of the land, and winning her wild love by the arts which had been successful with Parisian dames. A war-party of French and Indians were issuing from the gate to lay waste some village of New England. Near the fortress there was a group of dancers. The merry soldiers footing it with the swart savage maids; deeper in the wood, some red men were growing frantic around a keg of the fire-water; and elsewhere a Jesuit preached the faith of high cathedrals beneath a canopy of forest boughs, and distributed crucifixes to be worn beside English scalps.

I tried to make a series of pictures from the old French war, when fleets were on the lake and armies in the woods, and especially of Abercrombie's disastrous repulse, where thousands of lives were utterly thrown away; but being at a loss how to order the battle, I chose an evening scene in the barracks after the fortress had surrendered to Sir Jeffrey Amherst. What an immense fire blazes on that hearth, gleaming on swords, bayonets, and musket barrels, and blending with the hue of the scarlet coats till the whole barrack-room is quivering with ruddy light! One soldier has thrown himself down to rest, after a deer-hunt, or perhaps a long run through the woods, with Indians on his trail. Two stand up to wrestle, and are on the point of coming to blows. A fifer plays a shrill accompaniment to a drummer's song—a strain of light love and bloody war, with a chorus thundered forth by twenty voices. Meantime, a veteran in the corner is prosing about Dettingen and Fontenoye, and relates camp-traditions of Marlborough's battles; till his pipe, having been roguishly charged with gunpowder, makes a terrible explosion under his nose. And now they all vanish in a puff of smoke from the chimney.

I merely glanced at the ensuing twenty years, which glided peacefully over the frontier fortress, till Ethan Allen's shout was heard, summoning it to surrender "in the name of the great Jehovah and of the Continental Congress." Strange allies! thought the British captain. Next came the hurried muster of the soldiers of liberty, when the cannon of Burgoyne, pointing down upon their strong-hold from the brow of Mount Defiance, announced a new conqueror of Ticonderoga. No virgin fortress, this! Forth rushed the motley throng from the barracks, one man wearing the blue and buff of the Union, another the red coat of Britain, a third a dragoon's jacket, and a fourth a cotton frock; here was a pair of leather breeches, and striped trowsers there; a grenadier's cap on one head, and a broad-brimmed hat, with a tall feather, on the next; this fellow shouldering a king's arm, that might throw a bullet to Crown Point, and his comrade a long fowling-piece, admirable to shoot ducks on the lake. In the midst of the bustle, when the fortress was all alive with its last warlike scene, the ringing of a bell on the lake made me suddenly unclose my eyes, and behold only the gray and weed-grown ruins. They were as peaceful in the sun as a warrior's grave.

Hastening to the rampart, I perceived that the signal had been given by the steam-boat Franklin, which landed a passenger from Whitehall at the tavern, and resumed its progress northward, to reach Canada the next morning. A sloop was pursuing the same track; a little skiff had just crossed the ferry; while a scow, laden with lumber, spread its huge square sail and went up the lake. The whole country was a cultivated farm. Within musket shot of the ramparts lay the neat villa of Mr. Pell, who, since the Revolution, has become proprietor of a spot for which France, England, and America have so often struggled. How forcibly the lapse of time and change of circumstances came home to my apprehension! Banner would never wave again, nor cannon roar, nor blood be shed, nor trumpet stir up a soldier's heart, in this old fort of Ticonderoga. Tall trees had grown upon its ramparts, since the last garrison marched out, to return no more, or only at some dreamer's summons, gliding from the twilight past to vanish among realities.

THE WIVES OF THE DEAD

T HE FOLLOWING STORY, the simple and domestic incidents of which may be deemed scarcely worth relating, after such a lapse of time, awakened some degree of interest, a hundred years ago, in a principal seaport of the Bay Province. The rainy twilight of an autumn day; a parlor on the second floor of a small house, plainly furnished, as beseemed the middling circumstances of its inhabitants, yet decorated with little curiosities from beyond the sea, and a few delicate specimens of Indian manufacture, —these are the only particulars to be premised in regard to scene and season. Two young and comely women sat together by the fireside, nursing their mutual and peculiar sorrows. They were the recent brides of two brothers, a sailor and a landsman, and two successive days had brought tidings of the death of each, by the chances of Canadian warfare, and the tempestuous Atlantic. The universal sympathy excited by this bereavement, drew numerous condoling guests to the habitation of the widowed sisters. Several, among whom was the minister, had remained till the verge of evening; when one by one, whispering many comfortable passages of Scripture, that were answered by more abundant tears, they took their leave and departed to their own happier homes. The mourners, though not insensible to the kindness of their friends, had yearned to be left alone. United, as they had been, by the relationship of the living, and now more closely so by that of the dead, each felt as if whatever consolation her grief admitted, were to be found in the bosom of the other. They joined their hearts, and wept together silently. But after an hour of such indulgence, one of the sisters, all of whose emotions were influenced by her mild, quiet, yet not feeble character, began to recollect the precepts of resignation and endurance, which piety had taught her, when she did not think to need them. Her misfortune, besides, as earliest known, should earliest cease to interfere with her regular course of duties; accordingly, having placed the table before the fire, and arranged a frugal meal, she took the hand of her companion.

'Come, dearest sister; you have eaten not a morsel to-day,' she said. 'Arise, I pray you, and let us ask a blessing on that which is provided for us.'

Her sister-in-law was of a lively and irritable temperament, and the first pangs of her sorrow had been expressed by shrieks and passionate lamentation. She now shrunk from Mary's words, like a wounded sufferer from a hand that revives the throb.

'There is no blessing left for me, neither will I ask it,' cried Margaret, with a fresh burst of tears. 'Would it were His will that I might never taste food more.'

Yet she trembled at these rebellious expressions, almost as soon as they were uttered, and, by degrees, Mary succeeded in bringing her sister's mind nearer to the situation of her own. Time went on, and their usual hour of repose arrived. The brothers and their brides, entering the married state with no more than the slender means which then sanctioned such a step, had confederated themselves in one household, with equal rights to the parlor, and claiming exclusive privileges in two sleeping rooms contiguous to it. Thither the widowed ones retired, after heaping ashes upon the dying embers of

their fire, and placing a lighted lamp upon the hearth. The
doors of both chambers were left open, so that a part of the
interior of each, and the beds with their unclosed curtains,
were reciprocally visible. Sleep did not steal upon the sisters
at one and the same time. Mary experienced the effect often
consequent upon grief quietly borne, and soon sunk into
temporary forgetfulness, while Margaret became more disturbed and feverish, in proportion as the night advanced
with its deepest and stillest hours. She lay listening to the
drops of rain, that came down in monotonous succession,
unswayed by a breath of wind; and a nervous impulse continually caused her to lift her head from the pillow, and gaze
into Mary's chamber and the intermediate apartment. The
cold light of the lamp threw the shadows of the furniture
up against the wall, stamping them immoveably there, except
when they were shaken by a sudden flicker of the flame. Two
vacant arm-chairs were in their old positions on opposite sides
of the hearth, where the brothers had been wont to sit in
young and laughing dignity, as heads of families; two humbler
seats were near them, the true thrones of that little empire,
where Mary and herself had exercised in love, a power that
love had won. The cheerful radiance of the fire had shone
upon the happy circle, and the dead glimmer of the lamp
might have befitted their reunion now. While Margaret
groaned in bitterness, she heard a knock at the street-door.

'How would my heart have leapt at that sound but yesterday!' thought she, remembering the anxiety with which she
had long awaited tidings from her husband. 'I care not for it
now; let them begone, for I will not arise.'

But even while a sort of childish fretfulness made her
thus resolve, she was breathing hurriedly, and straining her
ears to catch a repetition of the summons. It is difficult to be
convinced of the death of one whom we have deemed another
self. The knocking was now renewed in slow and regular

strokes, apparently given with the soft end of a doubled fist, and was accompanied by words, faintly heard through several thicknesses of wall. Margaret looked to her sister's chamber, and beheld her still lying in the depths of sleep. She arose, placed her foot upon the floor, and slightly arrayed herself, trembling between fear and eagerness as she did so.

'Heaven help me!' sighed she. 'I have nothing left to fear, and methinks I am ten times more a coward than ever.'

Seizing the lamp from the hearth, she hastened to the window that overlooked the street-door. It was a lattice, turning upon hinges; and having thrown it back, she stretched her head a little way into the moist atmosphere. A lantern was reddening the front of the house, and melting its light in the neighboring puddles, while a deluge of darkness overwhelmed every other object. As the window grated on its hinges, a man in a broad brimmed hat and blanket-coat, stepped from under the shelter of the projecting story, and looked upward to discover whom his application had aroused. Margaret knew him as a friendly innkeeper of the town.

'What would you have, Goodman Parker?' cried the widow.

'Lack-a-day, is it you, Mistress Margaret?' replied the innkeeper. 'I was afraid it might be your sister Mary; for I hate to see a young woman in trouble, when I haven't a word of comfort to whisper her.'

'For Heaven's sake, what news do you bring?' screamed Margaret.

'Why, there has been an express through the town within this half hour,' said Goodman Parker, 'travelling from the eastern jurisdiction with letters from the governor and council. He tarried at my house to refresh himself with a drop and a morsel, and I asked him what tidings on the frontiers. He tells me we had the better in the skirmish you wot of, and that thirteen men reported slain are well and sound, and your husband among them. Besides, he is appointed of the escort to bring the captivated Frenchers and Indians home to the province jail. I judged you wouldn't mind being broke of your rest, and so I stept over to tell you. Good night.'

So saying, the honest man departed; and his lantern gleamed along the street, bringing to view indistinct shapes of things, and the fragments of a world, like order glimmering through chaos, or memory roaming over the past. But Margaret staid not to watch these picturesque effects. Joy flashed into her heart, and lighted it up at once, and breathless, and with winged steps, she flew to the bedside of her sister. She paused, however, at the door of the chamber, while a thought of pain broke in upon her.

'Poor Mary!' said she to herself. 'Shall I waken her, to feel her sorrow sharpened by my happiness? No; I will keep it within my own bosom till the morrow.'

She approached the bed to discover if Mary's sleep were peaceful. Her face was turned partly inward to the pillow, and had been hidden there to weep; but a look of motionless contentment was now visible upon it, as if her heart, like a deep lake, had grown calm because its dead had sunk down so far within. Happy is it, and strange, that the lighter sorrows are those from which dreams are chiefly fabricated. Margaret shrunk from disturbing her sister-in-law, and felt as if her own better fortune, had rendered her involuntarily unfaithful, and as if altered and diminished affection must be the consequence of the disclosure she had to make. With a sudden step, she turned away. But joy could not long be repressed, even by circumstances that would have excited heavy grief at another moment. Her mind was thronged with delightful thoughts, till sleep stole on and transformed them to visions, more delightful and more wild, like the breath of winter, (but what a cold comparison!) working fantastic tracery upon a window.

When the night was far advanced, Mary awoke with a sudden start. A vivid dream had latterly involved her in its unreal life, of which, however, she could only remember that it had been broken in upon at the most interesting point. For a little time, slumber hung about her like a morning mist, hindering her from perceiving the distinct outline of her situation. She listened with imperfect consciousness to two or three volleys of a rapid and eager knocking; and first she deemed the noise a matter of course, like the breath she drew; next, it appeared a thing in which she had no concern; and lastly, she became aware that it was a summons necessary to be obeyed. At the same moment, the pang of recollection darted into her mind; the pall of sleep was thrown back from the face of grief; the dim light of the chamber, and the objects therein revealed, had retained all her suspended ideas, and restored them as soon as she unclosed her eyes. Again, there was a quick peal upon the street-door. Fearing that her sister would also be disturbed, Mary wrapped herself in a cloak and hood, took the lamp from the hearth, and hastened to the window. By some accident, it had been left unhasped, and yielded easily to her hand.

'Who's there?' asked Mary, trembling as she looked forth.

The storm was over, and the moon was up; it shone upon broken clouds above, and below upon houses black with moisture, and upon little lakes of the fallen rain, curling into silver beneath the quick enchantment of a breeze. A young man in a sailor's dress, wet as if he had come out of the depths of the sea, stood alone under the window. Mary recognized him as one whose livelihood was gained by short voyages along the coast; nor did she forget, that, previous to her marriage, he had been an unsuccessful wooer of her own.

'What do you seek here, Stephen?' said she.

'Cheer up, Mary, for I seek to comfort you,' answered the rejected lover. 'You must know I got home not ten minutes ago, and the first thing my good mother told me was the news about your husband. So, without saying a word to the old woman, I clapt on my hat, and ran out of the house. I couldn't have slept a wink before speaking to you, Mary, for the sake of old times.'

'Stephen, I thought better of you!' exclaimed the widow, with gushing tears, and preparing to close the lattice; for she was no whit inclined to imitate the first wife of Zadig.

'But stop, and hear my story out,' cried the young sailor. 'I tell you we spoke a brig yesterday afternoon, bound in from Old England. And who do you think I saw standing on deck, well and hearty, only a bit thinner than he was five months ago?'

Mary leaned from the window, but could not speak.

'Why, it was your husband himself,' continued the generous seaman. 'He and three others saved themselves on a spar, when the Blessing turned bottom upwards. The brig will beat into the bay by daylight, with this wind, and you'll see him here tomorrow. There's the comfort I bring you, Mary, and so good night.'

He hurried away, while Mary watched him with a doubt of waking reality, that seemed stronger or weaker as he alternately entered the shade of the houses, or emerged into the broad streaks of moonlight. Gradually, however, a blessed flood of conviction swelled into her heart, in strength enough to overwhelm her, had its increase been more abrupt. Her first impulse was to rouse her sister-in-law, and communicate the new-born gladness. She opened the chamber-door, which had been closed in the course of the night, though not latched, advanced to the bedside, and was about to lay her hand upon the slumberer's shoulder. But then she remembered that Margaret would awake to thoughts of death and woe, rendered not the less bitter by their contrast with her own felicity. She suffered the rays of the lamp to fall upon the unconscious form of the bereaved one. Margaret lay in unquiet sleep, and the drapery was displaced around her; her young cheek was rosy-tinted, and her lips half opened in a vivid smile; an expression of joy, debarred its passage by her sealed eyelids, struggled forth like incense from the whole countenance.

'My poor sister! you will waken too soon from that happy dream,' thought Mary.

Before retiring, she set down the lamp and endeavored to arrange the bed-clothes, so that the chill air might not do harm to the feverish slumberer. But her hand trembled against Margaret's neck, a tear also fell upon her cheek, and she suddenly awoke.

LITTLE DAFFYDOWNDILLY

DAFFYDOWNDILLY was so called, because in his
nature he resembled a flower, and loved to do only
what was beautiful and agreeable, and took no
delight in labor of any kind. But, while Daffydowndilly was
yet a little boy, his mother sent him away from his pleasant
home, and put him under the care of a very strict schoolmaster, who went by the name of Mr. Toil. Those who knew
him best, affirmed that this Mr. Toil was a very worthy
character; and that he had done more good, both to children
and grown people, than anybody else in the world. Certainly,
he had lived long enough to do a great deal of good; for,
if all stories be true, he had dwelt upon earth ever since
Adam was driven from the garden of Eden.

Nevertheless, Mr. Toil had a severe and ugly countenance,
especially for such little boys or big men as were inclined
to be idle; his voice, too, was harsh; and all his ways and
customs seemed very disagreeable to our friend Daffydowndilly. The whole day long, this terrible old schoolmaster sat
at his desk overlooking the scholars, or stalked about the
schoolroom, with a certain awful birch rod in his hand.
Now came a rap over the shoulders of a boy, whom Mr. Toil
had caught at play; now he punished a whole class, who
were behindhand with their lessons; and, in short, unless a

lad chose to attend quietly and constantly to his book, he had no chance of enjoying a quiet moment in the school-room of Mr. Toil.

"This will never do for me," thought Daffydowndilly.

Now the whole of Daffydowndilly's life had hitherto been passed with his dear mother, who had a much sweeter face than old Mr. Toil, and who had always been very indulgent to her little boy. No wonder, therefore, that poor Daffy-downdilly found it a woful change, to be sent away from the good lady's side, and put under the care of this ugly-visaged schoolmaster, who never gave him any apples or cakes, and seemed to think that little boys were created only to get lessons.

"I can't bear it any longer," said Daffydowndilly to himself, when he had been at school about a week. "I'll run away, and try to find my dear mother; and, at any rate, I shall never find anybody half so disagreeable as this old Mr. Toil!"

So the very next morning, off started poor Daffydowndilly, and began his rambles about the world, with only some bread and cheese for his breakfast, and very little pocket-money to pay his expenses. But he had gone only a short distance, when he overtook a man of grave and sedate appearance, who was trudging at a moderate pace along the road.

"Good morning, my fine lad," said the stranger; and his voice seemed hard and severe, but yet had a sort of kindness in it; "whence do you come so early, and whither are you going?"

Little Daffydowndilly was a boy of very ingenuous dis-position, and had never been known to tell a lie in all his life. Nor did he tell one now. He hesitated a moment or two, but finally confessed that he had run away from school, on account of his great dislike to Mr. Toil, and that he was resolved to find some place in the world, where he should never see or hear of the old schoolmaster again.

"Oh, very well, my little friend!" answered the stranger. "Then we will go together; for I, likewise, have had a good deal to do with Mr. Toil, and should be glad to find some place where he was never heard of."

Our friend Daffydowndilly would have been better pleased with a companion of his own age, with whom he might have gathered flowers along the road-side, or have chased butterflies, or have done many other things to make the journey pleasant. But he had wisdom enough to understand, that he should get along through the world much easier, by having a man of experience to show him the way. So he accepted the stranger's proposal, and they walked on very sociably together.

They had not gone far, when the road passed by a field where some haymakers were at work, mowing down the tall grass and spreading it out in the sun to dry. Daffydowndilly was delighted with the sweet smell of the new-mown grass, and thought how much pleasanter it must be to make hay in the sunshine, under the blue sky, and with the birds singing sweetly in the neighboring trees and bushes, than to be shut up in a dismal schoolroom, learning lessons all day long, and continually scolded by old Mr. Toil. But, in the midst of these thoughts, while he was stopping to peep over the stone-wall, he started back and caught hold of his companion's hand.

"Quick, quick!" cried he. "Let us run away, or he will catch us!"

"Who will catch us?" asked the stranger.

"Mr. Toil, the old schoolmaster!" answered Daffydowndilly. "Don't you see him amongst the haymakers?"

And Daffydowndilly pointed to an elderly man, who seemed to be the owner of the field and the employer of the men at work there. He had stripped off his coat and waistcoat, and was busily at work in his shirt-sleeves. The drops of sweat stood upon his brow; but he gave himself not a moment's rest, and kept crying out to the haymakers to make haste while the sun shone. Now, strange to say, the figure and features of this old farmer were precisely the same as those of old Mr. Toil, who, at that very moment, must have been just entering his schoolroom.

"Don't be afraid," said the stranger. "This is not Mr. Toil the schoolmaster, but a brother of his, who was bred a farmer; and people say he is the most disagreeable man of the two. However, he won't trouble you, unless you become a laborer on the farm."

Little Daffydowndilly believed what his companion said, but was very glad, nevertheless, when they were out of sight of the old farmer, who bore such a singular resemblance to Mr. Toil. The two travellers had gone but a little farther, when they came to a spot where some carpenters were erecting a house. Daffydowndilly begged his companion to stop a moment; for it was a very pretty sight to see how neatly the carpenters did their work, with their broad-axes, and saws, and planes, and hammers, shaping out the doors, and putting in the window-sashes, and nailing on the clapboards; and he could not help thinking that he should like to take a broad-axe, a saw, a plane, and a hammer, and build a little house for himself. And then, when he should have a house of his own, old Mr. Toil would never dare to molest him.

But, just while he was delighting himself with this idea, little Daffydowndilly beheld something that made him catch hold of his companion's hand, all in a fright.

"Make haste! Quick, quick!" cried he. "There he is again!"

"Who?" asked the stranger, very quietly.

"Old Mr. Toil," said Daffydowndilly, trembling. "There! he that is overseeing the carpenters. 'Tis my old schoolmaster, as sure as I'm alive!"

The stranger cast his eyes where Daffydowndilly pointed his finger; and he saw an elderly man, with a carpenter's rule and compasses in his hand. This person went to and fro about the unfinished house, measuring pieces of timber, and marking out the work that was to be done, and continually exhorting the other carpenters to be diligent. And wherever he turned his hard and wrinkled visage the men seemed to feel that they had a taskmaster over them, and sawed, and hammered, and planed, as if for dear life.

"Oh, no! this is not Mr. Toil, the schoolmaster," said the stranger. "It is another brother of his, who follows the trade of carpenter!"

"I am very glad to hear it," quoth Daffydowndilly; "but, if you please, sir, I should like to get out of his way as soon as possible."

Then they went on a little farther, and soon heard the sound of a drum and fife. Daffydowndilly pricked up his ears at this, and besought his companion to hurry forward, that they might not miss seeing the soldiers. Accordingly, they made what haste they could, and soon met a company of soldiers, gaily dressed, with beautiful feathers in their caps, and bright muskets on their shoulders. In front, marched two drummers and two fifers, beating on their drums and playing on their fifes with might and main, and making such lively music, that little Daffydowndilly would gladly have followed them to the end of the world. And if he was only a soldier, then, he said to himself, old Mr. Toil would never venture to look him in the face.

"Quick step! Forward march!" shouted a gruff voice.

Little Daffydowndilly started, in great dismay; for this voice, which had spoken to the soldiers, sounded precisely the same as that which he had heard every day in Mr. Toil's schoolroom, out of Mr. Toil's own mouth. And, turning his eyes to the captain of the company, what should he see but the very image of old Mr. Toil himself, with a smart cap and feather on his head, a pair of gold epaulets on his shoulders, a laced coat on his back, a purple sash round his waist, and a long sword instead of a birch rod in his hand! And though he held his head so high, and strutted like a turkey-cock, still he looked quite as ugly and disagreeable as when he was hearing lessons in the schoolroom.

"This is certainly old Mr. Toil," said Daffydowndilly in a trembling voice. "Let us run away, for fear he should make us enlist in his company!"

"You are mistaken again, my little friend," replied the stranger, very composedly. "This is not Mr. Toil, the school-master, but a brother of his, who has served in the army all his life. People say he's a terribly severe fellow; but you and I need not be afraid of him."

"Well, well," said little Daffydowndilly, "but, if you please, sir, I don't want to see the soldiers any more."

So the child and the stranger resumed their journey; and, by-and-by, they came to a house by the road-side, where a number of people were making merry. Young men and rosy-cheeked girls, with smiles on their faces, were dancing to the sound of a fiddle. It was the pleasantest sight that Daffy-downdilly had yet met with, and it comforted him for all his disappointments.

"Oh, let us stop here," cried he to his companion; "for Mr. Toil will never dare to show his face where there is a fiddler, and where people are dancing and making merry. We shall be quite safe here!"

But these last words died away upon Daffydowndilly's tongue; for, happening to cast his eyes on the fiddler, whom should he behold again, but the likeness of Mr. Toil, holding a fiddle-bow instead of a birch rod, and flourishing it with as much ease and dexterity as if he had been a fiddler all his life! He had somewhat the air of a Frenchman, but still looked exactly like the old schoolmaster; and Daffydowndilly even fancied that he nodded and winked at him, and made signs for him to join in the dance.

"Oh, dear me!" whispered he, turning pale. "It seems as if there was nobody but Mr. Toil in the world. Who could have thought of his playing on a fiddle!"

"This is not your old schoolmaster," observed the stranger, "but another brother of his, who was bred in France, where he learned the profession of a fiddler. He is ashamed of his family, and generally calls himself Monsieur le Plaisir; but his real name is Toil, and those who have known him best, think him still more disagreeable than his brothers."

"Pray let us go a little farther," said Daffydowndilly, "I don't like the looks of this fiddler at all."

Well; thus the stranger and little Daffydowndilly went wandering along the highway, and in shady lanes, and through pleasant villages; and whithersoever they went, behold! there was the image of old Mr. Toil. He stood like a scarecrow in the cornfields. If they entered a house, he sat in the parlor; if they peeped into the kitchen, he was there! He made himself at home in every cottage, and stole, under one disguise or another, into the most splendid mansions. Everywhere there was sure to be somebody wearing the likeness of Mr. Toil, and who, as the stranger affirmed, was one of the old schoolmaster's innumerable brethren.

Little Daffydowndilly was almost tired to death, when he perceived some people reclining lazily in a shady place, by the side of the road. The poor child entreated his companion that they might sit down there, and take some repose.

"Old Mr. Toil will never come here," said he; "for he hates to see people taking their ease."

But, even while he spoke, Daffydowndilly's eyes fell upon a person who seemed the laziest, and heaviest, and most torpid, of all those lazy, and heavy, and torpid people, who had lain down to sleep in the shade. Who should it be, again, but the very image of Mr. Toil!

"There is a large family of these Toils," remarked the stranger. "This is another of the old schoolmaster's brothers, who was bred in Italy, where he acquired very idle habits, and goes by the name of Signor Far Niente. He pretends to lead an easy life, but is really the most miserable fellow in the family."

"Oh, take me back!—take me back!" cried poor little Daffydowndilly, bursting into tears. "If there is nothing but Toil all the world over, I may just as well go back to the schoolhouse!"

"Yonder it is—there is the schoolhouse!" said the stranger; for though he and little Daffydowndilly had taken a great many steps, they had travelled in a circle, instead of a straight line. "Come; we will go back to school together."

There was something in his companion's voice that little Daffydowndilly now remembered; and it is strange that he had not remembered it sooner. Looking up into his face, behold! there again was the likeness of old Mr. Toil; so that the poor child had been in company with Toil all day, even while he was doing his best to run away from him. Some people to whom I have told little Daffydowndilly's story, are of opinion that old Mr. Toil was a magician, and possessed the power of multiplying himself into as many shapes as he saw fit.

Be this as it may, little Daffydowndilly had learned a good lesson, and from that time forward was diligent at his task, because he knew that diligence is not a whit more toilsome than sport or idleness. And when he became better acquainted with Mr. Toil, he began to think that his ways were not so very disagreeable, and that the old schoolmaster's smile of approbation made his face almost as pleasant as even that of Daffydowndilly's mother.

MY KINSMAN, MAJOR MOLINEUX

A FTER the kings of Great Britain had assumed the right of appointing the colonial governors, the measures of the latter seldom met with the ready and general approbation, which had been paid to those of their predecessors, under the original charters. The people looked with most jealous scrutiny to the exercise of power, which did not emanate from themselves, and they usually rewarded the rulers with slender gratitude, for the compliances, by which, in softening their instructions from beyond the sea, they had incurred the reprehension of those who gave them. The annals of Massachusetts Bay will inform us, that of six governors, in the space of about forty years from the surrender of the old charter, under James II., two were imprisoned by a popular insurrection; a third, as Hutchinson inclines to believe, was driven from the province by the whizzing of a musket ball; a fourth, in the opinion of the same historian, was hastened to his grave by continual bickerings with the House of Representatives; and the remaining two, as well as their successors, till the Revolution, were favored with few and brief intervals of peaceful sway. The inferior members of the court party, in times of high political excitement, led scarcely a more desirable life. These remarks may serve as preface to the following adventures, which chanced upon a summer night, not far from a hundred years ago. The reader, in order to avoid a long and dry detail of colonial affairs, is requested to dispense with an account of the train of circumstances, that had caused much temporary inflammation of the popular mind.

It was near nine o'clock of a moonlight evening, when a boat crossed the ferry with a single passenger, who had obtained his conveyance, at that unusual hour, by the promise of an extra fare. While he stood on the landing-place, searching in either pocket for the means of fulfilling his agreement, the ferryman lifted a lantern, by the aid of which, and the newly risen moon, he took a very accurate survey of the stranger's figure. He was a youth of barely eighteen years, evidently country-bred, and now, as it should seem, upon his first visit to town. He was clad in a coarse grey coat, well worn, but in excellent repair; his under garments were durably constructed of leather, and sat tight to a pair of serviceable and well-shaped limbs; his stockings of blue yarn, were the incontrovertible handiwork of a mother or a sister; and on his head was a three-cornered hat, which in its better days had perhaps sheltered the graver brow of the lad's father. Under his left arm was a heavy cudgel, formed of an oak sapling, and retaining a part of the hardened root; and his equipment was completed by a wallet, not so abundantly stocked as to incommode the vigorous shoulders on which it hung. Brown, curly hair, well-shaped features, and bright, cheerful eyes, were nature's gifts, and worth all that art could have done for his adornment.

The youth, one of whose names was Robin, finally drew from his pocket the half of a little province-bill of five shillings, which, in the depreciation of that sort of currency, did but satisfy the ferryman's demand, with the surplus of a sexangular piece of parchment valued at three pence. He then walked forward into the town, with as light a step, as if his day's journey had not already exceeded thirty miles, and with as eager an eye, as if he were entering London city, instead of the little metropolis of a New England colony. Before Robin had proceeded far, however, it occurred to him, that he knew not whither to direct his steps; so he paused, and looked up and down the narrow street, scrutinizing the small and mean wooden buildings, that were scattered on either side.

'This low hovel cannot be my kinsman's dwelling,' thought he, 'nor yonder old house, where the moonlight enters at the broken casement; and truly I see none hereabouts that might be worthy of him. It would have been wise to inquire my way of the ferryman, and doubtless he would have gone with me, and earned a shilling from the Major for his pains. But the next man I meet will do as well.'

He resumed his walk, and was glad to perceive that the street now became wider, and the houses more respectable in their appearance. He soon discerned a figure moving on moderately in advance, and hastened his steps to overtake it. As Robin drew nigh, he saw that the passenger was a man in years, with a full periwig of grey hair, a wide-skirted coat of dark cloth, and silk stockings rolled about his knees. He carried a long and polished cane, which he struck down perpendicularly before him, at every step; and at regular intervals he uttered two successive hems, of a peculiarly solemn and sepulchral intonation. Having made these observations, Robin laid hold of the skirt of the old man's coat, just when the light from the open door and windows of a barber's shop, fell upon both their figures.

'Good evening to you, honored Sir,' said he, making a low bow, and still retaining his hold of the skirt. 'I pray you to tell me whereabouts is the dwelling of my kinsman, Major Molineux?'

The youth's question was uttered very loudly; and one of the barbers, whose razor was descending on a well-soaped chin, and another who was dressing a Ramillies wig, left their occupations, and came to the door. The citizen, in the meantime, turned a long favored countenance upon Robin, and answered him in a tone of excessive anger and annoyance. His two sepulchral hems, however, broke into the very centre of his rebuke, with most singular effect, like a thought of the cold grave obtruding among wrathful passions.

"Let go my garment, fellow! I tell you, I know not the man you speak of. What! I have authority, I have—hem, hem—authority; and if this be the respect you show your betters, your feet shall be brought acquainted with the stocks, by daylight, tomorrow morning!'

Robin released the old man's skirt, and hastened away, pursued by an ill-mannered roar of laughter from the barber's shop. He was at first considerably surprised by the result of his question, but, being a shrewd youth, soon thought himself able to account for the mystery.

'This is some country representative,' was his conclusion, 'who has never seen the inside of my kinsman's door, and lacks the breeding to answer a stranger civilly. The man is old, or verily—I might be tempted to turn back and smite him on the nose. Ah, Robin, Robin! even the barber's boys laugh at you, for choosing such a guide! You will be wiser in time, friend Robin.'

He now became entangled in a succession of crooked and narrow streets, which crossed each other, and meandered at no great distance from the water-side. The smell of tar was obvious to his nostrils, the masts of vessels pierced the moonlight above the tops of the buildings, and the numerous signs, which Robin paused to read, informed him that he was near the centre of business. But the streets were empty, the shops were closed, and lights were visible only in the

second stories of a few dwelling-houses. At length, on the
corner of a narrow lane, through which he was passing, he
beheld the broad countenance of a British hero swinging
before the door of an inn, whence proceeded the voices of
many guests. The casement of one of the lower windows was
thrown back, and a very thin curtain permitted Robin to
distinguish a party at supper, round a well-furnished table.
The fragrance of the good cheer steamed forth into the
outer air, and the youth could not fail to recollect, that the
last remnant of his travelling stock of provision had yielded
to his morning appetite, and that noon had found, and left
him, dinnerless.

'Oh, that a parchment three-penny might give me a right
to sit down at yonder table,' said Robin, with a sigh. 'But
the Major will make me welcome to the best of his victuals;
so I will even step boldly in, and inquire my way to his
dwelling.'

He entered the tavern, and was guided by the murmur of
voices, and fumes of tobacco, to the public room. It was a
long and low apartment, with oaken walls, grown dark in
the continual smoke, and a floor, which was thickly sanded,
but of no immaculate purity. A number of persons, the
larger part of whom appeared to be mariners, or in some way
connected with the sea, occupied the wooden benches, or
leather-bottomed chairs, conversing on various matters, and
occasionally lending their attention to some topic of general
interest. Three or four little groups were draining as many
bowls of punch, which the great West India trade had long
since made a familiar drink in the colony. Others, who had
the aspect of men who lived by regular and laborious handicraft, preferred the insulated bliss of an unshared potation,
and became more taciturn under its influence. Nearly all,
in short, evinced a predilection for the Good Creature in
some of its various shapes, for this is a vice, to which, as the
Fast-day sermons of a hundred years ago will testify, we

have a long hereditary claim. The only guests to whom Robin's sympathies inclined him, were two or three sheepish countrymen, who were using the inn somewhat after the fashion of a Turkish Caravansary; they had gotten themselves into the darkest corner of the room, and, heedless of the Nicotian atmosphere, were supping on the bread of their own ovens, and the bacon cured in their own chimney-smoke. But though Robin felt a sort of brotherhood with these strangers, his eyes were attracted from them, to a person who stood near the door, holding whispered conversation with a group of ill-dressed associates. His features were separately striking almost to grotesqueness, and the whole face left a deep impression in the memory. The forehead bulged out into a double prominence, with a vale between; the nose came boldly forth in an irregular curve, and its bridge was of more than a finger's breadth; the eyebrows were deep and shaggy, and the eyes glowed beneath them like fire in a cave.

While Robin deliberated of whom to inquire respecting his kinsman's dwelling, he was accosted by the innkeeper, a little man in a stained white apron, who had come to pay his professional welcome to the stranger. Being in the second generation from a French Protestant, he seemed to have inherited the courtesy of his parent nation; but no variety of circumstance was ever known to change his voice from the one shrill note in which he now addressed Robin.

'From the country, I presume, Sir?' said he, with a profound bow. 'Beg to congratulate you on your arrival, and trust you intend a long stay with us. Fine town here, Sir, beautiful buildings, and much that may interest a stranger. May I hope for the honor of your commands in respect to supper?'

'The man sees a family likeness! the rogue has guessed that I am related to the Major!' thought Robin, who had hitherto experienced little superfluous civility.

All eyes were now turned on the country lad, standing at the door, in his worn three-cornered hat, grey coat, leather breeches, and blue yarn stockings, leaning on an oaken cudgel, and bearing a wallet on his back.

Robin replied to the courteous innkeeper, with such an assumption of consequence, as befitted the Major's relative.

'My honest friend,' he said, 'I shall make it a point to patronize your house on some occasion, when—' here he could not help lowering his voice—'I may have more than a parchment three-pence in my pocket. My present business,' continued he, speaking with lofty confidence, 'is merely to inquire the way to the dwelling of my kinsman, Major Molineux.'

There was a sudden and general movement in the room, which Robin interpreted as expressing the eagerness of each individual to become his guide. But the innkeeper turned his eyes to a written paper on the wall, which he read, or seemed to read, with occasional recurrences to the young man's figure.

'What have we here?' said he, breaking his speech into little dry fragments. ' "Left the house of the subscriber, bounden servant, Hezekiah Mudge—had on, when he went away, grey coat, leather breeches, master's third best hat. One pound currency reward to whoever shall lodge him in any jail in the province." Better trudge, boy, better trudge!'

Robin had begun to draw his hand towards the lighter end of the oak cudgel, but a strange hostility in every countenance, induced him to relinquish his purpose of breaking the courteous innkeeper's head. As he turned to leave the room, he encountered a sneering glance from the bold-featured personage whom he had before noticed; and no sooner was he beyond the door, than he heard a general laugh, in which the innkeeper's voice might be distinguished, like the dropping of small stones into a kettle.

'Now is it not strange,' thought Robin, with his usual shrewdness, 'is it not strange, that the confession of an empty pocket, should outweigh the name of my kinsman, Major Molineux? Oh, if I had one of these grinning rascals in the woods, where I and my oak sapling grew up together, I would teach him that my arm is heavy, though my purse be light!'

On turning the corner of the narrow lane, Robin found himself in a spacious street, with an unbroken line of lofty houses on each side, and a steepled building at the upper end, whence the ringing of a bell announced the hour of nine. The light of the moon, and the lamps from numerous shop windows, discovered people promenading on the pavement, and amongst them, Robin hoped to recognize his hitherto inscrutable relative. The result of his former inquiries made him unwilling to hazard another, in a scene of such publicity, and he determined to walk slowly and silently up the street, thrusting his face close to that of every elderly gentleman, in search of the Major's lineaments. In his progress, Robin encountered many gay and gallant figures. Embroidered garments, of showy colors, enormous periwigs, gold-laced hats, and silver hilted swords, glided past him and dazzled his optics. Travelled youths, imitators of the European fine gentlemen of the period, trod jauntily along, half-dancing to the fashionable tunes which they hummed, and making poor Robin ashamed of his quiet and natural gait. At length, after many pauses to examine the gorgeous display of goods in the shop windows, and after suffering some rebukes for the impertinence of his scrutiny into people's faces, the Major's kinsman found himself near the steepled building, still unsuccessful in his search. As yet, however, he had seen only one side of the thronged street; so Robin crossed, and continued the same sort of inquisition down the opposite pavement, with stronger hopes than the philosopher seeking an honest man, but with no better fortune. He had arrived about midway towards the lower end, from which his course began, when he overheard the approach of some one, who struck down a cane on the flag-stones at every step, uttering, at regular intervals, two sepulchral hems.

'Mercy on us!' quoth Robin, recognizing the sound.

Turning a corner, which chanced to be close at his right hand, he hastened to pursue his researches, in some other part of the town. His patience was now wearing low, and he seemed to feel more fatigue from his rambles since he crossed the ferry, than from his journey of several days on the other side. Hunger also pleaded loudly within him, and Robin began to balance the propriety of demanding, violently and with lifted cudgel, the necessary guidance from the first solitary passenger, whom he should meet. While a resolution to this effect was gaining strength, he entered a street of mean appearance, on either side of which, a row of ill-built houses was straggling towards the harbor. The moonlight fell upon no passenger along the whole extent, but in the third domicile which Robin passed, there was a half-opened door, and his keen glance detected a woman's garment within.

'My luck may be better here,' said he to himself.

Accordingly, he approached the door, and beheld it shut closer as he did so; yet an open space remained, sufficing for the fair occupant to observe the stranger, without a corresponding display on her part. All that Robin could discern was a strip of scarlet petticoat, and the occasional sparkle of an eye, as if the moonbeams were trembling on some bright thing.

'Pretty mistress,'—for I may call her so with a good conscience, thought the shrewd youth, since I know nothing to the contrary—'my sweet pretty mistress, will you be kind enough to tell me whereabouts I must seek the dwelling of my kinsman, Major Molineux?'

Robin's voice was plaintive and winning, and the female, seeing nothing to be shunned in the handsome country youth, thrust open the door, and came forth into the moonlight. She was a dainty little figure, with a white neck, round arms, and a slender waist, at the extremity of which her scarlet petticoat jutted out over a hoop, as if she were standing in a balloon. Moreover, her face was oval and pretty, her hair dark beneath the little cap, and her bright eyes possessed a sly freedom, which triumphed over those of Robin.

'Major Molineux dwells here,' said this fair woman.

Now her voice was the sweetest Robin had heard that night, the airy counterpart of a stream of melted silver; yet he could not help doubting whether that sweet voice spoke Gospel truth. He looked up and down the mean street, and then surveyed the house before which they stood. It was a small, dark edifice of two stories, the second of which projected over the lower floor; and the front apartment had the aspect of a shop for petty commodities.

'Now truly I am in luck,' replied Robin, cunningly, 'and so indeed is my kinsman, the Major, in having so pretty a housekeeper. But I prithee trouble him to step to the door; I will deliver him a message from his friends in the country, and then go back to my lodgings at the inn.'

'Nay, the Major has been a-bed this hour or more,' said the lady of the scarlet petticoat; 'and it would be to little purpose to disturb him to-night, seeing his evening draught was of the strongest. But he is a kind-hearted man, and it would be as much as my life's worth, to let a kinsman of his turn away from the door. You are the good old gentleman's very picture, and I could swear that was his rainy-weather hat. Also, he has garments very much resembling those leather—But come in, I pray, for I bid you hearty welcome in his name.'

So saying, the fair and hospitable dame took our hero by the hand; and though the touch was light, and the force was gentleness, and though Robin read in her eyes what he did not hear in her words, yet the slender waisted woman, in the scarlet petticoat, proved stronger than the athletic country youth. She had drawn his half-willing footsteps nearly to the threshold, when the opening of a door in the neighborhood, startled the Major's housekeeper, and, leaving the Major's kinsman, she vanished speedily into her own domicile. A heavy yawn preceded the appearance of a man, who, like the Moonshine of Pyramus and Thisbe, carried a lantern, needlessly aiding his sister luminary in the heavens. As he walked sleepily up the street, he turned his broad, dull face on Robin, and displayed a long staff, spiked at the end.

'Home, vagabond, home!' said the watchman, in accents that seemed to fall asleep as soon as they were uttered. 'Home, or we'll set you in the stocks by peep of day!'

'This is the second hint of the kind,' thought Robin. 'I wish they would end my difficulties, by setting me there to-night.'

Nevertheless, the youth felt an instinctive antipathy towards the guardian of midnight order, which at first prevented him from asking his usual question. But just when the man was about to vanish behind the corner, Robin resolved not to lose the opportunity, and shouted lustily after him—

'I say, friend! will you guide me to the house of my kinsman, Major Molineux?'

The watchman made no reply, but turned the corner and was gone; yet Robin seemed to hear the sound of drowsy laughter stealing along the solitary street. At that moment, also, a pleasant titter saluted him from the open window above his head; he looked up, and caught the sparkle of a saucy eye; a round arm beckoned to him, and next he heard light footsteps descending the staircase within. But Robin, being of the household of a New England clergyman, was a good youth, as well as a shrewd one; so he resisted temptation, and fled away.

He now roamed desperately, and at random, through the town, almost ready to believe that a spell was on him, like that, by which a wizard of his country, had once kept three pursuers wandering, a whole winter night, within twenty paces of the cottage which they sought. The streets lay before him, strange and desolate, and the lights were extinguished in almost every house. Twice, however, little parties of men, among whom Robin distinguished individuals in outlandish attire, came hurrying along, but though on both occasions they paused to address him, such intercourse did not at all enlighten his perplexity. They did but utter a few words in some language of which Robin knew nothing, and perceiving his inability to answer, bestowed a curse upon him in plain English, and hastened away. Finally, the lad determined to knock at the door of every mansion that might appear worthy to be occupied by his kinsman, trusting that perseverance would overcome the fatality which had hitherto thwarted him. Firm in this resolve, he was passing beneath the walls of a church, which formed the corner of two streets, when, as he turned into the shade of its steeple, he encountered a bulky stranger, muffled in a cloak. The man was proceeding with the speed of earnest business, but Robin planted himself full before him, holding the oak cudgel with both hands across his body, as a bar to further passage.

'Halt, honest man, and answer me a question,' said he, very resolutely. 'Tell me, this instant, whereabouts is the dwelling of my kinsman, Major Molineux?'

'Keep your tongue between your teeth, fool, and let me pass,' said a deep, gruff voice, which Robin partly remembered. 'Let me pass, I say, or I'll strike you to the earth!'

'No, no, neighbor!' cried Robin, flourishing his cudgel, and then thrusting its larger end close to the man's muffled face. 'No, no, I'm not the fool you take me for, nor do you pass, till I have an answer to my question. Whereabouts is the dwelling of my kinsman, Major Molineux?'

The stranger, instead of attempting to force his passage, stept back into the moonlight, unmuffled his own face and stared full into that of Robin.

'Watch here an hour, and Major Molineux will pass by,' said he.

Robin gazed with dismay and astonishment, on the unprecedented physiognomy of the speaker. The forehead with its double prominence, the broad-hooked nose, the shaggy eyebrows, and fiery eyes, were those which he had noticed at the inn, but the man's complexion had undergone a singular, or, more properly, a two-fold change. One side of the face blazed of an intense red, while the other was black as midnight, the division line being in the broad bridge of the nose; and a mouth, which seemed to extend from ear to ear, was black or red, in contrast to the color of the cheek. The effect was as if two individual devils, a fiend of fire and a fiend of darkness, had united themselves to form this infernal visage. The stranger grinned in Robin's face, muffled his parti-colored features, and was out of sight in a moment.

'Strange things we travellers see!' ejaculated Robin.

He seated himself, however, upon the steps of the church-door, resolving to wait the appointed time for his kinsman's appearance. A few moments were consumed in philosophical speculations, upon the species of the *genus homo*, who had just left him, but having settled this point shrewdly, rationally, and satisfactorily, he was compelled to look elsewhere for amusement. And first he threw his eyes along the street; it was of more respectable appearance than most of those into which he had wandered, and the moon, 'creating, like the imaginative power, a beautiful strangeness in familiar objects,' gave something of romance to a scene, that might not have possessed it in the light of day. The irregular, and often quaint architecture of the houses, some of whose roofs were broken into numerous little peaks; while others ascended, steep and narrow, into a single point; and others again were square; the pure milk-white of some of their complexions, the aged darkness of others, and the thousand sparklings, reflected from bright substances in the plastered walls of many; these matters engaged Robin's attention for awhile, and then began to grow wearisome. Next he endeavored to define the forms of distant objects, starting away with almost ghostly indistinctness, just as his eye appeared to grasp them; and finally he took a minute survey of an edifice, which stood on the opposite side of the street, directly in front of the church-door, where he was stationed. It was a large square mansion, distinguished from its neighbors by a balcony, which rested on tall pillars, and by an elaborate Gothic window, communicating therewith.

'Perhaps this is the very house I have been seeking,' thought Robin.

Then he strove to speed away the time, by listening to a murmur, which swept continually along the street, yet was scarcely audible, except to an unaccustomed ear like his; it was a low, dull, dreamy sound, compounded of many noises, each of which was at too great a distance to be separately heard. Robin marvelled at this snore of a sleeping town, and marvelled more, whenever its continuity was broken, by now and then a distant shout, apparently loud where it originated. But altogether it was a sleep-inspiring sound, and to shake off its drowsy influence, Robin arose, and climbed a window-frame, that he might view the interior of the church. There the moonbeams came trembling in, and fell down upon the deserted pews, and extended along the quiet aisles. A fainter, yet more awful radiance, was hovering round the pulpit, and one solitary ray had dared to rest upon the opened page of the great Bible. Had Nature, in that deep hour, become a worshipper in the house, which man had builded? Or was that heavenly light the visible sanctity of the place, visible because no earthly and impure feet were within the walls? The scene made Robin's heart shiver with a sensation of loneliness, stronger than he had ever felt in the remotest depths of his native woods; so he turned away, and sat down again before the door. There were graves around the church, and now an uneasy thought obtruded into Robin's breast. What if the object of his search, which had been so often and so strangely thwarted, were all the time mouldering in his shroud? What if his kinsman should glide through yonder gate, and nod and smile to him in passing dimly by?

'Oh, that any breathing thing were here with me!' said Robin.

Recalling his thoughts from this uncomfortable track, he sent them over forest, hill, and stream, and attempted to imagine how that evening of ambiguity and weariness, had been spent by his father's household. He pictured them assembled at the door, beneath the tree, the great old tree, which had been spared for its huge twisted trunk, and venerable shade, when a thousand leafy brethren fell. There, at the going down of the summer sun, it was his father's custom to perform domestic worship, that the neighbors might come and join with him like brothers of the family, and that the wayfaring man might pause to drink at that fountain, and keep his heart pure by freshening the memory of home. Robin distinguished the seat of every individual of the little audience; he saw the good man in the midst, holding the Scriptures in the golden light that shone from the western clouds; he beheld him close the book, and all rise up to pray. He heard the old thanksgivings for daily mercies, the old supplications for their continuance, to which he had so often listened in weariness, but which were now among his dear remembrances. He perceived the slight inequality of his father's voice when he came to speak of the Absent One; he noted how his mother turned her face to the broad and knotted trunk; how his elder brother scorned, because the beard was rough upon his upper lip, to permit his features to be moved; how his younger sister drew down a low hanging branch before her eyes; and how the little one of all, whose sports had hitherto broken the decorum of the scene, understood the prayer for her playmate, and burst into clamorous grief. Then he saw them go in at the door; and when Robin would have entered also, the latch tinkled into its place, and he was excluded from his home.

'Am I here, or there?' cried Robin, starting; for all at once, when his thoughts had become visible and audible in a dream, the long, wide, solitary street shone out before him.

He aroused himself, and endeavored to fix his attention steadily upon the large edifice which he had surveyed before. But still his mind kept vibrating between fancy and reality; by turns, the pillars of the balcony lengthened into the tall, bare stems of pines, dwindled down to human figures, settled again in their true shape and size, and then commenced a new succession of changes. For a single moment, when he deemed himself awake, he could have sworn that a visage, one which he seemed to remember, yet could not absolutely name as his kinsman's, was looking towards him from the Gothic window. A deeper sleep wrestled with, and nearly overcame him, but fled at the sound of footsteps along the opposite pavement. Robin rubbed his eyes, discerned a man passing at the foot of the balcony, and addressed him in a loud, peevish, and lamentable cry.

'Halloo, friend! must I wait here all night for my kinsman, Major Molineux?'

The sleeping echoes awoke, and answered the voice; and the passenger, barely able to discern a figure sitting in the oblique shade of the steeple, traversed the street to obtain a nearer view. He was himself a gentleman in his prime, of open, intelligent, cheerful, and altogether prepossessing countenance. Perceiving a country youth, apparently homeless and without friends, he accosted him in a tone of real kindness, which had become strange to Robin's ears.

'Well, my good lad, why are you sitting here?' inquired he. 'Can I be of service to you in any way?'

'I am afraid not, Sir,' replied Robin, despondingly; 'yet I shall take it kindly, if you'll answer me a single question. I've been searching half the night for one Major Molineux; now, Sir, is there really such a person in these parts, or am I dreaming?'

'Major Molineux! The name is not altogether strange to me,' said the gentleman, smiling. 'Have you any objection to telling me the nature of your business with him?'

Then Robin briefly related that his father was a clergyman, settled on a small salary, at a long distance back in the country, and that he and Major Molineux were brothers' children. The Major, having inherited riches, and acquired civil and military rank, had visited his cousin in great pomp a year or two before; had manifested much interest in Robin and an elder brother, and, being childless himself, had thrown out hints respecting the future establishment of one of them in life. The elder brother was destined to succeed to the farm, which his father cultivated, in the interval of sacred duties; it was therefore determined that Robin should profit by his kinsman's generous intentions, especially as he had seemed to be rather the favorite, and was thought to possess other necessary endowments.

'For I have the name of being a shrewd youth,' observed Robin, in this part of his story.

'I doubt not you deserve it,' replied his new friend, good naturedly; 'but pray proceed.'

'Well, Sir, being nearly eighteen years old, and well grown, as you see,' continued Robin, raising himself to his full height, 'I thought it high time to begin the world. So my mother and sister put me in handsome trim, and my father gave me half the remnant of his last year's salary, and five days ago I started for this place, to pay the Major a visit. But would you believe it, Sir? I crossed the ferry a little after dusk, and have yet found nobody that would show me the way to his dwelling; only an hour or two since, I was told to wait here, and Major Molineux would pass by.'

'Can you describe the man who told you this?' inquired the gentleman.

'Oh, he was a very ill-favored fellow, Sir,' replied Robin, 'with two great bumps on his forehead, a hook nose, fiery eyes, and, what struck me as the strangest, his face was of two different colors. Do you happen to know such a man, Sir?'

'Not intimately,' answered the stranger, 'but I chanced to meet him a little time previous to your stopping me. I believe you may trust his word, and that the Major will very shortly pass through this street. In the mean time, as I have a singular curiosity to witness your meeting, I will sit down here upon the steps, and bear you company.'

He seated himself accordingly, and soon engaged his companion in animated discourse. It was but of brief continuance, however, for a noise of shouting, which had long been remotely audible, drew so much nearer, that Robin inquired its cause.

'What may be the meaning of this uproar?' asked he. 'Truly, if your town be always as noisy, I shall find little sleep, while I am an inhabitant.'

'Why, indeed, friend Robin, there do appear to be three or four riotous fellows abroad to-night,' replied the gentleman. 'You must not expect all the stillness of your native woods, here in our streets. But the watch will shortly be at the heels of these lads, and—'

'Aye, and set them in the stocks by peep of day,' interrupted Robin, recollecting his own encounter with the drowsy lantern-bearer. 'But, dear Sir, if I may trust my ears, an army of watchmen would never make head against such a multitude of rioters. There were at least a thousand voices went to make up that one shout.'

'May not one man have several voices, Robin, as well as two complexions?' said his friend.

'Perhaps a man may; but Heaven forbid that a woman should!' responded the shrewd youth, thinking of the seductive tones of the Major's housekeeper.

The sounds of a trumpet in some neighboring street now became so evident and continual, that Robin's curiosity was strongly excited. In addition to the shouts, he heard frequent bursts from many instruments of discord, and a wild and confused laughter filled up the intervals. Robin rose from the steps, and looked wistfully towards a point, whither several people seemed to be hastening.

'Surely some prodigious merrymaking is going on,' exclaimed he. 'I have laughed very little since I left home, Sir, and should be sorry to lose an opportunity. Shall we just step round the corner by that darkish house, and take our share of the fun?'

'Sit down again, sit down, good Robin,' replied the gentleman, laying his hand on the skirt of the grey coat. 'You forget that we must wait here for your kinsman; and there is reason to believe that he will pass by, in the course of a very few moments.'

The near approach of the uproar had now disturbed the neighborhood; windows flew open on all sides; and many heads, in the attire of the pillow, and confused by sleep suddenly broken, were protruded to the gaze of whoever had leisure to observe them. Eager voices hailed each other from house to house, all demanding the explanation, which not a soul could give. Half-dressed men hurried towards the unknown commotion, stumbling as they went over the stone steps, that thrust themselves into the narrow foot-walk. The shouts, the laughter, and the tuneless bray, the antipodes of music, came onward with increasing din, till scattered individuals, and then denser bodies, began to appear round a corner, at the distance of a hundred yards.

'Will you recognize your kinsman, Robin, if he passes in this crowd?' inquired the gentleman.

'Indeed, I can't warrant it, Sir; but I'll take my stand here, and keep a bright look out,' answered Robin, descending to the outer edge of the pavement.

A mighty stream of people now emptied into the street, and came rolling slowly towards the church. A single horseman wheeled the corner in the midst of them, and close behind him came a band of fearful wind-instruments, sending forth a fresher discord, now that no intervening buildings kept it from the ear. Then a redder light disturbed the moonbeams, and a dense multitude of torches shone along the street, concealing by their glare whatever object they illuminated. The single horseman, clad in a military dress, and bearing a drawn sword, rode onward as the leader, and, by his fierce and variegated countenance, appeared like war personified; the red of one cheek was an emblem of fire and sword; the blackness of the other betokened the mourning which attends them. In his train, were wild figures in the

Indian dress, and many fantastic shapes without a model, giving the whole march a visionary air, as if a dream had broken forth from some feverish brain, and were sweeping visibly through the midnight streets. A mass of people, inactive, except as applauding spectators, hemmed the procession in, and several women ran along the sidewalks, piercing the confusion of heavier sounds, with their shrill voices of mirth or terror.

'The double-faced fellow has his eye upon me,' muttered Robin, with an indefinite but uncomfortable idea, that he was himself to bear a part in the pageantry.

The leader turned himself in the saddle, and fixed his glance full upon the country youth, as the steed went slowly by. When Robin had freed his eyes from those fiery ones, the musicians were passing before him, and the torches were close at hand; but the unsteady brightness of the latter formed a veil which he could not penetrate. The rattling of wheels over the stones sometimes found its way to his ear, and confused traces of a human form appeared at intervals, and then melted into the vivid light. A moment more, and the leader thundered a command to halt; the trumpets vomited a horrid breath, and held their peace; the shouts and laughter of the people died away, and there remained only a universal hum, nearly allied to silence. Right before Robin's eyes was an uncovered cart. There the torches blazed the brightest, there the moon shone out like day, and there, in tar-and-feathery dignity, sate his kinsman, Major Molineux!

He was an elderly man, of large and majestic person, and strong, square features, betokening a steady soul; but steady as it was, his enemies had found the means to shake it. His face was pale as death, and far more ghastly; the broad forehead was contracted in his agony, so that his eyebrows formed one grizzled line; his eyes were red and wild, and the foam hung white upon his quivering lip. His whole frame was

agitated by a quick, and continual tremor, which his pride
strove to quell, even in those circumstances of overwhelming
humiliation. But perhaps the bitterest pang of all was when
his eyes met those of Robin; for he evidently knew him on
the instant, as the youth stood witnessing the foul disgrace
of a head that had grown grey in honor. They stared at each
other in silence, and Robin's knees shook, and his hair
bristled, with a mixture of pity and terror. Soon, however,
a bewildering excitement began to seize upon his mind; the
preceding adventures of the night, the unexpected appearance of the crowd, the torches, the confused din, and the
hush that followed, the spectre of his kinsman reviled by
that great multitude, all this, and more than all, a perception of tremendous ridicule in the whole scene, affected him
with a sort of mental inebriety. At that moment a voice of
sluggish merriment saluted Robin's ears; he turned instinctively, and just behind the corner of the church stood the
lantern-bearer, rubbing his eyes, and drowsily enjoying the
lad's amazement. Then he heard a peal of laughter like the
ringing of silvery bells; a woman twitched his arm, a saucy
eye met his, and he saw the lady of the scarlet petticoat. A
sharp, dry cachinnation appealed to his memory, and, standing on tiptoe in the crowd, with his white apron over his
head, he beheld the courteous little innkeeper. And lastly,
there sailed over the heads of the multitude a great, broad
laugh, broken in the midst by two sepulchral hems; thus—
'Haw, haw, haw—hem, hem—haw, haw, haw, haw!'
The sound proceeded from the balcony of the opposite
edifice, and thither Robin turned his eyes. In front of the
Gothic window stood the old citizen, wrapped in a wide
gown, his grey periwig exchanged for a nightcap, which was
thrust back from his forehead, and his silk stockings hanging
down about his legs. He supported himself on his polished
cane in a fit of convulsive merriment, which manifested itself

on his solemn old features, like a funny inscription on a tomb-stone. Then Robin seemed to hear the voices of the barbers; of the guests of the inn; and of all who had made sport of him that night. The contagion was spreading among the multitude, when, all at once, it seized upon Robin, and he sent forth a shout of laughter that echoed through the street; every man shook his sides, every man emptied his lungs, but Robin's shout was the loudest there. The cloud-spirits peeped from their silvery islands, as the congregated mirth went roaring up the sky! The Man in the Moon heard the far bellow; 'Oho,' quoth he, 'the old Earth is frolicsome to-night!'

When there was a momentary calm in that tempestuous sea of sound, the leader gave the sign, the procession resumed its march. On they went, like fiends that throng in mockery round some dead potentate, mighty no more, but majestic still in his agony. On they went, in counterfeited pomp, in senseless uproar, in frenzied merriment, trampling all on an old man's heart. On swept the tumult, and left a silent street behind.

'Well, Robin, are you dreaming?' inquired the gentleman, laying his hand on the youth's shoulder.

Robin started, and withdrew his arm from the stone post, to which he had instinctively clung, while the living stream rolled by him. His cheek was somewhat pale, and his eye not quite so lively as in the earlier part of the evening.

'Will you be kind enough to show me the way to the ferry?' said he, after a moment's pause.

'You have then adopted a new subject of inquiry?' observed his companion, with a smile.

'Why, yes, Sir,' replied Robin, rather dryly. 'Thanks to you, and to my other friends, I have at last met my kinsman, and he will scarce desire to see my face again. I begin to grow weary of a town life, Sir. Will you show me the way to the ferry?'

'No, my good friend Robin, not to-night, at least,' said the gentleman. 'Some few days hence, if you continue to wish it, I will speed you on your journey. Or, if you prefer to remain with us, perhaps, as you are a shrewd youth, you may rise in the world, without the help of your kinsman, Major Molineux.'

UNCOLLECTED TALES

THE BATTLE-OMEN

THE LATEST INCIDENT of this nature is said to have occurred on a cold, bright evening, during the winter that preceded the first actual hostilities in our great War. Two young men were returning from one of those military meetings, which the aspect of the times had rendered common throughout the country, and in which their education and active talents had given each of them a degree of authority. Their path lay over the frozen surface of a lake, extending two or three miles between the northern and south-western shores. Behind the travellers was the village from which they came,—a few dark houses in distant visibility upon the snow, and the white spire of the Church as strongly relieved against the sky; before them, and at still a greater distance, appeared their own more solitary home; and around all the remaining horizon stretched the forest, as desolate as if human foot had never trod there. The frosty sky glittered as if with diamonds above their heads; while the lake beneath them was scarcely less brilliant, except where its snowy mantle had been blown aside, so as to afford a glimpse of its black and inscrutable heart. The young men pursued their way rapidly, inhaling fresh cheerfulness with each draught of the elastic atmosphere. Merrily trod they over the crumpling snow, or slid across the long intervals of glary ice, singing and laughing till the sky and the far shores caught the spirit of their lonely mirth and sent it back to them. At times, also, they spoke of the approaching contest, almost forgetting the threatened ruin of their country, in the stirring prospects which were opened to youthful ambition.

"Is it not strange," said one of the young men, laughingly, "that these near commotions are foretold by none of the wild oracles, which our fathers were wont to hear, on occasions of so much less interest? Their petty warfare,—in which the utmost damage amounted to no more than the burning of a few farm-houses, and here and there a husbandman slain in his corn field,—was invariably preceded by signs and omens, as if all Nature were affrighted at the prospect of an Indian campaign. Now, here we stand on the verge of a war that may chance to separate two worlds, and not so much as a trumpet in the air has sounded its approach."

"True; the Pilgrims were a favored people," said his companion, whose earlier life had not been spent in the vicinity where he now found himself. "But if we had inherited the gloom of their religious faith, the winds in the forest, and the meteors in the sky, would have prophesied also to us."

"You must not suppose," rejoined the other, "that these supernatural warnings were witnessed only by persons of peculiar sanctity, or that they were wholly confined to the earliest days of the country. Indeed, it was an instance to the contrary in both these respects, (the scene of which is not far distant,) that drew from me my first remark. Do you see yonder dark speck in the snow? Some fifty years since, a fisherman made his boat fast to that rock;—intent either on his hook and line, or upon a brown jug, he tarried till late in the summer evening; and when he landed, he had a strange story to astonish his neighbors withal."

"We will rest there awhile, and you shall tell me the legend on the very spot," said his friend.

The insulated rock rose two or three feet above the ice, and was covered with rudely engraved characters attributed to the Indians, a powerful tribe of whom have left the memorials of their existence and annihilation round all the borders of that lake. The story which has been alluded to was one of a numerous class, often to be met with in the traditions of New England, and sanctioned by the sober pages of her old historians. A benighted fisherman had heard a sound of martial music in the air above him, coming from the direction of the Canadas, (whence both the savage and civilized enemies of the country might be expected to advance,) and passing onward to the settlements on the sea coast. Most of the apocryphal beliefs of the Puritans were the result of strong, but not of elevated imagination, and what was terrible in them has lost its effect upon modern minds, by the too frequent admixture of the ludicrous and disgusting. But this remark is inapplicable to all the signs and wonders by which they were warned of approaching war. These superstitions (if it be consistent, just now, to term them so) were the coinage of perilous and awful moments; they imbibed a desolate romance from the circumstances which formed them, and neither purification nor ornament could render them more poetical than when they issued from the hearts of our forefathers. The presage by the sound of drum and trumpet was peculiarly grand and lofty, but it would have been too cold in its magnificence, if a most singular opinion had not increased its power over human sympathies. There was a dim and indefinite idea, that the shadowy tread of the destined victims, the future slain of unfought battle-fields, might be heard to accompany the prophetic music through the sky.

In such subjects as these the young men became gradually engaged, till their talk acquired the earnestness of deep belief. The wind, as it howled over the snowy waste and buried itself in the forest, began to startle them by its resemblance to the spiritual minstrelsy, and the ice-crack, thundering heavily from shore to shore, rang upon their ears like the roar of cannon. And the Northern Lights—(Fancy's own Watch-Fires, now gleaming and quivering far towards the middle sky, so as to throw their mysterious radiance over the Milky Way)—might readily have assumed the aspect of armed hosts and flaming towns, apparitions not unknown to the men of olden time. After a silence, which had fallen on them they knew not how, one of the travellers laid his hand upon his companion's arm.

"Surely our comrades had separated long ago," whispered he, looking towards the village—"why do they beat the drum at such an hour?"

The church steeple, its attendant houses, and the snowy ascent upon which they stood, were distinctly visible, but there was no token of wakefulness anywhere about them. As the young men gazed, another far off and uncertain swell, like the ghost of music, just grazed upon their ears.

"The sound came out from thence," said they both, shuddering as they drew closer to each other.

A third and nearer repetition of the same phenomenon now marked its origin as in the east, where the wilderness lay dark and desolate for many a mile, undisturbed from the creation till that hour by other notes than those of an Indian War Song. Again they heard it, low down towards the horizon, but ascending along the arch of the sky, alternately pealing forth as with the full breath of many instruments, and then dying away till the ear scarce caught its murmur— even in its loudest tones there was such unreality, that the listeners doubted whether all were not the echo of their own excited thoughts. The clarion was there, the drum, the cymbal, and every instrument of music that should quicken the soul to war; but the notes of all were sad and solemn, like the evening wind that sighs over a field of victory, or like the stately and mournful march with which a hero is borne to his grave. As the sound kept onward in its airy course, the stars still twinkled brightly, and there was neither substance nor shadow, nor so much as a thought-like cloud, between them and the earth. There was no echo from the shore and sky, but only that mysterious music, passing on in solitude. And yet, for one brief moment, the solitude seemed broken by the clash of arms, the rustle and waving of garments, the undefinable hum of a viewless multitude, journeying through the awful brightness of the night. Then came familiar voices—there were two that spoke and replied —and the young men gazed at each other, deeming that their own bloodless lips had moved. A mighty peal of harmony broke forth, as the omen swept above their heads; it died away in regular gradations till the western woods received it into their bosom; and there its distant wail was lost.

AN OLD WOMAN'S TALE

I N THE HOUSE where I was born, there used to be
an old woman crouching all day long over the kitchen
fire, with her elbows on her knees and her feet in the
ashes. Once in a while she took a turn at the spit, and she
never lacked a coarse gray stocking in her lap, the foot about
half finished; it tapered away with her own waning life and
she knit the toe-stitch on the day of her death. She made it
her serious business and sole amusement to tell me stories
at any time from morning till night, in a mumbling, toothless voice, as I sat on a log of wood, grasping her check-
apron in both my hands. Her personal memory included the
better part of a hundred years, and she had strangely jumbled
her own experience and observation with those of many old
people who died in her young days; so that she might have
been taken for a contemporary of Queen Elizabeth, or of
John Rogers in the Primer. There are a thousand of her
traditions lurking in the corners and by-places of my mind,
some more marvellous than what is to follow, some less so,
and a few not marvellous in the least, all which I should
like to repeat, if I were as happy as she in having a listener.
But I am humble enough to own, that I do not deserve a

listener half so well as that old toothless woman, whose narratives possessed an excellence attributable neither to herself, nor to any single individual. Her ground-plots, seldom within the widest scope of probability, were filled up with homely and natural incidents, the gradual accretions of a long course of years, and fiction hid its grotesque extravagance in this garb of truth, like the devil (an appropriate simile, for the old woman supplies it) disguising himself, cloven-foot and all, in mortal attire. These tales generally referred to her birth-place, a village in the Valley of the Connecticut, the aspect of which she impressed with great vividness on my fancy. The houses in that tract of country, long a wild and dangerous frontier, were rendered defensible by a strength of architecture that has preserved many of them till our own times, and I cannot describe the sort of pleasure with which, two summers since, I rode through the little town in question, while one object after another rose familiarly to my eye, like successive portions of a dream becoming realized. Among other things equally probable, she was wont to assert that all the inhabitants of this village (at certain intervals, but whether of twenty-five or fifty years, or a whole century, remained a disputable point) were subject to a simultaneous slumber, continuing one hour's space. When that mysterious time arrived, the parson snored over his half-written sermon, though it were Saturday night and no provision made for the morrow,—the mother's eyelids closed as she bent over her infant, and no childish cry awakened her,—the watcher at the bed of mortal sickness slumbered upon the death pillow,—and the dying man anticipated his sleep of ages by one as deep and dreamless. To speak emphatically, there was a soporific influence throughout the village, stronger than if every mother's son and daughter were reading a dull story; notwithstanding which, the old woman professed to hold the substance of the ensuing account from one of those principally concerned in it.

One moonlight summer evening, a young man and a girl sat down together in the open air. They were distant relatives, sprung from a stock once wealthy, but of late years so poverty stricken, that David had not a penny to pay the marriage fee, if Esther should consent to wed. The seat they had chosen was in an open grove of elm and walnut trees, at a right angle of the road; a spring of diamond water just bubbled into the moonlight beside them, and then whimpered away through the bushes and long grass, in search of a neighboring mill-stream. The nearest house (situate within twenty yards of them, and the residence of their great-grandfather in his life time) was a venerable old edifice, crowned with many high and narrow peaks, and all overrun by innumerable creeping plants, which hung curling about the roof like a nice young wig on an elderly gentleman's head. Opposite to this establishment was a tavern, with a well and horse-trough before it, and a low green bank running along the left side of the door. Thence, the road went onward, curving scarce perceptibly, through the village, divided in the midst by a narrow lane of verdure, and bounded on each side by a grassy strip of twice its own breadth. The houses had generally an odd look. Here, the moonlight tried to get a glimpse of one, a rough old heap of ponderous timber, which, ashamed of its dilapidated aspect, was hiding behind a great thick tree; the lower story of the next had sunk almost under ground, as if the poor little house were a-weary of the world, and retiring into the seclusion of its own cellar; farther on, stood one of the few recent structures, thrusting its painted face conspicuously into the street, with an evident idea that it was the fairest thing there. About midway in the village was a grist-mill, partly concealed by the descent of the ground towards the stream which turned its wheel. At the southern extremity, just so far distant that the window-panes dazzled into each other, rose the meeting-house, a dingy old barnlike building, with an enormously disproportioned steeple sticking up straight into Heaven, as high as the Tower of Babel, and the cause of nearly as much confusion in its day. This steeple, it must be understood, was an afterthought, and its addition to the main edifice, when the latter had already begun to decay, had excited a vehement quarrel, and almost a schism in the church, some fifty years before. Here the road wound down a hill and was seen no more, the remotest object in view being the grave-yard gate, beyond the meeting-house. The youthful pair sat hand in hand beneath the trees, and for several moments they had not spoken, because the breeze was hushed, the brook scarce tinkled, the leaves had ceased their rustling, and every thing lay motionless and silent as if Nature were composing herself to slumber.

"What a beautiful night it is, Esther," remarked David, somewhat drowsily.

"Very beautiful," answered the girl, in the same tone.

"But how still!" continued David.

"Ah, too still!" said Esther, with a faint shudder, like a modest leaf when the wind kisses it.

Perhaps they fell asleep together, and, united as their spirits were by close and tender sympathies, the same strange dream might have wrapt them both in its shadowy arms. But they conceived, at the time, that they still remained wakeful by the spring of bubbling water, looking down through the village, and all along the moonlighted road, and at the queer old houses, and at the trees which thrust their great twisted branches almost into the windows. There was only a sort of mistiness over their minds, like the smoky air of an early Autumn night. At length, without any vivid astonishment, they became conscious that a great many people were either entering the village or already in the street, but whether they came from the meeting-house, or from a little beyond it, or where the devil they came from, was more than could be determined. Certainly, a crowd of people seemed to be there, men, women, and children, all of whom were yawning, rubbing their eyes, stretching their limbs and staggering from side to side of the road, as if but partially awakened from a sound slumber. Sometimes they stood stock-still, with their hands over their brows to shade their sight from the moonbeams. As they drew near, most of their countenances appeared familiar to Esther and David, possessing the peculiar features of families in the village, and that general air and aspect by which a person would recognize his own townsmen in the remotest ends of the earth. But though the whole multitude might have been taken, in the mass, for neighbors and acquaintances, there was not a single individual whose exact likeness they had ever before seen. It was a noticeable circumstance, also, that the newest fashioned garment on the backs of these people might have been worn by the great-grand parents of the existing generation. There was one figure behind all the rest, and not yet near enough to be perfectly distinguished.

"Where on earth, David, do all these odd people come from?" said Esther, with a lazy inclination to laugh.

"No where on earth, Esther," replied David, unknowing why he said so.

As they spoke, the strangers showed some symptoms of disquietude, and looked towards the fountain for an instant, but immediately appeared to resume their own trains of thought and previous purposes. They now separated to different parts of the village, with a readiness that implied intimate local knowledge, and it may be worthy of remark, that, though they were evidently loquacious among themselves, neither their footsteps nor their voices reached the ears of the beholders. Wherever there was a venerable old house, of fifty years standing and upwards, surrounded by its elm or walnut trees, with its dark and weather-beaten barn, its well, its orchard and stone-walls, all ancient and in good repair around it, there a little group of these people assembled. Such parties were mostly composed of an aged man and woman, with the younger members of a family; their faces were full of joy, so deep that it assumed the shade of melancholy; they pointed to each other the minutest objects about the homesteads, things in their hearts, and were now comparing them with the originals. But where hollow places by the way-side, grass-grown and uneven, with unsightly chimneys rising ruinous in the midst, gave indications of a fallen dwelling and of hearths long cold, there did a few of the strangers sit them down on the mouldering beams, and on the yellow moss that had overspread the door-stone. The men folded their arms sad and speechless; the women wrung their hands with a more vivid expression of grief; and the little children tottered to their knees, shrinking away from the open grave of domestic love. And wherever a recent edifice reared its white and flashy front on the foundation of an old one, there a gray-haired man might be seen to shake his staff in anger at it, while his aged dame and their offspring appeared to join in their maledictions, forming a fearful picture in the ghostly moonlight. While these scenes were passing, the one figure in the rear of all the rest was descending the hollow towards the mill, and the eyes of David and Esther were drawn thence to a pair with whom they could fully sympathize. It was a youth in a sailor's dress and a pale slender maiden, who met each other with a sweet embrace in the middle of the street.

"How long it must be since they parted," observed David.

"Fifty years at least," said Esther.

They continued to gaze with unwondering calmness and quiet interest, as the dream (if such it were) unrolled its quaint and motley semblance before them, and their notice was now attracted by several little knots of people, apparently engaged in conversation. Of these one of the earliest collected and most characteristic was near the tavern, the persons who composed it being seated on the low green bank along the left side of the door. A conspicuous figure here was a fine corpulent old fellow in his shirt sleeves and flame-coloured breeches, and with a stained white apron over his paunch, beneath which he held his hands and wherewith at times he wiped his ruddy face. The stately decrepitude of one of his companions, the scar of an Indian tomahawk on his crown, and especially his worn buff-coat, were appropriate marks of a veteran belonging to an old Provincial garrison, now deaf to the roll-call. Another showed his rough face under a tarry hat and wore a pair of wide trowsers, like an ancient mariner who had tossed away his youth upon the sea, and was returned, hoary and weather beaten, to his inland home. There was also a thin young man, carelessly dressed, who ever and anon cast a sad look towards the pale maiden above mentioned. With these there sat a hunter, and one or two others, and they were soon joined by a miller, who came upward from the dusty mill, his coat as white as if besprinkled with powdered starlight. All these (by the aid of jests, which might indeed be old, but had not been recently repeated) waxed very merry, and it was rather strange, that just as their sides shook with the heartiest laughter, they appeared greatly like a group of shadows flickering in the moonshine. Four personages, very different from these, stood in front of the large house with its periwig of creeping plants. One was a little elderly figure, distinguished by the gold on his three-cornered hat and sky-blue coat, and by the seal of arms annexed to his great

gold watch-chain; his air and aspect befitted a Justice of
Peace and county Major, and all earth's pride and pomposity
were squeezed into this small gentleman of five foot high.
The next in importance was a grave person of sixty or
seventy years, whose black suit and band sufficiently indicated his character, and the polished baldness of whose
head was worthy of a famous preacher in the village, half
a century before, who had made wigs a subject of pulpit
denunciation. The two other figures, both clad in dark gray,
showed the sobriety of Deacons; one was ridiculously tall
and thin, like a man of ordinary bulk infinitely produced, as
the mathematicians say; while the brevity and thickness of
his colleague seemed a compression of the same man. These
four talked with great earnestness, and their gestures intimated that they had revived the ancient dispute about the
meeting-house steeple. The grave person in black spoke with
composed solemnity, as if he were addressing a Synod; the
short deacon grunted out occasional sentences, as brief as
himself; his tall brother drew the long thread of his argument through the whole discussion, and (reasoning from
analogy) his voice must indubitably have been small and
squeaking. But the little old man in gold-lace was evidently
scorched by his own red-hot eloquence; he bounced from
one to another, shook his cane at the steeple, at the two
deacons, and almost in the parson's face, stamping with his
foot fiercely enough to break a hole through the very earth;
though, indeed, it could not exactly be said that the green
grass bent beneath him. The figure, noticed as coming behind
all the rest, had now surmounted the ascent from the mill,
and proved to be an elderly lady with something in her hand.

"Why does she walk so slow?" asked David.

"Don't you see she is lame?" said Esther.

This gentlewoman, whose infirmity had kept her so far
in the rear of the crowd, now came hobbling on, glided

unobserved by the polemic group, and paused on the left brink of the fountain, within a few feet of the two spectators. She was a magnificent old dame, as ever mortal eye beheld. Her spangled shoes and gold-clocked stockings shone gloriously within the spacious circle of a red hoop-petticoat, which swelled to the very point of explosion, and was bedecked all over with embroidery a little tarnished. Above the petticoat, and parting in front so as to display it to the best advantage, was a figured blue damask gown. A wide and stiff ruff encircled her neck, a cap of the finest muslin, though rather dingy, covered her head, and her nose was bestridden by a pair of gold-bowed spectacles with enormous glasses. But the old lady's face was pinched, sharp, and sallow, wearing a niggardly and avaricious expression, and forming an odd contrast to the splendor of her attire, as did likewise the implement which she held in her hand. It was a sort of iron shovel (by housewives termed a "slice"), such as is used in clearing the oven, and with this, selecting a spot between a walnut tree and the fountain, the good dame made an earnest attempt to dig. The tender sods, however, possessed a strange impenetrability. They resisted her efforts like a quarry of living granite, and losing her breath, she cast down the shovel and seemed to bemoan herself most piteously, gnashing her teeth (what few she had) and wringing her thin yellow hands. Then, apparently with new hopes, she resumed her toil, which still had the same result,—a circumstance the less surprising to David and Esther, because at times they would catch the moonlight shining through the old woman, and dancing in the fountain beyond. The little man in gold-lace now happened to see her, and made his approach on tiptoe.

"How hard this elderly lady works," remarked David.

"Go and help her, David," said Esther, compassionately.

As their drowsy voices spoke, both the old woman and the pompous little figure behind her lifted their eyes, and for a moment they regarded the youth and damsel with something like kindness and affection; which, however, were dim and uncertain, and passed away almost immediately. The old woman again betook herself to the shovel, but was startled by a hand suddenly laid upon her shoulder; she turned round in great trepidation, and beheld the dignitary in the blue coat; then followed an embrace, of such closeness as would indicate no remoter connexion than matrimony between these two decorous persons. The gentleman next pointed to the shovel, appearing to enquire the purpose of his lady's occupation; while she as evidently parried his interrogatories, maintaining a demure and sanctified visage as every good woman ought, in similar cases. Howbeit, she could not forbear looking askew, behind her spectacles, towards the spot of stubborn turf. All the while, their figures had a strangeness in them, and it seemed as if some cunning jeweller had made their golden ornaments of the yellowest of the setting sun beams, and that the blue of their garments was brought from the dark sky near the moon, and that the gentleman's silk waistcoat was the bright side of a fiery cloud, and the lady's scarlet petticoat a remnant of the blush of morning,—and that they both were two unrealities of colored air. But now there was a sudden movement throughout the multitude. The Squire drew forth a watch as large as the dial on the famous steeple, looked at the warning hands and gat him gone, nor could his lady tarry; the party at the tavern door took to their heels, headed by the fat man in the flaming breeches; the tall deacon stalked away immediately, and the short deacon waddled after, making four steps to the yard; the mothers called their children about them and set forth, with a gentle and sad glance behind. Like cloudy fantasies that hurry by a viewless impulse from the sky, they all were fled, and the wind rose up and followed them with a strange moaning down the lonely street. Now whither these people went, is more than may be told;

only David and Esther seemed to see the shadowy splendor of the ancient dame, as she lingered in the moonshine at the grave-yard gate, gazing backward to the fountain.

"Oh, Esther! I have had such a dream!" cried David, starting up and rubbing his eyes.

"And I such another!" answered Esther, gaping till her pretty red lips formed a circle.

"About an old woman with gold-bowed spectacles," continued David.

"And a scarlet hoop-petticoat," added Esther.

They now stared in each other's eyes, with great astonishment and some little fear. After a thoughtful moment or two, David drew a long breath and stood upright.

"If I live till to-morrow morning," said he, "I'll see what may be buried between that tree and the spring of water."

"And why not to-night, David?" asked Esther; for she was a sensible little girl, and bethought herself that the matter might as well be done in secrecy.

David felt the propriety of the remark and looked round for the means of following her advice. The moon shone brightly on something that rested against the side of the old house, and, on a nearer view, it proved to be an iron shovel, bearing a singular resemblance to that which they had seen in their dreams. He used it with better success than the old woman, the soil giving way so freely to his efforts, that he had soon scooped a hole as large as the basin of the spring. Suddenly, he poked his head down to the very bottom of this cavity.

"Oho!—What have we here!" cried David.

THE HAUNTED QUACK

A TALE OF A CANAL BOAT

IN THE SUMMER OF 18—, I made an excursion
to Niagara. At Schenectady, finding the roads nearly
impassable, I took passage in a canal boat for Utica.
The weather was dull and lowering. There were but few
passengers on board; and of those few, none were sufficiently
inviting in appearance, to induce me to make any overtures
to a travelling acquaintance. A stupid answer, or a surly
monosyllable, were all that I got in return for the few simple
questions I hazarded. An occasional drizzling rain, and the
wet and slippery condition of the tow path, along which the
lazy beasts that dragged the vessel travelled, rendered it
impossible to vary the monotony of the scene by walking.
I had neglected to provide myself with books, and as we crept
along at the dull rate of four miles per hour, I soon felt the
foul fiend *Ennui* coming upon me with all her horrors.

'Time and the hour,' however, 'runs through the roughest
day,' and night at length approached. By degrees the passengers, seemingly tired of each other's company, began to
creep slowly away to their berths; most of them fortifying
themselves with a potation, before resigning themselves to
the embrace of Morpheus. One called for a glass of hot
whiskey punch, because he felt cold; another took some

brandy toddy to prevent his taking cold; some took mint julaps; some gin-slings, and some rum and water. One took his dram because he felt sick; another to make him sleep well; and a third because he had nothing else to do. The last who retired from the cabin, was an old gentleman who had been deeply engaged in a well thumbed volume all day, and whose mental abstraction I had more than once envied. He now laid down his book, and, pulling out a red night-cap, called for a pint of beer, to take the vapors out of his head.

As soon as he had left the cabin, I took up the volume, and found it to be Glanville's marvellous book, entitled the History of Witches, or the Wonders of the Invisible World Displayed. I began to peruse it, and soon got so deeply interested in some of his wonderful narrations, that the hours slipped unconsciously away, and midnight found me poring half asleep over the pages. From this dreamy state I was suddenly aroused by a muttering, as of a suppressed voice, broken by groans and sounds of distress. Upon looking round, I saw that they proceeded from the figure of a man enveloped in a cloak, who was lying asleep upon one of the benches of the cabin, whom I had not previously noticed. I recognized him to be a young man, with whose singular appearance and behaviour during the day, I had been struck. He was tall and thin in person, rather shabbily dressed, with long, lank, black hair, and large grey eyes, which gave a visionary char-acter to one of the most pallid, and cadaverous countenances I had ever beheld. Since he had come on board, he had appeared restless and unquiet, keeping away from the table at meal times, and seeming averse from entering into con-versation with the passengers. Once or twice, on catching my eye, he had slunk away as if, conscience smitten by the remembrance of some crime, he dreaded to meet the gaze of a fellow mortal. From this behaviour I suspected that he was either a fugitive from justice, or else a little disordered in mind; and had resolved to keep my eye on him and observe what course he should take when we reached Utica.

Supposing that the poor fellow was now under the influence of nightmare, I got up with the intention of giving him a shake to rouse him, when the words, 'murder,' 'poison,' and others of extraordinary import, dropping unconnectedly from his lips, induced me to stay my hand. 'Go away, go away,' exclaimed he, as if conscious of my approach, but mistaking me for another. 'Why do you continue to torment me? If I did poison you, I didn't mean to do it, and they can't make that out more than manslaughter. Besides, what's the use of haunting me now? An't I going to give myself up, and tell all? Begone! I say, you bloody old hag, begone!' Here the bands of slumber were broken by the intensity of his feelings, and with a wild expression of countenance and a frame shaking with emotion, he started from the bench, and stood trembling before me.

Though convinced that he was a criminal, I could not help pitying him from the forlorn appearance he now exhibited. As soon as he had collected his wandering ideas, it seemed as if he read in my countenance, the mingled sentiments of pity and abhorrence, with which I regarded him. Looking anxiously around, and seeing that we were alone, he drew the corner of the bench towards me, and sitting down, with an apparent effort to command his feelings, thus addressed me. His tone of voice was calm, and distinct; and his countenance, though deadly pale, was composed.

'I see, Sir, that from what I am conscious of having uttered in my disturbed sleep, you suspect me of some horrid crime. You are right. My conscience convicts me, and an awful nightly visitation, worse than the waking pangs of remorse, compels me to confess it. Yes, I am a murderer. I have been the unhappy cause of blotting out the life of a fellow being from the page of human existence. In these pallid features, you may read enstamped, in the same characters which the first murderer bore upon his brow, Guilt—guilt—guilt!'

Here the poor young man paused, evidently agitated by strong internal emotion. Collecting himself, however, in a few moments, he thus continued.

'Yet still, when you have heard my sad story, I think you will bestow upon me your pity. I feel that there is no peace for me, until I have disburthened my mind. Your countenance promises sympathy. Will you listen to my unhappy narrative?'

My curiosity being strongly excited by this strange exordium, I told him I was ready to hear whatever he had to communicate. Upon this, he proceeded as follows.

'My name is Hippocrates Jenkins. I was born in Nantucket, but my father emigrated to these parts when I was young. I grew up in one of the most flourishing villages on the borders of the canal. My father and mother both dying of the lake fever, I was bound apprentice to an eminent operative in the boot and shoe making line, who had lately come from New York. Would that I had remained content with this simple and useful profession. Would that I had stuck to my waxed ends and awl, and never undertaken to cobble up people's bodies. But my legs grew tired of being trussed beneath my haunches; my elbows wearied with their monotonous motion; my eyes became dim with gazing forever upon the dull brick wall which faced our shop window; and my whole heart was sick of my sedentary, and, as I foolishly deemed it, particularly mean occupation. My time was nearly expired, and I had long resolved, should any opportunity offer of getting into any other employment, I would speedily embrace it.

'I had always entertained a predilection for the study of medicine. What had given my mind this bias, I know not.

Perhaps it was the perusal of an old volume of Doctor Buchan, over whose pages it was the delight of my youthful fancy to pore. Perhaps it was the oddness of my Christian cognomen, which surely was given me by my parents in a prophetic hour. Be this as it may, the summit of my earthly happiness was to be a doctor. Conceive then my delight and surprise, one Saturday evening, after having carried home a pair of new white-topped boots for Doctor Ephraim Ramshorne, who made the cure of bodies his care, in the village, to hear him ask me, how I should like to be a doctor. He then very generously offered to take me as a student. From my earliest recollections, the person and character of Doctor Ramshorne, had been regarded by me with the most profound and awful admiration. Time out of mind the successful practitioner for many miles around, I had looked upon him as the *beau idéal* of a doctor—a very Apollo in the healing art. When I speak of him, however, as the *successful* practitioner, I mean it not to be inferred that death was less busy in his doings, or funerals scarcer during his dynasty; but only that he had, by some means or other, contrived to force all those who had ventured to contest the palm with him, to quit the field. He was large and robust in person, and his ruby visage showed that if he grew fat upon drugs, it was not by swallowing them himself. It was never exactly ascertained from what college the Doctor had received his diploma; nor was he very forward to exhibit his credentials. When hard pressed, however, he would produce a musty old roll of parchment, with a red seal as broad as the palm of his hand, which looked as if it might have been the identical diploma of the great Boerhaave himself, and some cramp manuscript of a dozen pages, in an unknown tongue, said by the Doctor to be his Greek thesis. These documents were enough to satisfy the doubts of the most sceptical. By the simple country people, far and near, the Doctor was regarded, in point of occult knowledge and skill, as a second Faustus.

It is true the village lawyer, a rival in popularity, used to whisper, that the Doctor's Greek thesis was nothing but a bundle of prescriptions for the bots, wind-galls, spavins, and other veterinary complaints, written in high Dutch by a Hessian horse doctor; that the diploma was all a sham, and that Ephraim was no more a doctor than his jack-ass. But these assertions were all put down to the score of envy on the part of the lawyer. Be this as it may, on the strength of one or two remarkable cures, which he was said to have performed, and by dint of wheedling some and bullying others, it was certain that Ramshorne had worked himself into very good practice. The Doctor united in his own person, the attributes of apothecary and physician; and as he vended, as well as prescribed his own drugs, it was not his interest to stint his patients in their enormous boluses, or nauseous draughts. His former medical student had been worried into a consumption over the mortar and pestle; in consequence of which, he had pitched upon me for his successor.

'By the kindness of a few friends, I was fitted out with the necessary requisitions for my metamorphosis. The Doctor required no fee, and, in consideration of certain little services to be rendered him, such as taking care of his horse, cleaning his boots, running errands, and doing little jobs about the house, had promised to board and lodge me, besides giving me my professional education. So with a rusty suit of black, and an old plaid cloak, behold equipped the disciple of Esculapius.

'I cannot describe my elation of mind, when I found myself fairly installed in the Doctor's office. Golden visions floated before my eyes. I fancied my fortune already made, and blessed my happy star, that had fallen under the benign influence of so munificent a patron.

'The Doctor's office, as it was called *par excellence*, was a little nook of a room, communicating with a larger apartment denominated the shop. The paraphernalia of this latter place had gotten somewhat into disorder since the last student had gone away, and I soon learnt that it was to be my task to arrange the heterogeneous mass of bottles, boxes, and gallipots, that were strewed about in promiscuous confusion. In the office, there was a greater appearance of order. A small regiment of musty looking books, were drawn up in line upon a couple of shelves, where, to judge from the superincumbent strata of dust, they appeared to have peacefully reposed for many years. A ricketty wooden clock, which the Doctor had taken in part payment from a pedlar, and the vital functions of which, to use his own expression, had long since ceased to act, stood in one corner. A mouldy plaster bust of some unknown worthy, a few bottles of pickled, and one or two dried specimens of morbid anatomy, a small chest of drawers, a table, and a couple of chairs, completed the furniture of this *sanctum*. The single window commanded a view of the church-yard, in which, it was said, many of the Doctor's former patients were quietly slumbering. With a feeling of reverence I ventured to dislodge one of the dusty tomes, and began to try to puzzle out the hard words with which it abounded; when suddenly, as if he had been conjured back, like the evil one by Cornelius Agrippa's book, the Doctor made his appearance. With a gruff air, he snatched the volume from my hands, and telling me not to meddle with what I could not understand, bade me go and take care of his horse, and make haste back, as he wanted me to spread a pitch plaster, and carry the same, with a bottle of his patent catholicon, to farmer Van Pelt, who had the rheumatism. On my return, I was ordered by Mrs. Ramshorne to split some wood, and kindle a fire in the parlour, as she expected company; after which Miss Euphemia Ramshorne, a sentimental young lady, who was as crooked in person and crabbed in temper as her own name, despatched me to the village circulating library, in quest of the Mysteries of Udolpho. I soon found out that my place was no sinecure. The greater part of my time was occupied in compounding certain quack medicines of Ramshorne's own invention, from which he derived great celebrity, and no inconsiderable profit. Besides his patent catholicon, and universal panacea, there was his anti-pertusso-balsamico drops, his patent calorific refrigerating anodyne, and his golden restorative of nature. Into the business of compounding these, and other articles with similar high-sounding titles, I was gradually initiated, and soon acquired so much skill in their manipulation, that my services became indispensable to my master; so much so, that he was obliged to hire a little negro to take care of his horse, and clean his boots. What chiefly reconciled me to the drudgery of the shop, was the seeing how well the Doctor got paid for his villainous compounds. A mixture of a little brick dust, rosin, and treacle, dignified with the title of the anthelminthic amalgam, he sold for half a dollar; and a bottle of vinegar and alum, with a little rose water to give it a flavor, yclept the antiscrofulous abstergent lotion, brought twice that sum. I longed for the day when I should dispense my own medicines, and in my hours of castle-building, looked forward to fortunes far beyond those of the renowned Dr. Solomon. Alas! my fond hopes have been blighted in their bud. I have drunk deeply of the nauseous draught of adversity, and been forced to swallow many bitter pills of disappointment. But I find I am beginning to smell of the shop. I must return to my sad tale. The same accident, which not unfrequently before had put a sudden stop to the Doctor's patients' taking any more of his nostrums, at length prevented him from reaping any longer their golden harvest. One afternoon, after having dined with his friend, Squire Gobbledown, he came home, and complained of not feeling very well. By his directions, I prepared for him some of his elixir sanitatis, composed of brandy and bitters, of which he took an inordinate dose. Shortly after, he was seized with a fit of apoplexy, and before bedtime, in spite of all the drugs in the shop, which I poured down with unsparing hand, he had breathed his last. In three days, Ramshorne was quietly deposited in the churchyard, in the midst of those he had sent there before him.

'Having resided with the Doctor for several years, I had become pretty well known throughout the neighbourhood, particularly among the old ladies, whose good graces I had always sedulously cultivated. I accordingly resolved to commence quacking—I mean practising—on my own account. Having obtained my late master's stock of drugs from his widow at an easy rate, and displaying my own name in golden letters as his successor, to work I went, with the internal resolve that where Ramshorne had given one dose, I would give six.

'For a time, Fortune seemed to smile upon me, and everything went on well. All the old women were loud in sounding my praises, far and near. The medicaments of my master continued to be in demand, and treacle, brick dust, and alum came to a good market. Some drawbacks, however, I occasionally met with. Having purchased the patent right of one of Thompson's steam baths, in my first experiment I came near flaying alive a rheumatic tanner, who had submitted himself to the operation. By an unfortunate mistake in regulating the steam, he was nearly parboiled; and it was supposed that the thickness of his hide alone preserved his vitals uninjured. I was myself threatened with the fate of Marsyas, by the enraged sufferer; which he was happily prevented from attempting to inflict, by a return of his malady, which has never since left him. I, however, after this gave up steaming, and confined myself to regular practice. At length, either the charm of novelty wearing off, or people beginning to discover the inefficacy of the old nostrums, I was obliged to exert my wit to invent new ones. These I generally took the precaution to try upon cats or dogs, before using them upon the human system. They were, however, mostly of an innocent nature, and I satisfied my conscience with the reflection, that if they did no good, they could at least do no harm. Happy would it have been for me, could I always have done thus. Meeting with success in my first efforts, I by degrees ventured upon more active ingredients. At length, in an evil hour, I invented a curious mixture, composed of forty-nine different articles. This I dubbed in high flowing terms, "The Antidote to Death, or the Eternal Elixir of Longevity;" knowing full well, that though

"A rose might smell as sweet by any other name,"

yet would not my drugs find as good a sale under a more humble title. This cursed compound proved the antidote to all my hopes of success. Besides forcing me to quit the village in a confounded hurry, it has embittered my life ever since, and reduced me to the ragged and miserable plight in which you see me.

'I dare say you have met with that species of old women, so frequent in all country towns, who, seeming to have outlived the common enjoyments of life, and outworn the ordinary sources of excitement, seek fresh stimulus in scenes of distress, and appear to take a morbid pleasure in beholding the varieties of human suffering, and misery. One of the most noted characters in the village was an old beldame of this description. Granny Gordon, so she was familiarly denominated, was the rib of the village Vulcan, and the din of her eternal tongue, was only equalled by the ringing of her husband's anvil. Thin and withered away in person and redolent with snuff, she bore no small resemblance to a newly exhumed mummy, and to all appearance promised to last as long as one of those ancient dames of Egypt. Not a death, a burial, a fit of sickness, a casualty, nor any of the common calamities of life ever occurred in the vicinity, but Granny Gordon made it her especial business to be present. Wrapped in an old scarlet cloak—that hideous cloak! the thought of it makes me shudder—she might be seen hovering about the dwelling of the sick. Watching her opportunity, she would make her way into the patient's chamber, and disturb his repose with long dismal stories and ill-boding predictions; and if turned from the house, which was not unfrequently the case, she would depart, muttering threats and abuse.

'As the Indians propitiate the favor of the devil, so had I, in my eagerness to acquire popularity, made a firm friend and ally, though rather a troublesome one, of this old woman. She was one of my best customers, and, provided it was something new, and had a high-sounding name to recommend it, would take my most nauseous compounds with the greatest relish. Indeed the more disgusting was the dose, the greater in her opinion was its virtue.

'I had just corked the last bottle of my antidote, when a message came to tell me, that Granny Gordon had one of her old fits, and wanted some new doctor-stuff, as the old physic didn't do her any more good. Not having yet given my new pharmaceutic preparation a trial, I felt a little doubtful about its effects; but trusting to the toughness of the old woman's system, I ventured to send a potion, with directions to take it cautiously. Not many minutes had elapsed, before the messenger returned, in breathless haste, to say that Mrs. Gordon was much worse, and that though she had taken all the stuff, they believed she was dying. With a vague foreboding of evil, I seized my hat, and hastened to the blacksmith's. On entering the chamber my eyes were greeted with a sad spectacle. Granny Gordon, bolstered up in the bed, holding in her hand the bottle I had sent her, drained of its contents, sate gasping for breath, and occasionally agitated by strong convulsions. A cold sweat rested on her forehead, her eyes seemed dim and glazed, her nose, which was usually of a ruby hue, was purple and peaked, and her whole appearance evidently betokened approaching dissolution.

'Around the bed were collected some half dozen withered beldames, who scowled upon me, as I entered, with ill omened visages. Her husband, a drunken brute, who used to beat his better half six times a week, immediately began to load me with abuse, accusing me of having poisoned his dear, dear wife, and threatening to be the death of me, if she died.

'My conscience smote me. I felt stupified and bewildered, and knew not which way to turn. At this moment, the patient perceiving me, with a hideous contortion of countenance, the expression of which I shall carry to my dying hour, and a voice between a scream and a groan, held up the empty bottle, and exclaimed, "This is your doing, you villainous quack you" (here she was seized with hiccup);—"you have poisoned me, you have" (here fearful spasms shook her whole frame); —"but I'll be revenged; day and night my ghost shall haunt" —here her voice became inarticulate, and shaking her withered arm at me, she fell back, and, to my extreme horror, gave up the ghost. This was too much for my nerves. I rushed from the house, and ran home with the dying curse ringing in my ears, fancying that I saw her hideous physiognomy, grinning from every bush and tree that I passed. Knowing that as soon as the noise of this affair should get abroad, the village would be too hot to hold me, I resolved to decamp as silently as possible. First throwing all my recently manu- factured anodyne into the canal, that it should not rise in judgment against me, I made up a little bundle of clothes, and taking my seat in the mail stage, which was passing at the time and fortunately empty, in a couple of days I found myself in the great city of New York. Having a little money with me, I hired a mean apartment in an obscure part of the city, in the hope that I might remain concealed till all search after me should be over, when I might find some opportunity of getting employment, or of resuming my old profession, under happier auspices. By degrees the few dollars I brought with me were expended, and after pawning my watch and some of my clothes, I found myself reduced to the last shilling. But not the fear of impending starvation, nor the dread of a jail, are to be compared to the horrors I nightly suffer. Granny Gordon has been as good as her word. Every night, at the solemn hour of twelve' (here he looked fearfully around)—'her ghost appears to me, wrapped in a red cloak, with her grey hairs streaming from beneath an old nightcap of the same color, brandishing the vial, and accusing me of having poisoned her. These visitations have at length become so insupportable, that I have resolved to return and give myself up to justice; for I feel that hanging itself is better than this state of torment.'

Here the young man ceased. I plainly saw that he was a little disordered in his intellect. To comfort him, however, I told him, that if he had killed fifty old women, they could do nothing to him, if he had done it professionally. And as for the ghost, we would take means to have that put at rest, when we reached Utica.

About the grey of the morning, we arrived at the place of our destination. My *protégé* having unburthened his mind, seemed more at his ease, and taking a mint julap, prepared to accompany me on shore. As we were leaving the boat, several persons in a wagon drove down to the wharf. As soon as my companion observed them, he exclaimed with a start of surprise, 'Hang me, if there isn't old Graham the sheriff, with lawyer Dickson, and Bill Gordon come to take me.' As he spoke, his foot slipping, he lost his balance, and fell backwards into the canal. We drew him from the water, and as soon as the persons in the wagon perceived him, they one and all sprang out, and ran up with the greatest expressions of joyful surprise. 'Why Hippy, my lad,' exclaimed the sheriff, 'where have you been? All our town has been in a snarl about you. We all supposed you had been forcibly abducted. Judge Bates offered a reward of twenty dollars for your corpse. We have dragged the canal for more than a mile, and found a mess of bottles, which made us think you had been spirited away. Betsey Wilkins made her affadavit, that she heard Bill Gordon swear that he would take your life, and here you see we have brought him down to have his trial. But come, come, jump in the wagon, we'll take you up to the tavern, to get your duds dried, and tell you all about it.'

Here a brawny fellow with a smutty face, who I found was Gordon the blacksmith, came up, and shaking Hippocrates by the hand, said, 'By goles, Doctor, I am glad to see you. If you hadn't come back, I believe it would have gone hard with me. Come, man, you must forgive the hard words I gave you. My old woman soon got well of her fit, after you went away, and says she thinks the stuff did her a mortal sight o' good.'

It is impossible to describe the singular expression the countenance of the young man now exhibited. For some time he stood in mute amazement, shaking with cold, and gazing alternately at each of his friends as they addressed him; and it required their reiterated assurances to convince him, that Granny Gordon was still in the land of the living, and that he had not been haunted by a veritable ghost.

Wishing to obtain a further explanation of this strange scene, I accompanied them to the tavern. A plain looking man in a farmer's dress, who was of the party, confirmed what the blacksmith had said, as to the supposed death of his wife, and her subsequent recovery. 'She was only in a swoon,' said he, 'but came to, soon after the Doctor had left her.' He added that it was his private opinion, that she would now last forever. He spoke of Hippocrates as a 'nation smart doctor, who had a power of larning, but gave severe doses.'

After discussing a good breakfast, my young friend thanked me for the sympathy and interest I had taken in his behalf. He told me he intended returning to the practice of his profession. I admonished him to be more careful in the exhibition of his patent medicines, telling him that all old women had not nine lives. He shook hands with me, and, gaily jumping into the wagon, rode off with his friends.

ALICE DOANE'S APPEAL

ON A PLEASANT AFTERNOON of June, it was my good fortune to be the companion of two young ladies in a walk. The direction of our course being left to me, I led them neither to Legge's Hill, nor to the Cold Spring, nor to the rude shores and old batteries of the Neck, nor yet to Paradise; though if the latter place were rightly named, my fair friends would have been at home there. We reached the outskirts of the town, and turning aside from a street of tanners and curriers, began to ascend a hill, which at a distance, by its dark slope and the even line of its summit, resembled a green rampart along the road. It was less steep than its aspect threatened. The eminence formed part of an extensive tract of pasture land, and was traversed by cow paths in various directions; but, strange to tell, though the whole slope and summit were of a peculiarly deep green, scarce a blade of grass was visible from the base upward. This deceitful verdure was occasioned by a plentiful crop of 'wood-wax,' which wears the same dark and glossy green throughout the summer, except at one short period, when it puts forth a profusion of yellow blossoms. At that season to a distant spectator, the hill appears absolutely overlaid with gold, or covered with a glory of sunshine, even beneath a clouded sky. But the curious wanderer on the hill will perceive that all the grass, and every thing that should nourish man or beast, has been destroyed by this vile and ineradicable weed; its tufted roots make the soil their own, and permit nothing else to vegetate among them; so that a physical curse may be said to have blasted the spot, where guilt and phrenzy consummated the most execrable scene, that our history blushes to record. For this was the field where superstition won her darkest triumph; the high place where our fathers set up their shame, to the mournful gaze of generations far remote. The dust of martyrs was beneath our feet. We stood on Gallows Hill.

For my own part, I have often courted the historic influence of the spot. But it is singular, how few come on pilgrimage to this famous hill; how many spend their lives almost at its base, and never once obey the summons of the shadowy past, as it beckons them to the summit. Till a year or two since, this portion of our history had been very imperfectly written, and, as we are not a people of legend or tradition, it was not every citizen of our ancient town that could tell, within half a century, so much as the date of the witchcraft delusion. Recently, indeed, an historian has treated the subject in a manner that will keep his name alive, in the only desirable connection with the errors of our ancestry, by converting the hill of their disgrace into an honorable monument of his own antiquarian lore, and of that better wisdom, which draws the moral while it tells the tale. But we are a people of the present and have no heartfelt interest in the olden time. Every fifth of November, in commemoration of they know not what, or rather without an idea beyond the momentary blaze, the young men scare the town with bonfires on this haunted height, but never dream of paying funeral honors to those who died so wrongfully, and without a coffin or a prayer, were buried here.

Though with feminine susceptibility, my companions caught all the melancholy associations of the scene, yet these could but imperfectly overcome the gayety of girlish spirits. Their emotions came and went with quick vicissitude, and sometimes combined to form a peculiar and delicious excitement, the mirth brightening the gloom into a sunny shower of feeling, and a rainbow in the mind. My own more sombre mood was tinged by theirs. With now a merry word and next a sad one, we trod among the tangled weeds, and almost hoped that our feet would sink into the hollow of a witch's grave. Such vestiges were to be found within the memory of man, but have vanished now, and with them, I believe, all traces of the precise spot of the executions. On the long and broad ridge of the eminence, there is no very decided elevation of any one point, nor other prominent marks, except the decayed stumps of two trees, standing near each other, and here and there the rocky substance of the hill, peeping just above the wood-wax.

There are few such prospects of town and village, woodland and cultivated field, steeples and country seats, as we beheld from this unhappy spot. No blight had fallen on old Essex; all was prosperity and riches, healthfully distributed. Before us lay our native town, extending from the foot of the hill to the harbor, level as a chess board, embraced by two arms of the sea, and filling the whole peninsula with a close assemblage of wooden roofs, overtopt by many a spire, and intermixed with frequent heaps of verdure, where trees threw up their shade from unseen trunks. Beyond, was the bay and its islands, almost the only objects, in a country unmarked by strong natural features, on which time and human toil had produced no change. Retaining these portions of the scene, and also the peaceful glory and tender gloom of the declining sun, we threw, in imagination, a veil of deep forest over the land, and pictured a few scattered villages, and this old town itself a village, as when the prince of hell bore sway there. The idea thus gained, of its former aspect, its quaint edifices standing far apart, with peaked roofs and projecting stories, and its single meeting house pointing up a tall spire in the midst; the vision, in short, of the town in 1692, served to introduce a wondrous tale of those old times.

I had brought the manuscript in my pocket. It was one of a series written years ago, when my pen, now sluggish and perhaps feeble, because I have not much to hope or fear, was driven by stronger external motives, and a more passionate impulse within, than I am fated to feel again. Three or four of these tales had appeared in the Token, after a long time and various adventures, but had incumbered me with no troublesome notoriety, even in my birth place. One great heap had met a brighter destiny: they had fed the flames; thoughts meant to delight the world and endure for ages, had perished in a moment, and stirred not a single heart but mine. The story now to be introduced, and another, chanced to be in kinder custody at the time, and thus by no conspicuous merits of their own, escaped destruction.

The ladies, in consideration that I had never before intruded my performances on them, by any but the legitimate medium, through the press, consented to hear me read. I made them sit down on a moss-grown rock, close by the spot where we chose to believe that the death-tree had stood. After a little hesitation on my part, caused by a dread of renewing my acquaintance with fantasies that had lost their charm, in the ceaseless flux of mind, I began the tale, which opened darkly with the discovery of a murder.

A hundred years, and nearly half that time, have elapsed since the body of a murdered man was found, at about the distance of three miles, on the old road to Boston. He lay in a solitary spot, on the bank of a small lake, which the severe frost of December had covered with a sheet of ice. Beneath this, it seemed to have been the intention of the murderer to conceal his victim in a chill and watery grave, the ice being deeply hacked, perhaps with the weapon that had slain him, though its solidity was too stubborn for the patience of a man with blood upon his hand. The corpse therefore reclined on the earth, but was separated from the road by a thick growth of dwarf pines. There had been a slight fall of snow during the night, and as if Nature were shocked at the deed, and strove to hide it with her frozen tears, a little drifted heap had partly buried the body, and lay deepest over the pale dead face. An early traveller, whose dog had led him to the spot, ventured to uncover the features, but was affrighted by their expression. A look of evil and scornful triumph had hardened on them, and made death so life-like and so terrible, that the beholder at once took flight, as swiftly as if the stiffened corpse would rise up and follow.

I read on, and identified the body as that of a young man, a stranger in the country, but resident during several preceding months in the town which lay at our feet. The story described, at some length, the excitement caused by the murder, the unavailing quest after the perpetrator, the funeral ceremonies, and other common place matters, in the course of which, I brought forward the personages who were to move among the succeeding events. They were but three. A young man and his sister; the former characterized by a diseased imagination and morbid feelings; the latter, beautiful and virtuous, and instilling something of her own excellence into the wild heart of her brother, but not enough to cure the deep taint of his nature. The third person was a wizard; a small, gray, withered man, with fiendish ingenuity in devising evil, and superhuman power to execute it, but senseless as an idiot and feebler than a child, to all better purposes. The central scene of the story was an interview between this wretch and Leonard Doane, in the wizard's hut, situated beneath a range of rocks at some distance from the town. They sat beside a mouldering fire, while a tempest of wintry rain was beating on the roof. The young man spoke of the closeness of the tie which united him and Alice, the concentrated fervor of their affection from childhood upwards, their sense of lonely sufficiency to each other, because they only of their race had escaped death, in a night attack by the Indians. He related his discovery, or suspicion of a secret sympathy between his sister and Walter Brome, and told how a distempered jealousy had maddened him. In the following passage, I threw a glimmering light on the mystery of the tale.

'Searching,' continued Leonard, 'into the breast of Walter Brome, I at length found a cause why Alice must inevitably love him. For he was my very counterpart! I compared his mind by each individual portion, and as a whole, with mine. There was a resemblance from which I shrank with sickness, and loathing, and horror, as if my own features had come and stared upon me in a solitary place, or had met me in struggling through a crowd. Nay! the very same thoughts would often express themselves in the same words from our lips, proving a hateful sympathy in our secret souls. His education, indeed, in the cities of the old world, and mine in this rude wilderness, had wrought a superficial difference. The evil of his character, also, had been strengthened and rendered prominent by a reckless and ungoverned life, while mine had been softened and purified by the gentle and holy nature of Alice. But my soul had been conscious of the germ of all the fierce and deep passions, and of all the many varieties of wickedness, which accident had brought to their full maturity in him. Nor will I deny, that in the accursed one, I could see the withered blossom of every virtue, which by a happier culture, had been made to bring forth fruit in me. Now, here was a man, whom Alice might love with all the strength of sisterly affection, added to that impure passion which alone engrosses all the heart. The stranger would have more than the love which had been gathered to me from the many graves of our household—and I be desolate!'

Leonard Doane went on to describe the insane hatred that had kindled his heart into a volume of hellish flame. It appeared, indeed, that his jealousy had grounds, so far as that Walter Brome had actually sought the love of Alice, who also had betrayed an undefinable, but powerful interest in the unknown youth. The latter, in spite of his passion for Alice, seemed to return the loathful antipathy of her brother; the similarity of their dispositions made them like joint possessors of an individual nature, which could not become wholly the property of one, unless by the extinction of the other. At last, with the same devil in each bosom, they chanced to meet, they two on a lonely road. While Leonard spoke, the wizard had sat listening to what he already knew, yet with tokens of pleasurable interest, manifested by flashes of expression across his vacant features, by grisly smiles and by a word here and there, mysteriously filling up some void in the narrative. But when the young man told, how Walter Brome had taunted him with indubitable proofs of the shame of Alice, and before the triumphant sneer could vanish from his face, had died by her brother's hand, the wizard laughed aloud. Leonard started, but just then a gust of wind came down the chimney, forming itself into a close resemblance of the slow, unvaried laughter, by which he had been interrupted. 'I was deceived,' thought he; and thus pursued his fearful story.

'I trod out his accursed soul, and knew that he was dead; for my spirit bounded as if a chain had fallen from it and left me free. But the burst of exulting certainty soon fled, and was succeeded by a torpor over my brain and a dimness before my eyes, with the sensation of one who struggles through a dream. So I bent down over the body of Walter Brome, gazing into his face, and striving to make my soul glad with the thought, that he, in very truth, lay dead before me. I know not what space of time I had thus stood, nor how the vision came. But it seemed to me that the irrevocable years, since childhood had rolled back, and a scene, that had long been confused and broken in my memory, arrayed itself with all its first distinctness. Methought I stood a weeping infant by my father's hearth; by the cold and blood-stained hearth where he lay dead. I heard the childish wail of Alice, and my own cry arose with hers, as we beheld the features of our parent, fierce with the strife and distorted with the pain, in which his spirit had passed away. As I gazed, a cold wind whistled by, and waved my father's hair. Immediately, I stood again in the lonesome road, no more a sinless child, but a man of blood, whose tears were falling fast over the face of his dead enemy. But the delusion was not wholly gone; that face still wore a likeness of my father; and because my soul shrank from the fixed glare of the eyes, I bore the body to the lake, and would have buried it there. But before his icy sepulchre was hewn, I heard the voices of two travellers and fled.'

Such was the dreadful confession of Leonard Doane. And now tortured by the idea of his sister's guilt, yet sometimes yielding to a conviction of her purity; stung with remorse for the death of Walter Brome, and shuddering with a deeper sense of some unutterable crime, perpetrated, as he imagined, in madness or a dream; moved also by dark impulses, as if a fiend were whispering him to meditate violence against the life of Alice; he had sought this interview with the wizard, who, on certain conditions, had no power to withhold his aid in unravelling the mystery. The tale drew near its close.

The moon was bright on high; the blue firmament appeared to glow with an inherent brightness; the greater stars were burning in their spheres; the northern lights threw their mysterious glare far over the horizon; the few small clouds aloft were burthened with radiance; but the sky with all its variety of light, was scarcely so brilliant as the earth. The rain of the preceding night had frozen as it fell, and, by that simple magic, had wrought wonders. The trees were hung with diamonds and many-colored gems; the houses were overlaid with silver, and the streets paved with slippery brightness; a frigid glory was flung over all familiar things, from the cottage chimney to the steeple of the meeting house, that gleamed upward to the sky. This living world, where we sit by our firesides, or go forth to meet beings like ourselves, seemed rather the creation of wizard power, with so much of resemblance to known objects, that a man might shudder at the ghostly shape of his old beloved dwelling, and the shadow of a ghostly tree before his door. One looked to behold inhabitants suited to such a town, glittering in icy garments, with motionless features, cold, sparkling eyes, and just sensation enough in their frozen hearts to shiver at each other's presence.

By this fantastic piece of description, and more in the same style, I intended to throw a ghostly glimmer round the reader, so that his imagination might view the town through a medium that should take off its every day aspect, and make it a proper theatre for so wild a scene as the final one. Amid this unearthly show, the wretched brother and sister were represented as setting forth, at midnight, through the gleaming streets, and directing their steps to a grave yard, where all the dead had been laid, from the first corpse in that ancient town, to the murdered man who was buried three days before. As they went, they seemed to see the wizard gliding by their sides, or walking dimly on the path before them. But here I paused, and gazed into the faces of my two fair auditors, to judge whether, even on the hill where so many had been brought to death by wilder tales than this, I might venture to proceed. Their bright eyes were fixed on me; their lips apart. I took courage, and led the fated pair to a new made grave, where for a few moments, in the bright and silent midnight, they stood alone. But suddenly, there was a multitude of people among the graves.

Each family tomb had given up its inhabitants, who, one by one, through distant years, had been borne to its dark chamber, but now came forth and stood in a pale group together. There was the gray ancestor, the aged mother, and all their descendants, some withered and full of years, like themselves, and others in their prime; there, too, were the children who went prattling to the tomb, and there the maiden who yielded her early beauty to death's embrace, before passion had polluted it. Husbands and wives arose, who had lain many years side by side, and young mothers who had forgotten to kiss their first babes, though pillowed so long on their bosoms. Many had been buried in the habiliments of life, and still wore their ancient garb; some were old defenders of the infant colony, and gleamed forth in their steel caps and bright breast-plates, as if starting up at an Indian war-cry; other venerable shapes had been pastors of the church, famous among the New England clergy, and now leaned with hands clasped over their grave stones, ready to call the congregation to prayer. There stood the early settlers, those old illustrious ones, the heroes of tradition and fireside legends, the men of history whose features had been so long beneath the sod, that few alive could have remembered them. There, too, were faces of former townspeople, dimly recollected from childhood, and others, whom Leonard and Alice had wept in later years, but who now were most terrible of all, by their ghastly smile of recognition. All, in short, were there; the dead of other generations, whose moss-grown names could scarce be read upon their tomb stones, and their successors, whose graves were not yet green; all whom black funerals had followed slowly thither, now re-appeared where the mourners left them. Yet none but souls accursed were there, and fiends counterfeiting the likeness of departed saints.

The countenances of those venerable men, whose very features had been hallowed by lives of piety, were contorted now by intolerable pain or hellish passion, and now by an unearthly and derisive merriment. Had the pastors prayed, all saintlike as they seemed, it had been blasphemy. The chaste matrons, too, and the maidens with untasted lips, who had slept in their virgin graves apart from all other dust, now wore a look from which the two trembling mortals shrank, as if the unimaginable sin of twenty worlds were collected there. The faces of fond lovers, even of such as had pined into the tomb, because there their treasure was, were bent on one another with glances of hatred and smiles of bitter scorn, passions that are to devils, what love is to the blest. At times, the features of those, who had passed from a holy life to heaven, would vary to and fro, between their assumed aspect and the fiendish lineaments whence they had been transformed. The whole miserable multitude, both sinful souls and false spectres of good men, groaned horribly and gnashed their teeth, as they looked upward to the calm loveliness of the midnight sky, and beheld those homes of bliss where they must never dwell. Such was the apparition, though too shadowy for language to portray; for here would be the moon-beams on the ice, glittering through a warrior's breast-plate, and there the letters of a tomb stone, on the form that stood before it; and whenever a breeze went by, it swept the old men's hoary heads, the women's fearful beauty, and all the unreal throng, into one indistinguishable cloud together.

I dare not give the remainder of the scene, except in a very brief epitome. This company of devils and condemned souls had come on a holiday, to revel in the discovery of a complicated crime; as foul a one as ever was imagined in their dreadful abode. In the course of the tale, the reader had been permitted to discover, that all the incidents were results of the machinations of the wizard, who had cunningly devised that Walter Brome should tempt his unknown sister to guilt and shame, and himself perish by the hand of his twin-brother. I described the glee of the fiends, at this hideous conception, and their eagerness to know if it were consummated. The story concluded with the Appeal of Alice to the spectre of Walter Brome; his reply, absolving her from every stain; and the trembling awe with which ghost and devil fled, as from the sinless presence of an angel.

The sun had gone down. While I held my page of wonders in the fading light, and read how Alice and her brother were left alone among the graves, my voice mingled with the sigh of a summer wind, which passed over the hill top with the broad and hollow sound, as of the flight of unseen spirits. Not a word was spoken, till I added, that the wizard's grave was close beside us, and that the wood-wax had sprouted originally from his unhallowed bones. The ladies started; perhaps their cheeks might have grown pale, had not the crimson west been blushing on them; but after a moment they began to laugh, while the breeze took a

livelier motion, as if responsive to their mirth. I kept an
awful solemnity of visage, being indeed a little piqued, that
a narrative which had good authority in our ancient superstitions, and would have brought even a church deacon to
Gallows Hill, in old witch times, should now be considered
too grotesque and extravagant, for timid maids to tremble at.
Though it was past supper time, I detained them a while
longer on the hill, and made a trial whether truth were more
powerful than fiction.

We looked again towards the town, no longer arrayed in
that icy splendor of earth, tree and edifice, beneath the glow
of a wintry midnight, which, shining afar through the gloom
of a century, had made it appear the very home of visions in
visionary streets. An indistinctness had begun to creep over
the mass of buildings and blend them with the intermingled
tree tops, except where the roof of a statelier mansion, and
the steeples and brick towers of churches, caught the brightness of some cloud that yet floated in the sunshine. Twilight
over the landscape was congenial to the obscurity of time.
With such eloquence as my share of feeling and fancy could
supply, I called back hoar antiquity, and bade my companions
imagine an ancient multitude of people, congregated on the
hill side, spreading far below, clustering on the steep old roofs,
and climbing the adjacent heights, wherever a glimpse of this
spot might be obtained. I strove to realize and faintly communicate, the deep, unutterable loathing and horror, the in-
dignation, the affrighted wonder, that wrinkled on every
brow, and filled the universal heart. See! the whole crowd
turns pale and shrinks within itself, as the virtuous emerge
from yonder street. Keeping pace with that devoted company, I described them one by one; here tottered a woman in
her dotage, knowing neither the crime imputed her, nor its
punishment; there another, distracted by the universal madness, till feverish dreams were remembered as realities, and

she almost believed her guilt. One, a proud man once, was so broken down by the intolerable hatred heaped upon him, that he seemed to hasten his steps, eager to hide himself in the grave hastily dug, at the foot of the gallows. As they went slowly on, a mother looked behind, and beheld her peaceful dwelling; she cast her eyes elsewhere, and groaned inwardly, yet with bitterest anguish; for there was her little son among the accusers. I watched the face of an ordained pastor, who walked onward to the same death; his lips moved in prayer, no narrow petition for himself alone, but embracing all, his fellow sufferers and the frenzied multitude; he looked to heaven and trod lightly up the hill.

Behind their victims came the afflicted, a guilty and miserable band; villains who had thus avenged themselves on their enemies, and viler wretches, whose cowardice had destroyed their friends; lunatics, whose ravings had chimed in with the madness of the land; and children, who had played a game that the imps of darkness might have envied them, since it disgraced an age, and dipped a people's hands in blood. In the rear of the procession rode a figure on horseback, so darkly conspicuous, so sternly triumphant, that my hearers mistook him for the visible presence of the fiend himself; but it was only his good friend, Cotton Mather, proud of his well won dignity, as the representative of all the hateful features of his time; the one blood-thirsty man, in whom were concentrated those vices of spirit and errors of opinion, that sufficed to madden the whole surrounding multitude. And thus I marshalled them onward, the innocent who were to die, and the guilty who were to grow old in long remorse—tracing their every step, by rock, and shrub, and broken track, till their shadowy visages had circled round the hill-top, where we stood. I plunged into my imagination for a blacker horror, and a deeper woe, and pictured the scaffold——

But here my companions seized an arm on each side; their

nerves were trembling; and sweeter victory still, I had reached the seldom trodden places of their hearts, and found the well-spring of their tears. And now the past had done all it could. We slowly descended, watching the lights as they twinkled gradually through the town, and listening to the distant mirth of boys at play, and to the voice of a young girl, warbling somewhere in the dusk, a pleasant sound to wanderers from old witch times. Yet ere we left the hill, we could not but regret, that there is nothing on its barren summit, no relic of old, nor lettered stone of later days, to assist the imagination in appealing to the heart. We build the memorial column on the height which our fathers made sacred with their blood, poured out in a holy cause. And here in dark, funereal stone, should rise another monument, sadly commemorative of the errors of an earlier race, and not to be cast down, while the human heart has one infirmity that may result in crime.

MY VISIT TO NIAGARA

NEVER did a pilgrim approach Niagara with deeper enthusiasm, than mine. I had lingered away from it, and wandered to other scenes, because my treasury of anticipated enjoyments, comprising all the wonders of the world, had nothing else so magnificent, and I was loth to exchange the pleasures of hope for those of memory so soon. At length, the day came. The stage-coach, with a Frenchman and myself on the back seat, had already left Lewiston, and in less than an hour would set us down in Manchester. I began to listen for the roar of the cataract, and trembled with a sensation like dread, as the moment drew nigh, when its voice of ages must roll, for the first time, on my ear. The French gentleman stretched himself from the window, and expressed loud admiration, while, by a sudden impulse, I threw myself back and closed my eyes. When the scene shut in, I was glad to think, that for me the whole burst of Niagara was yet in futurity. We rolled on, and entered the village of Manchester, bordering on the falls.

I am quite ashamed of myself here. Not that I ran, like a madman, to the falls, and plunged into the thickest of the spray—never stopping to breathe, till breathing was impossible; not that I committed this, or any other suitable extravagance. On the contrary, I alighted with perfect decency and composure, gave my cloak to the black waiter, pointed out my baggage, and inquired, not the nearest way to the cataract, but about the dinner-hour. The interval was spent in arranging my dress. Within the last fifteen minutes, my mind had grown strangely benumbed, and my spirits apathetic, with a slight depression, not decided enough to be termed sadness. My enthusiasm was in a deathlike slumber. Without aspiring to immortality, as he did, I could have imitated that English traveller, who turned back from the point where he first heard the thunder of Niagara, after crossing the ocean to behold it. Many a western trader, by-the-by, has performed a similar act of heroism with more heroic simplicity, deeming it no such wonderful feat to dine at the hotel and resume his route to Buffalo or Lewiston, while the cataract was roaring unseen.

Such has often been my apathy, when objects, long sought, and earnestly desired, were placed within my reach. After dinner—at which, an unwonted and perverse epicurism detained me longer than usual—I lighted a cigar and paced the piazza, minutely attentive to the aspect and business of a very ordinary village. Finally, with reluctant step, and the feeling of an intruder, I walked towards Goat Island. At the toll-house, there were further excuses for delaying the inevitable moment. My signature was required in a huge leger, containing similar records innumerable, many of which I read. The skin of a great sturgeon, and other fishes, beasts, and reptiles; a collection of minerals, such as lie in heaps near the falls; some Indian moccasins, and other trifles, made of deer-skin and embroidered with beads; several newspapers from Montreal, New-York, and Boston; all attracted me in turn. Out of a number of twisted sticks, the manufacture of a Tuscarora Indian, I selected one of curled maple, curiously convoluted, and adorned with the carved images of a snake and a fish. Using this as my pilgrim's staff, I crossed the bridge. Above and below me were the rapids, a river of impetuous snow, with here and there a dark rock amid its whiteness, resisting all the physical fury, as any cold spirit did the moral influences of the scene. On reaching Goat Island, which separates the two great segments of the falls, I chose the right-hand path, and followed it to the edge of the American cascade. There, while the falling sheet was yet invisible, I saw the vapor that never vanishes, and the Eternal Rainbow of Niagara.

It was an afternoon of glorious sunshine, without a cloud, save those of the cataracts. I gained an insulated rock, and beheld a broad sheet of brilliant and unbroken foam, not shooting in a curved line from the top of the precipice, but falling headlong down from height to depth. A narrow stream diverged from the main branch, and hurried over the crag by a channel of its own, leaving a little pine-clad island and a streak of precipice, between itself and the larger sheet. Below arose the mist, on which was painted a dazzling sun-bow, with two concentric shadows—one, almost as perfect as the original brightness; and the other, drawn faintly round the broken edge of the cloud.

Still, I had not half seen Niagara. Following the verge of the island, the path led me to the Horse-shoe, where the real, broad St. Lawrence, rushing along on a level with its banks, pours its whole breadth over a concave line of precipice, and thence pursues its course between lofty crags towards Ontario. A sort of bridge, two or three feet wide, stretches out along the edge of the descending sheet, and hangs upon the rising mist, as if that were the foundation of the frail structure. Here I stationed myself, in the blast of wind, which the rushing river bore along with it. The bridge was tremulous beneath me, and marked the tremor of the solid earth. I looked along the whitening rapids, and endeavored to distinguish a mass of water far above the falls, to follow it to their verge, and go down with it, in fancy, to the abyss of clouds and storm. Casting my eyes across the river, and every side, I took in the whole scene at a glance, and tried to comprehend it in one vast idea. After an hour thus spent, I left the bridge, and, by a staircase, winding almost interminably round a post, descended to the base of the precipice. From that point, my path lay over slippery stones, and among great fragments of the cliff, to the edge of the cataract, where the wind at once enveloped me in spray, and perhaps dashed the rainbow round me. Were my long desires fulfilled? And had I seen Niagara?

Oh, that I had never heard of Niagara till I beheld it! Blessed were the wanderers of old, who heard its deep roar, sounding through the woods, as the summons to an unknown wonder, and approached its awful brink, in all the freshness of native feeling. Had its own mysterious voice been the first to warn me of its existence, then, indeed, I might have knelt down and worshipped. But I had come thither, haunted with a vision of foam and fury, and dizzy cliffs, and an ocean tumbling down out of the sky—a scene, in short, which Nature had too much good taste and calm simplicity to realize. My mind had struggled to adapt these false conceptions to the reality, and finding the effort vain, a wretched sense of disappointment weighed me down. I climbed the precipice, and threw myself on the earth—feeling that I was unworthy to look at the Great Falls, and careless about beholding them again.

All that night, as there has been and will be, for ages past and to come, a rushing sound was heard, as if a great tempest were sweeping through the air. It mingled with my dreams, and made them full of storm and whirlwind. Whenever I awoke, and heard this dread sound in the air, and the windows rattling as with a mighty blast, I could not rest again, till, looking forth, I saw how bright the stars were, and that every leaf in the garden was motionless. Never was a summer-night more calm to the eye, nor a gale of autumn louder to the ear. The rushing sound proceeds from the rapids, and the rattling of the casements is but an effect of the vibration of the whole house, shaken by the jar of the cataract. The noise of the rapids draws the attention from the true voice of Niagara, which is a dull, muffled thunder, resounding between the cliffs. I spent a wakeful hour at midnight, in distinguishing its reverberations, and rejoiced to find that my former awe and enthusiasm were reviving.

Gradually, and after much contemplation, I came to know, by my own feelings, that Niagara is indeed a wonder of the world, and not the less wonderful, because time and thought must be employed in comprehending it. Casting aside all pre-conceived notions, and preparation to be dire-struck or delighted, the beholder must stand beside it in the simplicity of his heart, suffering the mighty scene to work its own impression. Night after night, I dreamed of it, and was gladdened every morning by the consciousness of a growing capacity to enjoy it. Yet I will not pretend to the all-absorbing enthusiasm of some more fortunate spectators, nor deny, that very trifling causes would draw my eyes and thoughts from the cataract.

The last day that I was to spend at Niagara, before my departure for the far west, I sat upon the Table Rock. This celebrated station did not now, as of old, project fifty feet beyond the line of the precipice, but was shattered by the fall of an immense fragment, which lay distant on the shore below. Still, on the utmost verge of the rock, with my feet hanging over it, I felt as if suspended in the open air. Never before had my mind been in such perfect unison with the scene. There were intervals, when I was conscious of nothing but the great river, rolling calmly into the abyss, rather descending than precipitating itself, and acquiring tenfold majesty from its unhurried motion. It came like the march of Destiny. It was not taken by surprise, but seemed to have anticipated, in all its course through the broad lakes, that it must pour their collected waters down this height. The perfect foam of the river, after its descent, and the ever-varying shapes of mist, rising up, to become clouds in the sky, would be the very picture of confusion, were it merely transient, like the rage of a tempest. But when the beholder has stood awhile, and perceives no lull in the storm, and considers that the vapor and the foam are as everlasting as the rocks which produce them, all this turmoil assumes a sort of calmness. It soothes, while it awes the mind.

Leaning over the cliff, I saw the guide conducting two adventurers behind the falls. It was pleasant, from that high seat in the sunshine, to observe them struggling against the eternal storm of the lower regions, with heads bent down, now faltering, now pressing forward, and finally swallowed up in their victory. After their disappearance, a blast rushed out with an old hat, which it had swept from one of their heads. The rock, to which they were directing their unseen course, is marked, at a fearful distance on the exterior of the sheet, by a jet of foam. The attempt to reach it, appears both poetical and perilous, to a looker-on, but may be accomplished without much more difficulty or hazard, than in stemming a violent northeaster. In a few moments, forth came the children of the mist. Dripping and breathless, they crept along the base of the cliff, ascended to the guide's cottage, and received, I presume, a certificate of their achievement, with three verses of sublime poetry on the back.

My contemplations were often interrupted by strangers, who came down from Forsyth's to take their first view of the falls. A short, ruddy, middle-aged gentleman, fresh from old

England, peeped over the rock, and evinced his approbation by a broad grin. His spouse, a very robust lady, afforded a sweet example of maternal solicitude, being so intent on the safety of her little boy that she did not even glance at Niagara. As for the child, he gave himself wholly to the enjoyment of a stick of candy. Another traveller, a native American, and no rare character among us, produced a volume of Captain Hall's tour, and labored earnestly to adjust Niagara to the captain's description, departing, at last, without one new idea or sensation of his own. The next comer was provided, not with a printed book, but with a blank sheet of foolscap, from top to bottom of which, by means of an ever-pointed pencil, the cataract was made to thunder. In a little talk, which we had together, he awarded his approbation to the general view, but censured the position of Goat Island, observing that it should have been thrown farther to the right, so as to widen the American falls, and contract those of the Horse-shoe. Next appeared two traders of Michigan, who declared, that, upon the whole, the sight was worth looking at; there certainly was an immense water-power here; but that, after all, they would go twice as far to see the noble stone-works of Lockport, where the Grand Canal is locked down a descent of sixty feet. They were succeeded by a young fellow, in a home-spun cotton dress, with a staff in his hand, and a pack over his shoulders. He advanced close to the edge of the rock, where his attention, at first wavering among the different components of the scene, finally became fixed in the angle of the Horse-shoe falls, which is, indeed, the central point of interest. His whole soul seemed to go forth and be transported thither, till the staff slipped from his relaxed grasp, and falling down—down—down—struck upon the fragment of the Table Rock.

In this manner, I spent some hours, watching the varied impression, made by the cataract, on those who disturbed me, and returning to unwearied contemplation, when left alone. At length, my time came to depart. There is a grassy footpath, through the woods, along the summit of the bank, to a point whence a causeway, hewn in the side of the precipice, goes winding down to the ferry, about half a mile below the Table Rock. The sun was near setting, when I emerged from the shadow of the trees, and began the descent. The indirectness of my downward road continually changed the point of view, and shewed me, in rich and repeated succession—now, the whitening rapids and the majestic leap of the main river, which appeared more deeply massive as the light departed; now, the lovelier picture, yet still sublime, of Goat Island, with its rocks and grove, and the lesser falls, tumbling over the right bank of the St. Lawrence, like a tributary stream; now, the long vista of the river, as it eddied and whirled between the cliffs, to pass through Ontario towards the sea, and everywhere to be wondered at, for this one unrivalled scene. The golden sunshine tinged the sheet of the American cascade, and painted on its heaving spray the broken semicircle of a rainbow, Heaven's own beauty crowning earth's sublimity. My steps were slow, and I paused long at every turn of the descent, as one lingers and pauses, who discerns a brighter and brightening excellence in what he must soon behold no more. The solitude of the old wilderness now reigned over the whole vicinity of the falls. My enjoyment became the more rapturous, because no poet shared it—nor wretch, devoid of poetry, profaned it: but the spot, so famous through the world, was all my own!

GRAVES AND GOBLINS

NOW TALK WE of graves and goblins! Fit themes —start not! gentle reader—fit for a ghost like me. Yes; though an earth-clogged fancy is laboring with these conceptions, and an earthly hand will write them down, for mortal eyes to read, still their essence flows from as airy a ghost as ever basked in the pale starlight, at twelve o'clock. Judge them not by the gross and heavy form in which they now appear. They may be gross, indeed, with the earthly pollution contracted from the brain, through which they pass—and heavy with the burthen of mortal language, that crushes all the finer intelligences of the soul. This is no fault of mine. But, should aught of ethereal spirit be perceptible, yet scarcely so, glimmering along the dull train of words—should a faint perfume breathe from the mass of clay—then, gentle reader, thank the ghost, who thus embodies himself for your sake! Will you believe me, if I say that all true and noble thoughts, and elevated imaginations, are but partly the offspring of the intellect, which seems to produce them? Sprites, that were poets once, and are now all poetry, hover round the dreaming bard, and become his inspiration; buried statesmen lend their wisdom, gathered on earth and mellowed in the grave, to the historian; and when the preacher rises nearest to the level of his mighty subject, it is because the prophets of old days have communed with him. Who has not been conscious of mysteries within his mind, mysteries of truth and reality, which will not wear the chains of language? Mortal, then the dead were with you! And thus shall the earth-dulled soul, whom I inspire, be conscious of a misty brightness among his thoughts, and strive to make it gleam upon the page—but all in vain. Poor author! How will he despise what he can grasp, for the sake of the dim glory that eludes him.

So talk we of graves and goblins. But, what have ghosts to do with graves? Mortal man, wearing the dust which shall require a sepulchre, might deem it more a home and resting-place than a spirit can, whose earthly clod has returned to earth. Thus, philosophers have reasoned. Yet, wiser they who adhere to the ancient sentiment, that a phantom haunts and hallows the marble tomb or grassy hillock, where its material form was laid. Till purified from each stain of clay; till the passions of the living world are all forgotten; till it have less brotherhood with the wayfarers of earth, than with spirits that never wore mortality—the ghost must linger round the grave. Oh! it is a long and dreary watch, to some of us.

Even in early childhood, I had selected a sweet spot, of shade and glimmering sunshine, for my grave. It was no burial-ground, but a secluded nook of virgin earth, where I used to sit, whole summer afternoons, dreaming about life and death. My fancy ripened prematurely, and taught me secrets, which I could not otherwise have known. I pictured the coming years—they never came to me, indeed; but I pictured them like life, and made this spot the scene of all that should be brightest, in youth, manhood, and old age. There, in a little while, it would be time for me to breathe the bashful and burning vows of first-love; thither, after gathering fame abroad, I would return to enjoy the loud plaudit of the world, a vast but unobtrusive sound, like the booming of a distant sea; and thither, at the far-off close of life, an aged man would come, to dream, as the boy was dreaming, and be as happy in the past as he was in futurity. Finally, when all should be finished, in that spot so hallowed, in that soil so impregnated with the most precious of my bliss, there was to be my grave. Methought it would be the sweetest grave, that ever a mortal frame reposed in, or an ethereal spirit haunted. There, too, in future times, drawn thither by the spell which I had breathed around the place, boyhood would sport and dream, and youth would love, and manhood would enjoy, and age would dream again, and my ghost would watch but never frighten them. Alas, the vanity of mortal projects—even when they centre in the grave! I died in my first youth, before I had been a lover; at a distance, also, from the grave which fancy had dug for me; and they buried me in the thronged cemetery of a town, where my marble slab stands unnoticed amid a hundred others. And there are coffins on each side of mine!

'Alas, poor ghost!' will the reader say. Yet I am a happy ghost enough, and disposed to be contented with my grave, if the sexton will but let it be my own, and bring no other dead man to dispute my title. Earth has left few stains upon me, and it will be but a short time that I need haunt the place. It is good to die in early youth. Had I lived out three-score years and ten, or half of them, my spirit would have been so earth-encrusted, that centuries might not have purified it for a better home than the dark precincts of the grave. Meantime, there is good choice of company amongst us. From twilight till near sunrise, we are gliding, to-and-fro, some in the grave-yard, others miles away; and would we speak with any friend, we do but knock against his tomb-stone, and pronounce the name engraved on it; in an instant, there the shadow stands!

Some are ghosts of considerable antiquity. There is an old man, hereabout; he never had a tomb-stone, and is often puzzled to distinguish his own grave; but hereabouts he haunts, and long is doomed to haunt. He was a miser in his life-time, and buried a strong-box of ill-gotten gold, almost fresh from the mint, in the coinage of William and Mary. Scarcely was it safe, when the sexton buried the old man and his secret with him. I could point out the place where the treasure lies; it was at the bottom of the miser's garden; but a paved thoroughfare now passes beside the spot, and the corner-stone of a market-house presses right down upon it. Had the workmen dug six inches deeper, they would have found the hoard. Now thither must this poor old miser go, whether in starlight, moonshine, or pitch-darkness, and brood above his worthless treasure, recalling all the petty crimes, by which he gained it. Not a coin must he fail to reckon in his memory, nor forget a pennyworth of the sin that made up the sum, though his agony is such as if the pieces of gold, red-hot, were stamped into his naked soul. Often, while he is in torment there, he hears the steps of living men, who love the dross of earth as well as he did. May they never groan over their miserable wealth, like him! Night after night, for above a hundred years, hath he done this penance, and still must he do it, till the iron box be brought to light, and each separate coin be cleansed by the grateful tears of a widow or an orphan. My spirit sighs for his long vigil at the corner of the market-house!

There are ghosts whom I tremble to meet, and cannot think of them without a shudder. One has the guilt of blood upon him. The soul, which he thrust untimely forth, has long since been summoned from our gloomy grave-yard, and dwells among the stars of Heaven, too far and high for even the recollection of mortal anguish to ascend thither. Not so the murderer's ghost! It is his doom to spend all the hours of darkness in the spot which he stained with innocent blood, and to feel the hot steam—hot as when it first gushed upon his hand—incorporating itself with his spiritual substance. Thus, his horrible crime is ever fresh within him. Two other wretches are condemned to walk arm in arm. They were guilty lovers in their lives, and still, in death, must wear the guise of love, though hatred and loathing have become their very nature and existence. The pollution of their mutual sin remains with them, and makes their souls sick continually. Oh, that I might forget all the dark shadows which haunt about these graves! This passing thought of them has left a stain, and will weigh me down among dust and sorrow, beyond the time that my own transgressions would have kept me here.

There is one shade among us, whose high nature it is good to meditate upon. He lived a patriot, and is a patriot still. Posterity has forgotten him. The simple slab, of red free-stone, that bore his name, was broken long ago, and is now covered by the gradual accumulation of the soil. A tuft of thistles is his only monument. This upright spirit came to his grave, after a lengthened life, with so little stain of earth, that he might, almost immediately, have trodden the pathway of the sky. But his strong love of country chained him down, to share its vicissitudes of weal or woe. With such deep yearning in his soul, he was unfit for Heaven. That noblest virtue has the effect of sin, and keeps his pure and lofty spirit in a penance, which may not terminate till America be again a wilderness. Not that there is no joy for the dead patriot. Can he fail to experience it, while he contemplates the mighty and increasing power of the land, which he protected in its infancy? No; there is much to gladden him. But sometimes I dread to meet him, as he returns from the bed-chambers of rulers and politicians, after diving into their secret motives and searching out their aims. He looks round him, with a stern and awful sadness, and vanishes into his neglected grave. Let nothing sordid or selfish defile your deeds or thoughts, ye great men of the day, lest ye grieve the noble dead!

Few ghosts take such an enduring interest as this, even in their own private affairs. It made me rather sad, at first, to find how soon the flame of love expires, amid the chill damps of the tomb; so much the sooner, the more fiercely it may have burned. Forget your dead mistress, youth! She has already forgotten you. Maiden, cease to weep for your buried lover! He will know nothing of your tears, nor value them, if he did. Yet, it were blasphemy to say that true love is other than immortal. It is an earthly passion, of which I speak, mingled with little that is spiritual, and must therefore perish with the perishing clay. When souls have loved, there is no falsehood or forgetfulness. Maternal affection, too, is strong as adamant. There are mothers here, among us, who might have been in Heaven fifty years ago, if they could forbear to cherish earthly joy and sorrow, reflected from the bosoms of their children. Husbands and wives have a comfortable gift of oblivion, especially when secure of the faith of their living halves. Jealousy, it is true, will play the devil with a ghost, driving him to the bedside of secondary wedlock, there to scowl, unseen, and gibber inaudible remonstrances. Dead wives, however jealous in their life-time, seldom feel this posthumous torment so acutely.

Many, many things, that appear most important while we walk the busy street, lose all their interest the moment we are borne into the quiet grave-yard, which borders it. For my own part, my spirit had not become so mixed up with earthly existence, as to be now held in an unnatural combination, or tortured much with retrospective cares. I still love my parents and a younger sister, who remain among the living, and often grieve me by their patient sorrow for the dead. Each separate tear of theirs is an added weight upon my soul, and lengthens my stay among the graves. As to other matters, it exceedingly rejoices me, that my summons came before I had time to write a projected poem, which was highly imaginative in conception, and could not have failed to give me a triumphant rank in the choir of our native bards. Nothing is so much to be deprecated as post-humous renown. It keeps the immortal spirit from the proper bliss of his celestial state, and causes him to feed upon the impure breath of mortal men, till sometimes he forgets that there are starry realms above him. Few poets—infatuated that they are!—soar upward, while the least whisper of their name is heard on earth. On Sabbath evenings, my sisters sit by the fireside, between our father and mother, and repeat some hymns of mine, which they have often heard from my own lips, ere the tremulous voice left them forever. Little do they think, those dear ones, that the dead stands listening in the glimmer of the firelight, and is almost gifted with a visible shape by the fond intensity of their remembrance!

Now shall the reader know a grief of the poor ghost that speaks to him; a grief, but not a hopeless one. Since I have dwelt among the graves, they bore the corpse of a young maiden hither, and laid her in the old ancestral vault, which is hollowed in the side of a grassy bank. It has a door of stone, with rusty iron hinges, and above it, a rude sculpture of the family-arms, and inscriptions of all their names who have been buried there, including sire and son, mother and daughter, of an ancient colonial race. All of her lineage had gone before, and when the young maiden followed, the portal was closed forever. The night after her burial, when the other ghosts were flitting about their graves, forth came the pale virgin's shadow, with the rest, but knew not whither to go, nor whom to haunt, so lonesome had she been on earth. She stood by the ancient sepulchre, looking upward to the bright stars, as if she would, even then, begin her flight. Her sadness made me sad. That night and the next, I stood near her, in the moonshine, but dared not speak, because she seemed purer than all the ghosts, and fitter to converse with angels than with men. But the third bright eve, still gazing upward to the glory of the Heavens, she sighed, and said, 'When will my mother come for me!' Her low, sweet voice emboldened me to speak, and she was kind and gentle, though so pure, and answered me again. From that time, always at the ghostly hour, I sought the old tomb of her fathers, and either found her standing by the door, or knocked and she appeared. Blessed creature, that she was; her chaste spirit hallowed mine, and imparted such a celestial buoyancy, that I longed to grasp her hand, and fly—upward, aloft, aloft! I thought, too, that she only lingered here, till my earthlier soul should be purified for Heaven. One night, when the stars threw down the light that shadows love, I stole forth to the accustomed spot, and knocked, with my airy fingers, at her door. She answered not. Again I knocked, and breathed her name. Where was she? At once, the truth fell on my miserable spirit, and crushed it to the earth, among dead men's bones and mouldering dust, groaning in cold and desolate agony. Her penance was over! She had taken her trackless flight, and had found a home in the purest radiance of the upper stars, leaving me to knock at the stone portal of the darksome sepulchre. But I know—I know, that angels hurried her away, or surely she would have whispered ere she fled!

She is gone! How could the grave imprison that unspotted one! But her pure, ethereal spirit will not quite forget me, nor soar too high in bliss, till I ascend to join her. Soon, soon be that hour! I am weary of the earth-damps; they burthen me; they choke me! Already, I can float on the moonshine; the faint starlight will almost bear up my footsteps; the perfume of flowers, which grosser spirits love, is now too earthly a luxury for me. Grave! Grave! thou art not my home. I must flit a little longer in thy night-gloom, and then be gone—far from the dust of the living and the dead—far from the corruption that is around me, but no more within!

A few times, I have visited the chamber of one who walks, obscure and lonely, on his mortal pilgrimage. He will leave not many living friends, when he goes to join the dead, where his thoughts often stray, and he might better be. I steal into his sleep, and play my part among the figures of his dream. I glide through the moonlight of his waking fancy, and whisper conceptions, which, with a strange thrill of fear, he writes down as his own. I stand beside him now, at midnight, telling these dreamy truths, with a voice so dream-like, that he mistakes them for fictions of a brain too prone to such. Yet he glances behind him, and shivers, while the lamp burns pale. Farewell, dreamer—waking or sleeping! Your brightest dreams are fled; your mind grows too hard and cold for a spiritual guest to enter; you are earthly, too, and have all the sins of earth. The ghost will visit you no more.

But where is the maiden, holy and pure, though wearing a form of clay, that would have me bend over her pillow, at midnight, and leave a blessing there? With a silent invocation, let her summon me. Shrink not, maiden, when I come! In life, I was a high-souled youth, meditative, yet seldom sad, full of chaste fancies, and stainless from all grosser sin. And now, in death, I bring no loathsome smell of the grave, nor ghastly terrors—but gentle, and soothing, and sweetly pensive influences. Perhaps, just fluttering for the skies, my visit may hallow the well-springs of thy thought, and make thee heavenly here on earth. Then shall pure dreams and holy meditations bless thy life; nor thy sainted spirit linger round the grave, but seek the upper stars, and meet me there!

SKETCHES FROM MEMORY

The Inland Port

I T WAS a bright forenoon, when I set foot on the beach at Burlington, and took leave of the two boatmen, in whose little skiff I had voyaged since daylight from Peru. Not that we had come that morning from South America, but only from the New-York shore of Lake Champlain. The highlands of the coast behind us stretched north and south, in a double range of bold, blue peaks, gazing over each other's shoulders at the Green Mountains of Vermont. The latter are far the loftiest, and, from the opposite side of the lake, had displayed a more striking outline. We were now almost at their feet, and could see only a sandy beach, sweeping beneath a woody bank, around the semi-circular bay of Burlington. The painted light-house, on a small green island, the wharves and warehouses, with sloops and schooners moored alongside, or at anchor, or spreading their canvass to the wind, and boats rowing from point to point, reminded me of some fishing town on the sea-coast.

But I had no need of tasting the water to convince myself that Lake Champlain was not an arm of the sea; its quality was evident, both by its silvery surface, when unruffled, and a faint, but unpleasant and sickly smell, forever steaming up in the sunshine. One breeze from the Atlantic, with its briny fragrance, would be worth more to these inland people than all the perfumes of Arabia. On closer inspection, the vessels at the wharves looked hardly sea-worthy—there being a great lack of tar about the seams and rigging, and perhaps other deficiencies, quite as much to the purpose. I observed not a single sailor in the port. There were men, indeed, in blue jackets and trowsers, but not of the true nautical fashion, such as dangle before slop-shops; others wore tight pantaloons and coats preponderously long-tailed—cutting very queer figures at the mast-head; and, in short, these fresh-water fellows had about the same analogy to the real 'old salt,' with his tarpaulin, pea-jacket and sailor-cloth trowsers, as a lake fish to a Newfoundland cod.

Nothing struck me more, in Burlington, than the great number of Irish emigrants. They have filled the British provinces to the brim, and still continue to ascend the St. Lawrence, in infinite tribes, overflowing by every outlet into the States. At Burlington, they swarm in huts and mean dwellings near the lake, lounge about the wharves, and elbow the native citizens entirely out of competition in their own line. Every species of mere bodily labor is the prerogative of these Irish. Such is their multitude, in comparison with any possible demand for their services, that it is difficult to conceive how a third part of them should earn even a daily glass of whiskey, which is doubtless their first necessary of life—daily bread being only the second. Some were angling in the lake, but had caught only a few perch, which little fishes, without a miracle, would be nothing among so many. A miracle there certainly must have been, and a daily one, for the subsistence of these wandering hordes. The men exhibit a lazy strength and careless merriment, as if they had fed well hitherto, and meant to feed better hereafter; the women strode about, uncovered in the open air, with far plumper waists and brawnier limbs, as well as bolder faces, than our shy and slender females; and their progeny, which was innumerable, had the reddest and the roundest cheeks of any children in America.

While we stood at the wharf, the bell of a steamboat gave two preliminary peals, and she dashed away for Plattsburgh, leaving a trail of smoky breath behind, and breaking the glassy surface of the lake before her. Our next movement brought us into a handsome and busy square, the sides of which were filled up with white houses, brick stores, a church, a court-house, and a bank. Some of these edifices had roofs of tin, in the fashion of Montreal, and glittered in the sun with cheerful splendor, imparting a lively effect to the whole square. One brick building, designated in large letters as the custom-house, reminded us that this inland village is a port of entry, largely concerned in foreign trade, and holding daily intercourse with the British empire. In this border country, the Canadian bank-notes circulate as freely as our own, and British and American coin are jumbled into the same pocket, the effigies of the king of England being made to kiss those of the goddess of liberty. Perhaps there was an emblem in the involuntary contact. There was a pleasant mixture of people in the square of Burlington, such as cannot be seen elsewhere, at one view: merchants from Montreal, British officers from the frontier garrisons, French Canadians, wandering Irish, Scotchmen of a better class, gentlemen of the south on a pleasure-tour, country 'squires on business; and a great throng of Green Mountain boys, with their horse-wagons and ox-teams, true Yankees in aspect, and looking more superlatively so, by contrast with such a variety of foreigners.

ROCHESTER

The gray, but transparent evening, rather shaded than obscured the scene—leaving its stronger features visible, and even improved, by the medium through which I beheld them. The volume of water is not very great, nor the roar deep enough to be termed grand, though such praise might have been appropriate before the good people of Rochester had abstracted a part of the unprofitable sublimity of the cascade. The Genesee has contributed so bountifully to their canals and mill-dams, that it approaches the precipice with diminished pomp, and rushes over it in foamy streams of various width, leaving a broad face of the rock insulated and unwashed, between the two main branches of the falling river. Still it was an impressive sight, to one who had not seen Niagara. I confess, however, that my chief interest arose from a legend, connected with these falls, which will become poetical in the lapse of years, and was already so to me, as I pictured the catastrophe out of dusk and solitude. It was from a platform, raised over the naked island of the cliff, in the middle of the cataract, that Sam Patch took his last leap, and alighted in the other world. Strange as it may appear—that any uncertainty should rest upon his fate, which was consummated in the sight of thousands—many will tell you that the illustrious Patch concealed himself in a cave under the falls, and has continued to enjoy posthumous renown, without foregoing the comforts of this present life.

But the poor fellow prized the shout of the multitude too much not to have claimed it at the instant, had he survived. He will not be seen again, unless his ghost, in such a twilight as when I was there, should emerge from the foam, and vanish among the shadows that fall from cliff to cliff. How stern a moral may be drawn from the story of poor Sam Patch! Why do we call him a madman or a fool, when he has left his memory around the falls of the Genesee, more permanently than if the letters of his name had been hewn into the forehead of the precipice? Was the leaper of cataracts more mad or foolish than other men who throw away life, or misspend it in pursuit of empty fame, and seldom so triumphantly as he? That which he won is as invaluable as any, except the unsought glory, spreading, like the rich perfume of richer fruit, from virtuous and useful deeds.

Thus musing, wise in theory, but practically as great a fool as Sam, I lifted my eyes and beheld the spires, warehouses, and dwellings of Rochester, half a mile distant on both sides of the river, indistinctly cheerful, with the twinkling of many lights amid the fall of evening.

The town had sprung up like a mushroom, but no presage of decay could be drawn from its hasty growth. Its edifices are of dusky brick, and of stone that will not be grayer in a hundred years than now; its churches are Gothic; it is impossible to look at its worn pavements, and conceive how lately the forest-leaves have been swept away. The most ancient town in Massachusetts appears quite like an affair of yesterday, compared with Rochester. Its attributes of youth are the activity and eager life with which it is redundant. The whole street, sidewalks and centre, was crowded with pedestrians, horsemen, stage-coaches, gigs, light wagons, and heavy ox-teams, all hurrying, trotting, rattling, and rumbling, in a throng that passed continually, but never passed away. Here, a country wife was selecting a churn, from several gaily-painted ones on the sunny sidewalk; there, a farmer was bartering his produce; and, in two or three places, a crowd of people were showering bids on a vociferous auctioneer. I saw a great wagon and an ox-chain knocked off to a very pretty woman. Numerous were the lottery-offices—those true temples of Mammon—where red and yellow bills offered splendid fortunes to the world at large, and banners of painted cloth gave notice that the 'lottery draws next Wednesday.' At the ringing of a bell, judges, jurymen, lawyers, and clients, elbowed each other to the court-house, to busy themselves with cases that would doubtless illustrate the state of society, had I the means of reporting them. The number of public houses benefitted the flow of temporary population; some were farmers' taverns—cheap, homely, and comfortable; others were magnificent hotels, with negro waiters, gentlemanly landlords in black broadcloth, and foppish bar-keepers in Broadway coats, with chased gold watches in their waistcoat pockets. I caught one of these fellows quizzing me through an eye-glass. The porters were lumbering up the steps with baggage from the packet-boats, while waiters plied the brush on dusty travellers, who, meanwhile, glanced over the innumerable advertisements in the daily papers.

In short, everybody seemed to be there, and all had something to do, and were doing it with all their might, except a party of drunken recruits for the western military posts, principally Irish and Scotch, though they wore uncle Sam's gray jacket and trowsers. I noticed one other idle man. He carried a rifle on his shoulder and a powder-horn across his breast, and appeared to stare about him with confused wonder, as if, while he was listening to the wind among the forest boughs, the hum and bustle of an instantaneous city had surrounded him.

A Night Scene

The steamboat in which I was passenger for Detroit, had put into the mouth of a small river, where the greater part of the night would be spent in repairing some damages of the machinery. As the evening was warm, though cloudy and very dark, I stood on deck, watching a scene that would not have attracted a second glance in the day-time, but became picturesque by the magic of strong light and deep shade. Some wild Irishmen were replenishing our stock of wood, and had kindled a great fire on the bank, to illuminate their labors. It was composed of large logs and dry brushwood, heaped together with careless profusion, blazing fiercely, spouting showers of sparks into the darkness, and gleaming wide over Lake Erie—a beacon for perplexed voyagers, leagues from land. All around and above the furnace, there was total obscurity. No trees, or other objects, caught and reflected any portion of the brightness, which thus wasted itself in the immense void of night, as if it quivered from the expiring embers of the world, after the final conflagration. But the Irishmen were continually emerging from the dense gloom, passing through the lurid glow, and vanishing into the gloom on the other side. Sometimes a whole figure would be made visible, by the shirt-sleeves and light-colored dress; others were but half seen, like imperfect creatures; many flitted, shadow-like, along the skirts of darkness, tempting fancy to a vain pursuit; and often, a face alone was reddened by the fire, and stared strangely distinct, with no traces of a body. In short, these wild Irish, distorted and exaggerated by the blaze, now lost in deep shadow, now bursting into sudden splendor, and now struggling between light and darkness, formed a picture which might have been transferred, almost unaltered, to a tale of the supernatural. As they all carried lanterns of wood, and often flung sticks upon the fire, the least imaginative spectator would at once compare them to devils, condemned to keep alive the flame of their own torment.

A VISIT TO THE CLERK OF THE WEATHER

I DON'T KNOW—I have not yet spoken to the clerk of the weather,"—said I, in common parlance to my friend and kinsman, who had asked me the wise question—"Do you think we shall have an early spring?" We stood on the steps of the M—— hotel. The night was not very dark, but sundry flakes of snow, that came wavering to the ground, served to render the vision indistinct. Nevertheless I could plainly perceive that a little old woman in a gray cloak, who was passing at the moment, had caught my words; and her small black eyes rayed up through the mist as I spoke, with an expression of intelligence rather uncomfortable to a sober citizen like myself. My friend, at the same moment, turned on his heel with a slight shudder, and sought a warmer climate within. The little old woman stood at my side in a twinkling, and when I would have withdrawn myself, I felt her bony hand encircling my arm as if I had been in the grasp of a skeleton.

"Unhand me, madam, or by Heaven——"

"You have taken *his* name in vain," said she, in a hoarse whisper, "often enough, and it is evident that you believe not in his existence. Come with me. Nay, do not hesitate, or I will weigh your manhood against the courage of an old woman."

"On, fool!" exclaimed I.

Away scampered the old woman, and I followed—drawn by an impulse which I could not resist. Streets, houses, woods, fences, seemed running back as we progressed, so rapid was our motion. At length I was lifted from my feet, and whirled through the air at such a rate that I nearly lost my breath. The gray cloak of the old woman could be discerned at some distance before me—clouds sprang apart, and rolled themselves in ridges on either hand of her as she passed, making a clear path for herself and follower. How far we travelled thus I am unable to say. But suddenly we struck the land, and I stood upon the green turf. The sun flamed full upon my head, and I now, for the first time, felt travel-worn and faint.

"I can assist you no farther," said the old woman; and in a moment she had disappeared.

At a little distance from the spot where I stood, was a pile of rocks of a singular form. About a dozen tall, slate-colored rocks—each one of which was several acres in height—had been thrown together in a circle in the form of a pyramid, the points meeting at the top. As I stood gazing at this singular structure, I observed a light smoke rising up through a small aperture on the very apex of this gigantic cone. I determined to obtain ingress to this strange dwelling, for that it was inhabited I no longer doubted. I walked around the natural fabric several times before I discovered an entrance; several rugged rocks had hidden it from my view. But the opening was large enough to admit a dozen horsemen abreast. Slowly and cautiously I entered the lofty chamber. It was about five hundred yards in circumference. Several singular objects immediately drew my attention; of course the animated forms were honored with my first notice. There were three gigantic beings lounging about in different parts of the room, while a venerable, stately old man, with long gray locks, sat at the farther side of the apartment busily engaged in writing. Before advancing to speak to any of my new acquaintances, I glanced around the rocky cavern. In one corner was piled a heap of red-hot thunderbolts. Against the wall hung several second-hand rainbows, covered with dust and much faded. Several hundred cart loads of hailstones, two large sacks of wind, and a portable tempest, firmly secured with iron bands, next engaged my attention. But I saw that the venerable personage mentioned above had become sensible of my presence, and as he had half risen from his seat, I hastened to present myself. As I drew near to him, I was struck by the size of his massive frame and the fierce expression of his eyes. He had stuck his pen behind his ear—which pen was neither more nor less than the top of a poplar tree, which some storm had rudely disengaged from its trunk, and the butt of which he had hewed down to a proper size for dipping into his inkhorn. He took my hand into his broad palm, and squeezed it too cordially for my bodily comfort, but greatly to the satisfaction of my mind, which had experienced some painful misgivings from my first entrance. I saluted him in the fashion of my country, and he replied,

"I am tolerably well, I thank you, for an old man of threescore centuries—from whence come you?"

"I am last from Boston, sir."

"I do not recollect any planet of that name," said he.

"I beg pardon—from the earth, I should have said."

He thought a moment. "Yes, yes, I do recollect a little mud-ball somewhere in this direction;"—he pointed with his arm—"but, truly, I had almost forgotten it. Hum! we have neglected you of late. It must be looked to. Our ally, Mr. John Frost, has had some claims on us, which we have liquidated by giving him permission to erect sundry ice-palaces, and throw up a few fortifications on your soil; but I fear the rogue has made too much of his privilege. He must be checked!"

"Really, sir, not only my gratitude, but the gratitude of all the world would be yours, if you would attend to us a little more vigilantly than you have done."

He looked grave a moment—shook his head, and rejoined —"But, sir, I have, myself, some complaints to make with regard to you. I have been somewhat slandered by your fellows, and, in truth, that was one inducement that led me to yield so readily to the request of my kinsman, Mr. Frost. You probably know there are some persons on your little planet who pretend to be of my council, and who send out little printed missiles, pretending to great ingenuity, wherein it is set forth that on such and such a day there shall be a snow-storm—a tempest—thunder and lightning—or fervent heat. Nay, some of them have carried it so far as to publish caricatures and grotesque drawings—have prophesied that there should be snow in August, and——"

Here we were interrupted by a loud hissing noise, which caused me to start and turn round.

"You must have a care. You have scorched your garments, I fear," cried my host to a squat figure, who came trudging towards us, wrapped in sheets of ice and wearing a huge wig powdered with snow.

"It is nothing, your Honor," answered the other, in a hollow voice which chilled my blood—"I only trod upon that cursed coil of chain lightning which your servant has placed so near the door to be my bane as often as I visit you!"

I was too much taken up with this uncouth visiter to notice the entrance of another guest, who had placed herself directly between me and the clerk of the weather before I beheld her. She was a lovely young damsel, dressed in a variegated gown, of the most beautiful colors, her head surmounted by a green turban, and her feet shod with moccasins of the same hue, bespangled with dew-drops. The icy dwarf shrunk aside as she approached, and lowered at her from under his thick brows. She cast a glance at him, and pouted like a spoiled child. She then turned to me, and said in a tone of ineffable sweetness,

"You are the stranger from the Earth, I conclude?"

"At your service, fair lady."

"I heard of your arrival," continued she; "and hastened to meet you. I wish to inquire after my good friends, the inhabitants of your globe. My name is Spring."

"My dear lady," said I, "your countenance would gladden the hearts of us all; I assure you that your presence has been desired and earnestly prayed for by all classes of my fellow-sufferers."

"It is too provoking!" cried she, dashing her green turban upon the ground, and stamping with her little foot until I was besprinkled with the dew-drops that it shed. "I suppose that I am blamed—nay, execrated, for my tardiness by my children of the earth—while heaven knows that I long to bound over your valleys and hills, and linger by the side of your running brooks as of yore. But that wretch—that mis-shapen wretch—" and she pointed at Jack Frost, for he it was, "that soulless, withering demon, holds me in his power. I brought an action against him last year; but, unfortunately, I was advised to put the case in Chancery, and summer arrived before it was decided. But assure your fellows that I will not neglect them in future. I shall be amongst them early. Mr. Frost is obliged to take a journey to the north to procure a polar bear for his wife, who has lingered amongst you, with her husband, so long, that she affects some of your customs, and must needs have a substitute for a lap-dog." She then turned away and held communion with the clerk of the weather, while I sauntered about the cavern to examine its singular contents. A gigantic fellow was sweating over the fire and cooking his master's breakfast. In a moment, I saw him ascend by a sort of rope ladder, and pick a small white cloud out of the heavens wherewith to settle the coffee.

I sauntered on until I came to a heap of granite, behind which sat a dozen little black fellows, cross-legged, who were laboring with all their might to weave a thunder gust. The part of the business which seemed to puzzle them most was, the working in of the bolts, which they were obliged to handle with long pincers. Another important point was sewing on the fringe, which was made of chain lightning. While I stood surveying these apprentices, a strapping fellow came reeling towards me, and inquired whether I had visited the forge. I told him that I had not. He said that it was not now in operation, as there was a sufficient quantity of thunderbolts manufactured for present use, although there might soon be a trifle of an earthquake to patch up. I observed that his wrist was swathed with a crimson bandage, and inquired if he was injured in that part. He said that he had received a trifling scratch there, for that last year he had been commissioned to discharge several thunderbolts upon our earth, which he did to his satisfaction until he came to the last, which, having been hurled like a rocket against our globe, unfortunately alighted on the head of a certain member of Congress, where it met with so much resistance that it bounded back to the skies and grazed his wrist.

At this moment somebody seized my arm from behind; I turned my head and saw the little old woman in the gray cloak. I was hurried from the massive hall, and conveyed, with as much speed as before, back to the world from which I had set out on this strange and wonderful adventure.

FRAGMENTS FROM THE JOURNAL
OF A SOLITARY MAN

M Y POOR FRIEND "OBERON"—for let me be
allowed to distinguish him by so quaint a name—
sleeps with the silent of ages. He died calmly.
Though his disease was pulmonary, his life did not flicker
out like a wasted lamp, sometimes shooting up into a strange
temporary brightness; but the tide of being ebbed away, and
the moon of his existence waned till, in the simple phraseology of Scripture, "he was not." The last words he said to me
were, "Burn my papers—all that you can find in yonder
escritoire; for I fear there are some there which you may be
betrayed into publishing. I have published enough; as for
the old disconnected journal in your possession ——" But
here my poor friend was checked in his utterance by that
same hollow cough which would never let him alone. So he
coughed himself tired, and sunk to slumber. I watched from
that midnight hour till high noon on the morrow for his
waking. The chamber was dark; till, longing for light, I
opened the window-shutter, and the broad day looked in on
the marble features of the dead!

I religiously obeyed his instructions with regard to the
papers in the escritoire, and burned them in a heap without
looking into one, though sorely tempted. But the old journal

I kept. Perhaps in strict conscience I ought also to have burned that; but, casting my eye over some half-torn leaves the other day, I could not resist an impulse to give some fragments of it to the public. To do this satisfactorily, I am obliged to twist this thread, so as to string together into a semblance of order my Oberon's "random pearls."

If any body that holds any commerce with his fellow-men can be called solitary, Oberon was a "solitary man." He lived in a small village at some distance from the metropolis, and never came up to the city except once in three months for the purpose of looking into a book-store, and of spending two hours and a half with me. In that space of time I would tell him all that I could remember of interest which had occurred in the interim of his visits. He would join very heartily in the conversation; but as soon as the time of his usual tarrying had elapsed, he would take up his hat and depart. He was unequivocally the most original person I ever knew. His style of composition was very charming. No tales that have ever appeared in our popular journals have been so generally admired as his. But a sadness was on his spirit; and this, added to the shrinking sensitiveness of his nature, rendered him not misanthropic, but singularly averse to social intercourse. Of the disease, which was slowly sapping the springs of his life, he first became fully conscious after one of those long abstractions in which he was so wont to indulge. It is remarkable, however, that his first idea of this sort, instead of deepening his spirit with a more melancholy hue, restored him to a more natural state of mind.

He had evidently cherished a secret hope that some impulse would at length be given him, or that he would muster sufficient energy of will to return into the world, and act a wiser and happier part than his former one. But life never called the dreamer forth; it was Death that whispered him. It is to be regretted that this portion of his old journal contains so few passages relative to this interesting period; since the little which he has recorded, though melancholy enough, breathes the gentleness of a spirit newly restored to communion with its kind. If there be any thing bitter in the following reflections, its source is in human sympathy, and its sole object is himself.

"It is hard to die without one's happiness; to none more so than myself, whose early resolution it had been to partake largely of the joys of life, but never to be burthened with its cares. Vain philosophy! The very hardships of the poorest laborer, whose whole existence seems one long toil, has something preferable to my best pleasures.

Merely skimming the surface of life, I know nothing, by my own experience, of its deep and warm realities. I have achieved none of those objects which the instinct of mankind especially prompts them to pursue, and the accomplishment of which must therefore beget a native satisfaction. The truly wise, after all their speculations, will be led into the common path, and, in homage to the human nature that pervades them, will gather gold, and till the earth, and set out trees, and build a house. But I have scorned such wisdom. I have rejected, also, the settled, sober, careful gladness of a man by his own fireside, with those around him whose welfare is committed to his trust and their guidance to his fond authority. Without influence among serious affairs, my footsteps were not imprinted on the earth, but lost in air; and I shall leave no son to inherit my share of life, with a better sense of its privileges and duties, when his father should vanish like a bubble; so that few mortals, even the humblest and the weakest, have been such ineffectual shadows in the world, or die so utterly as I must. Even a young man's bliss has not been mine. With a thousand vagrant fantasies, I have never truly loved, and perhaps shall be doomed to loneliness throughout the eternal future, because, here on earth, my soul has never married itself to the soul of woman.

Such are the repinings of one who feels, too late, that the sympathies of his nature have avenged themselves upon him. They have frustrated, with a joyless life and the prospect of a reluctant death, my selfish purpose to keep aloof from mortal disquietudes, and be a pleasant idler among care-stricken and laborious men. I have other regrets, too, savoring more of my old spirit. The time has been when I meant to visit every region of the earth, except the Poles and central Africa. I had a strange longing to see the Pyramids. To Persia and Arabia, and all the gorgeous East, I owed a pilgrimage for the sake of their magic tales. And England, the land of my ancestors! Once I had fancied that my sleep would not be quiet in the grave unless I should return, as it were, to my home of past ages, and see the very cities, and castles, and battle-fields of history, and stand within the holy gloom of its cathedrals, and kneel at the shrines of its immortal poets, there asserting myself their hereditary countryman. This feeling lay among the deepest in my heart. Yet, with this home-sickness for the father-land, and all these plans of remote travel,—which I yet believe that my peculiar instinct impelled me to form, and upbraided me for not accomplishing—the utmost limit of my wanderings has been little more than six hundred miles from my native village. Thus, in whatever way I consider my life, or what must be termed such, I cannot feel as if I have lived at all.

I am possessed, also, with the thought that I have never yet discovered the real secret of my powers; that there has been a mighty treasure within my reach, a mine of gold beneath my feet, worthless because I have never known how to seek for it; and for want of perhaps one fortunate idea, I am to die

'Unwept, unhonored, and unsung.'

Once, amid the troubled and tumultuous enjoyment of my life, there was one dreary thought that haunted me,—the terrible necessity imposed on mortals to grow old or die. I could not bear the idea of losing one youthful grace. True: I saw other men, who had once been young and now were old, enduring their age with equanimity, because each year reconciled them to its own added weight. But for myself, I felt that age would be not less miserable, creeping upon me slowly, than if it fell at once. I sometimes looked in the glass, and endeavored to fancy my cheeks yellow and interlaced with furrows, my forehead wrinkled deeply across, the top of my head bald and polished, my eye-brows and side-locks iron-gray, and a grisly beard sprouting on my chin. Shuddering at the picture, I changed it for the dead face of a young man, with dark locks clustering heavily round its pale beauty, which would decay, indeed, but not with years, nor in the sight of men. The latter visage shocked me least.

Such a repugnance to the hard conditions of long life is common to all sensitive and thoughtful men, who minister to the luxury, the refinements, the gaiety and lightsomeness, to any thing, in short, but the real necessities of their fellow-creatures. He who has a part in the serious business of life, though it be only as a shoemaker, feels himself equally respectable in youth and age, and therefore is content to live, and look forward to wrinkles and decrepitude in their due season. It is far otherwise with the busy idlers of the world. I was particularly liable to this torment, being a meditative person in spite of my levity. The truth could not be concealed, nor the contemplation of it avoided. With deep inquietude I became aware that what was graceful now, and seemed appropriate enough to my age of flowers, would be ridiculous in middle life; and that the world, so indulgent to the fantastic youth, would scorn the bearded man, still telling love-tales, loftily ambitious of a maiden's tear, and squeezing out, as it were, with his brawny strength, the essence of roses. And in his old age the sweet lyrics of Anacreon made the girls laugh at his white hairs the more. With such sentiments, conscious that my part in the drama of life was fit only for a youthful performer, I nourished a regretful desire to be summoned early from the scene. I set a limit to myself, the age of twenty-five, few years indeed, but too many to be thrown away. Scarcely had I thus fixed the term of my mortal pilgrimage, than the thought grew into a presentiment that, when the space should be completed, the world would have one butterfly the less, by my far flight.

Oh, how fond I was of life, even while allotting, as my proper destiny, an early death! I loved the world, its cities, its villages, its grassy roadsides, its wild forests, its quiet scenes, its gay, warm, enlivening bustle; in every aspect, I loved the world so long as I could behold it with young eyes and dance through it with a young heart. The earth had been made so beautiful, that I longed for no brighter sphere, but only an ever youthful eternity in this. I clung to earth as if my beginning and ending were to be there, unable to imagine any but an earthly happiness, and choosing such, with all its imperfections, rather than perfect bliss which might be alien from it. Alas! I had not yet known that weariness by which the soul proves itself ethereal."

Turning over the old journal, I open, by chance, upon a passage which affords a signal instance of the morbid fancies to which Oberon frequently yielded himself. Dreams like the following were probably engendered by the deep gloom sometimes thrown over his mind by his reflections on death.

"I dreamed that one bright forenoon I was walking through Broadway, and seeking to cheer myself with the warm and busy life of that far-famed promenade. Here a coach thundered over the pavement, and there an unwieldy omnibus, with spruce gigs rattling past, and horsemen prancing through all the bustle. On the side-walk people were looking at the rich display of goods, the plate and jewelry, or the latest caricature in the booksellers' windows; while fair ladies and whiskered gentlemen tripped gaily along, nodding mutual recognitions, or shrinking from some rough countryman or sturdy laborer whose contact might have ruffled their finery. I found myself in this animated scene, with a dim and misty idea that it was not my proper place, or that I had ventured into the crowd with some singularity of dress or aspect which made me ridiculous. Walking in the sunshine, I was yet cold as death. By degrees, too, I perceived myself the object of universal attention, and, as it seemed, of horror and affright. Every face grew pale; the laugh was hushed, and the voices died away in broken syllables; the people in the shops crowded to the doors with a ghastly stare, and the passengers on all sides fled as from an embodied pestilence. The horses reared and snorted. An old beggar woman sat before St. Paul's church, with her withered palm stretched out to all, but drew it back from me, and pointed to the graves and monuments in that populous church-yard. Three lovely girls, whom I had formerly known, ran shrieking across the street. A personage in black, whom I was about to overtake, suddenly turned his head, and showed the features of a long-lost friend. He gave me a look of horror and was gone.

I passed not one step further, but threw my eyes on a looking-glass which stood deep within the nearest shop. At the first glimpse of my own figure I awoke, with a horrible sensation of self-terror and self-loathing. No wonder that the affrighted city fled! I had been promenading Broadway in my shroud!"

I should be doing injustice to my friend's memory, were I to publish other extracts even nearer to insanity than this, from the scarcely legible papers before me. I gather from them,—for I do not remember that he ever related to me the circumstances,—that he once made a journey, chiefly on foot, to Niagara. Some conduct of the friends among whom he resided in his native village was construed by him into oppression. These were the friends to whose care he had been committed by his parents, who died when Oberon was about twelve years of age. Though he had always been treated by them with the most uniform kindness, and though a favourite among the people of the village rather on account of the sympathy which they felt in his situation than from any merit of his own, such was the waywardness of his temper, that on a slight provocation he ran away from the home that sheltered him, expressing openly his determination to die sooner than return to the detested spot. A severe illness overtook him after he had been absent about four months. While ill, he felt how unsoothing were the kindest looks and tones of strangers. He rose from his sick bed a better man, and determined upon a speedy self-atonement by returning to his native town. There he lived, solitary and sad, but forgiven and cherished by his friends till the day he died. That part of the journal which contained a description of this journey is mostly destroyed. Here and there is a fragment. I cannot select, for the pages are very scanty; but I do not withhold the following fragments, because they indicate a better and more cheerful frame of mind than the foregoing.

"On reaching the ferry-house, a rude structure of boards at the foot of the cliff, I found several of these wretches devoid of poetry, and lost some of my own poetry by contact with them. The hut was crowded by a party of provincials—a simple and merry set, who had spent the afternoon fishing near the Falls, and were bartering black and white bass and eels for the ferryman's whiskey. A greyhound and three spaniels, brutes of much more grace and decorous demeanor than their masters, sat at the door. A few yards off, yet wholly unnoticed by the dogs, was a beautiful fox, whose countenance betokened all the sagacity attributed to him in ancient fable. He had a comfortable bed of straw in an old barrel, whither he retreated, flourishing his bushy tail as I made a step towards him, but soon came forth and surveyed me with a keen and intelligent eye. The Canadians bartered their fish and drank their whiskey, and were loquacious on trifling subjects, and merry at simple jests, with as little regard to the scenery as they could have shown to the flattest part of the Grand Canal. Nor was I entitled to despise them; for I amused myself with all those foolish matters of fishermen, and dogs, and fox, just as if Sublimity and Beauty were not married at that place and moment; as if their nuptial band were not the brightest of all rainbows on the opposite shore; as if the gray precipice were not frowning above my head and Niagara thundering around me.

The grim ferryman, a black-whiskered giant, half drunk withal, now thrust the Canadians by main force out of his door, launched a boat, and bade me sit down in the stern-sheets. Where we crossed, the river was white with foam, yet did not offer much resistance to a straight passage, which brought us close to the outer edge of the American falls. The rainbow vanished as we neared its misty base, and when I leaped ashore, the sun had left all Niagara in shadow."

"A sound of merriment, sweet voices and girlish laughter, came dancing through the solemn roar of waters. In old times, when the French and afterwards the English, held garrisons near Niagara, it used to be deemed a feat worthy of a soldier, a frontier man, or an Indian, to cross the rapids to Goat Island. As the country became less rude and warlike, a long space intervened, in which it was but half believed, by a faint and doubtful tradition, that mortal foot had ever trod this wild spot of precipice and forest clinging between two cataracts. The island is no longer a tangled forest, but a grove of stately trees, with grassy intervals about their roots and woodland paths among their trunks. There was neither soldier nor Indian here now, but a vision of three lovely girls, running brief races through the broken sunshine of the grove, hiding behind the trees, and pelting each other with the cones of the pine. When their sport had brought them near me, it so happened that one of the party ran up and shook me by the hand—a greeting which I heartily returned, and would have done the same had it been tenderer. I had known this wild little black-eyed lass in my youth and her childhood, before I had commenced my rambles.

We met on terms of freedom and kindness, which elder ladies might have thought unsuitable with a gentleman of my description. When I alluded to the two fair strangers, she shouted after them by their Christian names, at which summons, with grave dignity, they drew near, and honored me with a distant curtsey. They were from the upper part of Vermont. Whether sisters, or cousins, or at all related to each other, I cannot tell; but they are planted in my memory like 'two twin roses on one stem,' with the fresh dew in both their bosoms; and when I would have pure and pleasant thoughts, I think of them. Neither of them could have seen seventeen years. They both were of a height, and that a moderate one. The rose-bloom of their cheeks could hardly be called bright in her who was the rosiest, nor faint, though a shade less deep, in her companion. Both had delicate eye-brows, not strongly defined, yet somewhat darker than their hair; both had small sweet mouths, maiden mouths, of not so warm and deep a tint as ruby, but only red as the reddest rose; each had those gems, the rarest, the most precious, a pair of clear, soft, bright blue eyes. Their style of dress was similar; one had on a black silk gown, with a stomacher of velvet, and scalloped cuffs of the same from the wrist to the elbow; the other wore cuffs and stomacher of the like pattern and material, over a gown of crimson silk. The dress was rather heavy for their slight figures, but suited to September. They and the darker beauty all carried their straw bonnets in their hands."

I cannot better conclude these fragments than with poor Oberon's description of his return to his native village after his slow recovery from his illness. How beautifully does he express his penitential emotions! A beautiful moral may be indeed drawn from the early death of a sensitive recluse, who had shunned the ordinary avenues to distinction, and with splendid abilities sank into an early grave, almost unknown to mankind, and without any record save what my pen hastily leaves upon these tear-blotted pages.

My Home Return

"When the stage-coach had gained the summit of the hill, I alighted to perform the small remainder of my journey on foot. There had not been a more delicious afternoon than this, in all the train of summer—the air being a sunny perfume, made up of balm, and warmth, and gentle brightness. The oak and walnut-trees, over my head, retained their deep masses of foliage, and the grass, though for months the pasturage of stray cattle, had been revived with the freshness of early June, by the autumnal rains of the preceding week. The garb of Autumn, indeed, resembled that of Spring. Dandelions and buttercups were sprinkled along the road-side, like drops of brightest gold in greenest grass, and a star-shaped little flower of blue, with a golden centre. In a rocky spot, and rooted under the stone-wall, there was one wild rose-bush, bearing three roses, very faintly tinted, but blessed with a spicy fragrance. The same tokens would have announced that the year was brightening into the glow of summer. There

were violets, too, though few and pale ones. But the breath of
September was diffused through the mild air, and became
perceptible, too thrillingly for my enfeebled frame, whenever
a little breeze shook out the latent coolness.

I was standing on the hill at the entrance of my native
village, whence I had looked back to bid farewell, and forward
to the pale mist-bow that over-arched my path, and was the
omen of my fortunes. How had I misinterpreted that augury,
the ghost of hope, with none of hope's bright hues! Nor could
I deem that all its portents were yet accomplished, though
from the same western sky the declining sun shone brightly
in my face. But I was calm and not depressed. Turning to
the village, so dim and dream-like at my last view, I saw the
white houses and brick stores, the intermingled trees, the
foot-paths with their wide borders of grass, and the dusty road
between; all a picture of peaceful gladness in the sunshine.

'Why have I never loved my home before?' thought I, as
my spirit reposed itself on the quiet beauty of the scene.

On the side of the opposite hill was the grave-yard, sloping
towards the farther extremity of the village. The sun shone
as cheerfully there as on the abodes of the living, and showed
all the little hillocks and the burial stones, white marble or
slate, and here and there a tomb, with the pleasant grass
about them all. A single tree was tinged with glory from
the west, and threw a pensive shade behind. Not far from
where it fell, was the tomb of my parents, whom I had
hardly thought of in bidding adieu to the village, but had
remembered them more faithfully among the feelings that
drew me homeward. At my departure their tomb had been
hidden in the morning mist. Beholding it in the sunshine
now, I felt a sensation through my frame as if a breeze had
thrown the coolness of September over me, though not a
leaf was stirred, nor did the thistle down take flight. Was I
to roam no more through this beautiful world, but only to

the other end of the village? Then let me lie down near my parents, but not with them, because I love a green grave better than a tomb.

Moving slowly forward, I heard shouts and laughter, and perceived a considerable throng of people, who came from behind the meeting-house and made a stand in front of it. Thither all the idlers of the village were congregated to witness the exercises of the engine company, this being the afternoon of their monthly practice. They deluged the roof of the meeting-house, till the water fell from the eaves in a broad cascade; then the stream beat against the dusty windows like a thunder storm; and sometimes they flung it up beside the steeple, sparkling in an ascending shower about the weather-cock. For variety's sake, the engineer made it undulate horizontally, like a great serpent flying over the earth. As his last effort, being roguishly inclined, he seemed to take aim at the sky, falling rather short of which, down came the fluid, transformed to drops of silver, on the thickest crowd of the spectators. Then ensued a prodigious rout and mirthful uproar, with no little wrath of the surly ones, whom this is an infallible method of distinguishing. The joke afforded infinite amusement to the ladies at the windows and some old people under the hay scales. I also laughed at a distance, and was glad to find myself susceptible, as of old, to the simple mirth of such a scene.

But the thoughts that it excited were not all mirthful. I had witnessed hundreds of such spectacles in my youth, and one precisely similar only a few days before my departure. And now, the aspect of the village being the same, and the crowd composed of my old acquaintances, I could hardly realize that years had past, or even months, or that the very drops of water were not falling at this moment which had been flung up then. But I pressed the conviction home, that, brief as the time appeared, it had been long enough for me to wander away and return again, with my fate accomplished, and little more hope in this world. The last throb of an adventurous and wayward spirit kept me from repining. I felt as if it were better, or not worse, to have compressed my enjoyments and sufferings into a few wild years, and then to rest myself in an early grave, than to have chosen the untroubled and ungladdened course of the crowd before me, whose days were all alike, and a long lifetime like each day. But the sentiment startled me. For a moment I doubted whether my dear-bought wisdom were any thing but the incapacity to pursue fresh follies, and whether, if health and strength could be restored that night, I should be found in the village after to-morrow's dawn.

Among other novelties, I noticed that the tavern was now designated as a Temperance House, in letters extending across the whole front, with a smaller sign promising Hot Coffee at all hours, and Spruce Beer to lodgers gratis. There were few new buildings, except a Methodist chapel and a printing office, with a book store in the lower story. The golden mortar still ornamented the apothecary's door, nor had the Indian Chief, with his gilded tobacco stalk, been relieved from doing centinel's duty before Dominicus Pike's grocery. The gorgeous silks, though of later patterns, were still flaunting like a banner in front of Mr. Nightingale's dry goods store. Some of the signs introduced me to strangers, whose predecessors had failed, or emigrated to the West, or removed merely to the other end of the village, transferring their names from the sign-boards to slabs of marble or slate. But, on the whole, Death and Vicissitude had done very little. There were old men, scattered about the street, who had been old in my earliest reminiscences; and, as if their venerable forms were permanent parts of the creation, they appeared to be hale and hearty old men yet. The less elderly were more altered, having generally contracted a stoop, with hair woefully thinned and whitened. Some I could hardly recognize; at my last glance they had been boys and girls, but were young men and women when I looked again; and there were happy little things too, rolling about on the grass, whom God had made since my departure.

But now, in my lingering course I had descended the hill, and began to consider, painfully enough, how I should meet my townspeople, and what reception they would give me. Of many an evil prophecy, doubtless, had I been the subject. And would they salute me with a roar of triumph or a low hiss of scorn, on beholding their worst anticipations more than accomplished?

'No,' said I, 'they will not triumph over me. And should they ask the cause of my return, I will tell them that a man may go far and tarry long away, if his health be good and his hopes high; but that when flesh and spirit begin to fail, he remembers his birthplace and the old burial-ground, and hears a voice calling him to come home to his father and mother. They will know, by my wasted frame and feeble step, that I have heard the summons and obeyed. And, the first greetings over, they will let me walk among them unnoticed, and linger in the sunshine while I may, and steal into my grave in peace.'

With these reflections I looked kindly at the crowd, and drew off my glove, ready to give my hand to the first that should put forth his. It occurred to me, also, that some youth among them, now at the crisis of his fate, might have felt his bosom thrill at my example, and be emulous of my wild life and worthless fame. But I would save him.

'He shall be taught,' said I, 'by my life, and by my death, that the world is a sad one for him who shrinks from its sober duties. My experience shall warn him to adopt some great and serious aim, such as manhood will cling to, that

he may not feel himself, too late, a cumberer of this over-
laden earth, but a man among men. I will beseech him not
to follow an eccentric path, nor, by stepping aside from the
highway of human affairs, to relinquish his claim upon
human sympathy. And often, as a text of deep and varied
meaning, I will remind him that he is an American.'

By this time I had drawn near the meeting-house, and
perceived that the crowd were beginning to recognize me."

These are the last words traced by his hand. Has not so
chastened a spirit found true communion with the pure in
Heaven?

"Until of late, I never could believe that I was seriously
ill: the past, I thought, could not extend its misery beyond
itself; life was restored to me, and should not be misused
again. I had day-dreams even of wedded happiness. Still, as
the days wear on, a faintness creeps through my frame and
spirit, recalling the consciousness that a very old man might
as well nourish hope and young desire as I at twenty-four.
Yet the consciousness of my situation does not always make
me sad. Sometimes I look upon the world with a quiet
interest, because it cannot concern me personally, and a loving one for the same reason, because nothing selfish can interfere with the sense of brotherhood. Soon to be all spirit, I
have already a spiritual sense of human nature, and see
deeply into the hearts of mankind, discovering what is hidden
from the wisest. The loves of young men and virgins are
known to me, before the first kiss, before the whispered word,
with the birth of the first sigh. My glance comprehends the
crowd, and penetrates the breast of the solitary man. I think
better of the world than formerly, more generously of its
virtues, more mercifully of its faults, with a higher estimate

of its present happiness, and brighter hopes of its destiny. My mind has put forth a second crop of blossoms, as the trees do in the Indian summer. No winter will destroy their beauty, for they are fanned by the breeze and freshened by the shower that breathes and falls in the gardens of Paradise!"

TIME'S PORTRAITURE

BEING THE CARRIER'S ADDRESS TO THE PATRONS
OF THE SALEM GAZETTE,
FOR THE FIRST OF JANUARY, 1838

KIND PATRONS,

We newspaper-carriers are Time's errand-boys; and all the year round, the old gentleman sends us from one of your doors to another, to let you know what he is talking about and what he is doing. We are a strange set of urchins; for, punctually on New-Year's morning, one and all of us are seized with a fit of rhyme, and break forth in such hideous strains, that it would be no wonder if the infant Year, with her step upon the threshold, were frightened away by the discord with which we strive to welcome her. On these occasions, most generous Patrons, you never fail to give us a taste of your bounty; but whether as a reward for our verses, or to purchase a respite from further infliction of them, is best known to your worshipful selves. Moreover, we, Time's errand-boys as aforesaid, feel it incumbent upon us, on the first day of every year, to present a sort of summary of our master's dealings with the world, throughout the whole of the preceding twelvemonth. Now it has so chanced, by a misfortune heretofore unheard-of, that I, your present petitioner, have been altogether forgotten by the Muse. Instead of being able (as I naturally expected) to measure my ideas into six-foot lines and tack a rhyme at each of their tails, I find myself, this blessed morning, the same simple proser that I was yesterday, and shall probably be to-morrow. And to my further mortification, being a humble-minded little sinner, I feel nowise capable of talking to your Worships with the customary wisdom of my brethren, and giving sage opinions as to what Time has done right, and what he has done wrong, and what of right or wrong he means to do hereafter. Such being my unhappy predicament, it is with no small confusion of face, that I make bold to present myself at your doors. Yet it were surely a pity, that my non-appearance should defeat your bountiful designs for the replenishing of my pockets. Wherefore I have bethought me, that it might not displease your Worships to hear a few particulars about the person and habits of Father Time; with whom, as being one of his errand-boys, I have more acquaintance than most lads of my years.

For a great many years past, there has been a wood-cut on the cover of the Farmer's Almanac, pretending to be a portrait of Father Time. It represents that respectable personage as almost in a state of nudity, with a single lock of hair on his forehead, wings on his shoulders, and accoutred with a scythe and an hour glass. These two latter symbols appear to betoken, that the old fellow works in haying time by the hour. But, within my recollection, Time has never carried a scythe and an hour glass, nor worn a pair of wings, nor shown himself in the half naked condition that the Almanac would make us believe. Now-a-days, he is the most fashionably dressed figure about town; and I take it to be his natural disposition, old as he is, to adopt every fashion of the day and of the hour. Just at the present period, you may meet him in a furred surtout, with pantaloons strapped under his narrow-toed boots; on his head, instead of a single forelock, he wears a smart auburn wig, with bushy whiskers of the same hue, the whole surmounted by a German-lustre hat.

He has exchanged his hour glass for a gold patent lever watch, which he carries in his vest pocket; and as for his scythe, he has either thrown it aside altogether, or converted its handle into a cane, not much stouter than a riding-switch. If you stare him full in the face, you will perhaps detect a few wrinkles; but, on a hasty glance, you might suppose him to be in the very hey-day of life, as fresh as he was in the garden of Eden. So much for the present aspect of Time; but I by no means insure that the description shall suit him a month hence, or even at this hour to-morrow.

It is another very common mistake, to suppose that Time wanders among old ruins and sits on mouldering walls and moss-grown stones, meditating about matters which every body else has forgotten. Some people, perhaps, would expect to find him at the burial-ground in Broad-street, poring over the half-illegible inscriptions on the tombs of the Higginsons, the Hathornes,* the Holyokes, the Brownes, the Olivers, the Pickmans, the Pickerings, and other worthies, with whom he kept company of old. Some would look for him on the ridge of Gallows-Hill, where, in one of his darkest moods, he and Cotton Mather hung the witches. But they need not seek him there. Time is invariably the first to forget his own deeds, his own history, and his own former associates. His place is in the busiest bustle of the world. If you would meet Time face to face, you have only to promenade in Essex-street, between the hours of twelve and one; and there, among beaus and belles, you will see old Father Time, apparently the gayest of the gay. He walks arm in arm with the young men, talking about balls and theatres, and afternoon rides, and midnight merry makings;

* Not 'Hawthorne,'—as one of the present representatives of the family, has seen fit to transmogrify a good old name. However, Time seldom has occasion to mention the gentleman's name, so that it is no great matter how he spells or pronounces it.

he recommends such and such a fashionable tailor, and sneers at every garment of six months' antiquity; and generally, before parting, he invites his friends to drink champagne—a wine in which Time delights, on account of its rapid effervescence. And Time treads lightly beside the fair girls, whispering to them (the Old Deceiver!) that they are the sweetest angels he ever was acquainted with. He tells them that they have nothing to do but dance and sing, and twine roses in their hair, and gather a train of lovers, and that the world will always be like an illuminated ball room. And Time goes to the Commercial News-Room, and visits the Insurance Offices, and stands at the corner of Essex and St. Peter's street, talking with the merchants about the arrival of ships, the rise and fall of stocks, the price of cotton and bread stuffs, the prospects of the Whaling-business and the cod-fishery and all other news of the day. And the young gentlemen, and the pretty girls, and the merchants, and all others with whom he makes acquaintance, are apt to think that there is nobody like Time, and that Time is all in all.

But Time is not near so good a fellow as they take him for. He is continually on the watch for mischief, and often seizes a sly opportunity to lay his cane over the shoulders of some middle-aged gentleman; and lo and behold! the poor man's back is bent, his hair turns gray, and his face looks like a shrivelled apple. This is what is meant by being 'time-stricken.' It is the worst feature in Time's character, that he always inflicts the greatest injuries on his oldest friends. Yet, shamefully as he treats them, they evince no desire to cut his acquaintance, and can seldom bear to think of a final separation.

Again, there is a very prevalent idea, that Time loves to sit by the fire-side, telling stories of the Puritans, the Witch persecutors, and the heroes of the Old French War and the Revolution; and that he has no memory of anything more

recent than the days of the first President Adams. This is
another great mistake. Time is so eager to talk of novelties,
that he never fails to give circulation to the most incredible
rumours of the day, though at the hazard of being compelled
to eat his own words to-morrow. He shows numberless
instances of this propensity, while the national elections are
in progress. A month ago, his mouth was full of the wonderful Whig victories; and to do him justice, he really seems
to have told the truth for once. Whether the same story will
hold good another year, we must leave Time himself to
show. He has a good deal to say, at the present juncture,
concerning the revolutionary movements in Canada; he blus-
ters a little, about the north-eastern boundary question; he
expresses great impatience at the sluggishness of our com-
manders in the Florida war; he gets considerably excited,
whenever the subject of abolition is brought forward, and so
much the more, as he appears hardly to have made up his
mind on one side or the other. Whenever this happens to be
the case—as it often does—Time works himself into such a
rage, that you would think he were going to tear the universe to pieces; but I never yet knew him to proceed, in
good earnest, to such terrible extremities. During the last six
or seven months, he has been seized with intolerable sulki-
ness at the slightest mention of the currency; for nothing
vexes Time so much as to be refused cash upon the nail.
The above are the chief topics of general interest, which
Time is just now in the habit of discussing. For his more
private gossip, he has rumours of new matches, or of old
ones broken off, with now and then a whisper of good-
natured scandal; sometimes, too, he condescends to criticise
a sermon, or a Lyceum lecture, or a performance of the
Glee-Club; and, to be brief, catch the volatile essence of
present talk and transitory opinions, and you will have Time's
gossip, word for word. I may as well add, that he expresses

great approbation of Mr. Russell's vocal abilities, and means to be present from beginning to end of his next concert. It is not every singer that could *keep Time* with his voice and instrument, for a whole evening.

Perhaps you will inquire, 'What are Time's literary tastes?' And here, again, there is a general mistake. It is conceived by many, that Time spends his leisure hours at the Athenaeum, turning over the musty leaves of those huge worm-eaten folios, which nobody else has disturbed since the death of the venerable Doctor Oliver. So far from this being the case, Time's profoundest studies are the new novels from Messrs. Ives and Jewett's Circulating Library. He skims over the lighter articles in the periodicals of the day, glances at the newspapers, and then throws them aside forever; all except the Salem Gazette, of which he preserves a file, for his amusement a century or two hence.

We will now consider Time as a man of business. In this capacity, our citizens are in the habit of complaining, not wholly without reason, that Time is sluggish and dull. You may see him occasionally at the end of Derby-Wharf, leaning against a post or sitting on the breech of an iron cannon, staring listlessly at an unrigged East-Indiaman. Or if you look through the windows of the Union Marine Insurance Office, you may get a glimpse of him there, nodding over a newspaper, among the old weather-beaten sea-captains who recollect when Time was quite a different sort of fellow. If you enter any of the dry good stores along Essex-street, you will be likely to find him with his elbows on the counter, bargaining for a yard of tape or a paper of pins. To catch him in his idlest mood, you must visit the office of some young lawyer. Still, however, Time does contrive to do a little business among us, and should not be denied the credit of it. During the past season he has worked pretty diligently upon the Rail-road, and promises to start the cars by the middle of next summer. Then we may fly from Essex-street to State-street, and be back again before Time misses us. In conjunction with our worthy Mayor (with whose ancestor, the Lord Mayor of London, Time was well acquainted, more than two hundred years ago) he has laid the corner stone of a new City Hall, the granite front of which is already an ornament to Court-street. But, besides these public affairs, Time busies himself a good deal in private. Just at this season of the year, he is engaged in collecting bills, and may be seen at almost any hour peregrinating from street to street, and knocking at half the doors in town, with a great bundle of these infernal documents. On such errands, he appears in the likeness of an under-sized, portly old gentleman, with gray hair, a bluff red face, and a loud tone of voice; and many people mistake him for the penny-post.

Never does a marriage take place, but Time is present among the wedding-guests; for marriage is an affair in which Time takes more interest than in almost any other. He generally gives away the bride, and leads the bridegroom by the hand, to the threshold of the bridal chamber. Although Time pretends to be very merry on these occasions, yet if you watch him well, you may often detect a sigh. Whenever a babe is born into this weary world, Time is in attendance and receives the wailing infant in his arms. And the poor babe shudders instinctively at his embrace, and sets up a feeble cry. Then again, from the birth chamber, he must hurry to the bedside of some old acquaintance, whose business with Time is ended forever, though their accounts remain to be settled at a future day. It is terrible, sometimes, to perceive the lingering reluctance, the shivering agony, with which the poor souls bid Time farewell, if they have gained no other friend to supply the gray deceiver's place. How do they cling to Time, and steal another and yet another glance at his familiar aspect! But Time, the hard hearted old fellow! goes through such scenes with infinite composure, and dismisses his best friends from memory, the moment they are out of sight. Others, who have not been too intimate with Time, as knowing him to be a dangerous character, and apt to ruin his associates—these take leave of him with joy, and pass away with a look of triumph on their features. They know, that in spite of all his flattering promises, he could not make them happy, but that now they shall be so, long after Time is dead and buried.

For Time is not immortal. Time must die, and be buried in the deep grave of eternity. And let him die! From the hour when he passed forth through the gate of Eden, till this very moment, he has gone to and fro about the earth staining his hands with blood, committing crimes innumerable, and bringing misery on himself and all mankind. Sometimes he has been a pagan; sometimes a persecutor. Sometimes he has spent centuries in darkness, where he could neither read nor write. These were called the Dark Ages. There has hardly been a single year, when he has not stirred up strife among the nations. Sometimes—as in France, less than fifty years ago—he has been seized with fits of frenzy, and murdered thousands of innocent people, at noon day. He pretends indeed that he has grown wiser and better now. Trust him who will, for my part, I rejoice that Time shall not live forever. He hath an appointed office to perform. Let him do his task, and die. Fresh and young as he would make himself appear, he is already hoary with age, and the very garments that he wears about the town, were put on thousands of years ago, and have been patched and pieced, to suit the present fashion. There is nothing new in him nor about him. Were he to die, while I am speaking, we could not pronounce it an untimely death. Methinks, with his heavy heart and weary brain, Time should himself be glad to die!

Meanwhile, gentle Patrons, as Time has brought round another New Year, pray remember your poor petitioner! For so small a lad, you will agree that I talk pretty passably well, and have fairly earned whatever spare specie Time has left in your pockets. Be kind to me; and I have good hope that Time will be kind to you.—After all the hard things which I have said about him, he is really—that is, if you take him for neither more nor less than he is worth, and use him as not abusing him—Time is really a very tolerable old fellow, and may be endured for the little while that we are to keep him company. Be generous kind Patrons, to Time's errand boy. So may he bring to the Merchant his ship safe from the Indies,—to the Lawyer, a goodly number of new suits,—to the Doctor, a crowd of patients with the dyspepsia and fat purses,—to the Farmer, a golden crop and a ready market,—to the Mechanic, steady employment and good wages,—to the idle Gentleman, some honest business,—to the Rich, kind hearts and liberal hands,—to the Poor, warm fire-sides and food enough, patient spirits and the hope of better days,—to our Country, a return of specie payments,—and to you, sweet Maid, the youth who stole into your dream, last night! And next New Year's day, (if I find nothing better to do in the meanwhile,) may Time again bring to your doors your loving little friend,

THE CARRIER.

THE ANTIQUE RING

"YES, INDEED; the gem is as bright as a star, and curiously set," said Clara Pemberton, examining an antique ring, which her betrothed lover had just presented to her, with a very pretty speech. "It needs only one thing to make it perfect."

"And what is that?" asked Mr. Edward Caryl, secretly anxious for the credit of his gift. "A modern setting, perhaps?"

"Oh, no! That would destroy the charm at once," replied Clara. "It needs nothing but a story. I long to know how many times it has been the pledge of faith between two lovers, and whether the vows, of which it was the symbol, were always kept or often broken. Not that I should be too scrupulous about facts. If you happen to be unacquainted with its authentic history, so much the better. May it not have sparkled upon a queen's finger? Or who knows, but it is the very ring which Posthumus received from Imogen? In short, you must kindle your imagination at the lustre of this diamond, and make a legend for it."

Now such a task—and doubtless Clara knew it—was the most acceptable that could have been imposed on Edward Caryl. He was one of that multitude of young gentlemen—

limbs, or rather twigs, of the law—whose names appear in gilt letters on the front of Tudor's Buildings, and other places in the vicinity of the Court-House, which seem to be the haunt of the gentler, as well as the severer muses. Edward, in the dearth of clients, was accustomed to employ his much leisure in assisting the growth of American literature; to which good cause he had contributed not a few quires of the finest letter paper, containing some thought, some fancy, some depth of feeling, together with a young writer's abundance of conceits. Sonnets, stanzas of Tennysonian sweetness, tales imbued with German mysticism, versions from Jean Paul, criticisms of the old English poets, and essays smacking of Dialistic philosophy, were among his multifarious productions. The editors of the fashionable periodicals were familiar with his autography, and inscribed his name in those brilliant bead-rolls of ink-stained celebrity, which illustrate the first page of their covers. Nor did fame withhold her laurel. Hillard had included him among the lights of the New-England metropolis, in his Boston Book; Bryant had found room for some of his stanzas, in the Selections from American Poetry; and Mr. Griswold, in his recent assemblage of the sons and daughters of song, had introduced Edward Caryl into the inner court of the temple, among his fourscore choicest bards. There was a prospect, indeed, of his assuming a still higher and more independent position. Interviews had been held with Ticknor, and a correspondence with the Harpers, respecting a proposed volume, chiefly to consist of Mr. Caryl's fugitive pieces in the Magazines, but to be accompanied with a poem of some length, never before published. Not improbably, the public may yet be gratified with this collection.

Meanwhile, we sum up our sketch of Edward Caryl, by pronouncing him, though somewhat of a carpet knight in literature, yet no unfavorable specimen of a generation of rising writers, whose spirit is such that we may reasonably expect creditable attempts from all, and good and beautiful results from some. And, it will be observed, Edward was the very man to write pretty legends, at a lady's instance, for an old-fashioned diamond ring. He took the jewel in his hand, and turned it so as to catch its scintillating radiance, as if hoping, in accordance with Clara's suggestion, to light up his fancy with that star-like gleam.

"Shall it be a ballad?—a tale in verse?" he inquired. "Enchanted rings often glisten in old English poetry, I think something may be done with the subject; but it is fitter for rhyme than prose."

"No, no," said Miss Pemberton.—"We will have no more rhyme than just enough for a posy to the ring. You must tell the legend in simple prose; and when it is finished, I will make a little party to hear it read."

The young gentleman promised obedience; and going to his pillow, with his head full of the familiar spirits that used to be worn in rings, watches, and sword-hilts, he had the good fortune to possess himself of an available idea in a dream. Connecting this with what he himself chanced to know of the ring's real history, his task was done. Clara Pemberton invited a select few of her friends, all holding the stanchest faith in Edward's genius, and therefore the most genial auditors, if not altogether the fairest critics, that a writer could possibly desire. Blessed be woman for her faculty of admiration, and especially for her tendency to admire with her heart, when man, at most, grants merely a cold approval with his mind!

Drawing his chair beneath the blaze of a solar lamp, Edward Caryl untied a roll of glossy paper, and began as follows:

THE LEGEND

After the death-warrant had been read to the Earl of
Essex, and on the evening before his appointed execution,
the Countess of Shrewsbury paid his lordship a visit, and
found him, as it appeared, toying childishly with a ring.
The diamond, that enriched it, glittered like a little star, but
with a singular tinge of red. The gloomy prison-chamber in
the Tower, with its deep and narrow windows piercing the
walls of stone, was now all that the earl possessed of worldly
prospect; so that there was the less wonder that he should
look stedfastly into the gem, and moralize upon earth's
deceitful splendor, as men in darkness and ruin seldom fail
to do. But the shrewd observations of the countess,—an
artful and unprincipled woman,—the pretended friend of
Essex, but who had come to glut her revenge for a deed
of scorn, which he himself had forgotten;—her keen eye
detected a deeper interest attached to this jewel. Even while
expressing his gratitude for her remembrance of a ruined
favorite, and condemned criminal, the earl's glance reverted
to the ring, as if all that remained of time and its affairs
were collected within that small golden circlet.

"My dear lord," observed the countess, "there is surely
some matter of great moment wherewith this ring is connected, since it so absorbs your mind. A token, it may be,
of some fair lady's love,—alas, poor lady, once richest in possessing such a heart! Would you that the jewel be returned
to her?"

"The queen! the queen! It was her majesty's own gift,"
replied the earl, still gazing into the depths of the gem. "She
took it from her finger, and told me, with a smile, that it was

an heir-loom from her Tudor ancestors, and had once been the property of Merlin, the British wizard, who gave it to the lady of his love. His art had made this diamond the abiding-place of a spirit, which, though of fiendish nature, was bound to work only good, so long as the ring was an unviolated pledge of love and faith, both with the giver and receiver. But should love prove false, and faith be broken, then the evil spirit would work his own devilish will, until the ring were purified by becoming the medium of some good and holy act, and again the pledge of faithful love. The gem soon lost its virtue; for the wizard was murdered by the very lady to whom he gave it."

"An idle legend!" said the countess.

"It is so," answered Essex, with a melancholy smile. "Yet the queen's favor, of which this ring was the symbol, has proved my ruin. When death is nigh, men converse with dreams and shadows. I have been gazing into the diamond, and fancying—but you will laugh at me,—that I might catch a glimpse of the evil spirit there. Do you observe this red glow—dusky, too, amid all the brightness? It is the token of his presence; and even now, methinks, it grows redder and duskier, like an angry sunset."

Nevertheless, the earl's manner testified how slight was his credence in the enchanted properties of the ring. But there is a kind of playfulness that comes in moments of despair, when the reality of misfortune, if entirely felt, would crush the soul at once. He now, for a brief space, was lost in thought, while the countess contemplated him with malignant satisfaction.

"This ring," he resumed, in another tone, "alone remains, of all that my royal mistress's favor lavished upon her servant. My fortunes once shone as brightly as the gem. And now, such a darkness has fallen around me, methinks it would be no marvel if its gleam,—the sole light of my prison-house, were to be forthwith extinguished; inasmuch as my last earthly hope depends upon it."

"How say you, my lord?" asked the Countess of Shrewsbury. "The stone is bright; but there should be strange magic in it, if it can keep your hopes alive, at this sad hour. Alas! these iron bars and ramparts of the Tower, are unlike to yield to such a spell."

Essex raised his head, involuntarily; for there was something in the countess's tone that disturbed him, although he could not suspect that an enemy had intruded upon the sacred privacy of a prisoner's dungeon, to exult over so dark a ruin of such once brilliant fortunes. He looked her in the face, but saw nothing to awaken his distrust. It would have required a keener eye than even Cecil's to read the secret of a countenance, which had been worn so long in the false light of a court, that it was now little better than a masque, telling any story save the true one. The condemned nobleman again bent over the ring, and proceeded:

"It once had power in it—this bright gem—the magic that appertains to the talisman of a great queen's favor. She bade me, if hereafter I should fall into her disgrace—how deep soever, and whatever might be my crime—to convey this jewel to her sight, and it should plead for me. Doubtless, with her piercing judgment, she had even then detected the rashness of my nature, and foreboded some such deed as has now brought destruction upon my head. And knowing, too, her own hereditary rigor, she designed, it may be, that the memory of gentler and kindlier hours should soften her heart in my behalf, when my need should be the greatest. I have doubted—I have distrusted—yet who can tell, even now, what happy influence this ring might have?"

"You have delayed full long to show the ring, and plead her majesty's gracious promise," remarked the countess—"your state being what it is."

"True," replied the earl; "but for my honor's sake, I was loth to entreat the queen's mercy, while I might hope for life, at least, from the justice of the laws. If, on a trial by my peers, I had been acquitted of meditating violence against her sacred life, then would I have fallen at her feet, and presenting the jewel, have prayed no other favor than that my love and zeal should be put to the severest test. But now, it were confessing too much—it were cringing too low—to beg the miserable gift of life, on no other score than the tenderness which her majesty deems me to have forfeited!"

"Yet it is your only hope," said the countess.

"And besides," continued Essex, pursuing his own reflections, "of what avail will be this token of womanly feeling, when, on the other hand are arrayed the all-prevailing motives of state policy, and the artifices and intrigues of courtiers, to consummate my downfall? Will Cecil or Raleigh suffer her heart to act for itself, even if the spirit of her father were not in her? It is in vain to hope it."

But still Essex gazed at the ring with an absorbed attention, that proved how much hope his sanguine temperament had concentrated here, when there was none else for him in the wide world, save what lay in the compass of that hoop of gold. The spark of brightness within the diamond, which gleamed like an intenser than earthly fire, was the memorial of his dazzling career. It had not paled with the waning sunshine of his mistress's favor; on the contrary, in spite of its remarkable tinge of dusky red, he fancied that it had never shone so brightly. The glow of festal torches—the blaze of perfumed lamps—the bonfires that had been kindled for him, when he was the darling of the people—the splendor of the royal court, where he had been the peculiar star—all seemed to have collected their moral or material glory into the gem, and to burn with a radiance caught from the future, as well as gathered from the past. That radiance might break forth again. Bursting from the diamond, into which it was

now narrowed, it might beam first upon the gloomy walls of
the Tower—then wider, wider, wider—till all England, and
the seas around her cliffs, should be gladdened with the light.
It was such an ecstasy as often ensues after long depression,
and has been supposed to precede the circumstances of darkest fate that may befall mortal man. The earl pressed the
ring to his heart as if it were indeed a talisman, the habitation of a spirit, as the queen had playfully assured him—but
a spirit of happier influences than her legend spake of.

"Oh, could I but make my way to her footstool!" cried he,
waving his hand aloft, while he paced the stone pavement
of his prison-chamber with an impetuous step.—"I might
kneel down, indeed, a ruined man, condemned to the block
—but how should I rise again? Once more the favorite of
Elizabeth!—England's proudest noble!—with such prospects
as ambition never aimed at! Why have I tarried so long in
this weary dungeon? The ring has power to set me free!
The palace wants me! Ho, jailer, unbar the door!"

But then occurred the recollection of the impossibility of
obtaining an interview with his fatally estranged mistress, and
testing the influence over her affections, which he still flat-
tered himself with possessing.—Could he step beyond the
limits of his prison, the world would be all sunshine; but
here was only gloom and death.

"Alas!" said he, slowly and sadly, letting his head fall upon
his hands.—"I die for lack of one blessed word."

The Countess of Shrewsbury, herself forgotten amid the
earl's gorgeous visions, had watched him with an aspect that
could have betrayed nothing to the most suspicious observer;
unless that it was too calm for humanity, while witnessing
the flutterings, as it were, of a generous heart in the death-
agony. She now approached him.

"My good lord," she said, "what mean you to do?"

"Nothing—my deeds are done!" replied he, despondingly.
—"Yet, had a fallen favorite any friends, I would entreat

one of them to lay this ring at her majesty's feet; albeit with little hope, save that, hereafter, it might remind her that poor Essex, once far too highly favored, was at last too severely dealt with."

"I will be that friend," said the countess. "There is no time to be lost. Trust this precious ring with me. This very night, the queen's eye shall rest upon it; nor shall the efficacy of my poor words be wanting, to strengthen the impression which it will doubtless make."

The earl's first impulse was to hold out the ring. But looking at the countess, as she bent forward to receive it, he fancied that the red glow of the gem tinged all her face, and gave it an ominous expression. Many passages of past times recurred to his memory. A preternatural insight, perchance caught from approaching death, threw its momentary gleam, as from a meteor, all round his position.

"Countess," he said, "I know not wherefore I hesitate, being in a plight so desperate, and having so little choice of friends. But have you looked into your own heart? Can you perform this office with the truth—the earnestness—the zeal, even to tears, and agony of spirit—wherewith the holy gift of human life should be pleaded for? Wo be unto you, should you undertake this task, and deal towards me otherwise than with utmost faith! For your own soul's sake, and as you would have peace at your death-hour, consider well in what spirit you receive this ring!"

The countess did not shrink.

"My lord!—my good lord!" she exclaimed, "wrong not a woman's heart by these suspicions. You might choose another messenger; but who, save a lady of her bed-chamber, can obtain access to the queen at this untimely hour? It is for your life—for your life—else I would not renew my offer."

"Take the ring," said the earl.

"Believe that it shall be in the queen's hands before the lapse of another hour," replied the countess, as she received this sacred trust of life and death.—"To-morrow morning, look for the result of my intercession."

She departed. Again the earl's hopes rose high. Dreams visited his slumber, not of the sable-decked scaffold in the Tower-yard, but of canopies of state, obsequious courtiers, pomp, splendor, the smile of the once more gracious queen, and a light beaming from the magic gem, which illuminated his whole future.

History records, how foully the Countess of Shrewsbury betrayed the trust, which Essex, in his utmost need, confided to her. She kept the ring, and stood in the presence of Elizabeth, that night, without one attempt to soften her stern hereditary temper, in behalf of the former favorite. The next day, the earl's noble head rolled upon the scaffold. On her death-bed, tortured, at last, with a sense of the dreadful guilt which she had taken upon her soul, the wicked countess sent for Elizabeth, revealed the story of the ring, and besought forgiveness for her treachery. But the queen, still obdurate, even while remorse for past obduracy was tugging at her heart-strings, shook the dying woman in her bed, as if struggling with death for the privilege of wreaking her revenge and spite. The spirit of the countess passed away, to undergo the justice, or receive the mercy, of a higher tribunal; and tradition says, that the fatal ring was found upon her breast, where it had imprinted a dark red circle, resembling the effect of the intensest heat. The attendants, who prepared the body for burial, shuddered, whispering one to another, that the ring must have derived its heat from the glow of infernal fire. They left it on her breast, in the coffin, and it went with that guilty woman to the tomb.

Many years afterwards, when the church that contained the monuments of the Shrewsbury family, was desecrated by Cromwell's soldiers, they broke open the ancestral vaults, and stole whatever was valuable from the noble personages who reposed there. Merlin's antique ring passed into the possession of a stout serjeant of the Ironsides, who thus became subject to the influences of the evil spirit that still kept his abode within the gem's enchanted depths. The serjeant was soon slain in battle, thus transmitting the ring, though without any legal form of testament, to a gay cavalier, who forthwith pawned it, and expended the money in liquor, which speedily brought him to the grave. We next catch the sparkle of the magic diamond at various epochs of the merry reign of Charles the Second. But its sinister fortune still attended it. From whatever hand this ring of portent came, and whatever finger it encircled, ever it was the pledge of deceit between man and man, or man and woman, of faithless vows, and unhallowed passion; and whether to lords and ladies, or to village-maids—for sometimes it found its way so low,—still it brought nothing but sorrow and disgrace. No purifying deed was done, to drive the fiend from his bright home in this little star. Again, we hear of it at a later period, when Sir Robert Walpole bestowed the ring, among far richer jewels, on the lady of a British legislator, whose political honor he wished to undermine. Many a dismal and unhappy tale might be wrought out of its other adventures. All this while, its ominous tinge of dusky red had been deepening and darkening, until, if laid upon white paper, it cast the mingled hue of night and blood, strangely illuminated with scintillating light, in a circle round about. But this peculiarity only made it the more valuable.

Alas, the fatal ring! When shall its dark secret be discovered, and the doom of ill, inherited from one possessor to another, be finally revoked?

The legend now crosses the Atlantic, and comes down to our own immediate time. In a certain church of our city, not many evenings ago, there was a contribution for a charitable object. A fervid preacher had poured out his whole soul in a rich and tender discourse, which had at least excited the tears, and perhaps the more effectual sympathy, of a numerous audience. While the choristers sang sweetly, and the organ poured forth its melodious thunder, the deacons passed up and down the aisles, and along the galleries, presenting their mahogany boxes, in which each person deposited what ever sum he deemed it safe to lend to the Lord, in aid of human wretchedness. Charity became audible—chink, chink, chink,—as it fell, drop by drop, into the common receptacle. There was a hum—a stir,—the subdued bustle of people putting their hands into their pockets; while, ever and anon, a vagrant coin fell upon the floor, and rolled away, with long reverberation, into some inscrutable corner.

At length, all having been favored with an opportunity to be generous, the two deacons placed their boxes on the communion-table, and thence, at the conclusion of the services, removed them into the vestry. Here these good old gentlemen sat down together, to reckon the accumulated treasure.

"Fie, fie, brother Tilton," said Deacon Trott, peeping into Deacon Tilton's box, "what a heap of copper you have picked up! Really, for an old man, you must have had a heavy job to lug it along. Copper! copper! copper! Do people expect to get admittance into Heaven at the price of a few coppers?"

"Don't wrong them, brother," answered Deacon Tilton, a simple and kindly old man. "Copper may do more for one person, than gold will for another. In the galleries, where I present my box, we must not expect such a harvest as you gather among the gentry in the broad-aisle, and all over the floor of the church. My people are chiefly poor mechanics and laborers, sailors, seamstresses, and servant-maids, with a most uncomfortable intermixture of roguish school-boys."

"Well, well," said Deacon Trott;—"but there is a great deal, brother Tilton, in the method of presenting a contribution-box. It is a knack that comes by nature, or not at all."

They now proceeded to sum up the avails of the evening, beginning with the receipts of Deacon Trott. In good sooth, that worthy personage had reaped an abundant harvest, in which he prided himself no less, apparently, than if every dollar had been contributed from his own individual pocket. Had the good deacon been meditating a jaunt to Texas, the treasures of the mahogany-box might have sent him on his way rejoicing. There were bank-notes, mostly, it is true, of the smallest denominations in the giver's pocket-book, yet making a goodly average upon the whole. The most splendid contribution was a check for a hundred dollars, bearing the name of a distinguished merchant, whose liberality was duly celebrated in the newspapers of the next day. No less than seven half eagles, together with an English sovereign, glittered amidst an indiscriminate heap of silver; the box being polluted with nothing of the copper kind; except a single bright new cent, wherewith a little boy had performed his first charitable act.

"Very well! very well indeed!" said Deacon Trott, self-approvingly. "A handsome evening's work! And now, brother Tilton, let's see whether you can match it."

Here was a sad contrast! They poured forth Deacon Tilton's treasure upon the table, and it really seemed as if the whole copper coinage of the country, together with an amazing quantity of shopkeepers' tokens, and English and Irish half-pence, mostly of base metal, had been congregated into the box. There was a very substantial pencil-case, and the semblance of a shilling; but the latter proved to be made of tin, and the former of German silver. A gilded brass button was doing duty as a gold coin, and a folded shop-bill had assumed the character of a bank-note. But Deacon Tilton's feelings were much revived, by the aspect of another bank-note, new and crisp, adorned with beautiful engravings, and stamped with the indubitable word, TWENTY, in large black letters. Alas! it was a counterfeit. In short, the poor old Deacon was no less unfortunate than those who trade with fairies, and whose gains are sure to be transformed into dried leaves, pebbles, and other valuables of that kind.

"I believe the Evil One is in the box," said he, with some vexation.

"Well done, Deacon Tilton!" cried his brother Trott, with a hearty laugh.—"You ought to have a statue in copper."

"Never mind, brother," replied the good Deacon, recovering his temper. "I'll bestow ten dollars from my own pocket, and may Heaven's blessing go along with it! But look! what do you call this?"

Under the copper mountain, which it had cost them so much toil to remove, lay an antique ring! It was enriched with a diamond, which, so soon as it caught the light, began to twinkle and glimmer, emitting the whitest and purest lustre that could possibly be conceived. It was as brilliant as if some magician had condensed the brightest star in heaven into a compass fit to be set in a ring, for a lady's delicate finger.

"How is this?" said Deacon Trott, examining it carefully, in the expectation of finding it as worthless as the rest of his colleague's treasure. "Why, upon my word, this seems to be a real diamond, and of the purest water. Whence could it have come?"

"Really, I cannot tell," quoth Deacon Tilton, "for my spectacles were so misty that all faces looked alike. But now I remember, there was a flash of light came from the box, at one moment; but it seemed a dusky red, instead of a pure white, like the sparkle of this gem. Well; the ring will make up for the copper; but I wish the giver had thrown its history into the box along with it."

It has been our good luck to recover a portion of that history. After transmitting misfortune from one possessor to another, ever since the days of British Merlin, the identical ring which Queen Elizabeth gave to the Earl of Essex was finally thrown into the contribution-box of a New-England church. The two deacons deposited it in the glass-case of a fashionable jeweller, of whom it was purchased by the humble rehearser of this legend, in the hope that it may be allowed to sparkle on a fair lady's finger. Purified from the foul fiend, so long its inhabitant, by a deed of unostentatious charity, and now made the symbol of faithful and devoted love, the gentle bosom of its new possessor need fear no sorrow from its influence.

"Very pretty!—Beautiful!—How original!—How sweetly written!—What nature!—What imagination!—What power! —What pathos!—What exquisite humor!"—were the exclamations of Edward Caryl's kind and generous auditors, at the conclusion of the legend.

"It is a pretty tale," said Miss Pemberton, who, conscious that her praise was to that of all others as a diamond to a pebble, was therefore the less liberal in awarding it. "It is really a pretty tale, and very proper for any of the Annuals. But, Edward, your moral does not satisfy me. What thought did you embody in the ring?"

"Oh, Clara, this is too bad!" replied Edward, with a half-reproachful smile.—"You know that I can never separate the idea from the symbol in which it manifests itself. However, we may suppose the Gem to be the human heart, and the Evil Spirit to be Falsehood, which, in one guise or another, is the fiend that causes all the sorrow and trouble in the world. I beseech you, to let this suffice."

"It shall," said Clara, kindly. "And believe me, whatever the world may say of the story, I prize it far above the diamond which enkindled your imagination."

A GOOD MAN'S MIRACLE

I N EVERY good action there is a divine quality, which
does not end with the completion of that particular
deed, but goes on to bring forth good works in an
infinite series. It is seldom possible, indeed, for human eyes
to trace out the chain of blessed consequences, that extends
from a benevolent man's simple and conscientious act, here
on earth, and connects it with those labors of love which
the angels make it their joy to perform, in Heaven above.
Sometimes, however, we meet with an instance in which
this wonderful and glorious connection may clearly be perceived. It has always appeared to me, that a well-known
incident in the life of Mr. Robert Raikes offers us one of
the most hopeful and inspiring arguments, never to neglect
even the humblest opportunities of doing good, as not knowing what vast purposes of Providence we may thereby sub-
serve. This little story has been often told, but may here be
related anew, because it so strikingly illustrates the remark
with which we began.

Mr. Raikes, being in London, happened one day to pass
through a certain street, which was inhabited chiefly by poor
and ignorant people. In great cities, it is unfortunately the
case, that the poor are compelled to be the neighbors and

fellow-lodgers of the vicious; and that the ignorant seeing so much temptation around them, and having no kind advisers to direct them aright, almost inevitably go astray and increase the number of the bad. Thus, though doubtless there are many virtuous poor people, amidst all the vice that hides itself in the obscure streets of a great city, like London, still it seems as if they were kept virtuous only by the special providence of God. If He should turn away His eyes for a single instant, they would be lost in the flood of evil that continually surrounds them. Now, Mr. Raikes, as he passed along, saw much to make him sad, for there were so many tokens of sin and wretchedness on all sides, that most persons, hopeless of doing any good, would have endeavored to forget the whole scene as soon as possible.

There is hardly a gloomier spectacle in the world than one of those obscure streets of London. The houses, which were old and ruinous, stood so close together as almost to shut out the sky, and even the sunshine, where a glimpse of it could be seen, was made dusky and dim by the smoke of the city. A kennel of muddy water flowed through the street. The general untidiness about the houses proved that the inhabitants felt no affection for their homes, nor took pride in making them decent and respectable. In these houses, it is to be feared that there were many people sick, suffering for food, and shivering with cold, and many, alas! who had fallen into the sore disease of sin, and sought to render their lives easier by dishonest practices. In short, the street seemed a place seldom visited by angels of mercy, or trodden by the footsteps of good men. Yet it were well that good men should often go thither, and be saddened by such reflections as now occurred to Mr. Raikes, in order that their hearts might be stirred up to attempt a reformation.

"Alas, what a spectacle is here!" thought this good man to himself. "How can any Christian remain idle, when there is so much evil to be remedied within a morning's walk of his own home?"

But we have not yet mentioned what it was that chiefly moved the heart of Mr. Raikes with sorrow and compassion. There were children at play in the street. Some were dabbling in the kennel, and splashing its dirty water over their companions, out of the mere love of mischief. Others, who had already been taught to gamble, were playing at pitch-and-toss for half-pence. Others, perhaps, were quarelling and fighting. In a word—for we will not describe what it was so sad to witness—these poor children were growing up in idleness, with none but bad examples before their eyes, and without the opportunity of learning anything but evil. Their little, unclean faces looked already old in naughtiness; it seemed as if the vice and misery of the world had been born with them, and would cling to them as long as they existed. How sad a spectacle was this for a man like Mr. Raikes, who had always delighted in little children, and felt as if the world was made more beautiful, and his own heart the better, by their bright and happy faces! But, as he gazed at these poor little creatures, he thought that the world had never looked so dark, ugly, and sorrowful, as it did then.

"Oh, that I could save them!" thought he. "It were better for them to have been born among the wildest savages, than to grow up thus in a Christian country."

Now, at the door of one of the houses, there stood a woman, who, though she looked poor and needy, yet seemed neater and more respectable than the other inhabitants of this wretched street. She, like Mr. Raikes, was gazing at the children; and perhaps her mind was occupied with reflections similar to his. It might be, that she had children of her own, and was ready to shed tears at the thought, that they must grow up in the midst of such bad examples. At all events, when Mr. Raikes beheld this woman, he felt as if he had found somebody that could sympathize with him in his grief and anxiety.

"My good woman," said he, pointing to the children, "this is a dismal sight—so many of God's creatures growing up in idleness and ignorance, with no instruction but to do evil."

"Alas, good Sir," answered the woman, "it is bad enough on week-days, as you see;—but if you were to come into the street on a Sunday, you would find it a thousand times worse. On other days some of the children find employment, good or bad; but the Sabbath brings them all into the street together—and then there is nothing but mischief from morning till night."

"Ah, that is a sad case indeed," said Mr. Raikes. "Can the blessed Sabbath itself bring no blessing to these poor children? This is the worst of all."

And then, again, he looked along the street, with pity and strong benevolence; for his whole heart was moved by what he saw. The longer he considered, the more terrible did it appear that those children should grow up in ignorance and sin, and that the germs of immortal goodness, which Heaven had implanted in their souls, should be for ever blighted by neglect. And the earnestness of his compassion quickened his mind to perceive what was to be done. As he stood gazing at the spectacle that had so saddened him, an expression of delightful hope broke forth upon his face, and made it look as if a bright gleam of sunshine fell across it. And, if moral sunshine could be discerned on physical objects, just such a brightness would have shone through the gloomy street, gladdening all the dusky windows, and causing the poor children to look beautiful and happy. Not only in that wretched street would the light of gladness have appeared; it might have spread from thence all round the earth; for there was now a thought on the mind of Mr. Raikes, that was destined, in no long time, to make the whole world brighter than it had been hitherto.

And what was that thought?

It must be considered that Mr. Raikes was not a very rich man. There were thousands of people in England, to whom Providence had assigned greater wealth than he possessed, and who, as one would suppose, might have done far more good to their fellow-creatures than it lay in his power to do. There was a king, too, and princes, lords and statesmen, who were set in lofty places, and entrusted with the making and administration of the laws. If the condition of the world was to be improved, were not these the men to accomplish it? But the true faculty of doing good consists not in wealth nor station, but in the energy and wisdom of a loving heart, that can sympathize with all mankind, and acknowledges a brother or a sister in every unfortunate man or woman, and an own child in each neglected orphan. Such a heart was that of Mr. Raikes; and God now rewarded him with a blessed opportunity of conferring more benefit on his race, than he, in his humility, had ever dreamed of. And it would not be too much to say, that the king and his nobles, and the wealthy gentlemen of England, with all their boundless means, had for many years, done nothing so worthy of grateful remembrance, as what was now to be effected by this humble individual.

And yet how simple was this great idea, and how small the means by which Mr. Raikes proceeded to put it in execution! It was merely, to hire respectable and intelligent women, at the rate of a shilling each, to come, every Sabbath, and keep little schools for the poor children whom he had seen at play. Perhaps the good woman with whom Mr. Raikes had spoken in the street, was one of his new school-mistresses. Be that as it might, the plan succeeded, and, attracting the notice of benevolent people, was soon adopted in many other dismal streets of London. And this was the origin of Sunday-schools. In course of time, similar schools were established all over that great city, and thence extended to the remotest parts of England, and across the ocean to America, and to countries at a world-wide distance, where the humble name of Robert Raikes had never been pronounced.

That good man has now long been dead. But still, on every Sabbath-morning, in the cities and country villages, and wheresoever the steeple of a church points upward to the sky, the children take their way to the Sunday-school. Thousands, and tens of thousands, have there received instruction, which has been more profitable to them than all the gold on earth. And we may be permitted to believe, that, in the celestial world, where the founder of the system now exists, he has often met with other happy spirits, who have blessed him as the earthly means by which they were rescued from hopeless ignorance and evil, and guided on the path to Heaven. Is not this a proof, that when the humblest person acts in the simplicity of a pure heart, and with no design but to do good, *God* may be expected to take the matter into His all-powerful hands, and adopt the action as His own?

A BOOK OF AUTOGRAPHS

W E HAVE before us a volume of autograph letters, chiefly of soldiers and statesmen of the Revolution, and addressed to a good and brave man, General Palmer, who himself drew his sword in the cause. They are profitable reading in a quiet afternoon, and in a mood withdrawn from too intimate relation with the present time; so that we can glide backward some three-quarters of a century, and surround ourselves with the ominous sublimity of circumstance that then frowned upon the writers. To give them their full effect, we should imagine that these letters have this moment been brought to town by the splashed and way-worn post-rider, or perhaps by an orderly dragoon, who has ridden in a perilous hurry to deliver his despatches. They are magic scrolls, if read in the right spirit. The roll of the drum and the fanfare of the trumpet is latent in some of them; and in others, an echo of the oratory that resounded in the old halls of the Continental Congress, at Philadelphia; or the words may come to us as with the living utterance of one of those illustrious men, speaking face to face, in friendly communion. Strange, that the mere identity of paper and ink should be so powerful. The same thoughts might look cold and ineffectual, in a printed book. Human nature craves a certain materialism, and clings pertinaciously to what is tangible, as if that were of more importance than the spirit accidentally involved in it. And, in truth, the original manuscript has always something which print itself must inevitably lose. An erasure, even a blot, a casual irregularity of hand, and all such little imperfections of mechanical execution, bring us close to the writer, and perhaps convey some of those subtle intimations for which language has no shape.

There are several letters from John Adams, written in a small, hasty, ungraceful hand, but earnest, and with no unnecessary flourish. The earliest is dated at Philadelphia, Sept. 26, 1774, about twenty days after the first opening of the Continental Congress. We look at this old yellow document, scribbled on half a sheet of foolscap, and ask of it many questions for which the words have no response. We would fain know what were their mutual impressions, when all those venerable faces, that have since been traced on steel or chiselled out of marble, and thus made familiar to posterity, first met one another's gaze! Did one spirit harmonize them, in spite of the dissimilitude of manners between the North and the South, which were now for the first time brought into political relations? Could the Virginian descendant of the Cavaliers, and the New-Englander with his hereditary Puritanism—the aristocratic Southern planter, and the self-made man from Massachusetts or Connecticut—at once feel that they were countrymen and brothers? What did John Adams think of Jefferson?—and Samuel Adams of Patrick Henry? Did not North and South combine in their deference for the sage Franklin—so long the defender of the Colonies in England, and whose scientific renown was already world-wide? And was there yet any whispered prophecy, any vague conjecture, circulating among the delegates, as to the destiny which might be in reserve for one stately man, who sat, for the most part silent, among them?—what station he was to assume in the world's history?—and how many statues would repeat his form and countenance, and successively crumble beneath his immortality?

The letter before us does not answer these inquiries. Its main feature is the strong expression of the uncertainty and awe that pervaded even the firm hearts of the Old Congress, while anticipating the struggle which was to ensue:—

> "The commencement of hostilities," it says, "is exceedingly dreaded here. It is thought that an attack upon the troops, even should it prove successful, would certainly involve the whole continent in a war. It is generally thought that the Ministry would rejoice at a rupture in Boston, because it would furnish an excuse to the people *at home*;"—[this was the last time, we suspect, that John Adams spoke of England thus affectionately]—"and unite them in an opinion of the necessity of pushing hostilities against us."

His next letter bears on the superscription—'Favored by General Washington.' The date is June 20, 1775, three days after the battle of Bunker Hill, the news of which could not yet have arrived at Philadelphia. But the war, so much dreaded, had begun, on the quiet banks of Concord river; an army of twenty thousand men was beleaguering Boston; and here was Washington journeying northward, to take the command. It seems to place us in a nearer relation with the hero, to find him performing the little courtesy of bearing a letter between friend and friend, and to hold in our hands the very document entrusted to such a messenger. John Adams says simply—'We send you Generals Washington and Lee for your comfort'—but adds nothing in regard to the character of the commander-in-chief. This letter displays much of the writer's ardent temperament; if he had been anywhere but in the hall of Congress, it would have been in the entrenchment before Boston.

> "I hope," he writes, "a good account will be given of Gage, Haldiman, Burgoyne, Clinton, and Howe, before

winter. Such a wretch as Howe, with a statue in honor of his family in Westminster Abbey, erected by the Massachusetts, to come over with the design to cut the throats of the Massachusetts people, is too much. I most sincerely, coolly, and devoutly wish, that a lucky ball or bayonet may make a signal example of him, in warning to all such unprincipled, unsentimental miscreants for the future!"

He goes on in a strain that smacks somewhat of aristocratic feeling:—"Our camp will be an illustrious school of military virtue, and will be resorted to and frequented, as such, by gentlemen in great numbers from the other colonies." The term "gentleman" has seldom been used in this sense subsequently to the Revolution. Another letter introduces us to two of these gentlemen, Messrs. Aquilla Hall and Josias Carvill, volunteers, who are recommended as "of the first families in Maryland, and possessing independent fortunes."

After the British had been driven out of Boston, Adams cries out,—"Fortify, fortify; and never let them get in again!" It is agreeable enough to perceive the filial affection with which John Adams, and the other delegates from the North, regard New England, and especially the good old capital of the Puritans. Their love of country was hardly yet so diluted as to extend over the whole thirteen colonies, which were rather looked upon as allies than as composing one nation. In truth, the patriotism of a citizen of the United States is a sentiment by itself, of a peculiar nature, and requiring a life-time, or at least the custom of many years, to naturalize it among the other possessions of the heart.

The collection is enriched by a letter—dated "Cambridge, August 26, 1775"—from Washington himself. He wrote it in that house—now so venerable with his memory—in that very room, where his bust now stands upon a poet's table. Down this sheet of paper passed the hand that held the leading-staff! Nothing can be more perfectly in keeping with all other manifestations of Washington, than the whole visible aspect and embodiment of this letter. The manuscript is as clear as daylight; the punctuation exact, to a comma. There is a calm accuracy throughout, which seems the production of a species of intelligence that cannot err, and which, if we may so speak, would affect us with a more human warmth, if we could conceive it capable of some slight human error. The chirography is characterized by a plain and easy grace, which, in the signature, is somewhat elaborated, and becomes a type of the personal manner of a gentleman of the old school, but without detriment to the truth and clearness that distinguish the rest of the manuscript. The lines are as straight and equi-distant as if ruled; and from beginning to end, there is no physical symptom—as how should there be?— of varying mood, of jets of emotion, or any of those fluctuating feelings that pass from the hearts into the fingers of common men. The paper itself (like most of those Revolutionary letters, which are written on fabrics fit to endure the burthen of ponderous and earnest thought) is stout, and of excellent quality, and bears the water-mark of Britannia, surmounted by the crown.

The subject of the letter is a statement of reasons for not taking possession of Point Alderton; a position commanding the entrance of Boston harbor. After explaining the difficulties of the case, arising from his want of men and munitions for the adequate defence of the lines which he already occupies, Washington proceeds:—

"To you, sir, who are a well-wisher to the cause, and can reason upon the effects of such conduct, I may open myself with freedom, because no improper disclosures will be made of our situation. But I cannot expose my weakness to the enemy (though I believe they are pretty well informed of everything that passes), by telling this and that man, who are daily pointing out this, and that, and t'other place, of all the motives that govern my actions; notwithstanding I know what will be the consequence of not doing it—namely, that I shall be accused of inattention to the public service, and perhaps of want of spirit to prosecute it. But this shall have no effect upon my conduct. I will steadily (as far as my judgment will assist me) pursue such measures as I think conducive to the interest of the cause, and rest satisfied under any obloquy that shall be thrown, conscious of having discharged my duty to the best of my abilities."

The above passage, like every other passage that could be quoted from his pen, is characteristic of Washington, and entirely in keeping with the calm elevation of his soul. Yet how imperfect a glimpse do we obtain of him, through the medium of this, or any of his letters! We imagine him writing calmly, with a hand that never falters; his majestic face neither darkens nor gleams with any momentary ebullition of feeling, or irregularity of thought; and thus flows forth an expression precisely to the extent of his purpose, no more, no less. Thus much we may conceive. But still we have not grasped the man; we have caught no glimpse of his interior; we have not detected his personality. It is the same with all the recorded traits of his daily life. The collection of them, by different observers, seems sufficiently abundant, and strictly harmonizes with itself, yet never brings us into intimate relationship with the hero, nor makes us feel the warmth and the human throb of his heart. What can be the reason? Is it, that his great nature was adapted to stand in relation to his country, as man stands towards man, but could not individualize itself in brotherhood to an individual?

There are two letters from Franklin, the earliest dated, "London, August 8, 1767," and addressed to "Mrs. Franklin, at Philadelphia." He was then in England, as agent for the Colonies in their resistance to the oppressive policy of Mr. Grenville's administration. The letter, however, makes no reference to political, or other business. It contains only ten or twelve lines, beginning—"My dear child"—and conveying an impression of long and venerable matrimony, which has lost all its romance, but retained a familiar and quiet tenderness. He speaks of making a little excursion into the country for his health; mentions a longer letter, despatched by another vessel; alludes with homely affability to "Mrs. Stevenson," "Sally," and "our dear Polly," desires to be remembered to "all inquiring friends;" and signs himself—"Your ever loving husband." In this conjugal epistle, brief and unimportant as it is, there are the elements that summon up the past, and enable us to create anew the man, his connexions, and circumstances. We can see the sage in his London lodgings— with his wig cast aside, and replaced by a velvet cap—penning this very letter; and then can step across the Atlantic, and behold its reception by the elderly, but still comely Madam Franklin, who breaks the seal and begins to read, first remembering to put on her spectacles. The seal, by the way, is a pompous one of armorial bearings, rather symbolical of the dignity of the Colonial Agent, and Postmaster General of America, than of the humble origin of the New England printer. The writings is in the free, quick style of a man with great practice of the pen, and is particularly agreeable to the reader.

Another letter, from the same famous hand, is addressed to General Palmer, and dated "Passy, October 27, 1779." By an endorsement on the outside it appears to have been transmitted to the United States through the medium of La Fayette. Franklin was now the ambassador of his country at the court of Versailles, enjoying an immense celebrity, caressed by the French ladies, and idolized alike by the fashionable and the learned, who saw something sublime and philosophic even in his blue yarn stockings. Still, as before, he writes with the homeliness and simplicity that cause a human face to look forth from the old, yellow sheet of paper, and in words that make our ears re-echo, as with the sound of his long extinct utterance. Yet this brief epistle, like the former, has so little of tangible matter that we are ashamed to copy it.

Next, we come to the fragment of a letter by Samuel Adams; an autograph more utterly devoid of ornament or flourish than any other in the collection. It would not have been characteristic, had his pen traced so much as one hair-line in tribute to grace, beauty, or the elaborateness of manner; for this earnest-hearted man had been produced out of the past elements of his native land, a real Puritan, with the religion of his forefathers, and likewise with their principles of government, taking the aspect of Revolutionary politics. At heart, Samuel Adams was never so much a citizen of the United States, as he was a New-Englander, and a son of the Old Bay Province. The following passage has much of the man in it:—

"I heartily congratulate you," he writes from Philadelphia, after the British have left Boston, "upon the sudden and important change in our affairs, in the removal of the barbarians from the capital. We owe our grateful acknowledgments to Him who is, as he is frequently styled in sacred Writ, 'The Lord of Hosts.' We have not yet been informed with certainty what course the enemy have steered. I hope we shall be on our guard against future attempts. Will not care be taken to fortify the harbor, and thereby prevent the entrance of ships of war hereafter?"

From Hancock, we have only the envelope of a document "on public service," directed to "The Hon. the Assembly, or the Council of Safety of New-Hampshire," and with the autograph affixed, that stands out so prominently in the Declaration of Independence. As seen in the engraving of that instrument, the signature looks precisely what we should expect and desire in the handwriting of a princely merchant, whose penmanship had been practised in the ledger which he is represented as holding, in Copley's brilliant picture, but to whom his native ability, and the circumstances and customs of his country had given a place among its rulers. But, on the coarse and dingy paper before us, the effect is very much inferior; the direction, all except the signature, is a scrawl, large and heavy, but not forcible; and even the name itself, while almost identical in its strokes with that of the Declaration, has a strangely different and more vulgar aspect. Perhaps it is all right, and typical of the truth. If we may trust tradition, and unpublished letters, and a few witnesses in print, there was quite as much difference between the actual man and his historical aspect, as between the manuscript signature and the engraved one. One of his associates, both in political life and permanent renown, is said to have characterized him as a "man without a head or heart." We, of an after generation, should hardly be entitled, on whatever evidence, to assume such ungracious liberty with a name that has occupied a lofty position until it has grown almost sacred, and which is associated with memories more sacred than itself, and has thus become a valuable reality to our countrymen, by the aged reverence that clusters round about it. Nevertheless it may be no impiety to regard Hancock not precisely as a real personage, but as a majestic figure, useful and necessary in its way, but producing its effect far more by an ornamental outside than by any intrinsic force or virtue. The page of history would be half unpeopled, if all such characters were banished from it.

From General Warren we have a letter dated January 14, 1775, only a few months before he attested the sincerity of his patriotism, in his own blood, on Bunker Hill. His handwriting has many ungraceful flourishes. All the small *d*'s spout upward in parabolic curves, and descend at a considerable distance. His pen seems to have had nothing but hairlines in it; and the whole letter, though perfectly legible, has a look of thin and unpleasant irregularity. The subject is a plan for securing to the Colonial party, the services of Colonel

Gridley, the engineer, by an appeal to his private interests. Though writing to General Palmer, an intimate friend, Warren signs himself, most ceremoniously, "Your obedient servant." Indeed, these stately formulas in winding up a letter, were scarcely laid aside, whatever might be the familiarity of intercourse: husband and wife were occasionally, on paper at least, the "obedient servants" of one another; and not improbably, among well-bred people, there was a corresponding ceremonial of bows and courtesies, even in the deepest interior of domestic life. With all the reality that filled men's hearts, and which has stamped its impress on so many of these letters, it was a far more formal age than the present.

It may be remarked, that Warren was almost the only man eminently distinguished in the intellectual phase of the Revolution, previous to the breaking out of the war, who actually uplifted his arm to do battle. The legislative patriots were a distinct class from the patriots of the camp, and never laid aside the gown for the sword. It was very different in the great civil war of England, where the leading minds of the age, when argument had done its office, or left it undone, put on their steel breast-plates and appeared as leaders in the field. Educated young men, members of the old colonial families—gentlemen, as John Adams terms them—seem not to have sought employment in the Revolutionary army, in such numbers as might have been expected. Respectable as the officers generally were, and great as were the abilities sometimes elicited, the intellect and cultivation of the country was inadequately represented in them, as a body.

Turning another page, we find the frank of a letter from Henry Laurens, President of Congress,—him whose destiny it was, like so many noblemen of old, to pass beneath the Traitor's Gate of the Tower of London,—him whose chivalrous son sacrificed as brilliant a future as any young American could have looked forward to, in an obscure skirmish. Likewise, we have the address of a letter to Messrs. Leroy and Bayard, in the handwriting of Jefferson; too slender a material to serve as a talisman for summoning up the writer; a most unsatisfactory fragment, affecting us like a glimpse of the retreating form of the sage of Monticello, turning the distant corner of a street. There is a scrap from Robert Morris, the financier; a letter or two from Judge Jay; and one from General Lincoln, written, apparently, on the gallop, but without any of those characteristic sparks that sometimes fly out in a hurry, when all the leisure in the world would fail to elicit them. Lincoln was the type of a New England soldier; a man of fair abilities, not especially of a warlike cast, without much chivalry, but faithful and bold, and carrying a kind of decency and restraint into the wild and ruthless business of arms.

From good old Baron Steuben, we find—not a manuscript essay on the method of arraying a battle—but a commercial draft, in a small, neat hand, as plain as print, elegant without flourish, except a very complicated one beneath the signature. On the whole, the specimen is sufficently characteristic, as well of the Baron's soldierlike and German simplicity, as of the polish of the Great Frederick's aide-de-camp, a man of courts and of the world. How singular and picturesque an effect is produced, in the array of our Revolutionary army, by the intermingling of these titled personages from the continent of Europe, with feudal associations clinging about them —Steuben, De Kalb, Pulaski, La Fayette!—the German veteran, who had ridden from the smoke of one famous battle-field to another for thirty years; and the young French noble, who had come hither, though yet unconscious of his high office, to light the torch that should set fire to the antiquated trumpery of his native institutions! Among these autographs, there is one from La Fayette, written long after our Revolution, but while that of his own country was in full progress. The note is merely as follows:—

> "Enclosed you will find, my dear Sir, two tickets for the sitting of this day. One part of the debate will be on the Honors of the Pantheon, agreeably to what has been decreed by the Constitutional Assembly."

It is a pleasant and comfortable thought, that we have no such classic folly as is here indicated, to lay to the charge of our Revolutionary fathers. Both in their acts, and in the drapery of those acts, they were true to their severe and simple selves, and thus left nothing behind them for a fastidious taste to sneer at. But it must be considered that our Revolution did not, like that of France, go so deep as to disturb the common sense of the country.

General Schuyler writes a letter, under date of February 22, 1780, relating not to military affairs, from which the prejudices of his countrymen had almost disconnected him, but to the salt springs of Onondaga. The expression is peculiarly direct, and the hand that of a man of business, free and flowing. The uncertainty, the vague, hearsay evidence respecting these springs, then gushing into dim daylight beneath the shadows of a remote wilderness, is such as might now be quoted in reference to the quality of the water that supplies the fountains of the Nile. The following sentence shows us an Indian woman and her son, practising their simple processes in the manufacture of salt, at a fire of wind-strewn boughs, the flame of which gleams duskily through the arches of the forest:—"From a variety of information, I find the smallest quantity made by a squaw, with the assistance of one boy, with a kettle of about ten gallons capacity, is half a bushel per day; the greatest, with the same kettle, about two bushels." It is particularly interesting to find out anything as to the embryo, yet stationary arts of life among the red people, their manufactures, their agriculture, their domestic labors. It is partly the lack of this knowledge—the possession of which would establish a ground of sympathy on the part of civilized men—that makes the Indian race so shadowlike and unreal to our conception.

We could not select a greater contrast to the upright and unselfish patriot whom we have just spoken of, than the traitor Arnold, from whom there is a brief note, dated, "Crown-Point, January 19, 1775," addressed to an officer under his command. The three lines, of which it consists, can prove bad spelling, erroneous grammar, and misplaced and superfluous punctuation; but, with all this complication of iniquity, the ruffian General contrives to express his meaning as briefly and clearly as if the rules of correct composition had been ever so scrupulously observed. This autograph, impressed with the foulest name in our history, has somewhat of the interest that would attach to a document on which a fiend-devoted wretch had signed away his salvation. But there was not substance enough in the man—a mere cross between the bull-dog and the fox—to justify much feeling of any sort about him personally. The interest, such as it is, attaches but little to the man, and far more to the circumstances amid which he acted, rendering the villainy almost sublime, which, exercised in petty affairs, would only have been vulgar.

We turn another leaf, and find a memorial of Hamilton. It is but a letter of introduction, addressed to Governor Jay in favor of Mr. Davies, of Kentucky; but it gives an impression of high breeding and courtesy, as little to be mistaken as if we could see the writer's manner and hear his cultivated accents, while personally making one gentleman known to another. There is likewise a rare vigor of expression and pregnancy of meaning, such as only a man of habitual energy of thought could have conveyed into so common-place a thing as an introductory letter. This autograph is a graceful one, with an easy and picturesque flourish beneath the signature, symbolical of a courteous bow at the conclusion of the social ceremony so admirably performed. Hamilton might well be the leader and idol of the Federalists; for he was pre-eminent in all the high qualities that characterized the great men of that party, and which should make even a democrat feel proud that his country had produced such a noble old band of aristocrats; and he shared all the distrust of the people, which so inevitably and so righteously brought about their ruin. With his autograph we associate that of another Federalist, his friend in life; a man far narrower than Hamilton, but endowed with a native vigor, that caused many partisans to grapple to him for support; upright, sternly inflexible, and of a simplicity of manner that might have befitted the sturdiest republican among us. In our boyhood we used to see a thin, severe figure of an ancient man, time-worn, but apparently indestructible, moving with a step of vigorous decay along the street, and knew him as "Old Tim Pickering."

Side by side, too, with the autograph of Hamilton, we would place one from the hand that shed his blood. It is a few lines of Aaron Barr, written in 1823; when all his ambitious schemes, whatever they once were, had been so long shattered that even the fragments had crumbled away, leaving him to exert his withered energies on petty law cases, to one of which the present note refers. The hand is a little tremulous with age, yet small and fastidiously elegant, as became a man who was in the habit of writing billet-doux on scented note-paper, as well as documents of war and state. This is to us a deeply interesting autograph. Remembering what has been said of the power of Burr's personal influence, his art to tempt men, his might to subdue them, and the fascination that enabled him, though cold at heart, to win the love of woman, we gaze at this production of his pen as into his own inscrutable eyes, seeking for the mystery of his nature. How singular that a character, imperfect, ruined, blasted, as this man's was, excites a stronger interest than if it had reached the highest earthly perfection of which its original elements would admit! It is by the diabolical part of Burr's character, that he produces his effect on the imagination. Had he been a better man, we doubt, after all, whether the present age would not already have suffered him to wax dusty and fade out of sight, among the more respectable mediocrities of his own epoch. But, certainly, he was a strange, wild offshoot to have sprung from the united stock of those two singular Christians, President Burr, of Princeton College, and Jonathan Edwards!

Omitting many, we have come almost to the end of these memorials of historical men. We observe one other autograph of a distinguished soldier of the Revolution, Henry Knox, but written in 1791, when he was Secretary of War. In its physical aspect, it is well worthy to be a soldier's letter. The hand is large, round, and legible at a glance; the lines far apart, and accurately equi-distant; and the whole affair looks not unlike a company of regular troops in marching order. The signature has a print-like firmness and simplicity. It is a curious observation, sustained by these autographs, though we know not how generally correct, that Southern gentlemen are more addicted to a flourish of the pen beneath their names, than those of the North.

And now we come to the men of a later generation, whose active life reaches almost within the verge of present affairs; people of great dignity, no doubt, but whose characters have not acquired, either from time or circumstances, the interest that can make their autographs valuable to any but the collector. Those whom we have hitherto noticed were the men of an heroic age. They are departed, and now so utterly departed, as not even to touch upon the passing generation through the medium of persons still in life, who can claim

to have known them familiarly. Their letters, therefore, come
to us like material things out of the hands of mighty shadows,
long historical and traditionary, and fit companions for the
sages and warriors of a thousand years ago. In spite of the
proverb, it is not in a single day, or in a very few years, that
a man can be reckoned "as dead as Julius Cæsar." We feel
little interest in scraps from the pens of old gentlemen,
ambassadors, governors, senators, heads of departments, even
presidents though they were, who lived lives of praiseworthy
respectability, and whose powdered heads and black knee-
breeches have but just vanished out of the drawing-room. Still
less do we value the blotted paper of those whose reputations
are dusty, not with oblivious time, but with present political
turmoil and newspaper vogue. Really great men, however,
seem, as to their effect on the imagination, to take their place
amongst past worthies, even while walking in the very sunshine that illuminates the autumnal day in which we write.
We look, not without curiosity, at the small, neat hand of
Henry Clay, who, as he remarks with his habitual deference
to the wishes of the fair, responds to a young lady's request
for his seal; and we dwell longer over the torn-off conclusion
of a note from Mr. Calhoun, whose words are strangely
dashed off without letters, and whose name, were it less illustrious, would be unrecognizable in his own autograph. But
of all hands that can still grasp a pen, we know not the one,
belonging to a soldier or a statesman, which could interest us
more than the hand that wrote the following:—

"SIR:
"Your note of the 6th inst. is received. I hasten to answer
that there was no man 'in the station of colonel, by the
name of J. T. Smith,' under my command, at the battle of
New Orleans; and am, respectfully,   Yours,
                         "ANDREW JACKSON.
"Octr. 19th, 1833."

The old general, we suspect, has been ensnared by a pardonable little stratagem on the part of the autograph collector. The battle of New Orleans would hardly have been won, without better aid than that of this problematical Colonel J. T. Smith!

Intermixed with and appended to these historical autographs, there are a few literary ones. Timothy Dwight—the "old Timotheus" who sang the Conquest of Canaan, instead of choosing a more popular subject, in the British conquest of Canada—is of eldest date. Colonel Trumbull, whose hand, at various epochs of his life, was familiar with sword, pen, and pencil, contributes two letters, which lack the picturesqueness of execution that should distinguish the chirography of an artist. The value of Trumbull's pictures is of the same nature with that of daguerreotypes, depending not upon the ideal but the actual. The beautiful signature of Washington Irving appears as the endorsement of a draft, dated in 1814, when, if we may take this document as evidence, his individuality seems to have been merged into the firm of "P. E. Irving & Co." Never was anything less mercantile than this autograph, though as legible as the writing of a bank-clerk. Without apparently aiming at artistic beauty, it has all the Sketch Book in it. We find the signature and seal of Pierpont, the latter stamped with the poet's almost living countenance. What a pleasant device for a seal is one's own face, which he may thus multiply at pleasure, and send letters to his friends, —the Head without, and the Heart within! There are a few lines in the school-girl hand of Margaret Davidson, at nine years old; and a scrap of a letter from Washington Allston, a gentle and delicate autograph, in which we catch a glimpse of thanks to his correspondent for the loan of a volume of poetry. Nothing remains, save a letter from Noah Webster, whose early toils were manifested in a spelling book, and those of his latter age in a ponderous dictionary. Under date of February 10, 1843, he writes in a sturdy, awkward hand, very fit for a lexicographer—an epistle of old man's reminiscences, from which we extract the following anecdote of Washington, presenting the patriot in a festive light:

"When I was travelling to the South, in the year 1785, I called on General Washington at Mount Vernon. At dinner, the last course of dishes was a species of pancakes, which were handed round to each guest, accompanied with a bowl of sugar and another of molasses for seasoning them, that each guest might suit himself. When the dish came to me, I pushed by me the bowl of molasses, observing to the gentlemen present, that I had enough of *that* in my own country. The General burst out with a *loud laugh*, a thing very unusual with him. 'Ah,' said he, 'there is nothing in that story about your eating molasses in New England.' There was a gentleman from Maryland at the table; and the General immediately told a story, stating that, during the Revolution, a hogshead of molasses was stove in West-Chester by the oversetting of a wagon; and a body of Maryland troops being near, the soldiers ran hastily, and saved all they could by filling their hats or caps with molasses."

There are said to be temperaments endowed with sympathies so exquisite, that, by merely handling an autograph, they can detect the writer's character with unerring accuracy, and read his inmost heart as easily as a less gifted eye would peruse the written page. Our faith in this power, be it a spiritual one, or only a refinement of the physical nature, is not unlimited, in spite of evidence. God has imparted to the human soul a marvellous strength in guarding its secrets, and He keeps at least the deepest and most inward record for His own perusal. But if there be such sympathies as we have alluded to, in how many instances would History be put to the blush by a volume of autograph letters, like this which we now close!

EDITORIAL APPENDIXES

The Snow-Image

I N "THE OLD MANSE" Hawthorne had formally bid farewell to short fiction and described his *Mosses from an Old Manse* collection as "the last offering . . . of this nature, which it is my purpose ever to put forth." A week after dispatching the essay he entered the Salem custom house, ready to put literary labors aside for the responsibilities of the surveyorship. In contrast to the pastoral privacy he had enjoyed in Concord, he became secretary of the Salem Lyceum, and involved himself in public affairs. Nevertheless, he was not quite accurate when, in "The Custom-House" of *The Scarlet Letter*, he characterized his interests during these years: "Literature, its exertions and objects, were now of little moment in my regard. I cared not, at this period, for books; . . . A gift, a faculty, if it had not departed, was suspended and inanimate within me." Actually, Hawthorne threw off his old writing habits for only about eighteen months. Before the summer of 1847 he apparently wrote nothing except occasional literary reviews for the local Democratic newspaper, the *Advertiser*—reviews that he came later to regret since, labelled political essays by the Salem Whigs, they led to his dismissal from the custom house on June 8, 1849.[1]

[1] Among the reviews were those of *Typee* and *Evangeline*. He did not review *Kavanaugh*, he wrote H. W. Longfellow, because he had been accused of "writing political articles" (June 5, 1849, MS, Houghton

By June, 1847, he resumed making regular journal entries, after having scanted them since October, 1845. Sophia Hawthorne wrote to her mother, September 10, 1847, "He has now lived in the nursery a year without a chance for one hour's uninterrupted musing and without his desk being once opened!" but later she added, "My husband began retiring to his study on the 1st of November, and writes every afternoon." [2] Hawthorne's report to Longfellow on November 11 casts doubt on her estimate of his success: "I am trying to resume my pen; but the influences of my situation and customary associates are so anti-literary, that I know not whether I shall succeed. Whenever I sit alone, or walk alone, I find myself dreaming about stories, as of old; but these forenoons in the Custom House undo all that the afternoons and evenings have done. I should be happier if I could write—also, I should like to add something to my income, which, though tolerable, is a tight fit. If you can suggest any work of pure literary drudgery, I am the very man for it." [3] The one suggestion Longfellow made—"a history of Acadia"—did not tempt Hawthorne sufficiently for him to pursue it. [4]

Library, Harvard University). He protested more fully to George Hillard: "My contributions . . . have been two theatrical criticisms, a notice of a ball at Ballard Vale, a notice of Longfellow's Evangeline, and perhaps half a dozen other books. Never one word of politics. Any . . . would have been perfectly proper for a Whig paper; and, indeed, most of them were copied into Whig papers elsewhere. You know, and the public know, what my contributions to the Democratic Review have been. They are all published in one or another of my volumes—all, with a single exception . . . the life of my early and very dear friend, Cilley, written shortly after his death, at the request of the Editor. . . . It cannot be called a political article; and, with that single exception, I have never, in all my life, written one word that had reference to politics" (June 12, 1849, MS, Maine Historical Society).

2 September 9–10, November 22–23, MSS, Berg Collection, New York Public Library.

3 MS, Houghton Library, Harvard University.

4 Hawthorne to Longfellow, February 10, 1848, MS, Houghton Library, Harvard University.

But he did, apparently, try to compose the sort of lengthy fiction that he had mentioned as a goal, with mock-seriousness, in "The Old Manse." It is most likely that he turned again to short fiction only after the development of "The Unpardonable Sin" proved infeasible. Between early 1848 and October, 1849, when he had begun the work that was to become *The Scarlet Letter*, Hawthorne wrote at least one other piece, "Main-street," and perhaps also "The Great Stone Face" and "The Snow-Image: A Childish Miracle."

Fixing exactly the dates of composition of these pieces is impossible, but it appears certain that Hawthorne, earnest about escaping from the constrained economics of magazine publication, tried first to produce a full-length romance and, only after failing, turned again to the sketch and the tale. Although "The Unpardonable Sin" did not appear in print until January 5, 1850, Hawthorne had completed this part of a larger work by early December, 1848. At that time, suppressing his doubts about the suitability of the piece and apparently writing a prefatory note about its fragmentary character, he offered it to his sister-in-law Elizabeth Peabody for her anthology, *Æsthetic Papers*. In sending the manuscript to her mother, Sophia identified the story unmistakably: "He wishes the note at the end of the manuscript to be placed at the beginning of the printed text as a preface; and he thinks it had better be upon a separate fore-leaf. It is a tremendous truth, written, as he often writes truth, with characters of fire, upon an infinite gloom,—softened so as not wholly to terrify, by divine touches of beauty,—revealing pictures of nature, and also the tender spirit of a child." [5] Miss Peabody, who at the time was deeply involved in other activities, was delayed in assembling her volume, and

[5] Julian Hawthorne, *Nathaniel Hawthorne and His Wife* (Boston and New York, 1884), I, 330–31.

she evidently did not read Hawthorne's manuscript until
March; then Mrs. Peabody wrote to Sophia, "E. says she
thinks the 'Unpardonable Sin' very interesting and full of
genius; but of course, if another story is to be written, *at any
rate*, she would like to make a choice, if Mr. H. is willing
to give her liberty to do so. This story is gloomy, but it is
the illustration of a great truth, with great power and she
will not give it up unless for something as great as well
as more cheerful." [6] Sophia's answer suggests that Hawthorne had made further attempts to write longer pieces of
fiction: "With regard to the article, my husband began
another—rather went on with another, after the first went to
New York; & finally it grew so very long that he said it
would make a little book. So he had to put that aside &
begin another. This has also grown altogether too long for
E.'s book, so now he must prepare another from some of his
journals." [7] However, the two other tales perhaps written in
the winter of 1848–49, "The Great Stone Face" and "The
Snow-Image," are not of such length as to be inappropriate
for Miss Peabody's volume. It is more likely that he was
temporizing with his sister-in-law. "Main-street"—almost as
long as "The Gentle Boy," which he had published separately
in book form in 1839—is probably the piece Hawthorne
thought of making into a small book. He finally gave it to
Miss Peabody for *Æsthetic Papers*, which was published in
May, 1849. Since "The Great Stone Face" was first printed
in the *National Era*, January 24, 1850, and "The Snow-
Image" in the November, 1850, *International Miscellany*,
these stories are likely the work of a later date. It is highly
improbable that Hawthorne completed lengthy tales during
this period, without publishing them.

Hawthorne had not waited for Miss Peabody to accept or

[6] March 7, 1849, MS, Berg Collection, New York Public Library.

[7] March 8–9, 1849, MS, Berg Collection, New York Public Library.
"New York" refers to publication elsewhere; see the following paragraph.

reject "The Unpardonable Sin," but, having been invited by Charles W. Webber to contribute to his projected magazine— to be called *The American Review*—he sent off another copy of the story on December 14, 1848. His accompanying letter does not mention the tale by name but makes clear that it was "The Unpardonable Sin" and suggests strongly that this story was the first he had been able to write: "At last, by main strength, I have wrenched and torn an idea out of my miserable brain; or rather, the fragment of an idea, like a tooth ill-drawn, and leaving the roots to torture me. . . . When shall you want another article? Now that the spell is broken, I hope to get into a regular train of scribbling." [8] Webber went so far as to have the first issue set in type, but he and his partner Victor Audubon lacked the funds necessary to carry the magazine into distribution and had to store the sheets in a New York warehouse.[9] About a year later, Webber passed along the story, probably in the magazine sheets, to the *Boston Weekly Museum*, a newspaper. Earlier, James T. Fields had urged Hawthorne to publish a new volume, in which Hawthorne planned to include "The Unpardonable Sin." [10] He was unhappy with the arrangement made by Webber and on December 18, 1849, complained to him:

[8] MS, University of Virginia. Hawthorne told Webber in banter to "make no ceremony about rejecting it. I am as tractable an author as you ever knew, so far as putting my articles into the fire goes." But it is unlikely that Hawthorne would have destroyed more than fragments of stories.

[9] From this warehouse E. A. Duyckinck procured the sheets of Hawthorne's story and an illustrative wood-cut used in reprinting the piece in *Dollar Magazine*, May, 1851, as "Ethan Brand; or, The Unpardonable Sin" (Webber to Duyckinck, December 4, 1850 and March 5, 1851, MSS, Duyckinck Collection, New York Public Library).

[10] Fields wrote to Hawthorne on May 24, 1849, offering $25.00 for an original contribution to the 1850 *Boston Book* (MS, Ticknor and Fields Letter Books, Domestic, I, 455, Houghton Library, Harvard University); he reprinted "Drowne's Wooden Image" to represent Hawthorne. Some six months later Fields visited Hawthorne and promised to publish whatever he might wish, in "an edition of two thousand copies" (James T. Fields, *Yesterdays with Authors* [Boston, 1872], pp. 49–50).

An acquaintance of mine told me, to day, that I am announced as having written a story for "The Museum," and that it is to appear on the 5th of January. Now, when we spoke together about the "Unpardonable Sin," I understood that it was to be published, not as a story written for this newspaper—The Museum—but as a specimen of a forthcoming book; and that the time of its appearance was to be all but co-incident with the publication of the book. On any other understanding, I should not have given my consent to your proposal, although sincerely desirous of doing you all the service in my power. . . . I shall not have the book ready so soon as I expected and I do not wish the appearance of this article to precede that of the book so long as it must, if the announcement of the Editor of the Museum be carried into effect. Neither (to tell you the truth) does it quite suit me to be blazoned abroad as a contributor to this weekly Museum; which may be the very best publication in the universe, but of which I know nothing whatever. So that I wish, in the first place, that you would enjoin it on the Editor to "hold on", until I give him notice to "go ahead"; and, secondly, that, if not published merely as a specimen from the proof-sheets of my forth-coming book, it shall at least be stated that the article was originally contributed to your magazine, and that it is transferred to the Museum by an arrangement with the editor of that magazine, and not with the author of the article.[11]

Whatever Webber did to remedy the case resulted only in the subhead "From an Unpublished Work" under the misleading "For the Boston Weekly Museum."

The "forthcoming book" Hawthorne referred to is the manuscript and the accompanying project he sent to Fields on January 15, 1850. Hawthorne wrote, "I shall call the book Old-Time Legends; together with SKETCHES, EXPERI-

[11] MS, University of Virginia. There is no record that Webber had paid for the story, and the editor of the *Museum* was complacent about publishing it without consulting the author (J. T. Trowbridge, *My Own Story* [Boston, 1903], p. 120). Hawthorne fared only slightly better with "The Great Stone Face," receiving $25.00 and an abject apology for compensation not only late but inadequate (J. G. Whittier to Hawthorne, February 22, 1850, MS, Huntington Library).

MENTAL AND IDEAL." [12] If his account of the collection, in which the still unfinished "The Scarlet Letter" was the central tale, is at all accurate, he would have had to use nearly all of the pieces later gathered in *The Snow-Image.* "Calculating the page of the new volume at the size of that of the 'Mosses'," he wrote, "I can supply 400 and probably more." Besides "The Unpardonable Sin," he meant also to include, as he remarked in "The Custom-House," the long sketch "Main-street," and probably "The Great Stone Face," as well as earlier uncollected pieces: "Some of the briefer articles, which contribute to make up the volume, have likewise been written since my involuntary withdrawal from the toils and honors of public life, and the remainder are gleaned from annuals and magazines, of such antique date that they have gone round the circle, and come back to novelty again." He had apparently not assembled his selections from the old magazines and annuals. On January 20, he expressed to Fields a fear that "The Scarlet Letter" would "weary very many people, and disgust some," and explained that for prudent variety, "it was my purpose to conjoin the one long story with half a dozen shorter ones." Now, however, he left it to Fields's judgment to decide in favor of the collection or to publish a smaller book consisting of "The Custom-House" and "The Scarlet Letter"—a form Hawthorne confessed preferable "as a matter of taste and beauty." [13]

With the publication of *The Scarlet Letter* in March, 1850, and the establishment beyond question of his reputation as a writer of romance, Hawthorne soon moved his family to Lenox and there, in the following August, began writing

[12] MS transcription, Hawthorne-Fields Letter Book, Houghton Library, Harvard University.

[13] MS transcription, Hawthorne-Fields Letter Book, Houghton Library, Harvard University.

The House of the Seven Gables. It is probable that in the interval between finishing *The Scarlet Letter* and beginning the second romance, Hawthorne wrote "The Snow-Image." [14] Rufus Griswold, offering payment, requested a contribution from Hawthorne for a volume memorializing Mrs. Fanny Osgood, and in a letter of August 23, 1850, Hawthorne authorized Fields to give Griswold "a story which I happened to have by me, intended for another purpose." [15] The piece duly appeared in *The Memorial,* published by Putnam in early January, 1851; but Griswold, under the guise of promoting the volume, with Putnam's permission printed "The Snow-Image" in his *International Miscellany* in November, 1850. It is not known whether Hawthorne also gave permission for this use; but it is a fact that he had to wait for some time before being paid by the publisher of *The Memorial.* On August 23, 1850, he had at first asked Fields, who took the story to New York, to request immediate payment, but then said that Griswold (as agent for Putnam) could pay "when he is ready." On November 9, Fields inquired of Hawthorne whether "they have paid you the $50 for your story in the Osgood Memorial Book." [16] Two days later Fields emphasized to Griswold that the money was "important to [Hawthorne] just now," and in a letter to Hawthorne on January 30, 1851,

[14] Julian Hawthorne had "a dim impression" of the story as read aloud to him during the fall of 1848, but the chances are slight that Hawthorne would have withheld from publication for three years so polished a story (*Nathaniel Hawthorne and His Wife,* I, 330). In the preface to *The Snow-Image,* Hawthorne spoke of tales "lying for years in manuscript" before "they at last skulked into the Annuals or Magazines," but those tales he wrote expressly for projected collections rather than for periodicals. There is no evidence that he followed this same practice after "The Story Teller" had been fragmented.

A "germ" of "The Snow-Image" is in an undated journal entry by Hawthorne, between March 16 and September 17, 1849 (see *The American Notebooks* [Centenary Edition, 1973], p. 287).

[15] MS, Columbia University.

[16] MS, Berg Collection, New York Public Library.

noted, "I have written to Griswold . . . but as yet not a word in reply." [17] Hawthorne evidently received the $50.00 at last, for he was later willing to send Griswold "Feathertop" for his magazine.

The experience only reconfirmed for Hawthorne the undesirability of writing short fiction. Meanwhile, his reluctance to continue to supply periodicals with his tales had been shown toward other propositions. Fields, in his November 9 letter, had forwarded George R. Graham's offer of $100.00 for a story the length of "The Snow-Image," and on December 6 Fields reminded Hawthorne, "if you will send him a *brief* article, any thing you please, by *Christmas* . . . he will pay you One Hundred Dollars." [18] Answering on November 29, in a letter which reported no payment for "The Snow-Image," Hawthorne had observed tartly, "I think I would write an article for Graham for $100. I am pretty certain that I would for $150," but on December 9 he was emphatic: "I can't without more personal botheration and disgust than I choose to incur for $100 (so long as there are any shots in the locker) write a story for Graham at this time. He will want it just as much, by-and-by;—if not, it will save me the trouble of writing it." [19] On December 30, he wrote courteously to Ralph Waldo Emerson, declining an offer to contribute to a projected magazine; he took satisfaction in relating Graham's offer and another, from the *New York Tribune*, for a long story to be published in chapters. But of the project, he commented, "The remuneration, which the publishers could afford to offer, must necessarily be small. . . . I have

[17] *Passages from the Correspondence . . . of Rufus W. Griswold,* ed. W. M. Griswold (Cambridge, 1898), p. 268; MS, Berg Collection, New York Public Library.

[18] MS, Berg Collection, New York Public Library.

[19] November 29, MS, Collection of Norman Holmes Pearson; December 9, MS transcription, Hawthorne-Fields Letter Book, Houghton Library, Harvard University.

no faith whatever in its success; so that I should not feel as if I were doing anybody good, while doing myself harm." [20]

Hawthorne finished *The House of the Seven Gables* in late January, 1851, shortly after he had written his celebrated Preface to the Ticknor, Reed, and Fields edition of the *Twice-told Tales*.[21] As soon as the new book was in press, Fields began again to impress upon Hawthorne the importance of keeping himself before the public. On March 12, 1851, he wrote urgently:

> And now a business word or two. To "Keep the pot a boiling" has always been the endeavor of all true Yankees. . . . Will it not be a good plan for you to get ready a volume of Tales for the fall, to include those uncollected stories, The Snow Image, the piece in the mag^e. got up by Audubon's son & friend, &c, &c, and to add to it any other not yet printed? And then to[o] a Book of Stories for children for next season would do wonderfully well. . . . It is a good thing to follow up success in the Book way and your works are becoming every day more popular and commanding extensive sales. . . . It is well to begin early for the fall Publications.[22]

As his prefaces and letters indicate, Hawthorne nearly always found a reexamination of old tales painful and disappointing. His interest and confidence in his short fiction seemed to decrease as the years passed, and he was reluctant to take another backward glance at pieces he had already rejected two or three times. On May 20, he wrote to his sister Louisa, as postscript to a letter announcing Rosebud's birth, that "Ticknor & Co. want to publish a volume of my tales

[20] MS, Houghton Library, Harvard University.

[21] Hawthorne's title form is used for reference: see the Textual Commentary, *Twice-told Tales* (Centenary Edition, 1974).

[22] MS, Berg Collection, New York Public Library.

& sketches, not hitherto collected. If you have any, or can obtain them, pray do so." When he began writing *A Wonder-Book* in June, he put off thinking about the new collection. Beyond asking Louisa again on July 10 to send along whatever pieces she had, he seems to have made little progress on the seemingly simple task of collecting his old tales.[23] Indeed, upon completion of the juvenile work, he announced to Fields on July 15 that he was "going to begin to enjoy the summer now . . . and think of nothing at all." [24] On August 14 Fields asked him again, hopefully, "Do you intend to give us a new vol. of the Twice Told Tales?" [25] Finally, on September 2, having received from Louisa the package of magazine sheets she had gathered, Hawthorne had become uneasy about the makeup of the collection. He wrote Louisa: "I am rather afraid that I shall not be able to collect articles enough for a volume." [26] At this point he presumably asked for Fields's help in collecting, for on September 22, Fields wrote to him that he had "got together all the Token articles for the new vol. of Tales together with 'A Bells Biography' (Knick[r]) & the 'Old News' and 'Devils Mss' from the N.E. Mag[e]." [27]

Hawthorne, then, had relatively little to do with gathering the pieces for his last major collection. Of the fifteen tales and sketches, four were recent works that he should have had easy access to: "Main-street" (*Æsthetic Papers*, 1849), "Ethan Brand" (*Dollar Magazine*, May, 1851), "The Great Stone Face" (*National Era*, January 24, 1850), and "The Snow-Image" (*International Miscellany*, November, 1850).

[23] May 20, MS, Huntington Library; July 10, MS, Carl H. Pforzheimer Library, New York City. On May 24, Fields had reminded Hawthorne that the volume was expected in the fall (MS, Berg Collection, New York Public Library).

[24] MS, Huntington Library.

[25] MS, Berg Collection, New York Public Library.

[26] MS, Huntington Library.

[27] MS, Berg Collection, New York Public Library.

Fields gathered six others: "A Bell's Biography" (*Knicker-bocker*, March, 1837), "Old News" (*New-England Maga-zine*, February, March, May, 1835), "The Devil in Manu-script" (*New-England Magazine*, November, 1835), and tales from the *Token* annuals—"The Canterbury Pilgrims" (1833), "The Man of Adamant" (1837), "Sylph Etherege" (1838). "The Wives of the Dead" and "My Kinsman, Major Molineux" (1832 *Token*) were found with Ticknor's help, and Hawthorne directed the inclusion of "Little Daffydown-dilly" (*Boys' and Girls' Magazine*, August, 1843).

How many old tales Hawthorne was able to recover copies of only to reject is uncertain. In his Preface, written on November 1, Hawthorne, as he had done in "The Old Manse," called these tales the last he would publish, and added: "Or, if a few still remain, they are either such as no paternal partiality could induce the author to think worth preserving, or else they have got into some very dark and dusty hiding-place, quite out of my own remembrance, and whence no researches can avail to unearth them." Given his concern about the book's length, it is not likely that he thoughtlessly rejected any that came to his attention. He included "The Man of Adamant" even though years before he had judged it a failure: "I recollect that the Man of Adamant seemed a fine idea to me when I looked at it prophetically; but I failed in giving shape and substance to the vision which I saw. I don't think it can be very good." [28] There is no way of knowing what tales Louisa had located for her brother, but if she found "Old Ticonderoga," she may also have come by "Fragments from the Journal of a Solitary Man," which had appeared in the *American Monthly* (July, 1837). Whether Fields had available a complete run of volumes of the *Token* is likewise not known. But if he

[28] Letter to Sophia Peabody, September 16, 1841, MS, Huntington Library.

saw the 1835 *Token*, he would have easily identified Hawthorne's "Alice Doane's Appeal" from its attribution. In that
case, either he or Hawthorne himself would have had to
reject the tale. Although Hawthorne was probably unable
to remember a few of his oldest stories—for example, "An
Old Woman's Tale" (*Salem Gazette*, December 21, 1830)—
he very likely did recall "Sketches from Memory" (*New-
England Magazine*, November, December, 1835) inasmuch
as he asked that it be used in 1854 for the expanded edition
of *Mosses*.

Hawthorne wrote to Horatio Bridge on October 11 that
the volume was in press.[29] He complained to Ticknor on
October 22 that proof-sheets were not reaching him, and
requested, "When the Preface is needed, please to let me
know." [30] Ticknor answered on October 24, "I think you
had best send the Preface at your Earliest Convenience." [31]
The ordering of the tales and sketches in the volume indicates that the first selections for *The Snow-Image* went to
the printers before Hawthorne had made all his choices of
tales and sent copy to Ticknor. The first four tales are those
Hawthorne wrote after the summer of 1848, none of which
did he have to revise significantly. These are followed by
six other selections which Fields himself had culled from the
magazines and *The Token*. It seems plausible, even likely,
that when Fields spoke of having got together "all the Token
articles" he was referring only to three and had not searched
as far back as the 1832 volume containing "The Wives of
the Dead" and "My Kinsman, Major Molineux." These two
tales were among the last printed, and "Major Molineux"
came into Ticknor's hands very late. The delay probably
explains why "Major Molineux" was printed as the final

[29] MS, Bowdoin College.
[30] MS, University of Virginia.
[31] MS, Houghton Library, Harvard University.

piece in *The Snow-Image*. It is immediately preceded by a juvenile piece, "Little Daffydowndilly," which Ticknor queried Hawthorne about on November 5: "It is not marked on the list which Mr. Fields prepared for the Volume—Did you design to have it printed?"[32] Hawthorne replied on November 7, "I intended that the sketch of 'Daffy-downdilly' would be included in the volume. . . . It is as good as any of them."[33] That this innocuous sketch and "My Kinsman, Major Molineux" stand side by side is perhaps another illustration of Hawthorne's desire to gain variety by juxtaposing radically different kinds of fiction.

Hawthorne, knowing that his introductory sketches for *Mosses from an Old Manse* and *The Scarlet Letter* had been well received—long extracts from them being given in the reviews—used his new preface to restate several of the sentiments he had expressed in "The Old Manse" and in his Preface to the 1851 *Twice-told Tales*. Cast in the form of a dedicatory letter to Bridge, the Preface to *The Snow-Image* celebrates the "long and unbroken" friendship between Hawthorne and his benefactor. Hawthorne adopted a self-deprecatory but mellow tone in describing the merits of the tales: "I am disposed to quarrel with the earlier sketches, both because a maturer judgment discerns many faults, and still more because they come so nearly up to the standard of the best that I can achieve now. . . . In youth, men are apt to write more wisely than they really know or feel; and the remainder of life may be not idly spent in realizing and convincing themselves of the wisdom which they uttered long ago."

The first edition of *The Snow-Image, and Other Twice-told Tales* was printed on December 11, 1851 (dated 1852) and published during the month in an issue of 2,425 copies.

[32] MS, Ticknor and Fields Letter Books, Domestic, II, 348, Houghton Library, Harvard University.

[33] MS, Collection of Norman Holmes Pearson.

Hawthorne's royalty was ten percent on 2,300 copies sold at the retail price of 75 cents—$172.50. Advance sheets were sold to Henry G. Bohn in London for an English edition with the title date 1851. A second American printing of 1,000 copies was issued on December 1, 1852, but after that the publishers waited until August 28, 1857, before issuing 500 copies, the last to be printed by them during Hawthorne's lifetime.[34] *The Snow-Image* was decidedly less popular than *Twice-told Tales* and *Mosses from an Old Manse* in their overall printing histories.

The volume precipitated few reviews, perhaps because attention was drawn to *A Wonder-Book*, issued in the same month, but more likely because, as Hawthorne's third such collection, it lacked the aspect of novelty. A brief notice in the *Southern Quarterly Review* stated simply: "These stories are gathered together from the Magazines and Annuals, where they were originally scattered by the hands of their tasteful and prolific author. They are all characteristic,—quiet, gentle, fanciful,—clothing naked facts in pleasing allegory, and beguiling to truth and virtue, through labyrinths of fiction."[35] The notice in *To-Day* was still briefer: "The public will readily welcome a new collection of some of the delightful stories of this favorite author."[36] Duyckinck renewed his praise in the *Literary World*, quoting long passages from the Preface, "The Man of Adamant," and "A Bell's Biography," and objecting that "My Kinsman, Major Molineux" should have had a "supernatural conclusion" rather than a "broad comic" one: "The joke winding up this series of beautifully

[34] *The Cost Books of Ticknor and Fields,* ed. Warren S. Tryon and William Charvat (New York, 1949), pp. 210, 234, 409. The sale to Bohn in conjunction with *A Wonder-Book*, for £40, is detailed in a letter to Bohn from Ticknor, November 18, 1851 (MS, Ticknor and Fields Letter Books, Foreign, II, 242, Houghton Library, Harvard University).

[35] II (January, 1852), 262.

[36] I (January 3, 1852), 8.

drawn pictures is, that the traveller's distinguished kinsman is that night to be tarred and feathered. Most lame and impotent conclusion!" [37] Like Duyckinck, E. P. Whipple had nothing new to say in his *Graham's* review.[38] The collection, he began, "can hardly add to his great reputation, though it fully sustains it." While approving all the pieces, he mentioned specifically the four recent tales as especially noteworthy. Hawthorne's stories, he concluded, "arrest, fasten, fascinate attention; but, to the thoughtful reader they are not merely tales, but contributions to the philosophy of the human mind."

None of the omnibus essays written during Hawthorne's later life focussed on *The Snow-Image* tales and sketches. And, although he was moved to write "Feathertop," his last tale, as *The Snow-Image* was going through the press, the book-length romance was clearly what Hawthorne had come to expect of himself. But before he had finished with the writing of tales and sketches—experimental and ideal—he had left behind him a rich legacy of achieved form as well as promising potential. With all his false starts and his failures he had created a number of the finest stories in the language. He had developed his craft during the infancy and adolescence of American magazines, amidst a "damned mob of scribbling women"—and men—and had established, with his individual talent, a set of possibilities that still continue to nourish the American literary imagination.

J. D. C.

---

[37] X (January 10, 1852), 22–24.
[38] XL (April, 1852), 443.

The Uncollected Tales

IN ADDITION TO THE PIECES in Hawthorne's three collections, nine uncollected tales and sketches published within the span of 1830-44 are undoubtedly his. Of these, "The Antique Ring," in *Sargent's*, February, 1843, "A Good Man's Miracle," in the *Child's Friend*, February, 1844, and "A Book of Autographs," in the *Democratic Review*, November, 1844, appeared under his name. A partial manuscript survives of "Time's Portraiture," but the sketch is identifiable even in its unsigned appearance as the *Salem Gazette* broadside Carrier's Address for New Year's, 1838, by the reference in it to the author's changed spelling of his family name. "Alice Doane's Appeal" was attributed in the 1835 *Token* to the author of "The Gentle Boy," and "My Visit to Niagara," in the *New-England Magazine*, February, 1835, to the author of "The Gray Champion." The evidence for acceptance is indirect but no less categorical for "Sketches from Memory. No. II," printed in the *New-England Magazine*, December, 1835, as "By a Pedestrian." In preparation for the 1854 *Mosses*, Hawthorne asked that James T. Fields, his trusted editor, search for sketches in the *New-England Magazine* through the year of Park Benjamin's editorship. "The beginning, and the conclusion, of the 'Itinerant Story-teller' are there at an interval of some months," he wrote.[1] Fields located and placed in *Mosses* as "Passages from a Relinquished Work" parts of the beginning of "The Story Teller." He also found through Hawthorne's reference the two "Sketches from Memory," and placed "The Canal-Boat"

[1] Hawthorne to W. D. Ticknor, June 7, 1854, MS, Berg Collection, New York Public Library.

from the second installment with the first, as sufficient novelty for the new collection. That Hawthorne did not later deny authorship provides proof that he wrote the remainder of the second number.[2] Fields apparently did not pursue "The Story Teller" into the *American Monthly Magazine*, where Benjamin had transferred bits of the collection and many months later, in July, 1837, had printed the conclusion as "Fragments from the Journal of a Solitary Man." There the name of the traveling storyteller, Oberon—a name used by Hawthorne at Bowdoin and the protagonist's name in "The Devil in Manuscript"—marks the sketch as Hawthorne's, as does the entire narrative mode. In the first paragraph of the section "The Home Return" is the description which had been printed as "An Afternoon Scene" in the second installment of "Sketches from Memory." "Fragments" is an integral, if perhaps revised, part of the scattered collection.

For just one other piece can a virtually indisputable claim be made for a place in the Hawthorne canon: "An Old Woman's Tale," published without signature in the *Salem Gazette*, December 21, 1830. Although no external evidence beyond its place of publication suggests Hawthorne's authorship, internal evidence precludes argument. The firmly wrought tale creates an ambiguous atmosphere where the marvellous and the commonplace, the imaginary and the real, can interpenetrate; and all its details call up at every point the leading qualities and concerns of Hawthorne's most characteristic and distinctive art.

Seven of these tales and sketches were first collected in the 1876 Little Classic and Illustrated Library editions of

[2] In the postscript of his letter to Ticknor cited above, Hawthorne specified "an evening at the mountain-house . . . part of a work, the whole of which was never published." The vignettes of the first "Sketches from Memory" relate to "The Great Carbuncle" and "The Ambitious Guest." "The Canal-Boat," placed with these in *Mosses*, is not related in time or place.

The Dolliver Romance, and Other Pieces.[3] "Alice Doane's Appeal" was first collected in 1883 in *Sketches and Studies;* in the same year it appeared also in *Tales, Sketches, and Other Papers,* where the editor, G. P. Lathrop, noted that Elizabeth Hawthorne had told him of "Alice Doane" and that after a three-year search he had come across an 1835 *Token* containing "Alice Doane's Appeal," which he described as "a reminiscence of one among the 'Seven Tales of My Native Land.' "[4] None of the publishers succeeding the Ticknor firm collected "A Good Man's Miracle."

Beyond these pieces the establishment of the canon of Hawthorne's short fiction becomes increasingly problematic. The editors are profoundly indebted to Nelson F. Adkins, whose investigation of all aspects of the Hawthorne canon has been an integral part of the preparation of the Centenary Edition, and whose working papers are gratefully made use of in the following discussion.

The first question arises in the identification of the editor who discovered the vagrant pieces of the 1876 volumes. Sophia Hawthorne apparently had little knowledge of her husband's earliest work; and Hawthorne's sisters, judging from their correspondence about *The Snow-Image,* had already offered up all their suggestions, aside from Elizabeth's recall of "Alice Doane." Lathrop's *Study of Hawthorne,* also published by Osgood in 1876, makes no mention of the tales and sketches that had recently come to light. The publisher may have had the unacknowledged assistance of J. E. Babson, a minor Boston writer and bibliophile. Such, at any rate, was the opinion of a reviewer in *Appleton's Journal:*

[3] Both editions were published by James R. Osgood and Company, successor to Ticknor and Fields, and to Fields, Osgood, and Company.

[4] Page 9. Both volumes were published by Houghton, Mifflin and Company, descended from the Ticknor firm. *Tales, Sketches, and Other Papers* was vol. XII of the Riverside Edition of *The Complete Works of Nathaniel Hawthorne,* and *Sketches and Studies* was vol. XXIV of the Little Classic Edition.

"Perhaps not the least enjoyable of these works of Hawthorne's will be found in the two volumes of miscellaneous pieces which the fastidious author had suppressed and forgotten, and for the resurrection of which we are indebted, it is said, to the indefatigable researches of the late Mr. J. E. Babson." [5] The question is important because of the attributed pieces, "An Old Woman's Tale" and "Graves and Goblins" (anonymous in the *New-England Magazine,* June, 1835), included in the 1876 imprints.[6] The latter story, like the first, makes a strong claim to be considered Hawthorne's; its presence with the other pieces recovered in 1876 argues circumstantially for its authenticity, and the date and place of its first publication conspire with its subject and narrative manner to persuade that the sketch is a part of "The Story Teller." [7] This whimsical, somewhat self-pitying meditation is clearly an apt narrative for Hawthorne's central character in that projected collection. Its sentiments are reminiscent at once of *Fanshawe* and of "Fragments from the Journal of a Solitary Man," and elements of Hawthorne's style echo throughout.

"The Haunted Quack" was first printed in the 1831 *Token* as "By Joseph Nicholson." Franklin B. Sanborn

[5] *Appleton's Journal,* n.s. I (August, 1876), 190. The second volume of "miscellaneous pieces" was *Fanshawe, and Other Pieces,* published by Osgood, which contained the biographical sketches from the *Salem Gazette,* the *American Monthly,* and the *Democratic Review.*

[6] "The Hollow of the Three Hills," published anonymously in the *Salem Gazette,* November 12, 1830, was collected by Hawthorne in *Twice-told Tales.* This circumstance drew attention to what became attributions of a cluster of anonymous *Salem Gazette* pieces: "The Battle-Omen," November 2, and "An Old Woman's Tale," December 21, and the biographical sketches "Sir William Phips," November 23, "Mrs. Hutchinson," December 7, and "Dr. Bullivant," January 11, 1831.

[7] Hawthorne's other pieces in the *New-England Magazine* for June were "The Ambitious Guest," credited to the author of "The Gray Champion," and "A Rill from the Town-Pump," like "Graves and Goblins" published anonymously.

claimed it for the Hawthorne canon in 1898.[8] Horace
Scudder then included the tale in the Autograph Edition of
1900. This piece, too, would have had a natural place in
the "Story Teller" group. Sanborn called attention to Hawthornian characteristics in the tale: a contempt for the
"meanness and triviality of village life," a persistent interest
in the physician's potentially magical powers, and references
to the potion, "The Antidote to Death, or the Eternal Elixir
of Longevity." In its farcical vein, the tale resembles "Mr.
Higginbotham's Catastrophe." Besides such internal evidence,
there is a letter of May 6, 1830, in which Hawthorne tells
Goodrich that he is sending "two pieces" for the 1831
Token.[9] The only known Hawthorne sketch in that volume
is "Sights from a Steeple." Assuming that Goodrich accepted
both contributions from Hawthorne, "The Haunted Quack"
is almost certainly the other piece.[10]

Two attributions of later dates are "A Visit to the Clerk of
the Weather" (*American Monthly*, May, 1836), ascribed to
Hawthorne by George E. Woodberry in his 1902 biography,[11]
and "The Battle-Omen" (*Salem Gazette*, November 2, 1830),
listed as a possible Hawthorne work in 1924, and defended
by Donald C. Gallup in 1936.[12] Although Woodberry gave
no evidence to support his claim, "A Visit to the Clerk of the

[8] "A new 'Twice-Told Tale' by Nathaniel Hawthorne," *New England Magazine*, n.s. XVIII (August, 1898), 688–96.

[9] MS transcription, Bowdoin College.

[10] Hawthorne observed in his letter, "I have complied with your wishes in regard to brevity." Although the twenty-one pages of "The Haunted Quack" are double the length of "Sights from a Steeple," *The Token* used many stories of twenty or more pages.

[11] *Nathaniel Hawthorne* (Boston, 1902), p. 61.

[12] In *The Stephen H. Wakeman Collection of Books of Nineteenth Century American Writers* (New York [1924]), item 376 lists a type-written copy of the story. Gallup's argument is "On Hawthorne's Author-ship of 'The Battle Omen,'" *New England Quarterly*, IX (December, 1936), 690–99.

Weather" convincingly anticipates both "A Select Party" and "The Hall of Fantasy" in numerous details and aspects of style. As Adkins has suggested, it seems to have been intended originally for "The Story Teller." [13] For "The Battle-Omen" Gallup presented persuasive evidence for Hawthorne's authorship, citing various strong parallels between the sketch and other Hawthorne tales, and he noted that its date of initial publication placed it in a series with five other *Salem Gazette* pieces either known or thought to be by Hawthorne.[14] Although these two pieces cannot be established definitively as part of the canon, they are printed here, despite the lateness of their discovery, as stories for which there is a very high probability of Hawthorne's authorship.

The question of whether Hawthorne wrote still other unacknowledged tales and sketches has excited and plagued critics and enthusiasts for more than a century. Numerous claims have been made; some have since been proved false, and all the others lack sufficient plausibility to be accepted here.

The earliest attributions, and some of the most curious, were published without comment in James M'Glashan's unauthorized 1850 Dublin edition of *Twice-told Tales*. To the volume, otherwise a virtual line-by-line reprint of the second volume of the 1842 Munroe edition, were added "Ethan Allen, and the Lost Children," "An Indian's Revenge," and "The Fairy Fountain," none of which can seriously be claimed as Hawthorne's work. It is even unlikely that all three of these pieces are by a single author.[15]

[13] "The Early Projected Works of Nathaniel Hawthorne," *Papers of the Bibliographical Society of America*, XXXIX (1945), 139.

[14] See note 6, above.

[15] One of these stories has been seen in a periodical appearance: "Indian Revenge," in the *New-York Mirror*, VII (October 3, 1829), 1–2; anonymous.

After Hawthorne's death, various biographers and bibliog-raphers—with a widely held belief in the young Haw-thorne as an extremely secretive writer, the knowledge of his suppression of *Fanshawe* followed by its posthumous republication with other fragments and notebooks, and the encouragement of remarks by Hawthorne in his letters and prefaces—developed an undiscriminating hope of finding large numbers of unsigned Hawthorne tales in newspapers, magazines, and annuals in which his known work had appeared. In 1898, Sanborn, commenting that "There are enough of these uncollected tales and sketches of the Salem recluse, written in the years from 1825 to 1835, to fill a small volume," [16] accepted seven pieces, five of which have since been proved false attributions. "The Adventures of a Rain Drop," in the 1828 *Token*, was identified in 1936 as by Lydia Maria Child.[17] In 1902, Woodberry asserted that "My Wife's Novel," in the 1833 *Token*, and "The Modern Job; or, The Philosophic Stone," in the 1835 *Token*, were the work of Edward Everett.[18] Luther Livingston pointed out that "The Bald Eagle," in the 1833 *Token*, was by Longfellow.[19] A fifth, "The Young Provincial," in the 1830 *Token*, was assigned by two newspaper reprints to W. B. O. Peabody.[20] Moncure Conway added a new attribution in 1901, "The Adventurer," in the 1831 *Token*, which had an editorial headnote coyly announcing the manuscript to be "in a handwriting much resembling that of our friend

[16] "A new 'Twice-Told Tale' by Nathaniel Hawthorne," p. 696.

[17] Ralph Thompson, *American Literary Annuals and Gift Books* (New York, 1936), p. 70.

[18] The *Nation*, LXXV (October 9, 1902), 283.

[19] Luther Samuel Livingston, *A Bibliography of . . . the Writings of Henry Wadsworth Longfellow* (New York, 1908), p. 12. Further evidence is in Lawrance Thompson, *Young Longfellow* (New York, 1938), pp. 134, 375, 387.

[20] *Springfield Republican*, November 25, 1829, p. 1; *Essex Register*, Salem, Mass., December 3, 1829, pp. 1–2.

J. Neal." [21] Lacking strong internal evidence to the contrary, more recent bibliographers have concluded that this hint about John Neal's authorship cannot be disregarded.[22]

Two more recent attributions have likewise been established as erroneous. In 1938, Louise Hastings argued that Hawthorne had written "The First and Last Dinner," which appeared in Samuel Phillips Newman's *A Practical System of Rhetoric* (Portland, 1829); the author, however, is William Mudford.[23] In 1970, C. E. Frazer Clark, Jr. attributed to Hawthorne "Eastern Lands. A Tale of Yesterday" (*Knickerbocker Magazine*, October, 1838) on the mistaken supposition that its signature "By the Author of 'The Old Town Pump'" refers to Hawthorne's "A Rill from the Town-Pump."[24] The reference, however, unquestionably points to "The Old Town Pump," a sketch that had appeared in the September issue of *Knickerbocker*.

A spectacular bulk attribution was made in 1948 by Samuel T. Sukel, a book collector, who claimed for Hawthorne the entire contents of *The Flower Basket*, a reprint of S. G. Goodrich's 1840 anthology *Moral Tales*, in which all the stories were anonymous, but with four recognizable Hawthorne reprints from *The Token* among them, and with the title-page attribution "By the Author of Peter Parley."[25] Adkins traced to volumes of *The Token* selections which were revealed there as by Catherine Sedgwick, Mrs. Seba

21"Hawthorne, His Uncollected Tales in 'The Token,' Beginning with 1830," *New York Times Saturday Review of Books and Art*, June 8, 1901, pp. 397-98.

22 *American Literary Annuals and Gift Books*, p. 68.

23 Louise Hastings, "An Origin for 'Dr. Heidegger's Experiment,'" *American Literature*, IX (January, 1938), 403-10. The Mudford identification was established by Nolan E. Smith, "Another Story Falsely Attributed to Hawthorne: 'The First and Last Dinner,'" *Papers of the Bibliographical Society of America*, LXV (1971), 172-73.

24 *The Merrill Checklist of Nathaniel Hawthorne*, ed. Clark (Columbus, Ohio, 1970), p. 6.

25 "14 'Unknown' Tales Held Hawthorne's," *New York Times*, September 13, 1948, p. 16.

Smith, and Goodrich himself. Only one sketch, "The Man with the ——," unidentified, but not from *The Token*, gave Adkins pause; though, as he said, "to assert absolute authorship for this tale would indeed be rash."[26] Although there is in the tale's use of the idea of gold as a talisman a parallel to a passage in the Hawthorne journals, the story's verbal and stylistic qualities and nuances share no similarity whatever with those that mark Hawthorne's fiction.[27]

"The Man with the ——" is one of eight attributions that, although not yet proven false, represent such slight possibilities as authentic Hawthorne items that they are not reprinted here in the Centenary Edition. Most of these unaccepted tales and sketches were ascribed to Hawthorne at the turn of the century, and perhaps the most accurate measure of their worth as attributions is that they have failed to attract the support of more than one or two scholars.

Horace Scudder, editor of the 1900 Autograph Edition of Hawthorne's works, without vouching for its genuineness, included "Hints to Young Ambition," from the *New-England Magazine*, June, 1832—for the simple reason, apparently, that it had been signed "H." It is easily conceivable, too, that Scudder, viewing the piece in terms of the biographical myth of seclusion, considered it an expression of Hawthorne's bitterness and discontent at his lack of success as a writer. Woodberry, however, commented in 1902 that the signature was a common one in the periodicals of the time and that, had Hawthorne contributed to the magazine in 1832, there would have been no need for Goodrich to have introduced him to its publishers in 1834.[28] He pointed out that Haw-

---

[26] Nelson F. Adkins, "Notes on the Hawthorne Canon," *Papers of the Bibliographical Society of America*, LX (1966), 364–67.

[27] The undated journal entry falls between 1842 and 1844; see *The American Notebooks*, (Centenary Edition, 1973), p. 242. The sketch has been seen, printed anonymously, in the Boston *American Traveller*, Dec. 6. 1833, p. 4, and in the *Monthly Traveller*, January 1834, pp. 2–6.

[28] *Nathaniel Hawthorne*, p. 46.

thorne was not known ever to have used such a pseudonym; he might also have added that the pious, self-righteous moralizing is entirely foreign to any sentiment Hawthorne ever expressed about the aspirations, worthy or presumptuous, of young people. The total lack of both sympathy and irony in the heavy-handed attitudes expressed is so uncharacteristic of Hawthorne that the sketch has been almost completely ignored by later students.

Conway made two other attributions of questionable authenticity: "The Fated Family" in the 1831 *Token*, and "A Cure for Dyspepsia" in the 1833 *Token*. The first of these is most probably the result of his ignorance that *The Token* was postdated, or possibly his misreading the date of Goodrich's letter of May 31, 1831, to Hawthorne naming the titles of four tales accepted for the 1832 *Token*. Conway interpreted the letter as naming "four of his pieces in this volume of 1831." [29] Supporting Sanborn's attribution of "The Haunted Quack," Conway concluded that "The Fated Family" and "The Adventurer," together with "Sights from a Steeple," were the other contributions from Hawthorne. The only extant letter referring to the 1831 *Token*, however, is Hawthorne's of May 6, 1830, in which he mentions sending to Goodrich just the "two pieces" cited earlier. Although a few superficial, and thoroughly conventional, details of "The Fated Family" are vaguely similar to Hawthorne's standard devices, the internal evidence is resoundingly negative. This historical-sentimental tale, an undistinguished imitation of Scott's manner, has far too much overt physical action and far too little psychological interest to suggest that it is Hawthorne's work. The narrator, an active clergyman-widower

---

[29] "Hawthorne, His Uncollected Tales." The Goodrich letter is in Julian Hawthorne, *Nathaniel Hawthorne and His Wife* (1884) I, 132. Conway, in an earlier confusion about the Goodrich letter, had it that four tales were inserted in the 1830 *Token* (*Life of Nathaniel Hawthorne* [London, 1895], p. 43).

"desirous to spend the short remainder of my life in the service of my heavenly Master," makes, as Adkins has observed, "certain formal references to fundamentalist Christianity . . . atypical of Hawthorne." [30] Instead of being an immature or half-hearted effort of Hawthorne's own, the tale is one of those countless productions forming the underbrush of nineteenth-century periodical literature which Hawthorne's short historical fiction always transcends. As far afield as "The Fated Family" is, there is still less justification for Conway's attributing "A Cure for Dyspepsia" to Hawthorne. The tale's stereotyped love plot concerns a man who, suffering from a disease the author struggles unsuccessfully to swathe in mystery—it is affirmed to be acute "indigestion of the heart"—recovers his health and overcomes his solitariness through his love for a young girl, who, we learn in the conclusion's unsubtle irony, is in love herself with the hero's young companion. Although the story is not without a psychological dimension, Conway radically overstates the matter when he compares it to "Egotism; or, the Bosom Serpent." And he completely disregards the tale's setting in the South. As Adkins has commented, "names of towns and rivers, such as Milledgeville, Macon, Tuscaloosa, Oconee River, Flint River, Hawthorne would never have introduced into a tale." [31]

Woodberry proposed as Hawthorne's "The Downer's Banner" (*American Monthly*, September, 1829) on the grounds of its possible place in "Provincial Tales," the collection Hawthorne projected in 1829–31.[32] But he does not explain why Hawthorne would have published separately a tale intended for a collection that, two years later, he was still seeking a publisher for. Although the narrative of Revolu-

[30] "The Hawthorne Canon," unpublished typescript (Ohio State University Center for Textual Studies), p. 21.

[31] Ibid., p. 19.

[32] *Nathaniel Hawthorne*, pp. 34–35.

tionary struggles contains a reference to a willow blasted by lightning, calling to mind Hawthorne's use of a similar symbol in "Roger Malvin's Burial," the internal properties of the tale are not convincingly Hawthornian. The focus is on violent physical combat and the righteous revenge that a brother and sister take upon rapacious British troops; the plot is loose and disjointed, the language unrelieved melodrama. Altogether lacking is the characteristic economy of plot and the internalization of action that Hawthorne gains by taking up Roger Malvin's story immediately after the well-known incident of Lovell's Fight. Historical tales such as "The Downer's Banner" were a staple product in the popular literature of the day, but they rarely manifest Hawthorne's ability to transform historical incidents into symbolic and psychological events.

"The New England Village" is another contribution to the 1831 *Token* ascribed to Hawthorne; it was included in the Autograph Edition without evidence of authorship and also in Sanborn's list of attributions. The possibility that it is by Hawthorne has recently been revived by Gerald Griffin, who argues that the characterization of the guilt-plagued Mr. Forester anticipates Hawthorne's development of Arthur Dimmesdale.[33] But the guilt of Mr. Forester, a convicted felon long since rehabilitated and virtuous, and the confession that dispels all the mystery of his suffering are rubrics almost unavoidable in the conventions of nineteenth-century sentimental fiction. They contain little of the intensity and ambiguity of Hawthorne's treatment of such situations in "Roger Malvin's Burial," "The Minister's Black Veil," *The Scarlet Letter*, or even "Fancy's Show Box." Like "The Fated Family" and "The Adventurer," "The New England Village"

[33] Gerald R. Griffin, "Hawthorne and 'The New England Village': Internal Evidence and a New Genesis of *The Scarlet Letter*," *Essex Institute Historical Collections*, CVII (1971), 268–79.

does not compete seriously with "The Haunted Quack" as the second Hawthorne contribution to the 1831 *Token*.

The only attribution taken seriously by several Hawthorne students in the twentieth century is "The Interrupted Nuptials" (*Salem Gazette*, October 12, 1827), first proposed as Hawthorne's work by the bibliophile P. K. Foley and more recently, in elaborate detail, by C. E. Frazer Clark, Jr., who cites as major reasons for tentative attribution the similarity of motif and plot devices in "The Interrupted Nuptials," *Fanshawe*, "The May-Pole of Merry Mount," "The Shaker Bridal," "The Wedding-Knell" and other tales; the appearance in the tale of an image recurrent in Hawthorne's fiction (the sun's rays on a church steeple); the incidence of names beginning with "E" in Hawthorne's stories; Hawthorne's close relationship with the newspaper; and the signature "N****," which could mean either "Nath. H." or "Nath¹." [34] Although some of these points are plausible enough to compel a close examination of the little tale, they are far from conclusive. First-initial "E" names were quite commonplace in the literature of sensibility, and Hawthorne's fascination with the play of light on various objects was shared by the majority of nineteenth-century romancers. Several of the parallels claimed seem merely mechanical, even far-fetched. The marriage ceremony cancelled because of a traumatic discovery is as old as folklore. Hawthorne used this motif quite often, but never in his known fictions did he simply wrap the hackneyed circumstance in stereotyped details. The recognition scene in "The Interrupted Nuptials" consists, pathetically, of the announcement, at the altar, that the betrothed have been discovered to be brother and sister. The bride dies on the spot; the bridegroom, struck speechless, succumbs precisely a year

[34] C. E. Frazer Clark, Jr., " 'The Interrupted Nuptials,' A Question of Attribution," *Nathaniel Hawthorne Journal, 1971* (Washington, 1971), pp. 49–66.

later. In all this there is not the slightest hint of an emergent vision suggestive of the emotional complexity of "The Shaker Bridal" or the cultural ambivalence of "The May-Pole of Merry Mount." Nor is there a sign of what characterizes *Fanshawe*: a delicate, subtle, mature prose style that outstrips the subject matter. "The Interrupted Nuptials" is stylistically immature even when compared to Hawthorne's youthful letters. The question is not whether Hawthorne would or, as Clark says, "would not consider the attribution a favor . . . " The question is whether or not there is evidence compelling enough to suggest his authorship.

One other recent attribution is still more questionable. In 1962, Irving Richards claimed that "David Whicher," in the 1832 *Token*, is probably a tale Hawthorne wrote in imitation of John Neal.[35] Two other critics, on the other hand, assigned the work to Longfellow and to Neal himself.[36] The story, part hoax and part cruel revenge melodrama, moves so uncertainly in its seriocomic ways and suffers from such looseness of syntax and absence of stylistic control that Hawthorne's authorship seems out of the question. Moreover, Goodrich's letter of May 31, 1831, in which he identifies four tales he had already inserted in the volume for 1832 and is conscious of "having so many pages by one author," makes the addition of a fifth tale quite improbable.

Although it is possible that future scholars will unearth external evidence to show that one or another of these attributions is a genuine, if atypical, work by Hawthorne, the present state of our knowledge offers little chance indeed that further additions to the Hawthorne canon of short fiction

[35] "A Note on the Authorship of 'David Whicher,' " *Jahrbuch für Amerikastudien*, VII (Heidelberg, 1962), 294.

[36] Attribution to Neal was by Hans-Joachim Lang, "The Authorship of 'David Whicher,' " *Jahrbuch für Amerikastudien*, VII (1962), 288–93. Alfred Weber discussed the Longfellow possibility in "Der Autor von 'David Whicher' und das Geheimnis der grünen Brille," *Jahrbuch*, X (1965), 106–25.

remain to be discovered. The few newspapers, magazines, and annuals in which Hawthorne was likely to publish occasional early tales and sketches have been examined closely by various researchers, and the fruits of that scholarship in the last seventy years have not been abundant. The present editors have examined numerous additional tales and sketches without unearthing any that bear clear evidence of Hawthorne's stamp. Any effort to discover Hawthorne's earliest publication or another possible item in his "Provincial Tales" must be tempered henceforth by two facts that scholars have too often carelessly disregarded. First, it should be recognized that Hawthorne's astute assessment of the difficult conditions attached to periodical publication led him, from the beginning of his career, to strive to publish his tales and sketches in book form. Secondly, his comment in the 1851 preface to *Twice-told Tales*—"Much more, indeed, he wrote; and some very small part of it might yet be rummaged out (but it would not be worth the trouble) among the dingy pages of fifteen-or-twenty-year-old periodicals, or within the shabby morocco-covers of faded Souvenirs"—must be heeded. The remark suggests that much of what he wrote he may have destroyed before it could be printed. And it validates the fact that in *The Snow-Image* and the 1854 expanded edition of *Mosses from an Old Manse* he "rummaged out" twelve more old pieces. These, together with the other dozen items known or considered to be his, could account handsomely indeed for the production of a young writer conscientiously learning his craft.

J. D. C.

TEXTUAL COMMENTARY

T HE SNOW-IMAGE, and Other Twice-told Tales
was published through James T. Fields's insistence
in 1851 on yet another volume, and was perhaps
more commercially motivated than *Mosses from an Old
Manse*; and, the cupboard being relatively bare, Hawthorne's
use of earlier stories was more extensive than before and his
care to correct and revise these for the printer was slight
indeed. We know that he read proof for the volume; on
October 22, 1851, he complained to Ticknor that proof had
not arrived during the preceding week. Ticknor replied on
October 24 that new proof went on the 21st, 22nd, and 23rd;
this would presumably be three sheets or forty-eight pages.[1]
"In your last stories," Ticknor continued, "I requested the
printer to mail the proofs. Else I should have discovered the
delinquency." This statement appears to have no particular
significance except as indicating that the printer had been
instructed to mail proof directly to Hawthorne instead of to
Ticknor for distribution to him. Proofreading in the publisher's editorial offices would not have been affected by the

[1] Hawthorne to Ticknor & Co., MS, University of Virginia; Ticknor to
Hawthorne, MS, Ticknor and Fields Letter Books, Domestic, II, 320,
Houghton Library, Harvard University.

difference in arrangement, for whether proof was customarily read simultaneously or only after Hawthorne had returned it is not known. In most cases when the 1852 readings suggest authorial change, the alterations are so minor as to be more appropriate for proof-corrections than for revision of printer's copy, although the two can scarcely be distinguished with certainty save in "Old News" and "Old Ticonderoga." As an example, in the first three stories, for which Hawthorne himself probably provided copy—"The Snow-Image," "The Great Stone Face," and "Main-street"—none of the 1852 variants appears to be authorial, and it seems probable that these three recent tales went to the printer in their periodical form without alteration.

How much duplication there was between the tales and sketches he received from his sister Louisa, and Fields's recoveries reported on September 22, is impossible to determine.[2] In this group "Old News" is the only one to be given unusual treatment. "A Bell's Biography," "Sylph Etherege," "The Devil in Manuscript," "John Inglefield's Thanksgiving," "The Wives of the Dead," "Ethan Brand," and "Little Daffydowndilly" appear to have no variant readings in 1852 for which the printer was not exclusively responsible. In "The Man of Adamant" the 1852 alteration "fleshy" of "fleshly" (164.4) is clearly a printer's error, but the change from "female" to "woman" (165.4) appears to be Hawthorne's on the analogy of two similar changes from first appearances of "The Great Carbuncle" and "The Hollow of the Three Hills" to the 1837 *Twice-told Tales* form.

In 1841, when Hawthorne was collecting copy for the second volume of *Twice-told Tales*, he revised a copy of the 1833 *Token* containing "The Seven Vagabonds" and "The Canterbury Pilgrims." It seems probable that the markings for "The Seven Vagabonds" were transferred to the printer's

[2] See the discussion in the Historical Commentary, pp. 388–91.

copy, since this copy of *The Token* was at the time, or shortly thereafter, in the possession of his aunt Rebecca Manning.[3] "The Canterbury Pilgrims" was not used in *Twice-told Tales*, however, and at the time of collecting *The Snow-Image* in 1851, it would seem that the annotated *Token* copy, long ago prepared, might not have been available. This matter is not certain, however. Only six alterations had been marked, of which the 1852 printing observes four: the alterations of "etherial" and "wintery" to "ethereal" and "wintry" at 124.7 and 130.13, and the misprint "father's" to "fathers" at 124.22, and, finally, the removal of a comma after "But" at 121.9. On the other hand, two substantive changes of the marked *Token* were not observed: the deletion of the personal reference "as the writer has" in the opening sentence of *The Token* "no traveller, toiling as the writer has, up the hilly road" (120.4) was not made in *Snow-Image*, and the misprint "moral" was corrected to "mortal" in *Snow-Image* instead of the marked *Token* "human" (131.11). One may query whether the four common changes were not indeed fortuitous. In the present edition all these alterations from the marked *Token* are adopted since they represent what Hawthorne wanted when he revised the tale in 1841 and are hence more authoritative than his revision in 1851.

"My Kinsman, Major Molineux" appears to be a special case. It can be established from a Ticknor & Co. letter of September 27, 1851, to the editors of *Literary World* requesting assistance in securing copies of "John Inglefield's Thanksgiving," "Old Ticonderoga," "Ethan Brand," and "Major Molineux," that the copy for these pieces was not supplied by Hawthorne.[4] Moreover, it can also be established that he could not have seen "Major Molineux" before it was sent to

---

[3] See C. E. Frazer Clark, Jr., "New Light on the Editing of the 1842 Edition of *Twice-Told Tales*," *Nathaniel Hawthorne Journal 1972* (Washington, 1973), pp. 91–138.

[4] MS, Duyckinck Collection, New York Public Library.

the printer. Typesetting for the collection had started on October 11,[5] but on November 3 when sending the manuscript of the Preface to Ticknor, Hawthorne offered to rewrite what was missing in "Major Molineux" if a perfect copy from the *Token* could not be turned up.[6] Clearly, the copy supplied by *Literary World* had been found to be imperfect on examination at the publisher's or printer's. On November 5 Ticknor found a *Token* for 1832 but evidently was not permitted to borrow it for printer's copy since he wrote Hawthorne, "I am having it copied & it will go into the printers hands tomorrow."[7] This exchange of letters establishes not only the unique status of the printer's copy for "My Kinsman, Major Molineux" but also the impossibility that Hawthorne could have made any alterations except in proof, as he seems, doubtfully, to have done for one or two readings.

"The Wives of the Dead" had been printed in the same 1832 *Token*; that it appears near the end of the 1852 collection with "Major Molineux" may point to its having been recovered at the same time, but the situation is obscure. No mention is made of this piece in any of the preserved correspondence about assembling *The Snow-Image*, whereas Ticknor inquired about "Daffydowndilly" when he did not find it on the contents list left with him by Fields. It is improbable that in his examination of the 1832 *Token* Ticknor would recognize as Hawthorne's an anonymously published story and retrieve it. Yet if it had been on Hawthorne's list, the question arises why "My Kinsman, Major Molineux" was not acquired at the same time as "Wives of the Dead." Just possibly, Hawthorne was in possession of a clipping of "Wives."

[5] Hawthorne to Horatio Bridge, MS, Bowdoin College.

[6] MS, University of Virginia.

[7] MS, Ticknor and Fields Letter Books, Domestic, II, 348, Houghton Library, Harvard University.

"Old Ticonderoga" also presents a problem, for when this sketch was printed in 1852 the opening two paragraphs were omitted and the account began abruptly with what had been the third paragraph, "The greatest attraction, in this vicinity, is the famous old fortress of Ticonderoga". It is only in the original two paragraphs that we learn that "this vicinity" is the town of Orwell on Lake Champlain. The removal of these two paragraphs can be defended, since their account of the town of Orwell, its commerce, and the travellers awaiting its ferry, has nothing to do with the fortress and its description. One cannot imagine Ticknor excising them on his own responsibility, and thus—whatever the motive—Hawthorne seems to have been responsible. The problem remains, however, of when the deletion was made and if it were short of the proof-stage. The earliest known record of the start of Hawthorne's collection is a postscript in a letter of May 20, 1851, to his sister Louisa, asking her to send him any of his uncollected tales and sketches she had or could obtain.[8] On July 10 he requested again, "If you have any of the magazine articles mentioned in my last, I wish you [would] have them sent to Mr Burchmore . . . as he is going to send a package to me within a week or two."[9] On August 1, Louisa wrote to her sister Elizabeth, whom she had been visiting, "I came away in such a hurry that I forgot to ask you any more about those articles for Nathaniel you said you had Old Ticonderoga, where is it? can I get it, or must you come over? let me know about all there are as soon as you can, for I expect Mr Burchmore is waiting for us to send, and is in a hurry. It is a fortnight since Nathaniel wrote."[10] It

[8] MS, Huntington Library.

[9] MS, Carl H. Pforzheimer Library, New York City. Although Hawthorne was having trouble finding his old pieces, he asserted in this letter that he did not intend to publish anything from the *American Magazine* which he had edited under such difficulties in 1836.

[10] MS, Berg Collection, New York Public Library.

would appear that Hawthorne had recalled "Old Ticonderoga" and mentioned it by name; if Louisa located the
sketch, the clipping should have been in the packet that
Hawthorne acknowledged to Louisa on September 2. But
it is odd that Ticknor lists it specifically as among his four
wants in the September 27 letter to the Duyckincks at
Literary World. Given the presumably authoritative deletion
of the first two paragraphs, and the probability that this was
not done in proof, one may speculate that Hawthorne had in
fact sent in the copy, thus marked, and that through some
error Ticknor was informed that it was wanting. Only guess-
work can operate in this lack of any concrete evidence. In
the present edition the deletion of the opening paragraphs
has been accepted as authoritative; the cancelled passage is
entered in the Historical Collation.

In short, with this exception, no piece save "Old News"
shows any demonstrable authorial alteration of the printer's
copy, and there is every reason to believe that the rest of
the *Snow-Image* collection was put together by Hawthorne's
sending to Fields a few unmarked clippings to which Fields
added a larger number that he had himself found in periodicals. Whether or not Hawthorne ever saw these Fields copies
before they were sent to the press is completely dependent
on the circumstances surrounding the revision of "Old News."
Insofar as can be determined on the evidence of substantive
variants from copy, proofreading was desultory and was more
concerned with correction than with improvement and revision. "Old News" is a marked exception, however. How
Hawthorne came to see this copy is not very clear, since the
clipping was one of those collected by Fields and reported
to Hawthorne on September 22. Perhaps Fields sent these
clippings to Hawthorne for his approval, after all; or perhaps
the piece had also been among those collected by Louisa.
What is clear is that in one way or another Hawthorne saw

the copy and revised it before printing: the changes, including the omission of some footnotes but the incorporation of others into the text, are too extensive to permit the adjustments to have been made in proof. Possibly it was the problem posed by these footnotes that led Fields to send the clippings to Hawthorne for this one sketch; and when Hawthorne read it over with a view to dropping or including the footnotes, he found various examples of just the kind of printer's error that he was accustomed to deplore. He could only have been shocked, for instance, at the magazine corruption "salutatory" for his careful word "saltatory" (137.28), "discoveries" for "discourses" (140.31), or "disparity" for "dignity" (152.22). These he corrected, along with such errors as "county" for "country" (134.18), and "round" for "sound" (152.6), and probably "trampling" for "tramping" (152.12). He revised other readings, such as substituting "a member of the council" (133.4) for "councillor", "quaffed to the lees" (133.20) for "consumed", "human' (138.35) for "black and woolly", and so on, and placed some footnotes in the text while omitting others. This is the only piece that he seems to have marked in any way for the printer, except for the deletion of the original chatty opening of "Old Ticonderoga."

Thus the problem of the revision of copy before typesetting does not affect the stories in *The Snow-Image and Other Tales* as it does in *Twice-told Tales* or *Mosses from an Old Manse*. Problems in transmission do, however, affect the editorial treatment of two tales. The first of these is "Ethan Brand." Hawthorne had first sent the piece to Elizabeth Peabody for her book *Æsthetic Papers* and then, within a matter of days (before Miss Peabody had read it), submitted another copy on December 14, 1848, to Charles W. Webber in New York, for a projected magazine which reached printed form but was never distributed. A year later,

Webber passed a copy to the *Boston Weekly Museum*, where it was first published on January 5, 1850, as "The Unpardonable Sin." In the December of 1850, Evert Duyckinck came across the Webber magazine sheets in a warehouse, and asked Hawthorne's permission to publish the story in the *Dollar Magazine*, where it appeared in May, 1851, with Duyckinck's suggestion for a title, "Ethan Brand; or, The Unpardonable Sin." It is clear that Hawthorne had nothing to do with providing the copy and had no opportunity to correct or revise the story for the *Dollar Magazine* even if he had been interested. Hence no evidence exists that he concerned himself at all with the text, or even that he marked in any way the *Dollar Magazine* appearance that was used as copy for the 1852 *Snow-Image* text.[11]

Insofar as the external evidence goes, it looks as if Hawthorne had made two manuscript fair copies of "Ethan Brand" from the same draft, which presumably was close to the final form. The first copy, sent to Elizabeth Peabody, seems to have disappeared; certainly it never entered the textual transmission. The second manuscript, presumably, was destroyed by Webber after the story had been set in type for the proposed *American Review*. It follows that both the *Boston Museum* and the *Dollar Magazine* texts radiate independently from the lost printed *Review* sheets and thus that each is at two removes from the manuscript and of equal authority. Under these circumstances the choice of copy-text is indifferent on genealogical grounds,[12] and a selection is generally made from that one of the two equally authoritative documents that is more convenient; that is, the one that seems in its accidentals to conform most closely to those of the author and thus to need the less emendation. In this

[11] These events are discussed at length in the Historical Commentary, pp. 381–84.

[12] See Bowers, "Multiple Authority: New Problems and Concepts of Copy-Text," *The Library*, Fifth Series, XXVII (June, 1972), 81–115.

case, the *Boston Museum* seems to have received somewhat less house styling than the *Dollar Magazine* and hence has been selected as the copy-text. On the other hand, the conjectured authority of the accidentals need have no intimate connection with that of the substantives, since the family tree for the transmission of the text indicates that both printings are technically of equal authority. Thus in the lack of bibliographical evidence, only critical judgment can decide between the variant substantive readings. On the whole, the substantives of the *Boston Museum* seem to be more faithful to the conjectured readings of the copy and have ordinarily been adopted when indifferent—as most of them are. The readings of the *Dollar Magazine* at 83.19–21 and 85.6–7 have been preferred, however. The first seems to represent some sort of misunderstanding in the *Boston Museum*, and the second a reduction in the *Museum* of rather stilted phraseology reproduced by the *Dollar Magazine*, an expression it would be difficult to attribute to the editor's or compositor's invention as a substitute.

The second problem in the volume concerns "My Kinsman, Major Molineux." From Ticknor's letter to Hawthorne we know that there had been trouble finding a perfect copy of *The Token*. Ticknor responded to Hawthorne's offer to rewrite the missing part by a letter announcing that he had found a copy, and was having it transcribed, and would send it to the printer the next day. On the evidence of the evenly distributed and extraordinarily large number of substantive variants, the copyist did not transcribe just the missing part but the whole of the *Token* printing. Since Hawthorne would have had no chance to see the transcribed form of the story before the stage of proof, and since certain of the variants are clearcut errors—such as "confidence" for "consequence" (214.6) or "he seemed" for "he had seemed" (225.1–2), and many show no possible reason for authorial alteration, like "kinsman" for "kinsman, Robin" (227.13)—it would seem that the variant readings in the 1852 text all come under the suspicion of being copyist errors or sophistications; they can scarcely represent an unexampled care in the proofreading. Moreover, the external evidence—as well as the internal evidence of their nature—prevents them from being classified as authorial markings of copy as in "Old News." It is possible to conjecture that because of his knowledge of the transcription, Hawthorne may have read proof with some extra care; hence a few readings that seem likely to be authorial instead of copyist variants are adopted, such as the substitution of "grizzled" for "dark grey" (228.33) and the omission of "deep" (229.26). On the whole, however, when *The Token* is not obviously in error, the odds favor the general authority of its substantives over those of the 1852 edition which have run the gauntlet of copyist and another compositor.

According to the usual editorial procedures of the Centenary edition, the earliest document—meaning the one closest to the lost manuscript—has been invariably chosen as copytext. In the special case of "Ethan Brand" the fact that the *Boston Museum* was earlier in point of publication than the *Dollar Magazine* has had no effect on the choice of copy-text since a collateral, and not a linear, relationship exists between them. A single manuscript—that of "The Snow-Image"—is known to be preserved for any of the material collected in the *Snow-Image* volume. In the majority of the tales only a handful of conjectured authorial substantive proof-alterations have been accepted from 1852 as displacing copy-text readings, although a small number of indifferent questions of usage characteristic of Hawthorne have been adopted from 1852 even if of highly dubious authority, and a few corrections. For "Ethan Brand" there are no sure signs of 1852 proof-correction; hence the choice of variant readings has been made between the two magazines, each of equal authority. That the 1852 edition follows the *Dollar Magazine* readings is of no consequence as relating to their authority, for this is merely a question of printer's copy. Since the printer's copy for "Old News" is conjectured to have been revised by Hawthorne, the 1852 substantive variants have been given general authority over those of *New-England Magazine*, which was selected as copy-text on the specific grounds of its transmissional closeness to the accidentals of Hawthorne's lost manuscript.

In this collection, copy-texts have general authority for accidentals, and substantive emendations are judged by the authority of their sources; editorial corrections reject printer's errors presumably missed by Hawthorne in his reviews, and return his characteristic spellings when misreading or house-styling is considered the agent of variance. Normalizations of spelling, capitalization, and word-division are made in the individual texts by use of the prevailing form. Hawthorne's undifferentiated use of "further" and "farther" is kept, and his spelling is modernized only when the obsolete would confuse the sense. A full statement of editorial principles is included in the first four volumes of the Centenary Edition.

F. B.

Note: copy-texts for the uncollected tales of Hawthorne are their first printed appearances, except where partial manuscript takes precedence in "Time's Portraiture"; none had later authoritative emendation. Centenary accepts two substantive variants and some punctuations of an extract from "My Home Return" printed earlier than the complete sketch by the editor who held the manuscript; they are adjudged to be nearer Hawthorne's original manuscript, though corruption is recognized in both printings. Centenary emendations otherwise correct obvious errors, return characteristic spellings, and normalize spelling and hyphenation usage within the reference of each separate sketch.

L. N. S.

BIBLIOGRAPHICAL INFORMATION

THE FOLLOWING DESCRIPTIONS are in three sections, the first dealing with the Ticknor, Reed, and Fields edition of *The Snow-Image, and Other Twice-told Tales*, the second with individual tales and sketches in that collection, and the third with uncollected sketches, and attributions to Hawthorne.

I

Published in December, 1851—possibly December 18 [1]— the stereotype first edition of *The Snow-Image* included fifteen tales, from "The Snow-Image: A Childish Miracle" to "Major Molineux" (the latter titled "My Kinsman, Major Molineux" in the running heads). *Cost Books* entry A238a

---

[1] Sophia Hawthorne wrote to Louisa Hawthorne, December 25, 1851, "This new volume of Twice T. T. was published on Thursday & yesterday Ticknor told Nathaniel that he had already sold a thousand copies & had not enough bound to supply the demand." MS, Berg Collection, New York Public Library.

dates the first printing of 2,425 copies on December 11, 1851.[2] The volume retailed for 75 cents.

THE | SNOW-IMAGE, | AND | OTHER TWICE-TOLD TALES | BY | NATHANIEL HAW-THORNE. | BOSTON: | TICKNOR, REED, AND FIELDS. | M DCCC LII.
[1]⁸ 2–17⁸; 136 leaves; pp. [3–7] 8–10 [11–13] 14–273 [274], with initial pages of tales unnumbered; pp. 3–4 are blank; the title is on p. 5; p. 6 has the copyright and stereotype notices; pp. 7–10 have the preface, dated November 1, 1851; the contents are listed on p. 11 (p. 12 blank); pp. 13–273 have the text, with p. 274 blank.

Page-edge evidence in seven copies examined at Ohio State University yields the two imposition formulas within the general formula of half-sheet of 16's, work-and-tumble. The *Cost Books* entry gives the sheet size as 29 by 18 1/2 inches, verifying that 16 pages measuring 7 by 4 1/2 inches would be imposed on a side of one sheet, 32 pages per sheet.

Formula 1: Savage #53,[3] for sigs. 1–2, 4–6, and 8–14, a total of twelve gatherings.

Formula 2: Variation of Savage #53, with page 1 at the outside left edge, centered (see illustration, p. 425), for sigs. 3, 7, and 15–17, a total of five gatherings. In each use of formula 2 imposition, the compositor avoided placing half-blank pages or initial pages of tales on the outside bottom or top edges of the forme.

The *Cost Books* and unpublished Cost Books show that

---

[2] *The Cost Books of Ticknor and Fields*, ed. Warren S. Tryon and William Charvat (New York, 1949), p. 210. Records of the unpublished Cost Books (MSS, Houghton Library, Harvard University) are also referred to, below.

[3] William Savage, *A Dictionary of the Art of Printing* (London, 1841), p. 351.

Imposition formulas for the first printing of *The Snow-Image, and Other Twice-told Tales.*

Formula 1

2	15	14	3
7	10	11	6
8	9	12	5
1	16	13	4

Formula 2

9	11	10	7
3	14	15	2
4	13	16	1
5	12	9	8

the plates were imposed thirteen times up to 1876, the last known printing, in the Tinted Edition. The total number of copies for the entire edition is 11,150. Machine collation of a first printing with a copy of the volume in the Tinted Edition shows no substantive variants throughout the plate history. *The Snow-Image* collection was included in the second volume of a two-volume Blue and Gold Edition by Ticknor and Fields of 1865, which included *Twice-told Tales* and was so titled.

The first English edition, *The Snow-Image, and Other Tales* (London: Henry G. Bohn, 1851), was contracted by Bohn from the Ticknor firm and was set from advance sheets of the first printing for simultaneous publication with the American edition. Although the title-page date is 1851, William D. Ticknor's letter to Bohn of November 18, 1851, establishes the textual priority of the Ticknor, Reed, and Fields edition.[4]

A piracy of *The Snow-Image*, apparently published soon after the Bohn edition, appeared as *The Canterbury Pilgrims, and Other Twice-told Tales* (London: Knight & Son, n. d.).

II

Recorded here are the individual pieces of *The Snow-Image* in their descent from copy-text first printed appearance (copy-text manuscript in the case of the story "The Snow-Image") to the stereotype 1852 Ticknor, Reed, and Fields collection. Hawthorne's journal sources are remarked, as "*Notebooks*, 25.26–30, 30, 11," for "Ethan Brand"; the numbers are page / line citations to text and associated

[4] MS, Ticknor and Fields Foreign Letter Books, 2, 242, Houghton Library, Harvard University.

Explanatory Notes in *The American Notebooks*, ed. Claude M. Simpson (Centenary Edition, [Columbus, Ohio, 1973]). Further references to the tales may be found in the index of *The American Notebooks*.

The numerous unauthoritative reprintings of the tales are not listed, since they have no bearing on the Centenary text.

The 1852 *Snow-Image* collection is referred to as *SI*.

Preface

First printed appearance, copy-text: *The Snow-Image*, 1852 (described pp. 423–26), pp. 7–10.

The Snow-Image

Manuscript (The Henry Huntington Library) copy-text: Seven sheets 9 15/16 by 15 1/4 inches, folded to make two-leaf folios 9 15/16 by 7 5/8 inches, and a half sheet of the latter dimensions. Blind-stamped oval in upper left corner of each folded sheet, depicting a ship with pennon flying at top center and anchor in foreground. Hawthorne wrote only on the 15 rectos, and foliated them top center [1] 2–15. Now also foliated in pencil at upper right corners. No printer's marks, except possibly the '39' in ink on fol. 5ᵛ, opposite the beginning of p. 47 of *Memorial* text, marked also with inked vertical in text, 'and|were', fol. 6. The editor, R. W. Griswold, wrote 'By Nathaniel Hawthorne' beneath the subtitle.

First printed appearance: *The Memorial*. New York: George P. Putnam, 1851, pp. 41–58. By Nathaniel Hawthorne. Reprinted as *Laurel Leaves*. New York: Lamport, Blakeman and Law, 1854.

BIBLIOGRAPHICAL INFORMATION

Second printed appearance: *International Miscellany of Literature, Art, and Science,* I (November 1, 1850), 537–43. By Nathaniel Hawthorne.

Note: The publisher of *The Memorial* permitted, for publicity, the appearance in the *International,* which made the story known long before the volume which had served as printer's copy. The magazine form served as printer's copy for *The Snow-Image, and Other Twice-told Tales.*

SI pp. 13–35.

The Great Stone Face

Notebooks 184.19.
National Era, IV (January 24, 1850), I. By Nathaniel Hawthorne.
SI pp. 36–62.

Main-street

Notebooks 26.12–15, 30.11, 165.14–16, 169.4–7, 181.5–8.
Æsthetic Papers. Boston: Elizabeth P. Peabody; New York: G. P. Putnam, 1849, pp. 145–74. Article VIII, identified on contents page as by N. Hawthorne, Esq.
SI pp. 63–101.

Ethan Brand

Notebooks 25.26–30, 30.11, 89.15–19, 226.30–33, 237.7–9, 251.8.
First printed appearance, copy-text (see Textual Commentary): *Boston Weekly Museum,* II (January 5, 1850), 234–35. Titled "The Unpardonable Sin. From an Unpublished Work." By Nathaniel Hawthorne.
Second printed appearance, copy-text (see Textual Commentary): *Dollar Magazine,* VII (May, 1851), 193–201.

Titled "Ethan Brand; or, The Unpardonable Sin." By Nathaniel Hawthorne.

SI pp. 102–24.

A Bell's Biography

Notebooks 13.12.
Knickerbocker, or New-York Monthly Magazine, IX
(March, 1837), 219–23. By the author of *Twice-told Tales*,
"The Fountain of Youth," etc.

SI pp. 125–33.

Sylph Etherege

The Token and Atlantic Souvenir. Boston: American
Stationers' Company, 1838, pp. 22–32. No attribution.

Note: reprints of the 1838 *Token* plates have been seen
as follows: Hartford: S. Andrus and Son, n. d. (*The Token,
or Affection's Gift*); New York: A. Edwards, n. d.; New York;
Leavitt and Allen, n. d.

SI pp. 134–44.

The Canterbury Pilgrims

The Token and Atlantic Souvenir. Boston: Gray and
Bowen, 1833, pp. 153–66. By the author of "The Gentle
Boy."

SI pp. 145–58.

Old News

New-England Magazine. The appearance was as follows:
"Old News. No. I.", VIII (February, 1835), 81–88; "Old
News. No. II. The Old French War.", VIII (March, 1835),

170–78; "Old News. No. III. The Old Tory.", VIII (May, 1835), 365–70. No attribution.
SI pp. 159–92.

The Man of Adamant

Notebooks 13.1–11, 13.20–22.
The Token and Atlantic Souvenir. Boston: Charles Bowen, 1837, pp. 119–28. By the author of "The Gentle Boy."
SI pp. 193–202.

The Devil in Manuscript

New-England Magazine, IX (November, 1835), 340–45. By Ashley A. Royce.
SI pp. 203–12.

John Inglefield's Thanksgiving

United States Magazine and Democratic Review, VII (March, 1840), 209–12. By Rev. A. A. Royce.
SI pp. 213–20.

Old Ticonderoga

American Monthly Magazine, VII (February, 1836), 138–42. No attribution.
SI pp. 221–27.

The Wives of the Dead

The Token. Boston: Gray and Bowen, 1832, pp. 74–82. No attribution.
SI pp. 228–36.

Little Daffydowndilly

Boys' and Girls' Magazine, II (August, 1843), 264–69. By Nathaniel Hawthorne.
SI pp. 237–46.

My Kinsman, Major Molineux

The Token. Boston: Gray and Bowen, 1832, pp. 89–116. By the author of "Sights from a Steeple."
SI pp. 247–73, "Major Molineux."

III

The uncollected pieces and attributions included in the Centenary edition are described in their first printed appearances during Hawthorne's lifetime, all copy-texts with the exception of "Time's Portraiture," for which partial manuscript provides copy-text as detailed below.

The Battle-Omen

Salem Gazette, XLIV, n. s. VIII (November 2, 1830), 1. No attribution.

An Old Woman's Tale

Salem Gazette, XLIV, n. s. VIII (December 21, 1830), 1–2. No attribution.

The Haunted Quack

The Token. Boston: Gray and Bowen, 1831, pp. 117–37. By Joseph Nicholson.

Alice Doane's Appeal

The Token and Atlantic Souvenir. Boston: Charles Bowen, 1835, pp. 84–101. By the author of "The Gentle Boy."

My Visit to Niagara

New-England Magazine, VIII (February, 1835), 91–96. By the author of "The Gray Champion."

Graves and Goblins

New-England Magazine, VIII (June, 1835), 438–44. No attribution.

Sketches from Memory

New-England Magazine, IX (December, 1835), 404–9 ("Sketches from Memory. No. II."—including editorial introduction, "The Canal-Boat," "An Afternoon Scene"). By a Pedestrian.

A Visit to the Clerk of the Weather

American Monthly, VII (May, 1836), 483–87. No attribution.

Fragments from the Journal of a Solitary Man

American Monthly, X (July, 1837), 45–56. No attribution. Note: the passage at Centenary 322.16–323.4 "There. . . . coolness." was published as "An Afternoon Scene" in

"Sketches from Memory. No. II.", *New-England Magazine*, IX (December, 1835).

Time's Portraiture

Partial manuscript, copy-text: Two fragments written in black ink on white wove paper. Fragment 1 (Berg Collection, New York Public Library) is a single leaf 9 3/4 by 7 7/8 inches. The recto (which has at top left corner the ink inscription "This is Hawthorne's | Autograph | E. P. Peabody | Feb 7th 1856") carries the text from the title through "errand-boys, I have" (at Centenary p. 330.15). The verso, marked by Hawthorne at head "(4th page)", has "he has no" through "word for word." (332.34–333.34) and "Perhaps" through "reason," (334.5–334.19). Following "word for word." is a caret and "(see last page)". Fragment 2 (University of Virginia) is a cut strip of 1 by 7 7/8 inches, recto (second page of MS) carrying "[in]scriptions" through "of old." (331.16–19) and "But they need not seek him" (331.21–22); on verso (third page of MS), "It is" through "separation." (332.26–30). Following "of old." is a caret, with "(see last page)" interlined below. The manuscript fragments show no printer's markings.

The full manuscript, judging by the fragments, had at least two more pages, on one or more leaves.

First printed appearance, partial copy-text: *Salem Gazette* broadside, January 1, 1838. No attribution.

Standing type of the broadside was rearranged without alterations in the typesetting, to become part of the front page of the *Salem Gazette*, January 2, and entitled "The Carrier's Address." The appearance is thus the second printing of the original form.

Note: The Essex Institute has the broadside printed on a pink silk handkerchief as a souvenir.

The Antique Ring

Sargent's New Monthly Magazine of Literature, Fashion, and the Fine Arts, I (February, 1842), 80–86. By Nathaniel Hawthorne.

A Good Man's Miracle

Notebooks 28.21
Child's Friend, I (February, 1844), 151–56. By Nathaniel Hawthorne.

A Book of Autographs

United States Magazine and Democratic Review, XV (November, 1844), 454–61. By Nathaniel Hawthorne.

J. M.

TEXTUAL NOTES

50.10 tract] The 1852 "track" is a cunning sophistication by reference to "track" at 50.25. But the original "tract" in *Æsthetic Papers* must be right, for one first sees the spread or *tract* of land, and then only at 50.22 is the "path" noticed that is then called a "track" at 50.25.

99.5 star-light] The magazines' reading is correct and the 1852 'star-lit' a sophistication. It is not so much that the eminence was lighted by the stars as that it was high, metaphorically speaking, as star-light—that is, it towered well above the earth. For a similar phrase, see "My Kinsman, Major Molineux," where "moonlight evening" at 209.7 means less an evening that was lighted by the moon than an evening of moonlight.

137.11 councillor] The 1852 "counsellor" may be either a Hawthorne confusion or a printer's sophistication. At 133.4 which in *NE* read, "There he sits, a major, a councillor, and a weighty merchant", the "councillor" was altered in 1852 to "member of the council", perhaps because of the latent ambiguity of the spellings "councillor" and "counsellor" which were practically interchangeable in the eighteenth century. We can be certain, no matter what the spelling, that at 137.11 Hawthorne also intended a *member of the council* and not a legal counsel, or lawyer.

152.12 tramping] The general authority of the 1852 corrections and revisions must admit the change from *NE* "trampling" despite the older occasional confusion between the two words. It is possible—if the *NE* reading were not in error—that Hawthorne himself modernized the reading by correction.

203.2 haste] Although 1852 "hay" for the magazine "haste" could theoretically be a proof variant, its purpose is obscure, and it is probably the compositor's memorial lapse.

217.33 leather—] The *Token's* "leather—"is not likely to represent a dash filling a space for a word the compositor could not read, nor is there any reason to suppose that the woman broke off from any delicacy in pronouncing the word *breeches*. She had had to qualify her recognition of his hat as the Major's "rainy weather hat", which in itself stretched plausibility the limit. When it came to her pretending to find a relationship between Robin's leather breeches and the Major's elegant city attire, we may suppose that her mirth at the notion did not permit her to finish and she broke off in order to issue her invitation to enter—an interpretation perhaps assisted by the "But" that begins the sentence after the dash. The problem is less the meaning of the dash than it is whether it was Hawthorne who made the change to "small-clothes" in proof. To this no certain answer can be made. In the introductory description of Robin, "his under garments were durably constructed of leather" (209.17–18). The "small-clothes" is appropriate for the period and could well be his instead of the copyist's. On the other hand, it is as possible to conjecture that the copyist did not understand the purpose of the dash and himself substituted what seemed to be an appropriate word. One can be relatively sure that the dash is authorial; the question of the substitution of "small-clothes" is uncertain. In this dilemma it is safer to stick to what one knows and not to risk sophistication of the text. The status of "small-clothes" being so doubtful, therefore, the 1852 reading is rejected and the original *Token* dash retained.

229.26 two sepulchral] The omission of *Token* "deep" in 1852 is interesting, since it may coincide with another possible authorial proof revision at 228.32–33. To be both "deep" and "sepulchral" is to be tautological. The previous appearances of this old gentleman and his "hems" have all used the word "sepulchral"; but only at 210.27 is "solemn and" prefixed (see 211.7, 216.5).

EDITORIAL EMENDATIONS IN THE
COPY-TEXT

Except for silent typographical modernizations remarked
on in The Centenary Texts: Editorial Procedures, prefixed
to Volume I (as A Preface to the Text) and appended to
Volumes II–IV of this edition, every editorial change from
copy-text is listed here. Also noted are certain editorial de-
cisions against emendation, marked *stet*. The titles of individual pieces are followed by symbols (identified below) for
copy-text and for texts in which emended forms could have
appeared. For each entry, the accepted reading, at the left
of the bracket, is followed by the first appearance of the
emendation, and then by any rejected reading and its text.
An asterisk indicates that the crux is discussed in a Textual
Note. In recording punctuation variants, a wavy dash ∼
represents a word before the bracket, and a caret ∧ indicates
the absence of a punctuation mark. Hawthorne's characteristic spellings are restored (as his 'z' misread as 's' by com-
positors), but copy-texts cover a period of years during which
Hawthorne's spelling habits varied, especially for doublet
forms (as 'stopt / stopped') and for hyphenation of compounds; no attempt has been made to impose uniformity on
such spellings between one periodical or annual and another.

AM   *American Monthly Magazine*
AP   *Æsthetic Papers*
BG   *Boys' and Girls' Magazine*
BW   *Boston Weekly Museum*
DM   *Dollar Magazine*
DR   *United States Magazine and Democratic Review*
E   *National Era*
IM   *International Miscellany of Literature, Art, and Science*
K   *Knickerbocker, or New-York Monthly Magazine*
M   *The Memorial*
NE   *New-England Magazine*
SG   *Salem Gazette*
T   *The Token*
52   *The Snow-Image, and Other Twice-told Tales*, 1852

The Snow-Image (MS, *M*, *IM*, 52)

7.4	elder] 52; eldest MS-*IM*
7.12 *et seq.*	Mr.] *M*; Mᵣ MS (*stet* Mr., 18.17,25.30)
11.20	this."] *M*; ~.ₐ MS
13.9	Indistinctly] *M*; Indistinclly MS
13.12	it.] *M*; ~ₐ MS
14.29	west-wind] Centenary; ~ₐ~ MS-52
17.15	mamma] *M*; Mamma MS
19.9	she.] *M*; ~ₐ MS
19.25	child."] *M*; ~.ₐ MS
20.6	"Run] *M*; ₐ~ MS
22.5	Why,] 52; ~ₐ MS-*IM*

The Great Stone Face (*E*,52)

29.14	recognized] 52; recognised *E*
30.16	suited] 52; saited *E*

31.26,34.11	Man] CENTENARY; man E-52
31.34–32.1,34.3,41.10	mountain-side] CENTENARY; ∼∧∼ E-52
32.13	he] 52; *omit* E
32.14	forcibly together] 52; forcibly he together E
33.31	oddest] 52; eddest E
35.17	General's] CENTENARY; general's E-52
37.4	recognize] 52; recognise E
40.16	marvellous.] 52; ∼∧ E
42.5	centuries.] 52; ∼∧ E
43.16	mightier] 52; migthier E
44.9	truth.] 52; ∼∧ E
45.33	eyes.] 52; ∼∧ E
46.12	fulfilment] 52; filfulment E
46.24	poet.] 52; ∼∧ E
47.31	them] 52; ∼∧ E
48.5	distinctly] 52; distincly E

MAIN-STREET (AP,52)

49	Main-street] 52; Art. VIII.—Main-street. AP
*50.10	tract] *stet* AP
55.13	name—] CENTENARY; ∼,— AP-52
56.21	centuries,] 52; ∼∧ AP
57.3	you] 52; ∼. AP
61.16	nature,—] 52; ∼,∧ AP
61.24	breast;] 52; ∼: AP
61.32	him;] 52; ∼: AP
65.6	gray] 52; grey AP
67.31	next;] 52; ∼: AP
70.30	cleanse] 52; clease AP
71.7	neighbors] 52; neighbours AP
72.20	breaking out] 52; ∼-∼ AP
72.20	Philip's] 52; Phillip's AP
73.34	Captain] 52; Capt. AP
74.15	Jacobs'] 52; Jacob's AP
75.1	County] 52; county AP

75.5	Sewall] CENTENARY; Sewell *AP*-52
75.22	one] CENTENARY; *omit AP*-52
76.7	Reverend]CENTENARY; Rev. *AP*-52
77.28	infirmity;] 52; ~: *AP*

ETHAN BRAND (*BW*,*DM*,52)

83	Ethan Brand . . . Romance] 52; The Unpardonable Sin. | From an Unpublished Work. *BW*; Ethan Brand; | or, The Unpardonable Sin. *DM*
83.10	Oh] *DM*; O *BW*
83.13	So] *DM*; ~, *BW*
83.19	man, I do believe; there] *DM*; ~. ~ ~ ~ ~ *BW*
83.20–21	startle you] *DM*; to startle her *BW*
84.6	IDEA] *DM*; *ital. BW*
85.6–7	the . . . requisite] *DM*; those necessary *BW*
90.29	drunk] *DM*; drank *BW*
91.19	ragamuffin] 52; ragmuffin *BW*; raggamuffin *DM*
92.3	misfortunes] *DM*; misfortune *BW*
93.5	doubt—] *DM*; ~,— *BW*
93.15	Doctor] CENTENARY; doctor *BW*-52
93.25	travellers] *DM*; travelers *BW*
93.27	of] *DM*; or *BW*
94.23	travelling] *DM*; traveling *BW*
94.32	courtesy] *DM*; ~, *BW*
95.12	brown,] *DM*; ~_∧ *BW*
96.6	Nuremberg] CENTENARY; Nuremburgh *BW*; Nuremburg *DM*-52
96.26	barking,] *DM*; ~_∧ *BW*
97.11	the] *DM*; an *BW*
97.33	advised, them] *DM*; ~_∧~, *BW*
98.11	an] *DM*; no *BW*
98.14	spirts] *DM*; sprits *BW*

98.26	had first begun] *DM*; had began *BW*
*99.5	star-light] *stet BW,DM*
100.26	Heaven,] *DM*; ~$_\wedge$ *BW*
101.13	into] *DM*; in *BW*
101.13	towards] *DM*; toward *BW*
101.30	cheerily] *DM*; cheerly *BW*
102.1	spoilt] *DM*; spolt *BW*
102.15	and,] *DM*; ~$_\wedge$ *BW*
102.17	him."] *DM*; ~·$_\wedge$ *BW*

A Bell's Biography (K,52)

105.12	Puritan] 52; puritan *K*
107.26	towards] Centenary; toward *K-52*
110.14	ecstasy] 52; ecstacy *K*

Sylph Etherege (T,52)

112.31	Sylvia] 52; Silvia *T*

The Canterbury Pilgrims (T,52)

Note: (H) is annotated *T*; see Textual Commentary, pp. 412–13.

120.4	toiling] (H); toiling as the writer has, *T*; toiling, as the writer has, 52
120.15	Nature] Centenary; nature *T-52*
121.9	But] (H) 52; ~, *T*
121.10	life-like] 52; ~$_\wedge$~ *T*
122.23	people,] 52; ~$_\wedge$ *T*
123.10	cistern;] 52; ~, *T*

123.10	children,] 52; ~∧ T
124.7	ethereal] (H) 52; etherial T
124.9	forever] 52; for ever T
124.22	fathers] (H) 52; father's T
124.29	Nature,] 52; ~∧ T
125.10	thee,] 52; ~∧ T
125.15	Now,] 52; ~∧ T
126.21	road-side] 52; ~∧~ T
126.21	ours,] 52; ~∧ T
127.18	sect] 52; set T
128.23,129.35	didn't] 52; did'nt T
128.32	and,] 52; ~∧ T
129.12	Miriam? Oh] 52 (i.e.,O); ~?' '~ T
130.13	wintry] (H) 52; wintery T
130.24	hungry!] 52; ~, T
130.27	other's] 52; others' T
130.27	threshold] 52; threshhold T
131.11	human] (H); moral T; mortal 52

OLD NEWS (NE,52)

132	Old News | I] 52; Old News. | No. I. NE
133.4	a member of the council] 52; a councillor NE
133.20	quaffed to the lees] 52; consumed NE
134.18	country] 52; county NE
134.34	bring] 52; brings NE
135.9	liquor. Some] 52; ~: some NE
135.24	travellers] 52; travelers NE
135.31	wretches.] 52; see Historical Collation NE
136.4	land.] 52; see Historical Collation NE
136.9–10	seems, . . . as that] 52; see Historical Collation NE
136.11 et seq.	-street] 52; ∧~ NE
136.17	Legislature] 52; legislature NE
136.24	Puritanism] 52; puritanism NE
*137.11	councillor] stet NE

137.28	saltatory] 52; salutatory *NE*
137.30	movement.] 52; *see* Historical Collation *NE*
138.2	Common] 52; common *NE*
38.2	Beach] 52; beach *NE*
138.16	calendar; for the] 52; callender. The *NE*
138.18	Castle] 52; castle *NE*
138.22	Second] 52; second *NE*
138.30	birth-day.] 52; *see* Historical Collation *NE*
138.32	was] 52; is *NE*
138.35	human] 52; black and woolly *NE*
139.7	were] 52; are *NE*
139.19	harassed] 52; harrassed *NE*
139.23	blaze] 52; blazed *NE*
139.28	bidder. Slave] 52; *see* Historical Collation *NE*
139.30	people;] 52; ~: *NE*
139.32	times.] 52; *see* Historical Collation *NE*
140.5,141.16	-lane] 52; ∧~ *NE*
140.9	jeweller;] CENTENARY; ~: *NE-52*
140.14	cap] 52; quilted cap *NE*
140.16	sorts;] 52; ~: *NE*
140.27	common;] 52; ~: *NE*
140.29 *et seq.*	-street] 52; ∧~ *NE*
140.31	discourses] 52; discoveries *NE*
141.1	famed] 52; found *NE*
141.11	mellow] 52; aged *NE*
141.17	There] 52; ~, *NE*
141.23	II The Old French War] 52; Old News. No. II. | The Old French War. *NE*
142.14,152.10	-street] 52; ∧~ *NE*
142.22	travelled] 52; traveled *NE*
142.27	paste, at] 52; paste, perhaps diamonds, at *NE*
142.33	Smollett] CENTENARY; Smollet *NE-52*
143.2	peruke-makers.] 52; *see* Historical Collation *NE*
143.4,17	Puritans] 52; puritans *NE*
143.16	New-England] CENTENARY; ~∧~ *NE-52*
144.12,145.2	Revolution] 52; revolution *NE*
145.17	Secretary] 52; secretary *NE*

145.23	Fort] 52; fort *NE*
145.28	jovial] 52; social *NE*
145.34–146.1	Protestant . . . Catholic] 52; *lower case NE*
147.2	officer;] 52; ~: *NE*
147.4–9	Wolfe. . . . ¶ In the] 52; *see* Historical Collation *NE*
147.18	lakes;] 52; ~, *NE*
147.22	month.] 52; *see* Historical Collation *NE*
147.24	forces;] 52; ~: *NE*
147.35	Lake] 52; lake *NE*
148.14	Imagine] 52; I imagine *NE*
148.31–149.2	life. . . . Many] 52; *see* Historical Collation *NE*
149.4	Deacon] 52; deacon *NE*
150.1	Two] 52; two *NE*
150.3	Poem;] 52; ~: *NE*
150.19–21	music. . . . ¶ There] 52; *see* Historical Collation *NE*
150.27	mansion. Wine] 52; *see* Historical Collation *NE*
151.1	Quaker-] 52; quaker- *NE*
151.25	—the] 52; ∧~ *NE*
151.27	-bottom] 52; -Bottom *NE*
152.6	sound] 52; round *NE*
152.9–10	built . . . ground,] 52; *omit NE*
152.11	Beacon-hill.] 52; *see* Historical Collation *NE*
*152.12	tramping] 52; trampling *NE*
152.13	King's Chapel] 52; king's chapel *NE*
152.18	Brazen-Head] 52; ~∧~ *NE*
152.22	dignity] 52; disparity *NE*
153.12	III The Old Tory] 52; Old News. No. III. | The Old Tory *NE*
154.9	Doctor Caner] 52; Mather Byles *NE*
154.10	King] CENTENARY; king *NE*-52
154.11	Plains] 52; plains *NE*
154.15	gentlemen] 52; gentleman *NE*
155.5	arm's] 52; arms' *NE*
155.12	motto] 52; ~— *NE*

157.1	Hewes,] 52; ∼∧ NE
157.8	heavenly] 52; Heavenly NE
157.29	petticoats] 52; peticoats NE
158.3	anointed] 52; annointed NE
158.5	Scripture] Centenary; scripture NE 52
158.18	thieves] 52; theives NE
158.27	to] 52; as NE
159.2	Yea;] Centenary; ∼: NE-52
159.20	friends,] 52; ∼∧ NE
159.33–34	routine; and . . . them. One] 52; routine. One NE

The Man of Adamant (*T*,52)

| 165.4 | woman] 52; female *T* |
| 169.17 | grandchildren] 52; ∼|∼ *T* |

The Devil in Manuscript (*NE*,52)

171.2	who, indeed,] 52; ∼∧∼∧ NE
172.19	examination—'] Centenary; ∼'— NE; ∼. 52
173.5	"trade"] Centenary; '∼' NE-52

John Inglefield's Thanksgiving (*DR*,52)

180.27	Inglefield.] 52; ∼, DR
181.27	Providence] 52; providence DR
182.16	do] 52; Do DR
183.2	you] 52; You DR
183.8	deeds.] 52; ∼∧ DR

Old Ticonderoga (*AM*,52)

186.1	The] 52; *see* Historical Collation *AM*
186.7	recognized] 52; recognised *AM*
187.9	pine-tree] 52; ~ₐ~ *AM*
190.21	Meantime,] 52; ~~ₐ *AM*
191.9	fowling-piece] 52; ~ₐ~ *AM*
191.23	Revolution] 52; revolution *AM*

The Wives of the Dead (*T*,52)

193.14	to-day] 52; to day *T*
193.15	said. 'Arise] 52 (~. "~); ~, '~ *T*
195.20,28	Goodman] 52; goodman *T*
195.21	Mistress] 52; mistress *T*
197.27	recognized] 52; recognised *T*
199.10	awoke.] 52; awoke.	F . . . . . . *T*

Little Daffydowndilly (*BG*,52)

202.7	road-side] Centenary; roadside *BG*-52
*203.2	haste] *stet BG*

My Kinsman, Major Molineux (*T*,52)

208.18	House of Representatives] 52; *lower-case T*
211.10	you,] 52; ~. *T*
213.23	Protestant] 52; protestant *T*

214.8	patronize] 52; patronise *T*
214.21	' "Left] 52 (i.e., " '∼); ∧"∼ *T*
214.25	Better] 52; '∼ *T*
214.26	begun] 52; began *T*
215.14,227.16	recognize 52; recognise *T*
216.6	recognizing] 52; recognising *T*
217.15	Gospel] 52; gospel *T*
217.25	more,'] 52 (i.e., ∼,"); ∼,∧ *T*
217.27	to-night] 52; to night *T*
*217.33	leather]— *stet T*
220.19	or,] 52; ∼∧ *T*
220.26	parti-] 52; party- *T*
221.22	Gothic] 52; gothic *T*
222.6	Bible] 52; bible *T*
223.2	Scriptures] 52; scriptures *T*
223.10	trunk;] 52; ∼, *T*
226.17	Heaven] 52; heaven *T*
227.26	kept] 52; keep *T*
228.24	a universal] 52; an universal *T*
228.32–33	his . . . line] 52; the eyebrows formed one dark grey line *T*
*229.26	two sepulchral] 52; two deep sepulchral *T*
230.28,231.3	ferry] 52; Ferry *T*

CENTENARY Emendations in the Uncollected Tales

THE BATTLE-OMEN (SG)

236.22	us."] ∼.'
238.1	minstrelsy] minstrelsey
238.12	why] Why
239.7	solitude] ∼.
239.14	heads] head

An Old Woman's Tale (SG)

241.22	point)] ~,)
242.18	young] youg
247.1	watch-chain] watchchain
247.9	gray] grey
247.16	meeting-house] ~∧~
247.24	steeple] steple
248.17	slice")] ~,")∧
248.30	gold-lace] ~∧~
249.12	interrogatories] interregatories
249.13	similar] simlar

The Haunted Quack (T)

251.18	other's] others'
251.19	berths] births
252.22	recognized] recognised
254.6,259.31,260.3	, however,] ∧~∧
255.3	Christian] christian
255.27	however,] ~∧
256.12,20	Doctor] doctor
257.30,261.28	Mrs.] Mrs
258.23	Dr.] Dr
260.9	forty-nine] fortynine
262.17	villainous] villanous
263.26	*protégé*] *protégee*
264.17	hadn't] had'nt
264.34	to] too

Alice Doane's Appeal (T)

267.22,272.10	indeed,] ~∧

268.1	feminine] femenine
268.10	hollow] hallow
269.24	moss-grown] ~ᴧ~
270.9	Nature] nature
272.32–273.1	A space between sections of narrative is obscured by pagination.
277.29	wood-wax] ~ᴧ~

My Visit to Niagara (*NE*)

281.21–22	impossible;] ~:
282.10,287.6	traveller] traveler
282.20	cigar] ciger
282.23,283.6,287.15,288.13	Island] island
284.22	Nature] nature
287.7	Captain] captain

Graves and Goblins (*NE*)

289.12,291.9,296.30	ethereal] etherial *NE*
291.14	mortal] mrotal
295.1	theirs] ~'

Sketches from Memory (*NE*)

298	Sketches from Memory] Sketches from Memory. | By a Pedestrian. | No. II. *NE* ["The Canal-Boat" appears in "Sketches from Memory," and the introductory paragraph is in the Historical Collation, *Mosses from an Old Manse* (Centenary Edition, 1974); "An Afternoon Scene" is restored to context on pp. 322–23 of this volume.]

298.5,19; 304.18	Lake] lake
299.14	analogy] analagy
301.11,302.8	Genesee] Genessee
303.24	travellers] travelers

A Visit to the Clerk of the Weather (*AM*)

| 309.25 | chain lightning] ~-~ |
| 311.5 | bolts] bolis |

Fragments from the Journal of a Solitary Man (*AM*)

Note: spaces are inserted for symmetry following 314.5, 317.21, 26, 322.3, 327.8,11

315.31	'Unwept . . . unsung.'] *double quotes*
320.19	crossed,] crossed |
325.3	kept] keep
326.28	of my] of his

Note: 322.16–323.4 "There. . . . coolness." appeared as "An Afternoon Scene" in *New-England Magazine*, December, 1835, p. 408, omitting 322.26 "of blue" and 323.2–3 "and . . . frame,"; variants accepted from that appearance are listed below.

322.17	this,] ~∧
322.17	summer—] ~∧
322.19	-trees,] ~∧
322.19	head,] ~∧
322.22	June,] ~∧
322.23	Autumn . . . Spring] *lower case*
322.24	buttercups] butterflies
322.25	grass;] ~,

322.27	stone-wall] stone walk
322.27	rose-bush,] ~-~∧
323.1	violets,] ~∧

TIME'S PORTRAITURE (partial MS,SG)

Note: all emendations are of *SG* copy-text

330.17	wood-cut] ~∧~
331.14	people,] ~∧
332.2	months'] month's,
332.23	middle-aged gentleman] ~∧~-~
334.5	What] what
334.31	however,] ~∧
335.26	cry.] ~∧
336.3	sight.] ~∧
336.20	Sometimes] ~,
336.24	for] For
337.1,11	Patrons] patrons
337.18	hands,—] ~,∧
337.20	you,] ~∧

THE ANTIQUE RING
(*Sargent's New Monthly Magazine*)

339.21	Mr.] ~,
340.14	Pemberton.] ~,
346.5	countess.] ~∧
346.23	undertake] uudertake
349.21	Heaven] heaven
352.9	What pathos] what pathos
352.12	who,]~∧

A Good Man's Miracle (*Child's Friend*)

354.8	His] his
356.1	sympathize] sympathise
358.22	His own] his own

A Book of Autographs (*DR*)

363.3	daylight] ~-~
363.17,366.12	Revolutionary] revolutionary
366.33	handwriting] ~-~
373.16	Revolution] revolution

WORD-DIVISION

1. *End-of-the-Line Hyphenation in the Centenary Edition*

Possible compounds hyphenated at the end of a line in the Centenary text are listed here if they are hyphenated within the line in the copy-text. Exclusion from this list means that a possible compound appears as one unhyphenated word in the copy-text. Also excluded are hyphenated compounds in which both elements are capitalized.

10.22	snow-image	60.25	frame-work
11.18	snow-sister	70.15	Main-street
11.22	angel-children	70.30	blood-stain
11.34	half-dreaming	72.8	school-boys
13.14	snow-images	72.12	fire-water
18.15	fur-cap	72.27	buff-coat
21.17	snow-child's	73.20	first-born
21.27	well-meaning	78.21	hat-bands
23.9	North-pole	78.34	white-bearded
24.35	common-sensible	83.10	lime-burner
28.21	old-fashioned	84.10	tower-like
29.3	log-cottage	86.5	country-made
36.17	mountain-visage	89.6, 90.34	lime-kiln
37.13, 84.6	mountain-side	92.13	purple-visaged
38.1	well-considered	93.26	circus-performers
50.21	faintly-traced	94.18	sun-burnt
51.12	stone-front	101.22	stage-coach
59.33	town-forces	102.8	snow-white

105.7	thick-strewn	285.22	all-absorbing
107.31	Heave-oh!	288.2	foot-path
116.28	drawing-room	290.13	resting-place
132.2	time-stained	291.25	three-score
133.21	waste-paper	291.32	tomb-stone
140.22	town-dock	293.17	free-stone
141.11	wine-cellar	307.18	slate-colored
142.22	petit-maitre	308.5	hail-stones
145.25	stone-mansion	308.32	ice-palaces
146.3	Sabbath-day	310.10	fellow-sufferers
147.17	batteaux-men	315.5	care-stricken
148.10	pine-boughs	315.18	home-sickness
148.16	scarlet-coated	316.9	iron-gray
149.6	ornamental-work	316.18	fellow-creatures
149.22	twenty-three	316.30	love-tales
153.29	sour-visaged	320.18	stern-sheets
157.14	town-house	332.25	time-stricken
157.15	bloody-minded	333.29	good-natured
162.9	meeting-house	345.31	death-agony
175.28	laughing-stock	350.16	self-approvingly
213.7	chimney-smoke	350.27	shop-bill
214.30	bold-featured	352.18	half-reproachful
217.31	rainy-weather	357.32	school-mistresses
220.29	church-door	358.11	Sunday-school
221.34	window-frame	360.30	world-wide
225.8	well-grown	366.7	hair-line
230.8	cloud-spirits	367.32	hair-lines
240.10	check-apron	371.18	fiend-devoted
242.14	great-grandfather	372.17	time-worn
245.17	door-stone	373.10	off-shoot
259.5	church-yard	374.10	knee-breeches
285.17	dire-struck		

2. *End-of-the-Line Hyphenation in the Copy-Texts*

The following possible compounds are hyphenated at the ends of lines in the copy-texts. The form adopted in the

Centenary Edition, as listed below, represents Hawthorne's predominant usage as ascertained by other appearances within the copy-text.

5.9, 39.28	wayside	86.13	wayfarer
6.12	summertime	88.2	hobgoblins
10.31	snow-image	88.15	footsteps
13.9,	snow-child	89.30	prison-house
18.11, 20.3		90.23	mountain-side
17.2	west-wind	91.11	bar-room
19.18	common-sensible	91.17	well-remembered
19.32	snow-girl	91.20	tow-cloth
21.7	snow-drift	91.26	soap-vat
24.6	snow-sister	92.14	half-gentlemanly
26.12	hill-sides	92.30	hell-fire
30.31	weather-beaten	95.8	tobacco-smoke
37.17	cloud-vesture	95.14	showman's
48.20	by-and-|by	95.22	overflowing
49.6	thoroughfare	97.10	self-pursuing
49.22	noontide	97.23	fire-light
50.16	snowfall	98.6	above-mentioned
50.28, 51.27	underbrush	98.20	night-dew
50.33	half-seen	99.29	lime-kiln
55.34	sad-colored	101.7	weathercocks
56.11	linsey-woolsey	105.5	birthday
59.21	meeting-house	108.10	home-tenderness
60.3	steel-caps	113.6	fancy-picture
62.13	lovelock	113.25	life-long
64.25	long-accustomed	115.16	day-dreams
65.8	street-corners	119.7	moonlight
66.32	town-born	133.19, 150.30	broadcloths
67.5	do-nothing	135.32	forebodings
67.7	tithing-man	133.35	blackguarding
74.22	witch-meeting	137.20	coachmaker
82.1	tomorrow	139.7	cross-legged
84.31, 90.7,19	lime-burner	140.2	mother-|of-pearl
85.17	half-frightened	142.14, 149.20	coffee-house
85.34	fireside	143.11	mother-country

144.34	twenty-three	248.12	gold-bowed
147.21	able-bodied	248.28	moonlight
147.31	pay-rolls	257.18	church-yard
148.5	overshadowing	258.20	antiscrofulous
148.12	spruce-beer	261.22	doctor-stuff
149.18	great-grandmothers	275.2	midnight
150.12	copper-plate	282.4	dinner-hour
150.26	pier-glasses	283.7	right-hand
151.17	sidewalks	287.12	ever-pointed
153.28	nickname	289.3	earth-clogged
155.6	figure-head	289.18	offspring
158.13	Brattle-street	298.15	alongside
168.12	darksome	299.13	fresh-water
177.27, 190.24 gunpowder		302.21	forest-leaves
187.5	zigzags	317.4	twenty-five
188.3	church-yards	318.24	looking-glass
202.24	stone-wall	323.30	sunshine
202.34	shirt-sleeves	326.8	townspeople
204.7, 205.32 schoolmaster		326.17	birthplace
209.10	landing-place	329.15	errand-boys
215.25	half-dancing	329.18	twelvemonth
220.15	forehead	330.3	to-morrow
227.9	Half-dressed	330.17	wood-cut
240.17	by-places	340.6	old-fashioned
241.8	cloven-foot	346.30	bed-chamber
242.13	mill-stream	347.5	Tower-yard
244.11	moonbeams	349.13–14 communion-table	
245.13	grass-grown	353.11	well-known
245.23	gray-haired	359.7	three-quarters
246.30	moonshine	374.9	praiseworthy
246.34	sky-blue		

3. *Special Cases*

In the following list, the possible compound is hyphenated at the end of the line in the copy-text and in the Centenary text.

19.14	snow-sister	84.19	hill-side
24.13	horror-stricken	94.18	sun-burnt
36.14	thunder-breath	118.26	drawing-room
50.10	leaf-strewn	151.28	bedizzened
53.19	psalm-tune	172.31	booksellers
54.9, 63.33	forest-track	201.2	school-room
59.21	too-frequented	201.10	ugly-visaged
60.14	mother-country	202.33	waistcoat
61.5	meeting-house	286.7	ever-varying
63.35	Main-street	293.32	bed-chambers
78.10	rose-color	367.29	handwriting

HISTORICAL COLLATION

Substantive variants from copy-text are listed chronologically in descent of the texts of individual pieces of the *Snow-Image* collection through the stereotype 1852 edition to the Centenary Edition. Also listed are copy-text errors not forming accepted words. For the uncollected tales, it has not been thought necessary to list a separate Historical Collation, since Centenary substantive variants (and two accepted from *New-England Magazine*) are easily to be seen in the Editorial Emendations in the Copy-Text.

Rejected first-edition substantive variants, when they occur, head all lists but that of "The Snow-Image," where two rejections of manuscript copy-text are noticed.

Following the title of each piece are the symbols (identified below) for copy-text and successive appearances. For each entry, the Centenary reading to the left of the bracket is followed by the rejected variant with its origin and other editions using it. Unlisted editions may be taken to agree with Centenary.

AM   *American Monthly Magazine*
AP   *Æsthetic Papers*
BG   *Boys' and Girls' Magazine*
BW   *Boston Weekly Museum*
DM   *Dollar Magazine*

DR   *United States Magazine and Democratic Review*
E   *National Era*
IM   *International Monthly Magazine*
K   *Knickerbocker, or New-York Monthly Magazine*
M   *The Memorial*
NE   *New-England Magazine*
T   *The Token*
52   *The Snow-Image, and Other Twice-told Tales,* 1852

The Snow-Image (MS,M,IM,52)

7.4	elder] eldest MS-*IM*
13.9	Indistinctly] Indistinclly MS
8.34	thought] idea *M*-52
11.16	'ittle] little *M*-52
14.5	pilgrimage] a pilgrimage *M*-52
15.26	hair] hue *M*-52
18.20–21	at sight] at the sight *M*-52
19.29	a hand] the hand *M*-52
21.13	and how] *omit M*-52
22.11	were] was *M*-52
22.28	very] same *M*-52
23.20	window] windows *M*-52
24.1	had] has *M-IM*
24.5	his] her *M-IM*
7.16	people's] peoples' *IM*
10.20	look as handsome as possible] look handsome *IM*-52
11.10	furthest] farthest *IM*
13.14	Then]*omit IM*-52
15.23	see] *omit IM*-52
19.3,27, 23.20	towards] toward *IM*-52
19.15	not she] she not *IM*-52
21.11	now] *omit IM*-52

21.29	towards] toward *IM*
23.14	kind] *omit IM*-52
23.32	round] around *IM*-52
24.3	way] away *IM*
7.7	that] who 52
18.19	all day] all the day 52
23.4	farthest] furthest 52

The Great Stone Face (*E*,52)

30.16	suited] saited *E*
32.13	he] *omit E*
32.14	forcibly together] forcibly he together *E*
33.31	oddest] eddest *E*
43.16	mightier] migthier *E*
46.12	fulfilment] filfulment *E*
48.5	distinctly] distincly *E*
27.16	farther] further 52
35.7	grand] great 52
36.21	a] an 52
39.9–10	as a candidate] *omit* 52
46.18	those of] *omit* 52

Main-street (*AP*,52)

49	Main-street] Art. VIII—Main-street *AP*
70.30	cleanse] clease *AP*
72.20	Philip's] Phillip's *AP*
74.15	Jacobs'] Jacob's *AP*
75.22	one]*omit AP*-52
50.10	tract] track 52
61.30	Farther] Further 52

65.24	past] passed 52
77.20	ones] one 52
81.5	leave] leaves 52

ETHAN BRAND (BW,DM,52)

83	Ethan Brand . . . Romance] The Unpardonable Sin. | From an Unpublished Work. BW; see also DM
83.19	man, I do believe; there] man. I do believe there BW
83.20–21	startle you] to startle her BW
85.6–7	the very few that were requisite] those necessary BW
90.29	drunk] drank BW
92.3	misfortunes] misfortune BW
93.27	of] or BW
96.6	Nuremberg] Nuremburgh BW
97.11	the] an BW
98.11	an] no BW
98.14	spirts] sprits BW; see also 52
98.26	had first begun] had began BW
101.13	into] in BW
101.13	towards] toward BW
101.30	cheerily] cheerly BW
102.1	spoilt] spolt BW; see also 52
83	Ethan Brand . . . Romance] Ethan Brand; | or, The Unpardonable Sin. DM
84.13	that blocks] that the blocks DM-52
84.34	chat] a chat DM-52
85.11	was] were DM-52
86.34	I myself] I am myself DM-52
88.20	the only] the one only DM-52
89.12	abide in the] abide the DM-52
90.8	farther] further DM-52
90.11	the pride] a pride DM-52
91.30	gripe] grip DM-52

92.2	on] *omit* DM
92.9	more] many more DM-52
94.3	is] was DM-52
96.6	Nuremberg] Nuremburg DM-52
96.20	notion] motion DM-52
97.19	homeward] homewards DM-52
98.10	to] at DM-52
101.6	upward] upwards DM-52
92.11–12	we should have introduced] we introduced 52
98.14	spirts] spirits 52
99.5	star-light] star-lit 52
102.1	spoilt] spoiled 52

A Bell's Biography (K,52)

107.26	towards] toward K-52
103.6	farther] further 52
109.20	mistress's] mistress' 52

Sylph Etherege (T,52)

112.31	Sylvia] Silvia T

The Canterbury Pilgrims (T,52)

120.4	toiling] toiling as the writer has T-52
124.22	fathers] father's T
127.18	sect] set T
130.13	wintry] wintery T
130.27	other's] others' T
130.27	threshold] threshhold T

131.11   human] moral *T; see also* 52
121.24   farther] further 52
130.19   past] passed 52
131.11   human] mortal 52

OLD NEWS (*NE*,52)

132   Old News | I] Old News. | No. I. *NE*
133.4   a member of the council] a councillor *NE*
133.20   quaffed to the lees] consumed *NE*
134.18   country] county *NE*
134.34   bring] brings *NE*
135.31   wretches.] wretches.* (*footnote*) *It might well
              have been the case, as there were no light-
              ning-rods. *NE*
136.4   land.] land.* (*footnote*) *The printer intimates
              a doubt, whether any sound auguries could
              be drawn from these unaccountable noises.
              We have no patience with such a would-be
              sadducee, who, so long as general opinion
              countenances the belief, could struggle to be
              a sceptic, in regard to this most thrilling and
              sublime superstition. *NE*
136.9–10   seems, . . . as that] seems to have been re-
              garded with as much affright, though so
              familiar a scourge, as that *NE*
137.28   saltatory] salutatory *NE*
137.30   movement.] movement.* (*footnote*) *There was
              a dancing-school in Boston, for a short period,
              so long ago, we think, as in 1685. *NE*
138.16   calendar; for the] callender. The *NE*
138.30   birth-day.] birth-day.* (*footnote*) *In some old
              pamphlet, we recollect a proposal to erect an
              equestrian statue of the 'glorious King Wil-
              liam,' in front of the town-house, looking
              down King-street. It would have been pleas-
              ant to have had an historic monument, of

any kind, in that street of historic recollections. Even the whig monarch, however, would hardly have kept his saddle through the Revolution, though himself a revolutionary king. *NE*

138.32   was] is *NE*
138.35   human] black and woolly *NE*
139.7   were] are *NE*
139.19   harassed] harrassed *NE*
139.23   blaze] blazed *NE*
139.28   bidder. Slave] bidder. Setting fine sentiment aside, slavery, as it existed in New-England, was precisely the state most favorable to the humble enjoyments of an alien race, generally incapable of self-direction, and whose claims to kindness will never be acknowledged by the whites, while they are asserted on the ground of equality. Slave *NE*

139.32   times.] times.* (*footnote*) *Nevertheless, some time after this period, there is an advertisement of a run-|away slave from Connecticut, who carried with him an iron collar rivetted round his neck, with a chain attached. This must have been rather galling. Undoubtedly, there had been a previous attempt at escape. *NE*

140.14   cap] quilted cap *NE*
140.31   discourses] discoveries *NE*
141.1   famed] found *NE*
141.11   mellow] aged *NE*
141.23   II The Old French War] Old News. No. II. | The Old French War. *NE*
142.27   paste, at] paste, perhaps diamonds, at *NE*
142.33   Smollett] Smollet *NE*-52
143.2   peruke-makers.] peruke-makers.* (*footnote*) *There was a great competition among these artists. Two or three were French; of the Englishmen, one professed to have worked in the best shops about London, and another had studied the science in the chief cities of

Europe. The price of white wigs and grizzels, made of picked human hair, was £20, old tenor; of light grizzels, £15; and of dark grizzels, £12 10s. These prices are not so formidable as they appear—money, in old tenor, being worth only about a fourth of its original value. *NE*

145.28	jovial] social *NE*
147.4–9	Wolfe. Somewhere . . . soldiers. ¶ In] Wolfe.* ¶ In (*footnote*) *Somewhere in this volume, though we cannot now lay our finger upon the passage, we recollect a report, that General Wolfe was slain, not by the enemy, but by a shot from his own soldiers. *NE*
147.22	month.] month.† (*footnote*) †At one time, there was an impress for this ship, sanctioned by the provincial authorities. Throughout the war, the British frigates seized upon the crews of all vessels, without ceremony, to the great detriment of trade. But, some years before, a British admiral threw Boston into a memorable ferment, by recruiting, in the same arbitrary manner, from the wharves. *NE*
148.14	Imagine] I imagine *NE*
148.31–149.2	life. During . . . bridges. Many] life.* (*footnote*) *During the winter of 1759, it was computed that about a thousand sled-loads of country produce were daily brought into Boston market. Commerce had declined. It was a symptom of an irregular and unquiet course of affairs, that innumerable lotteries were projected, ostensibly for the purpose of public improvements, such as roads and bridges. (*text*) Many *NE*
150.19–21	music. There . . . exhibitions. ¶ There] music.* (*footnote*) *There had already been an attempt at theatrical exhibitions. ¶ There *NE*
150.27	mansion. Wine] mansion; more so, indeed, than

the slighter elegancies of our own days. Wine
NE

152.6   sound] round *NE*
152.9–10   built . . . ground,] *omit NE*
152.11   Beacon hill,] Beacon hill,* (*footnote.*) *These
                bonfires were built on scaffolds, raised several
                stories above the ground. *NE*
152.12   tramping] trampling *NE*
152.22   dignity] disparity *NE*
153.12   III | The Old Tory] Old News. No. III. | The
                Old Tory. *NE*
154.9   Doctor Caner] Mather Byles *NE*
154.15   gentlemen] gentleman *NE*
155.5   arm's] arms' *NE*
157.29   petticoats] peticoats *NE*
158.3   anointed] annointed *NE*
158.18   thieves] theives *NE*
158.27   false to] false as *NE*
159.33–34   routine; and . . . them. One] routine. One *NE*
135.26   farther] further 52
137.11   councillor] counsellor 52
140.14   Jenkins's] Jenkins' 52
158.33   those] these 52
159.31   virtue] virtues 52

THE MAN OF ADAMANT (T,52)

165.4   woman] female *T*
162.28   onward] onwards 52
164.4   fleshly] fleshy 52

THE DEVIL IN MANUSCRIPT (NE,52)

171.10   would] could 52
176.10   those] these 52

John Inglefield's Thanksgiving (DR,52)

No substantive variants.

Old Ticonderoga (AM,52)

186.1 ¶ The greatest] ¶ In returning once to New England, from a visit to Niagara, I found myself, one summer's day, before noon, at Orwell, about forty miles from the southern extremity of Lake Champlain, which has here the aspect of a river or a creek. We were on the Vermont shore, with a ferry, of less than a mile wide, between us and the town of Ti, in New-York. ¶ On the bank of the lake, within ten yards of the water, stood a pretty white tavern, with a piazza along its front. A wharf and one or two stores were close at hand, and appeared to have a good run of trade, foreign as well as domestic; the latter with Vermont farmers, the former with vessels plying between Whitehall and the British dominions. Altogether, this was a pleasant and lively spot. I delighted in it, among other reasons, on account of the continual succession of travellers, who spent an idle quarter of an hour in waiting for the ferry-|boat; affording me just time enough to make their acquaintance, penetrate their mysteries, and be rid of them without the risk of tediousness on either part. ¶ The greatest *AM*

The Wives of the Dead (T,52)

No substantive variants.
Token appearance ends with signature: F . . . . . .

Little Daffydowndilly (BG,52)

203.2	haste] hay 52
203.14	but a little] but little 52
203.14, 204.13, 206.10	farther] further 52

My Kinsman, Major Molineux (T,52)

214.26	begun] began T
227.26	kept] keep T
228.24	a universal] an universal T
228.32–33	his eyebrows formed one grizzled line] the eyebrows formed one dark grey line T
229.26	two sepulchral] two deep sepulchral T
208	My Kinsman, Major Molineux] Major Molineux 52
208.8	the rulers] their rulers 52
209.1	preface] a preface 52
209.18	sat] fitted 52
209.20	handiwork] work 52
210.23	about] above 52
210.32–33	to tell] tell 52
211.12	show] show for 52
212.19	fumes] the fumes 52
212.28	great] *omit* 52
212.30	aspect] appearance 52

212.34	the] *omit* 52
213.13	in] on 52
213.25	circumstance] circumstances 52
213.28	Beg to] Beg leave to 52
214.6	consequence] confidence 52
214.7	¶ My] *no* ¶ My 52
214.9	I] when I 52
214.12	the way] my way 52
214.24	whoever] whosoever 52
214.25	in] of 52
215.4	these] those 52
215.12	numerous] the numerous 52
216.9	was now] now was 52
217.33	leather—But] leather small-clothes. But 52
218.2	though] *omit* 52
219.23	which] that 52
220.10	own] *omit* 52
220.20	blazed of] blazed 52
220.30–31	kinsman's appearance.] kinsman. 52
220.32	the *genus homo*] man 52
221.1	amusement] his amusement 52
221.10	milk-white] snow-white 52
221.12	plastered] *omit* 52
222.4	round] around 52
222.18	passing dimly] dimly passing 52
223.2	shone] fell 52
223.12	his] the 52
223.27	in] into 52
225.2	had seemed] seemed 52
225.9	raising himself to] drawing himself up to 52
225.15	dusk] dark 52
226.13–14	went to make up] went up to make 52
226.15	one] a 52
226.30	just] *omit* 52
227.13	onward] onwards 52
227.16	Robin] *omit* 52
227.34	which] that 52
228.6	sidewalks] side-walk 52
228.10	uncomfortable] an uncomfortable 52

228.22	held] then held 52
228.24	nearly] *omit* 52
228.30	the] *omit* 52
229.6	that had] *omit* 52
229.27	¶ 'Haw] *no* ¶ 'Haw 52
229.33	down] *omit* 52
230.14	sign, the] sign, and the 52
230.16	round] around 52
230.24	while] as 52
230.26	so] as 52
231.5	continue to] *omit* 52

ALTERATIONS IN THE MANUSCRIPTS

A Centenary key is given to the left of the bracket, and a description of the alteration follows; "above" indicates interlineation, and "over," inscription in the same space. The presence of a caret is always noticed. Not listed are interlineations repeating originals for clarity, mendings for clarity, or alterations over undecipherable originals.

THE SNOW-IMAGE

7.10	phiz] over wiped-out 'Phiz'
7.12	a certain] the article over wiped-out initial strokes of 'M'
7.15	common-sense] followed by cancelled 'of'
7.17	head] 'd' over wiped-out 'rd'
8.1	Violet] 'Vi' over 'Pe'
8.2	in] over cancelled 'with'
8.8	plum-] 'plu' over wiped-out '[l]'
8.16	up] over 'a' and an ascender, perhaps of 'l'
8.32	when] 'w' over 'a'
8.33	Violet] 'i' over 'o'
9.10	make] 'e' over wiped-out 'er'
9.22	one,] semicolon partially wiped, leaving comma
9.28	like] interlined with a caret in pencil, probably by Hawthorne
10.2	help] 'l' over wiped-out 'p'

10.8	with] 'h' of initially inscribed 'wh' abandoned after upstroke and 'i' written below it
11.18	thoughtfully] second 't' over 'f'
11.24	help] 'lp' over wiped-out 'pp'
12.6	Violet] interlined with a caret above cancelled 'Violet', which was inscribed over 'Peon'
12.14	on] over wiped-out 'of'
12.25	then] 'en' over 'a'
12.29	sun—] dash cancels comma
12.30	year—] dash cancels comma
13.6	image—] dash cancels comma
13.11	nor] 'r' over wiped-out 'ne'
14.5	gone] 'go' over wiped-out 'tra'
14.8	Come] preceded by partially erased opening quotation mark
14.33–34	with one] over wiped-out 'at once.'
15.10	are!] exclamation point cancels period and closing quotation mark
15.14	delay] 'd' over 'to'
15.24	was a] the article over 'as'
15.29	as] over 'and'
15.32	neighbors] 'ei' mended from 'ie'
15.34	kind] above cancelled 'good'
16.20	airily] above cancelled 'airily', which was inscribed over wiped-out 'airl'
16.23	in] over wiped-out 'up', the 'p' incomplete
16.28	Almost] followed by wiped-out comma
16.32	better] 'be' over wiped-out 'not'
17.7	snow-drift could] 'ri' over wiped-out 'if'
17.9	name?"] question mark mended from exclamation point after initial inscription of comma
17.16	-image!] exclamation point cancels question mark
17.17	child] 'i' over wiped-out 'l'
17.22	claim] 'im' mended from 'me'
17.25	her, and] comma mended from period; 'and' over wiped-out 'She'
17.28	their] 'ir' over 're'
17.31	in] over 'as'

17.31	may] interlined with a caret
18.3	perplexed,] 'er' over wiped-out 'ex'; comma cancels period
18.5	mamma] initial 'm' over 'M'
18.18–19	frost-pinched] 'frost' above cancelled 'cold'
18.19	face,] followed by cancelled 'and was glad to get back to his wife and children, and his quiet,'
18.27	girl may] 'girl m' over wiped-out 'may th'
18.33	Violet] 'V' over 'P'
19.10	mother?] question mark cancels comma
19.29	a] over 'an'
20.2	This] 'T' over 'o'
20.6	Run] 'R' over 'O'
20.16	souls?] question mark cancels comma
20.20	as Violet] 'as' over wiped-out 'are'
21.5	seeing] 'see' over wiped-out 'loo'
21.11	observe] over wiped-out 'see h'
21.27	all . . . cold,] interlined with a caret
22.1	face—their eyes] dash cancels comma; 'their ey' over wiped-out 'with tears'
22.25	threshold] 'r' over 'e'
22.26	She] 'S' over left arm of 'H'
22.28	Without] 'u' over wiped-out 't'
23.2	fume] 'fum' over wiped-out 's[ ]'
23.4	wall farthest] above cancelled 'wall farthest', which was inscribed over wiped-out 'opposite wall'
23.26	But] 'u' over wiped-out 'ef'
23.18	woollen] above 'woollen', of which the second 'o' was inscribed over partially wiped-out 'l'
24.9	had] 'ad' over wiped-out 'ard'
24.16	Violet] 'V' over 'P'
25.1	man.] period cancels comma
25.3	Heidenberg] 'H' over 's'
25.3	isinglass] 'l' over top loop of incomplete 'g'
25.10	but] 'b' over 'c'
25.12	edification] 'e' over wiped-out 'd'
25.18	prove] followed by cancelled 'to be'

25.23	there] 're' over wiped-out 'ere'
25.27	Providence] a following comma erased

Time's Portraiture

329.21	naturally] 'ly' over wiped-out 'y'
329.21	expected)] parenthesis deletes comma
331.19	old.] followed by caret and '(see last page)'
333.5	shows] above cancelled 'gives'
333.26	The above are] over wiped-out 'I have written'
333.34	word.] followed by caret and '(see last page)'

THE COMPLETE TALES

HERE IN alphabetical order are listed the titles and variant titles of all the tales printed in volumes IX, X, and XI of the Centenary Edition. When the title is a variant from Centenary, a cross-reference follows. Abbreviations of the titles of the volumes are: volume IX, *TT*, *Twice-told Tales*; volume X, *MOM*, *Mosses from an Old Manse*; and volume XI, *SI*, *The Snow-Image, and Uncollected Tales*.

Afternoon Scene, An [attributed], *within text of* Fragments from the Journal of a Solitary Man *SI*
Alice Doane's Appeal *SI*
Allegories of the Heart, The, *i.e.* Egotism; or, The Bosom-Serpent *and* The Christman Banquet *MOM*
Ambitious Guest, The *TT*
Antique Ring, The *SI*
Artist of the Beautiful, The *MOM*
At Home, *in* Passages from a Relinquished Work *MOM*

Battle-Omen, The [attributed] *SI*
Bell's Biography, A *SI*
Bertram the Lime-Burner, *i.e.* Ethan Brand *SI*
Birth-mark, The *MOM*
Book of Autographs, A *SI*
Bosom Serpent, The, *i.e.* Egotism *MOM*
Buds and Bird-Voices *MOM*

Canal-Boat, The, *in* Sketches from Memory *MOM*
Canterbury Pilgrims, The *SI*

John Inglefield's Thanksgiving *SI*

Lady Eleanore's Mantle *TT*
Legends of the Province-House, *incl.* I. Howe's Masquerade; II.
    Edward Randolph's Portrait; III. Lady Eleanore's Mantle; IV.
    Old Esther Dudley *TT*
Lily's Quest, The *TT*
Little Annie's Ramble *TT*
Little Daffydowndilly *SI*

Main-street *SI*
Major Molineux, *i.e.* My Kinsman, Major Molineux *SI*
Man of Adamant, The *SI*
May-Pole of Merry Mount, The *TT*
Mermaid, The; A Reverie, *i.e.* The Village Uncle *TT*
Minister's Black Veil, The *TT*
Monsieur du Miroir *MOM*
Mr. Higginbotham's Catastrophe *TT*
Mrs. Bullfrog *MOM*
My Home Return [attributed], *in* Fragments from the Journal
    of a Solitary Man *SI*
My Kinsman, Major Molineux *SI*
My Visit to Niagara *SI*

New Adam and Eve, The *MOM*
Night Scene, A [attributed], *in* Sketches from Memory *SI*
Night Sketches *TT*
Night Sketches beneath an Umbrella, *i.e.* Night Sketches *TT*
Night Sketches under an Umbrella, *i.e.* Night Sketches *TT*
Notch, The, *in* Sketches from Memory *MOM*
Notch of the White Mountains, The, *i.e.* The Notch, *in* Sketches
    from Memory *MOM*

Old Apple-Dealer, The *MOM*
Old Esther Dudley *TT*
Old French War, The, *in* Old News *SI*
Old Maid in the Winding-Sheet, The, *i.e.* The White Old Maid
    TT
Old Manse, The *MOM*
Old News, *incl.* I.; II. The Old French War; III. The Old Tory
    SI

Old Ticonderoga *SI*
Old Tory, The, *in* Old News *SI*
Old Woman's Tale, An [attributed] *SI*
Our Evening Party among the Mountains, *in* Sketches from Memory *MOM*

Passages from a Relinquished Work, *incl.* At Home, A Flight in the Fog, A Fellow-Traveller, The Village Theatre *MOM*
Peter Goldthwaite's Treasure *TT*
Procession of Life, The *MOM*
Prophetic Pictures, The *TT*
P.'s Correspondence *MOM*

Rappaccini's Daughter *MOM*
Rill from the Town-Pump, A *TT*
Rochester [attributed], *in* Sketches from Memory *SI*
Roger Malvin's Burial *MOM*

Select Party, A *MOM*
Seven Vagabonds, The *TT*
Shaker Bridal, The *TT*
Sights from a Steeple *TT*
Sister Years, The *TT*
Sketches from Memory No. I, *incl.* The Notch, Our Evening Party among the Mountains, *i.e.* Sketches from Memory *MOM*
Sketches from Memory No. II, *incl.* The Canal-Boat, *i.e.* Sketches from Memory *MOM*; *incl.* The Inland Port, Rochester, A Night Scene [attributed], *i.e.* Sketches from Memory *SI*
Snow-flakes *TT*
Snow-Image, The *SI*
Story Teller, The, *incl.* No. I: At Home, A Flight in the Fog, A Fellow-Traveller; No. II: The Village Theatre, *i.e.* Passages from a Relinquished Work *MOM*; No. II: Mr. Higginbotham's Catastrophe, *i.e.* Mr. Higginbotham's Catastrophe *TT*
Sunday at Home *TT*
Sylph Etherege *SI*

Tales of the Province-House, *i.e.* Legends of the Province-House *TT*
Threefold Destiny, The *TT*
Time's Portraiture *SI*

Toll-Gatherer's Day, The *TT*
Two Widows, The, *i.e.* The Wives of the Dead *SI*

Unpardonable Sin, The, *i.e.* Ethan Brand *SI*

Village Theatre, The, *in* Passages from a Relinquished Work
   MOM
Village Uncle, The *TT*
Virtuoso's Collection, A *MOM*
Vision of the Fountain, The *TT*
Visit to the Celestial City, A, *i.e.* The Celestial Rail-road *MOM*
Visit to the Clerk of the Weather, A [attributed] *SI*

Wakefield *TT*
Wedding-Knell, The *TT*
White Old Maid, The *TT*
Wives of the Dead, The *SI*
Writings of Aubépine, *i.e.* Rappaccini's Daughter *MOM*

Young Goodman Brown *MOM*

CHRONOLOGICAL LIST

ALL TALES included in volume IX, *Twice-told Tales*, volume X, *Mosses from an Old Manse*, and volume XI, *The Snow-Image, and Uncollected Tales*, of the Centenary Edition, are here listed by dates of the first printed appearances. The Centenary title is followed by the name or symbol of first publication and date, any variant original title, and first collection; tales uncollected in Hawthorne's lifetime are indicated. *The Token*, annually issued in the fall preceding its year of identification, is listed by title-page date. Symbols for publications are these:

TT 37, 42, 51   *Twice-told Tales* 1837, 1842, 1851
MOM 46, 54   *Mosses from an Old Manse* 1846, 1854

SI	*The Snow-Image, and Other Twice-told Tales* 1852
AM	*American Monthly Magazine*
DR	*United States Magazine and Democratic Review*
K	*Knickerbocker, or New-York Monthly Magazine*
NE	*New-England Magazine*
SG	*Salem Gazette*
T	*The Token*

1830

The Battle-Omen [attributed] *SG* Nov. 2; uncollected
The Hollow of the Three Hills *SG* Nov. 12; *TT* 37
An Old Woman's Tale [attributed] *SG* Dec. 21; uncollected

1831

Sights from a Steeple *T*; *TT* 37
The Haunted Quack [attributed] *T*; uncollected

1832

The Wives of the Dead *T*; *SI*
My Kinsman, Major Molineux *T*; *SI*
Roger Malvin's Burial *T*; *MOM* 46
The Gentle Boy *T*; *TT* 37

1833

The Seven Vagabonds *T*; *TT* 42
The Canterbury Pilgrims *T*; *SI*

1834

Passages from a Relinquished Work *NE* Nov.-Dec. (The Story Teller No. I and No. II *except* Mr. Higginbotham's Catastrophe); *MOM* 54

Mr. Higginbotham's Catastrophe *NE* Dec. *in* The Story Teller No. II; *TT* 37

1835

The Haunted Mind *T*; *TT* 42

Alice Doane's Appeal *T*; uncollected

The Village Uncle *T* (The Mermaid; A Reverie); *TT* 42

Little Annie's Ramble *Youth's Keepsake*; *TT* 37

The Gray Champion *NE* Jan.; *TT* 37

My Visit to Niagara *NE* Feb.; uncollected

Old News I *NE* Feb.; *SI* Old News II The Old French War *NE* Mar.; *SI* Old News III The Old Tory *NE* May; *SI*

Young Goodman Brown *NE* Apr.; *MOM* 46

Wakefield *NE* May; *TT* 37

The Ambitious Guest *NE* June; *TT* 42

Graves and Goblins [attributed] *NE* June; uncollected

A Rill from the Town-Pump *NE* June; *TT* 37

The White Old Maid *NE* July (The Old Maid in the Winding-Sheet); *TT* 42

The Vision of the Fountain *NE* Aug.; *TT* 37

The Devil in Manuscript *NE* Nov.; *SI*

Sketches from Memory *NE* Nov. (Sketches from Memory. By a Pedestrian. No. I. *incl.* The Notch *and* Our Evening Party among the Mountains); *MOM* 54

Sketches from Memory *NE* Dec. (Sketches from Memory. By a Pedestrian. No. II. *incl.* The Canal-Boat); *MOM* 54; (*also incl.* The Inland Port, Rochester, An Afternoon Scene, A Night Scene [attributed]); uncollected

1836

The Wedding-Knell *T*; *TT* 37

The May-Pole of Merry Mount *T; TT* 37
The Minister's Black Veil *T; TT* 37
Old Ticonderoga *AM* Feb.; *SI*
A Visit to the Clerk of the Weather [attributed] *AM* May; un-
  collected

1837

Monsieur du Miroir *T; MOM* 46
Mrs. Bullfrog *T; MOM* 46
Sunday at Home *T; TT* 37
The Man of Adamant *T; SI*
David Swan *T; TT* 37
The Great Carbuncle *T; TT* 37
Fancy's Show Box *T; TT* 37
The Prophetic Picures *T; TT* 37
Dr. Heidegger's Experiment *K* Jan. (The Fountain of Youth);
  TT 37
A Bell's Biography *K* Mar.; *SI*
Fragments from the Journal of a Solitary Man [attributed] *AM*
  July (*incl.* I., II. My Home Return); uncollected
Edward Fane's Rosebud *K* Sept.; *TT* 42
The Toll-Gatherer's Day *DR* Oct.; *TT* 42

1838

Sylph Etherege *T; SI*
Peter Goldthwaite's Treasure *T; TT* 42
Endicott and the Red Cross *T; TT* 42
Night Sketches *T; TT* 42
The Shaker Bridal *T; TT* 42
Foot-prints on the Sea-shore *DR* Jan.; *TT* 42
Time's Portraiture *SG* broadside Jan. 1; uncollected
Snow-flakes *DR* Feb.; *TT* 42
The Threefold Destiny *AM* Mar.; *TT* 42
Howe's Masquerade *DR* May (Tales of the Province-House. No.
  I. Howe's Masquerade); *TT* 42

Edward Randolph's Portrait *DR* July (Tales of the Province-House. No. II. Edward Randolph's Portrait); *TT* 42
Chippings with a Chisel *DR* Sept.; *TT* 42
Lady Eleanor's Mantle *DR* Dec. (Tales of the Province-House. No. III. Lady Eleanor's Mantle); *TT* 42

1839

Old Esther Dudley *DR* Jan. (Tales of the Province-House. No. IV. Old Esther Dudley); *TT* 42
The Sister Years *SG* pamphlet, Jan. 1; *TT* 42
The Lily's Quest *Southern Rose* Jan. 19; *TT* 42

1840

John Inglefield's Thanksgiving *DR* Mar.; *SI*

1842

A Virtuoso's Collection *Boston Miscellany* May; *MOM* 46

1843

The Old Apple-Dealer *Sargent's Magazine* Jan.; *MOM* 46
The Antique Ring *Sargent's Magazine* Feb.; uncollected
The Hall of Fantasy *Pioneer* Feb.; *MOM* 46
The New Adam and Eve *DR* Feb.; *MOM* 46
The Birth-mark *Pioneer* Mar.; *MOM* 46
Egotism; or, the Bosom-Serpent *DR* Mar.; *MOM* 46
The Procession of Life *DR* Apr.; *MOM* 46
The Celestial Rail-road *DR* May; *MOM* 46
Buds and Bird-Voices *DR* June; *MOM* 46
Little Daffydowndilly *Boys' and Girls' Magazine* Aug.; *SI*
Fire-Worship *DR* Dec.; *MOM* 46

1844

The Christmas Banquet *DR* Jan.; *MOM* 46
A Good Man's Miracle *Child's Friend* Feb.; uncollected
The Intelligence Office *DR* Mar.; *MOM* 46
Earth's Holocaust *Graham's Magazine* May; *MOM* 46
The Artist of the Beautiful *DR* June; *MOM* 46
Drowne's Wooden Image *Godey's Magazine* July; *MOM* 46
A Select Party *DR* July; *MOM* 46
A Book of Autographs *DR* Nov.; uncollected
Rappaccini's Daughter *DR* Dec. (Writings of Aubépine. Rappaccini's Daughter); *MOM* 46

1845

P.'s Correspondence *DR* Apr.; *MOM* 46

1846

The Old Manse *MOM* 46

1849

Main-street *Æsthetic Papers*; SI

1850

Ethan Brand *Boston Weekly Museum* Jan. 5 (The Unpardonable Sin. From an Unpublished Work); SI
The Great Stone Face *National Era* Jan. 24;
The Snow-Image *International Miscellany* Nov. 1; SI

1852

Feathertop *International Monthly Magazine* Feb. 1–Mar. 1; *MOM* 54